A Blazing Vengeance

Robert Fisher

authorHOUSE®

AuthorHouse™
1663 Liberty Drive
Bloomington, IN 47403
www.authorhouse.com
Phone: 1 (800) 839-8640

Published by AuthorHouse 07/29/2016

ISBN: 978-1-5246-2114-8 (sc)
ISBN: 978-1-5246-2113-1 (e)

Print information available on the last page.

This book is printed on acid-free paper.

Chapter One

The knocking at the door of room 832 continued for five seconds followed by a pause then another five seconds.

"Mr. and Mrs. Chen, this is housekeeping. May I make up your room now?"

Lucinda Ramos was a very polite maid. She had arrived in Canada three years ago from her native Philippines; and had astutely continued to regularly display her usual pleasant demeanor. It had paid dividends. She was five feet four inches tall, weighed one hundred and twenty pounds and had a lovely face. She smiled a lot which showed off her perfectly white teeth against her light brown skin. Her smile didn't mean she was permanently happy but it pleased the management and the clientele of the five star hotel where she worked. That also paid dividends.

She missed her homeland. She missed its sunshine and warm weather. Winter in Vancouver was too rainy for her liking. However the weather was not the determinant factor in her selection of location. She had chosen Vancouver because of its cosmopolitan composition. It had a very large Asian population, therefore she, as a Philippina, fitted in well. But most of all she missed her daughter.

Nevertheless she had determinately stuck to her plan. In the Philippines she had worked as a qualified pediatric nurse and had been distressed, when she arrived in Canada, to discover her level of expertise was not instantly recognized. She was told she had to spend many months of training to earn a similar status. That amount of time did not fit in with her plan.

She had made one major mistake in her life. A mistake which left her pregnant and to her utter horror it was followed by the shocking revelation her boyfriend didn't love her as much as he had professed, and had abandoned her. Life in San Pablo south of Manila was not easy. She recognized she could not raise her daughter in a decent manner on her salary. But she could not afford to uproot her mother, with whom she lived, and move to the capital city of Manila for a better paying position. Therefore, her plan was to move to Canada for a few years, save enough money to purchase a small apartment in Manila, and there find appropriate well paying work in one of the larger hospitals.

In Vancouver she soon discovered by using her intelligence and industriousness she was making much more as a maid than she could have done as a nurse. She quickly mastered the technique of always remembering the names of the constantly changing guests and never failed to greet them graciously with her charming smile. Her bright brain also taught her to use every opportunity to meet the guests and to inquire if there was any thing she could do to make their stay more comfortable. Most times this lead to a conversation during which the guest would inquire about her background. She would shyly mention her need to leave home to earn money to support her mother back in the Philippines. That was a bit of a stretch but it had some semblance of truth as her mother did suffer from asthma.

Her other skill was the mastery of origami. She would leave a paper crane on the pillow of a guest along with the obligatory chocolate. And on the night before the guest's departure she would leave a hand written note in an envelope saying she hoped her service had been satisfactory. Ninety percent of guests filled the envelope with a handsome tip, often a very generous one. In fact on several occasions wealthy elderly guests had left over five hundred dollars. She made much more in tips than her salary.

After three years she had just enough to buy that small apartment in Manila. However, as further financial security for her daughter's future, she had decided to stay for up to another year then go home.

As her knocking on the door of the Chens elicited no response, she used her passkey and entered the room. The room was stifling hot but it was not that which troubled her. It was the sight of the chest drawers wide open with their contents strewn around the floor that caused her hand to fly to her mouth. The inside of both suitcases were slashed as obviously someone had sought something inside the lining. Mr. Chen's briefcase had received similar treatment and its papers littered the carpet. With a pounding heart she walked towards the telephone on the desk to call security. It was then she thought of looking in the bathroom. Almost instinctively her brain told her not to do so; however, her feet seemed to operate independently as her shoes scuffed inexorably along the carpet.

Her screams were the closest possible to being inhuman.

Sitting in the bathtub, fully clothed and facing each other, were Mr. and Mrs. Chen, with a single bullet hole in each of their foreheads.

Two weeks later Lucinda Ramos returned to the Philippines with enough money to buy her apartment in Manila but with a horrific memory which would haunt her for a long, long time.

Chapter Two

Detective Inspector McKay of the Vancouver police homicide department was equally shocked at this sight. He was five feet ten inches tall with prematurely grey hair for his forty six years of age. He liked to believe he was fit and trim but his wife occasionally deflated his balloon by pointing to his growing paunch. His blue grey eyes always smiled at this as they, in turn, mischievously stared at her slightly swelling tummy. That earned him a playful clip on the ear. She loved her husband, but fervently wished he had taken up some other vocation. The long, irregular hours and dangers of his position had been a cause for concern on several occasions. When trouble arose in Vancouver he inevitably was in the thick of it. Today would be no exception.

He and his team consisting of forensic specialists, a medical examiner and his trusty sergeant, Johnny Thomas, hadn't taken long to arrive at the scene. McKay was regarded as the best detective in Vancouver and had deservedly earned this accolade by his outstanding record of successful investigations.

Hugh McKay had been evacuated from Scotland in 1940 at the age of four. Germany's heavy bombing of Britain caused this exodus from urban areas. Many parents, fearful for the lives of their children, sent the youngsters to relatives in America or Canada; hoping to be reunited at war's end. He, along with many other young children, had made the dangerous crossing to Canada where his aunt and uncle awaited him. He was lucky as many ships with young evacuees were sunk by German U-boats.

He still had a photograph taken at a Glasgow railway station showing him in his best suit with a clear plastic envelope strung around his neck.

The card inside indicated his name, date of birth and address to which he was being sent. A year later at ten minutes past nine on Thursday night March 13th 1941, German bombers launched a blitz on the area surrounding his Scottish home. Wave after wave periodically pounded the area until six twenty the following morning. His home with many, many others was obliterated. And his parents were among the thousands to be killed. Therefore, he had remained in Canada to be raised by his doting aunt and uncle.

While they showered him with unstinting love, they also instilled in him values such as decency, honesty and a sense of caring for others. When he graduated from college, it was perhaps almost inevitable he would continue to hold true to those values by turning to public service for a career. The police force provided just such an opportunity and he took to it like a duck to water.

Today his eyes were clouded as he surveyed the scene.

"In all my years I've never seen anything like this," he said to his sergeant. "Make sure to get plenty of photographs before Angela removes the bodies."

Sergeant Thomas was just as shocked as his boss at the positioning of the victims. Therefore took no offence at this gratuitous instruction. After all he had been on the force for over ten years and knew his job well.

Angela Rossini, the medical examiner, had been born in Palermo, but left when she was two years old. Like many other Europeans her parents immigrated to Canada looking for greater opportunity. She had graduated medical university with high honors and was extremely competent. She overheard McKay's instruction to Johnny Thomas but like him was not offended on this occasion. Normally McKay was extremely appreciative and complimentary of her skills. Of course he always wanted results much quicker than thorough science dictated. She only had to fix her dark eyes on him and give him her stern Sicilian stare, to put him in his place. She could see this homicide was having a profoundly negative impact on McKay and silently forgave him for the insinuation she would prematurely remove the victims.

"Both shot at close range judging by the powder burns. Looks like a small caliber, probably a twenty two. Not much blood so the bodies have been moved. Correct, Angela?"

She nodded her assent.

"Time of death? Best guess."

Normally this would have elicited her famous stare but not this time.

"The perpetrator knew what he was doing by turning up the thermostat to keep the bodies artificially warm, so I may be off, but my best guess is between one and four this morning. I'll use my lamp to check for any blood stains that may have been cleaned up."

"Thanks, Angela. Johnny ---,"

"I know, get the CCTV tapes for that time."

"Right."

The team worked thoroughly but rapidly and had finished with the hotel in a few hours. From experience they all knew the importance of the first day in a homicide investigation.

At five o'clock that afternoon McKay and Rossini sat in the office of Hugh's boss, Superintendent Sven Larsen. A Miss Carson from the CSIS, The Canadian Security Intelligence Service, the equivalent of the United States CIA, was there at the request of McKay. As usual, coffee and cookies had been supplied, but remained untouched. This alone indicated the tension existing in the room. Sergeant Thomas was the last one to arrive and was introduced to Miss Carson.

"Were you born in Canada?" he asked peremptorily.

She was visibly surprised at this question and annoyed at its tone.

"Of course I was," she replied indignantly.

"Don't be offended," he said. "It's just that I am fed up being the token Canadian round here. The Superintendent was born in Stockholm, Angela in Italy and my boss in Scotland," he explained with a wide grin.

Larsen's weak smile quickly faded from his face. He normally enjoyed Johnny's quick wit but today he was in no mood for jokes.

"Bring me up-to-date Hugh," he ordered rather brusquely.

"Okay. The victims were a Mr. and Mrs. Chen from Los Angeles according to their US passports. We know they arrived by plane from Los Angeles a few days ago and intended to stay at the hotel for another three days. They had a return flight booked for that day. At first we didn't know if it was business or pleasure. We initially thought pleasure since they were always seen leaving the hotel and returning to it together. But we haven't found their names on any of the main tour groups operating in the city. We know they returned to the hotel at about eleven last night and did not appear to be under the influence of either drugs or alcohol. They were discovered when the maid entered the room at eleven twenty this morning. They were an unusually well-buttoned-up couple. There was never any trash left in the room, not one scrap of paper. They ate breakfast and dinner each day from room service. Never had a drink with dinner or in the bar, and often left the hotel after dinner returning before midnight. This all seemed odd to me so I asked the FBI to check them out. These guys are getting good. They came back with a reply in less than two hours. The passports numbers are fictitious as was the address in Los Angeles. That's why I requested CSIS to send someone along to this meeting. Something about this case deeply worries me, Sven. Angela, tell us what you have learned."

"The victims were shot at close range by a point two two handgun, fitted with a silencer. They were killed as they attempted to enter an elevator on their floor. Then dragged to their room and placed facing each other in the bathtub with his hand on her shoulder. I found blood spatter traces in the elevator and along the corridor to their room. Someone had used a strong detergent to remove the blood but my lamp clearly showed the initial stains. Time of death was between one and four this morning. Once I have finished a more complete autopsy I can be more precise. The perpetrator had turned up the thermostat to its maximum to disguise the time of death."

"Thanks Angela. Now what did you find out Johnny?"

"We checked the CCTV recording from the lobby. No one entered an elevator between one and four. We did discover a man reserved a room on the same floor yesterday. He did it by telephone and picked up his key at five yesterday afternoon. He was Asian and registered as Phan Tran giving an address in Toronto. Both name and address were fictitious. He did not check out and there is no sign of him. The room was spotlessly clean – no fingerprints. In reviewing later CCTV recordings in the lobby we noticed someone with a hat pulled over his face and an upturned collar exited an elevator along with eleven other people at eight o'clock. It could have been him. If so, he chose one of the busiest times to mingle with other guests."

"Anything else, Sergeant?" asked Larsen.

"Yes, sir. The Chens made no outside telephone calls from their room nor did they receive any. The maid confirmed the bed sheets she changed each day showed no signs of semen. The couple slept quite apart in the bed. As requested by DI McKay I checked every one who spoke to the Chens. Interestingly, every one of the hotel's staff I questioned said they only talked to the woman. They never heard the man speak. No apparent trace of an accent. However the woman never engaged in long conversations. She always used the minimum of words."

"Your conclusions, Hugh?"

"This was not a robbery gone wrong. It was an execution. However the killer did thoroughly search their room and definitely did remove items. The maid told us there had been a portable computer in the room. And one evening a desk clerk going off duty saw Mr. Chen using a portable telephone outside the hotel. There was no sign of either of these items. I'm guessing the killer took them. And the positioning of the bodies was meant as a message. To whom, and its significance, are unknowns at this time. The killer planned this meticulously and in my opinion did not believe his use of a detergent to remove bloodstains, or his trick with the thermostat, would not be discovered. He expected them to be discovered. They were only to buy time to allow him to slip out of the hotel at one of its busiest times as Johnny said."

"I see," said Larson. "Anything further?"

"Yes. The Chens or whatever their real names are, were a highly trained team sent here on a mission. They were not a married couple. It is my opinion they were foreign agents operating on our soil. And whoever they were seeking got wind of them and assassinated them. They must have found out something or someone close to their quarry and that alerted him. Unless the Chens had extraordinary memories they would have made notes on the portable computer. There were no written notes in the room. The assassin killed them and cleaned all traces of the Chens' progress from the room to end the trail. More importantly he did so as soon as he knew they were getting too close. All of which means he can not only plan meticulously but also act immediately. In my opinion he is a highly skilled and extremely dangerous person and must be involved in something very big. And since foreign agents were sent after him, it may be something outside of Canada. That's why I asked CSIS to send someone here."

"Perhaps you may have to speak to your boss in Ottawa, Miss Carson. See what he can find out. The Chens could well have been foreign agents as Hugh suggests." said the superintendent.

"I will, Superintendent, but for now I have three questions," she said and turned to face McKay. "First, what did you learn from their clothes?"

"All were American brands, some with labels from Los Angeles stores," responded McKay.

"Secondly, if they were foreign agents wouldn't you have found guns?"

"I thought about that. I agree they would have had guns. Either they acquired them here or brought them with them. I tend to believe they brought them with them and the killer took them as the type of gun could have given us a clue as to their nationality."

"I see. Lastly, if they were a well trained team why were they taken by surprise and shot at close range?"

McKay smiled. This woman was pretty intelligent.

"This being a new hotel it has all sorts of the latest fancy controls. One of them is a log of the two elevators. We noticed that at just before two o'clock one elevator was stationary on the ground floor. The other went from the eighth floor where the Chens stayed, to the seventh floor. Then it was called to the eighth floor, presumably by the Chens. I am guessing the killer made a call from his room to the Chens saying he was someone with critical knowledge. Probably someone they had previously talked to and now professed to have information they would be vitally interested in; and he would wait for them in the lobby. Remember the Chens had been here for several days and must have talked to a lot of people. Also the killer had intentionally wakened them early in the morning hoping they would still be groggy with sleep. Probably that's why the elevator originating on the seventh floor and not the lobby didn't register as suspicious. They would hardly have expected an assassin to be in the elevator. That would give our killer the second or two he required to shoot both of them. As I said this guy is scarily smart. Everything was planned down to the minutest detail."

"You too seem to have thought out every detail, Inspector."

"No, not everything. The positioning of the bodies still eludes me. However if this guy is as intelligent as I think he is. He would know it would mean nothing to us. But it would be highly significant to someone. He would expect us to seek help and to involve you as we would soon find out the Chens were not who they purported to be. He is deliberately drawing CSIS into this. There is one other thing. If I had been hunting someone and a contact I had previously made, suddenly came forward with important information. I would have expected him to demand money. I was not surprised to find that Mr. Chen had two thousand dollars in his pocket. The question is, why didn't the killer take the money?"

"Now you are starting to scare me too with this guy's capability," said Miss Carson. "If you'll excuse me Superintendent Larson, I'll leave now and see what I can find out."

He nodded his consent and she quickly left the office.

"You certainly spooked our spook, boss," said Johnny.

"Then she can join the club. Because I'm spooked too!"

Chapter Three

Belinda Carson wasted no time. As soon as she was seated in her car she used her secure telephone to call her boss in the office in Vancouver. It would not have been proper to go over his head to the top man in Ottawa as Larson had suggested. She gave him a detailed report. He too was the son of immigrants, his from Germany. In his earlier years he had to endure many taunts about Germans leaving around the end of the war and vehemently professing they were not Nazis. It left him with a significant chip on his shoulder. And although he had risen to Deputy Director of CSIS, a powerful position in Canada which, with the requisite vetting, surely proved his parents were not followers of the Nazi party, his sense of insecurity still lingered.

"Do you agree with DI McKay's assessment?" he demanded.

"Yes sir, I do. There can be little doubt they were foreign agents."

"Listen Belinda, stay close to this guy McKay. I've heard of his reputation. He's a brilliant detective, but likes to do things his way. I don't want him holding anything back from us."

"Got it, sir."

"I'll do a little poking around here and report to Ottawa. I'll let you know if I come up with anything. I don't like his deduction this was deliberately intended to draw us into this assassination. Take extra care Belinda. There is a strong foul odor about this situation."

"Yes sir."

Jason Brandt, her boss, hadn't needed to warn her. But his twenty years of service, including many overseas posts, had honed his instincts and he sensed something evil and felt compelled to issue his warning. He had a nose for trouble. Actually he had a rather large nose. And if it smelled danger it only heightened the concern she already felt. She decided to go straight home, kick off her shoes, pour a generous glass of her favorite Chardonnay, and type up the notes from today. Actually she didn't need to submit typed notes. As standard operating procedure, her conversation was recorded. But a typed record always helped her focus.

When she finished she decided to have a bath. But no sooner had she turned on the taps when the thought of the Chens sitting facing each other raced through her brain. Quickly she turned off the taps and decided to have a shower instead. She wondered when she would be able to enjoy a bath again.

McKay and Thomas were still in the office. Thomas had typed their notes. McKay had scrawled several large question marks in a red pen on his copy and stared at them. There were too many unanswered questions for his liking. His brow was furrowed and his eyes almost closed in concentration. Thomas sat quietly. He knew not to disturb his boss while he was like this. Finally he looked at Thomas who waited expectantly.

"Why did the Chens go out at night after dinner and not return until late?"

"They could have been meeting people."

"Could be, but I think not. No Johnny, if they had names to follow up on they would have conducted their interviews during the day. The only exception would be if they had turned up a hot lead; which I don't think they had yet. I believe they were doing something else. But what?"

"Late night shopping," said Thomas jocularly to lighten the mood.

"Bingo! You're a genius Johnny!"

Thomas looked stunned.

"I was only kidding, boss."

"What type of stores are open late at night?" persisted McKay.

"One or two department stores. Small local general stores."

"Go on – and."

"Pharmacies."

"Exactly! And what do they sell?"

"Prescription drugs, over-the-counter drugs, medical supplies,"

"What else, think Johnny!"

"Chemicals of various types."

"You got it, son. Get photographs printed up of the Chens. Use the ones from their passports not the ones with bullet holes in their heads. Get half a dozen men to go round the pharmacies. See if anyone recognizes them and if so what they were interested in."

"What about you, boss?"

"Me? I'm going home. The wife warned me not to be late, she's making a roast."

He shook himself as though terrified of his wife's wrath. Thomas burst into laughter. But McKay was only partly acting. His wife had been hounding him to either get a desk job or take early retirement and he didn't want an argument tonight. He knew this case was about to cause him to work long hours and he wanted to break the news to her gently. Maybe after a bottle of wine? Yes wine. However he recognized she had long had the ability to see through such efforts. They would have wine – but only because they both enjoyed it – he knew it would not assuage her distress at his news. Nevertheless he would attempt to make her understand how critical this was. His gut told him this case was perhaps the most dangerous he had ever undertaken. The man who had committed the Chen murders was up to something monstrous. He could feel it. This killer was too meticulous not to be planning something sensational. And what really worried McKay was he felt instinctively the man had the capability to carry out his plan.

With that gloomy thought he started his car and headed for home.

As he anticipated, Cathy, his wife was not happy with his news.

"We're not getting any younger and we should be spending more time together. Take vacations like normal people," she complained. "Don't you want that, Hugh?"

"A long vacation would be nice," he admitted. "But Cathy please believe me, this is a special case. I feel it in my bones."

She had heard similar protests before. Her husband truly loved his job. However she saw something in his blue grey eyes she had never seen before – fear. She quickly put her arms around him.

"What is it, Hugh?"

"I'll know better tomorrow when I get reports from the men canvassing certain stores. But I'll bet my pension someone is planning the most heinous crime I've ever heard of. And my instincts tell me he intends killing hundreds if not thousands of people. I believe a foreign agent is here in our city and he was being hunted by the people who were assassinated today. Cathy, I have to find out who he is, what he is up to, and stop him."

Not only had she never seen fear in her husband's eyes but she had never heard it so clearly in his voice. She shivered and clung close to him.

"Okay, Hugh, you find him," she whispered in his ear.

The next morning he received all the reports. A sleepy Thomas summarized them for him. He had waited for the results until one in the morning and then worked through the night.

"Many of the staff at the pharmacies recalled seeing the Chens. They had asked if anyone had purchased any of these three chemicals."

He gave the list to McKay who sighed loudly.

"Bomb making chemicals. Did you check with the lab?"

"Of course, and you're right. But they would be used in making a relatively small bomb. If killing about a hundred people is considered small! And that would only happen if they all stood close to one another. Like at a sports event. Of course the guy could be planning on making several of these bombs."

"That's not the main objective," averred McKay. "God knows the lives of a hundred people are not a trivial matter, but there is something much, much, bigger afoot. As I told Cathy last night, I feel it in my bones. What else, Johnny?"

"Three of the pharmacies told the Chens an Asian man had made enquiries about those chemicals in the last two weeks. But when the suspicious pharmacists asked why he wanted them, the man quickly left. And a different pharmacy was burglarized ten days ago and those chemicals were stolen. But the good news is one of the pharmacists recognized the Asian man who came to his store. Apparently he had obtained a prescription over a month ago. He was unusually big for a Chinese and had a badly pock-marked face. After checking his prescription register he gave the Chens the man's name and address. We checked the address – a boarding house – and the man has not been seen for a week. However we showed the landlord a photograph of the Chens and sure enough they had been at the boarding house the day before they were murdered."

"You've been a busy boy, Johnny. When did you get to bed?"

"The night before last," he replied as he attempted to stifle a huge yawn.

"You've been working all night?"

"Someone had to do it since you're too scared of your wife to do it," he said, demonstrating his impish waggishness had not deserted him.

McKay grinned and patted him on the shoulder.

"Good man. This is proof the Chens had a lead. But only to a message boy. He's not the man we are after. Now before I send you packing to bed. Do you have anything further for me?"

"The big Chinese man's name is Hsieh Siang Lee and I am guessing either he's our killer or that's the name our killer used to lure the Chens out of bed at two in the morning."

"Good thinking, Johnny, and I agree with you," responded McKay as he quickly reached for the phone.

Thomas was slightly deflated as his brain accepted McKay had already come to that conclusion. He was even more put out when he heard his boss ask the morgue to check if they had an accidental death in the last few days of a Hsieh Siang Lee.

"No one of that name," was the reply.

"He's a big Chinese with a severely pock-marked face," persisted McKay. "You do - a John Doe. What was the cause of death? I see. Thanks, one of my men will be down to photograph the body."

"What was it?" asked Thomas not surprised at his boss's rapid deductive process.

"He was fished out of the docks two days ago. He had no identification and his alcohol level was through the roof. It was put down as an accidental drowning. But I'll bet it was the work of our killer. He was tying up a loose end."

"Look boss, I'm not going home. I'm past the stage of sleeping. I'll leave early this afternoon. Meantime I'll send someone to the morgue to photograph and fingerprint Hsieh and I'll update the crime board I started in the squad room."

Chapter Four

While Thomas was in the squad room, McKay restudied his notes in a discontented manner. He continually shifted around in his chair. He knew he was missing something. A little voice in his head mocked him, telling him to study harder. He tried – and – tried. It wasn't that the notes lacked coherence; but, he found it impossible to draw a satisfactory conclusion from them. His frustration was within seconds of exploding into a stream of angry expletives, when, at last, the light bulb in his head lit. Exuberantly he yelled out to Thomas.

"Johnny, come in here!"

Thomas entered with a large mug of steaming coffee in his hand. He had lost count of how many coffees he had consumed as he attempted to keep his head clear. But one look at his boss was better than all the coffee he had taken. His boss had that look on his face which Thomas immediately recognized and that look cleared his head immediately. He knew something important had entered that brilliant police mind of McKay.

"Let me bounce an idea off you. I've been guilty of looking for a convoluted solution regarding the origins of the Chens. But what if it's not so complicated? What if it's simple?"

It may have been Johnny's tiredness, he sat looking dazed.

"Let me explain," said McKay. "At first it seemed they were making a show of not speaking too much - he, not at all. That seemed to indicate they were disguising their accents as they were from some far off land – probably in Asia. However, they flew in from Los Angeles; they were wearing clothes purchased in Los Angeles; they had expert forgeries for passports. So let's not try to be too clever. Let's assume they actually did live in Los Angeles and they were in fact foreign agents. But only foreign to Canada not to North America. Eh?"

"The CIA," blurted out Thomas.

"Exactly!"

"But why didn't they get in touch with us?"

"The CIA is not authorized to work on cases inside the USA. That's the prerogative of the FBI. So I'm guessing they were given a tip of a danger to the USA originating here in Canada. And they were attempting to verify this information before raising it with us. That could only mean, if the threat was valid, it was one of such a magnitude as to cause huge concern."

"But the only thing we have uncovered is the possible manufacture of a relatively low grade bomb."

"That's right, Johnny. That's what's troubling me. The man who killed the Chens let's call him Mr. X, has been leading us around by our noses. I think this whole affair is a set up. For example, if he is only half as intelligent as I think he is, and he wanted to cover his tracks regarding the pharmacies, he wouldn't have drowned Hsieh. The body was bound to be discovered. He would have disposed of the body in a manner which would never be found. After all who would have missed Hsieh? No, he wanted the body found. In the first place he didn't believe anyone in Canada could decipher the message of the Chens' bodies facing each other. But he calculated the CSIS would discover they worked for the CIA. Hsieh was just another clue to ensure the CSIS got the message and called the CIA. He wants to bring the CIA into this. He's planning something big but wants to embarrass them. He has a bone to pick with the CIA in general or with one or more of their operatives."

"So Mr. X is using Canada as bait to get even with the Americans?"

"That's the way I see it."

"But if all that is true, boss, he must be frighteningly brilliant to devise all these moves."

McKay nodded his agreement as he picked up the phone and dialed the number for Miss Carson.

"I was about to call you," she said.

"To tell us the Chens worked for the CIA?"

There was an explosive gasp of astonishment.

"How did you know that?" she exclaimed.

"I'm a detective."

"Their names were Sandra Choo and George Lim," she told him.

"I see, and they were following up on a tip concerning someone in Canada planning something catastrophic in America," he added

"Who have you been talking to? Was it my boss?" burst out a highly disquieted Carson, unable to conceal her agitation.

"No, I told you I'm a detective. But I wanted to talk to you before going to my boss in case I was completely wrong in my deductions."

"Well you really are a good detective. My boss, Jason Brandt, thought it possible the CIA could be involved but obviously wasn't sure. So he went on a fishing expedition by contacting the CIA chief in Ottawa. He called him and asked if he had lost a package. When there was a brief silence on the line he knew he was correct. He then asked if he had lost the Chens. That rocked him and a meeting was arranged with our chief in Ottawa early this morning and the whole story came out. I have been authorized to meet with Sven Larson and brief him; and to fully cooperate in the investigation. I assume he'll invite you to the meeting."

"I believe he will, I'll see you there."

She called Larson and arranged to meet him in his office at two o'clock. Then she was compelled to call Brandt to give him the startling news of McKay's deductive abilities. If she had been shocked at McKay's ability, Brandt was speechless with astonishment. When he finally stopped blustering he asked her, "Do you really believe McKay is so bright, Belinda? Or do I have a leak in my office?"

"If you didn't confide in anyone in your office, how could there have been a leak? Of course it could have come from the CIA but I think that's highly unlikely. No, it was all McKay's deductive powers."

"Hmm, I asked you to stay close to him. Now I ask that you stay *very* close to him. Is he married?"

"Don't you dare say what I believe you are hinting at!" thundered Carson.

"Calm down, Belinda. I apologize. But I just can't believe McKay worked all this out by himself. I still believe someone must have told him and it is vitally important that I discover his source."

"I'll see what I can find out. But never again suggest I stoop to such depravity. Never!" she barked, bristling with indignation.

"Once again I apologize, Belinda."

He knew he had overstepped the mark and their working relationship was permanently damaged. He didn't regret it. In his line of work knowing who to trust was critical. And if someone was leaking essential information, almost anything was worth the cost of finding out.

If Miss Carson had been impressed with McKay's ability before, she was absolutely overwhelmed with his account of his deductions at the two o'clock meeting. Several times she found herself snapping shut her gaping mouth as he related his findings. Superintendent Larson saw this and smiled inwardly. He was one person who never had to worry about job security. Not as long as he had Hugh McKay working for him. But although he had known his detective inspector for some time and had ceased to be amazed at his ability, even he was astounded at his insights into this case.

When both Miss Carson and McKay had related their information, Larson sat back in his chair.

"Well what do we do now?" he asked.

They looked towards McKay.

"If my instincts are correct there must be a meeting between the CIA, FBI, CSIS and the Canadian Police."

"You mean we should go over the heads of my boss and his contact in the CIA in Ottawa?" asked Carson incredulously.

"Damn right. This meeting must involve the director of the CIA in Langley or at the very least his deputy. And the same level from each of the services I mentioned."

"I doubt that's possible, Hugh," said Larson. "It would take the highest authority in America and Canada to move such people into action."

McKay stared intently into the eyes of Larson. When he spoke it was in a low voice, almost a whisper, but it was full of passionate concern.

"We have worked together for quite some time, Superintendent. Let me ask you a question. Have you ever known me to deliberately exaggerate a situation?"

"Never," admitted Larson.

"Then let me be the one to stick my neck out and put my reasoning in a memo and send it to you with copies to the people I mentioned. If they choose to disregard my advice the consequences are on their heads."

"And if I refuse to permit this. Will you do so anyway, Hugh?"

McKay sat silently. Carson was transfixed by this interplay. She had never been involved in such high stakes poker in her life and could not think of anything to add.

Finally Larson smiled resignedly.

"I would never hang you out to dry, Hugh. You prepare the memo and I'll sign the copies and send them on. If that famous gut of yours says it's so important; I'll back you all the way. Let's not waste any time, let's do it now. Miss Carson, I don't want to get you into difficulties with your boss, so if you would rather not participate in the composition of his memo, you should feel free to leave. I would just ask you not to mention this to your boss for an hour. I don't know him but I would not like anyone to go over my head and have someone much higher up the chain of command issue a directive to me ordering the memo not be sent."

The price of poker had just gone up for Miss Carson but she chose to stay in the game. Perhaps the licentious request her boss made of her still rankled. More likely she saw in McKay a man who didn't give a damn for potential political negative repercussions. He just wanted to protect people.

The memo, which in future would be informally described as 'McKay's Warning', was sent that afternoon.

Chapter Five

To say the memo caused a storm would be like saying the 1883 eruption on Krakatoa in Indonesia was a minor tremor. Chairs were overturned, flailing arms swept everything from the tops of desks, every known curse word was screeched at the top of lungs and flamed red eyes sought someone to crucify. But when the fury subsided it was replaced with a somewhat lower lever of anger, deeply tinged with fear.

The Canadians were furious at not receiving advance notice from their own people and directed their ire not at McKay but at Larson. He took all this criticism on his own broad shoulders and merely pointed out he wished to inform his own superiors and those of the CSIS simultaneously. The Americans were enraged for a different reason. They firmly believed this should have been handled more covertly by a personal visit and not in writing. But each branch was secretly annoyed at not being the only one to be told. In effect this had turned into a turf war between all four organizations clearly showing the parochial nature of all of them. Eventually, the potentially disastrous consequences outlined in the memo sank home and sanity was restored. They all agreed to meet in Ottawa as soon as possible. They also agreed, as this was of the greatest urgency, details like an agenda were not a prerequisite and should be arranged at the meeting.

A large room in a leading hotel was selected as the venue. And after technicians from all four organizations had ensured there were no listening devices, everyone trooped in. Tables and chairs were set out in a square with seating for ten people on each side. But this turned out to be woefully inadequate. The hubbub was almost deafening as all clamored for more seating and – importantly – a heated discussion broke out as to who should chair the meeting. Finally Hugh McKay, probably viewed by all as the least senior person there, banged his open palm on a table. This caused every one to stare at him.

"This chaos will get us nowhere. I am the one who mainly authored the memo we are here to discuss. Obviously, we are unable to have a sensible review of this potentially cataclysmic situation with so many people talking at once. We must reduce the numbers to have a cohesive and calmer discussion. Superintendent Larson, Miss Belinda Carson and I are, for the present, the people most involved in this investigation therefore we must be here. To get moving forward, we need no more than two senior representatives from each organization to attend at this stage."

There were loud protests. McKay once more pounded the table.

"The noise level only proves my point. We have reserved four other rooms for individual organization meetings. So let's get on with the smaller group as I suggest, then you can break up into the other rooms to brief your people. If at a later time it is deemed necessary to convene a larger group so be it. But let's get this critical matter moving forward quickly. We don't have time to waste. And as the murdered personnel were from the CIA, I suggest its senior representative takes the chair."

There was a stunned silence before the head of the CSIS spoke.

"That's okay with me."

The most senior person from the other organizations gradually nodded their agreement and all those not invited were told to quickly leave. They did so still mumbling their displeasure at not being able to participate.

Sven Larson smiled. His detective inspector was known to him as a take charge guy and he had just proved so again. Larson hoped it would not lead to a later vendetta towards McKay. He suspected the men in this room had long memories and large egos.

Jonathan Truman, Director of the CIA, took the chair. His creased face reflected the seriousness he attached to the matter. He ran his left hand through the thick grey hair at the side of his head, coughed, then made his opening remark.

"Thank you for your nomination, DI McKay – did I get the pronunciation of your name correct? McKay, like sky and not like way?"

"Yes sir."

"Since you have been the person most involved I invite you to make any opening comments you think appropriate."

If he intended Hugh to make a brief summary of his memorandum, he was mistaken. Not just mistaken but deeply shocked. He was not alone; most of the delegates could not refrain from gasping aloud at McKay's first words. Some of them even gave voice to their astonishment.

"Director Truman, you have been set up!"

"Explain that comment," demanded Truman in a voice he had not intended to be so harsh. He was a man who carried a great responsibility and was accustomed to commanding brief and thorough responses from his people. He never had time to waste. But even by his authoritarian standards, this was an extremely terse response. When the noise level had settled down, he held up his hand at Hugh in an apology for his tone and an invitation to continue.

"I can only tell you what my long experience as a homicide cop tells me. Nothing in this murder has been as simple as it first seemed. The perpetrator has been leaving misdirecting clues all the way along. He wanted us to struggle to interpret his motive. Struggle - yes - but finally solve it with the help of outside sources. He knew the ultimate clue to his identity would be beyond the Canadian police. My gut says this guy who murdered your agents is the smartest criminal I have ever come across. I believe he has been meticulously planning an egregious attack on America; possibly killing tens of thousands of people. But more than that he wants, what I detect to be, reprisal on the CIA. Someone has done something to him to make him a revenge-sated evil monster. And it is my belief that person is connected to your agency."

Once again they were murmurs of disquiet from those around the table.

Jonathan Truman remained deathly calm. He no longer barked at Hugh.

"Would you kindly elaborate on your theory, DI McKay?"

"Little things like cleaning the blood from the scene inside the room and outside the elevator. He *knew* we had the tools to discover this. Also, leaving the hotel at eight in the morning to mingle with the heavy morning traffic. What murderer has the audacity to kill his victims at two o'clock yet wait until eight to leave the scene? Only someone supremely intelligent and confident in his abilities. And by leaving the victims' passports he *knew* we would check their validity with the FBI and discover they were fakes. And he *intended* us to pursue this further and learn they were CIA agents."

"I see, is there anything further?"

"His masterstroke of timing. He had an accomplice, named Hsieh, go around pharmacies asking about the necessary chemicals to make a bomb. But not one capable of huge destruction. Once again he was misdirecting us. Then he closes the loop by killing Hsieh. But not in a way to completely cover his tracks. He drowns him which allows us to find the body. He wanted him found. And – this is the most terrifying part - he does all this *before* your agents arrive in Vancouver."

He paused to let that sink in to all in the room. There were no hysterical outbursts. Only many gasps and a few open mouths. The frightening consequences of his statement sent shock waves through all their bodies.

"It is my opinion," he continued, "he must have sent your agency messages indicating a Vancouver based plot to attack America. He spun his web and waited for your agents to entangle themselves in it. Somehow he calculated the time it would take for you to send your agents to Vancouver and timed the visits to pharmacies and the murder of Hsieh, to occur just before they came to Vancouver."

"That seems almost impossible," interjected the head of the FBI.

"But I suspect it is true," averred Hugh. "And if I am correct it demonstrates his genius; and it should cause us to lose sleep at night."

"Why do you believe he would go to such lengths," asked Truman.

"Because he wanted to catch bigger fish. Pardon me for saying this, Director, but your Los Angeles based agents, while competent, were relatively junior. Our killer used them as bait to attract the bigger fish he is really after. He *knew* you would have to assign a much more senior person to this case and he *hoped* it would be the one he really sought."

"That's preposterous, McKay," said the head of CSIS, afraid his fellow Canadian had gone too far.

Hugh McKay also knew he was on treacherous ground. All his instincts told him he was correct but he was sufficiently realistic to know how improbable his story sounded. He turned to face Truman.

"Perhaps, but the way to settle it, Director, is for you to tell us how the CIA came to hear of a proposed attack emanating from Vancouver."

The man sitting next to Truman smiled grimly. He admired the insightfulness of Hugh McKay. He was the second member of the CIA attending this meeting. It was his boss who responded.

"You are brilliant detective, McKay. I checked you out before coming here and was impressed by your record. But frankly I was not prepared for this depth of deduction. I hope all you have surmised is not correct as it terrifies me. However some of it is certainly factual. I did not ask my deputy to attend this limited attendance meeting. Instead I invited our Regional Director of South East Asia, Phil Hughes. I would like him to answer your question."

Phil Hughes was well known to many in the room as a man who had refused a very senior position in Langley. He preferred to be where the action was and not sit in a comfortable office at CIA headquarters. He was greatly respected for not only this but his highly effective service record. He stood to respond to Hugh's question as a token of his esteem for the man he had never met but who had quickly earned his admiration by his exceptional analysis. His eyes were on McKay's and his smile was an acknowledgement of the veracity of Hugh's assumption.

"I have no earthly idea how you came by your conclusion, DI McKay, but you are absolutely correct."

That admission brought murmuring of alarm from the group.

"It was almost a month ago when snippets of information came from three Asian sources to my office in Hawaii. They all indicated a pending attack on mainland America. I immediately visited all three sources to question them and found their information to be vague. But just like you, Detective Inspector, my gut told me there was something to be investigated further. With my associates in those three countries, we dug further. We came to the conclusion the essence of the stories was true and an attack was indeed being planned by someone."

Hughes paused to take a sip of water. Not that he was terribly thirsty but he was not above using this to create the desired theatrical effect his next statement would have on the group.

"However, the wispiness of the information made me very uneasy. And, just like you, I felt I was being played. I became convinced the stories had been planted. It was as though a series of veils had to be lifted to get to the truth. And it was not until one week later that one of our sources was informed the planner of the attack was in Canada. And another week went by before a second source identified Vancouver as his location. Now, I was certain this was the creation of a very, very crafty mind. Initially I had to consider the possibility this could be a tremendously elaborate hoax. Believe me, we receive a great many of them. Or it could be true. My recommendation to Langley was to send a team to quietly investigate, but being conscious of the possibility of a hoax, not to alert Canadian authorities until something more concrete was discovered."

The chiefs of the Canadian police, the CSIS and the FBI nodded their heads in understanding. They too received their fair share of hoaxes based on flimsy information.

"Therefore I have to conclude I agree with DI McKay. There is an incredibly gifted mind behind all this. A person who can create such a plan involving so many countries and do so with immaculate precision and timing is to be greatly feared. Whatever he intends, it will be commensurate in scale with his brainpower."

Hughes sat down and this time there was no murmuring from the group – only stunned silence. Ashen faces looked to the chairman for his summary.

"I suggest we break now. We should go to the rooms where our respective associates are waiting and brief them on all we have heard. Then I suggest we form a joint task force comprised of two of each of our best people to come up with a response. That task force should include DI McKay. Is that acceptable?"

All were in such a state of shock they couldn't think of anything to add. They unanimously agreed.

Chapter Six

The person who had caused such utter trepidation among the members of the meeting sat comfortably in his apartment in a middle-class section of Vancouver. He was the man referred to as Mr. X by Hugh McKay. It was one of his three residencies in the city; all of them under different names and none of them under his real name. In fact his real name was not registered anywhere in Canada. His other two residencies were in lower middle-class areas and from the outward appearance of all three residencies no one could have guessed at his great wealth.

One of his homes was sparsely furnished but the one he sat in now was full of the finest furniture including many oriental antiques. The third was crammed with the most sophisticated specialized equipment - equipment necessary for his malevolent plan. He referred to it as his war room. All three had heavily bolted steel doors with distressed wooden outer coverings as a disguise. The windows were sealed shut. No one could find a way in; and no one had ever visited any of his homes - and lived. The person from whom he had ordered his furniture and his two delivery people had vanished without trace. Mr. X had considered this as an appetizer on his way toward his plan of mass destruction. Such was his appetite for killing.

He felt well satisfied and proud with his progress as he sipped his strong liquor. It had taken more than two years to hatch his plan. As he listened to his stereo he reflected on that serendipitous day which made his plan possible.

It had all started soon after his arrival in Canada. He had sought out criminal elements in the city – mostly Asian. He did small deals with a chosen few. He carefully selected only those he recognized were too incompetent to be major players. He correctly assumed they must have relationships with the more established organizations to be able to stay in business. He skillfully worked his way up several ladders towards the leadership. Somehow it escaped the notice of the top criminal leaders and the police that his initial contacts all mysteriously disappeared; their bodies never to be found. Perhaps it was just the police didn't care about such small fry. But they did notice the disappearance of three of the countries top crime bosses. That fulfilled two of Mr. X's needs. The three organizations were in such turmoil, they launched attacks on each other believing these incidents to be gang related. In doing so they completely forgot about his slight involvement in their organizations. He became invisible. His second requirement was met by his association with the top man in all of Canada, Jacques Simone. His headquarters was in Montreal. By using his incredible brainpower, Mr. X was able to craft several operations for Simone which greatly enriched him. By doing so he managed to persuade Simone to keep their relationship on a strictly one-to-one basis. Therefore, after some time, Mr. X seemed to have vanished as far as Simone's senior lieutenants were concerned.

His serendipitous day was a frigid winter one in Montreal, when Simone took his friend - he called him Wong - to a large garage on the outskirts of the city. When they entered, Mr. Wong was amazed at the sight before his eyes. It was no longer a functioning garage. Much of the inner space was crammed with computer equipment and at the center, like a spider in its web, sat a young man. Jean Mercier was twenty six years old. At first glance his bushy hair and beard were his obvious features. But a closer look revealed pale blue eyes, a crooked nose, a small almost lipless mouth and an incredibly pale skin. He almost never went out. In the back of the garage was a bed, bathroom, table and chair, a huge refrigerator, a small stove, a chest of drawers and a small wardrobe which contained his three pairs of jeans and his four shirts.

This young man lived within a world created by his computers. Mr. X, or Wong, as Simone knew him, was instantly captivated. From that day, he spent most of his time for the next eight months vacuuming up every piece of knowledge imparted to him by Mercier. At the outset he was as much bamboozled as enthralled. But his enormous brain quickly learned. After only a week he asked a question which had puzzled him.

"If you hardly ever leave this place how do you manage to live?"

"You can have almost anything delivered these days."

"But how do you pay for everything?"

A sly smile crossed Mercier's face.

"I have no shortage of money. I just pick it up when I need more."

Seeing the confusion on his student's face, he explained.

"I just go into a bank's system and transfer money to my account."

His student's face displayed continued confusion but his brain was on high alert. He knew he was about to learn something of tremendous value.

"Look, Wong, every financial institution uses a secure coded protocol. They change their pass codes every few days. The bigger banks use a random selection device for their passwords. I had Simone's men steal one of these devices. Then I disassembled it and spent three months studying it. And finally I built one to do the reverse of the original designer's intention. Instead of selecting passwords, it finds them."

"Just like that?" asked Mr. X and snapped his fingers.

Mercier laughed loudly.

"No, not just like that; sometimes it can take up to five hours. But usually it takes less than two hours. Then I select a high value account and have small amounts transferred to my account. It's important to only take a few hundred dollars at a time. Often if the customer thoroughly checks his account and complains to the bank, the amount is refunded. It would take the bank too long to trace it and they consider it not worth their time for such a small amount."

"But surely if you were to do this to a bank several times, they would catch on and begin a comprehensive investigation."

"Let me explain something further, Wong. At school I was considered somewhat of a genius at mathematics. As soon as I heard about computers I began learning everything available. I left school at eighteen and immediately went to work for the best security company in Canada. Because of my knowledge I got an interesting position in their computer security department. And at night I attended a course on building computers from scratch; including understanding the construction of computer chips. After a year I had learned as much as I could so I quit and joined a large bank. Once again I was successful in getting a job in their computer department. That's where I learned their protocols and studied their security systems. After only nine months I left and began setting up this operation. There is no one in Canada as knowledgable in computer science as me. And there may only be a couple in America. That's not a boast – it's a fact. So if you want to learn all about computers you've come to the right place."

Mr. X believed him and diligently applied his superb brain to the learning process. After four months Mercier was amazed at the progress his pupil had made. He had already built two advanced computers and was logging into other computers with considerable ease. One afternoon in early spring, he was about to attempt his first computer theft from a bank, when a sudden thought occurred.

"Jean, it just struck me that a bank would be able to trace my account if I moved money from one of their accounts."

"Ah, that's a valuable lesson to learn," said Mercier. "I wondered when you would realize that. Come over here."

He unlocked a steel cabinet to reveal a large machine.

"This makes electronic thefts safe. It was built by a genius in Germany named Klaus Schultz. I believe there are no more than four or five in the entire world. Unfortunately, Klaus was caught and is now serving a long sentence in jail."

"What does it do?"

"It is a high speed digital message transfer device. It can route any message I send to any location around the world."

By the look on the face of Mr. X, Mercier knew he had to explain further.

"Let me give you an example. I have bank accounts in over twenty countries. When I intend stealing from a bank in Canada I break into one of their accounts. The transfer is sent to a fictitious account say in America and instantaneously from there to say France then Belgium then Egypt then Venezuela then Japan and so on. This machine can route that message to more than fifty countries. The money will eventually finish up in one of my accounts in some country. Then I do a normal transfer to my account in Canada. All of this takes no longer than three minutes."

"That's amazing," marveled Mr. X. "But how did you manage to purchase such a device?"

"Good question. Klaus was commissioned to develop this machine for German Intelligence. Then the Americans heard of it and the CIA requested one. The third went to MI6 in Britain and the fourth, to France or Israel, I'm not sure which. I initiated a purchase order supposedly from Canadian Intelligence, CSIS. But I requested Klaus to route it via Syria, Angola, Brazil, Venezuela, and finally Albany, New York. I said this was a security precaution. I'm not certain Klaus believed all this but since I paid him a huge amount of money, he did as I requested. I then drove down there and picked it up."

"You had no trouble getting it over the border?"

"None. It was labeled as a Cray computer and I had a license to import it."

"Ingenious!"

"Not really; quite simple actually. However as I implied earlier, I think Klaus suspected the machine was not intended for government use. This probably gave him the idea that selling his invention to certain private parties could be much more profitable. He thought he was being careful in contacting parties in the Middle East and certain gangs in France and America. He immediately received several orders and was in the process of building his first when the German authorities arrested him. But Klaus was smart enough not to keep blueprints; his design remained in his head. Therefore, no one can build such a machine. You see he built a safeguard into his machine in case someone wanted to reverse engineer it and copy it. As soon as a certain part is removed it automatically destroys several other components. He is probably hoping to be out in twenty years and to start all over again."

Jean Mercier could not know he had just signed his own death warrant by relating that story. Mr. X knew he must have that machine also the password one devised by Mercier. But not yet; he still had much more to learn.

Eight months after first entering the garage of Mercier, Mr. X was ready. He was now almost as great a genius as Mercier in using computers. He was so competent he had even added a few subtle improvements of his own. One, in particular, concerned reconfiguring telephone networks and would prove to be exceptionally useful in the future. Being a man who paid meticulous attention to all details of his plans, he asked Mercier to conduct a check on his improvements. Mercier was highly impressed and could only add one small final detail.

Two days later Jacques Simone and Jean Mercier vanished.

Their bodies would never be found. And now Mr. X had the greatest personal computer setup in all of North America. It wouldn't take him long before his plan was in place and ready to go. Then, with the aid of his powerful computers, it had been an almost routine matter to send untraceable messages to groups in three Asian countries. Groups he had carefully researched and become familiar with over this time. These groups became the sources of the CIA's snippets of information received in Hawaii.

This was the first major step in his plan and it had been a complete success.

The blazing vengeance which had long burned deep inside him was about to erupt into a searing ferocious reality.

Chapter Seven

Following the initial meeting in Ottawa, the heads of the four organizations agreed the Prime Minister of Canada and the President of the United States must be informed. But these leaders would be strongly advised to keep details of this matter severely restricted until further information could be gathered by the task force. A leak at this stage would have serious consequences.

The appointed task force decided to move to Vancouver where a spacious room was set up at police headquarters. The start of the first meeting was predictably confusing as several people were talking at the same time. Then, as if by divine intervention people stopped talking and everyone looked at Hugh McKay. He had brought the Ottawa meeting to order and they needed that same inspiration. Jeremy Mason, the Director of CSIS noticed this as he stood to address the meeting.

"Welcome to Vancouver. As you all know I am not a member of this task force. My deputy, Jason Brandt will be our representative. I merely wished to let you know if we can do anything to make your stay more comfortable you only have to ask. Naturally your first task is to appoint a leader; however, I want to commend my fellow Canadian, Hugh McKay, on all he has done so far including the compilation of the crime board you see along the wall. I will take my leave and perhaps Hugh will open the meeting by describing all he has started on the board."

With that he left the room, and McKay stood.

"In police parlance, this will be our incident room. Sergeant Thomas has pinned up all the information we have gathered so far. We can add to it as we go along. However there are two points I believe critical to our deliberations and which we should come to agreement on right away. Firstly, it is possible this whole thing is some sort of sick hoax perpetuated by a deranged mind. The purpose of such a hoax is beyond my reasoning. However I suggest we either consider this possibility or rule it out immediately."

"This is not hoax. The planning is too brilliantly meticulous to be the work of a madman. We should proceed as you are suggesting and eliminate that possibility," said Phil Hughes of the CIA.

They all agreed.

"Good. The second point is the killer's gathering of chemical materials which could only be used for a relatively small bomb or bombs. This may be important in unraveling his ultimate motive; however, I tend to rule it out as his primary objective. What do you think?"

"I agree for the same reason as Phil mentioned," responded special agent Larry Douglas of the FBI. "The amount of detailed planning which has been demonstrated doesn't seem to justify a small explosion. There is something decidedly evil about all of this. I am not afraid to say it scares me more than a little. I believe the killer is planning something extraordinary."

Once again everyone agreed.

"Okay, I just wanted to get those points out of the way."

"Have you come to any conclusion about the positioning of the bodies, Hugh?" continued Larry Douglas.

"Not a clue. I was hoping one of the other agencies could come up with something. If it's a traditional rite in some culture, I believe it must either be Asian or Eastern European. Could the CIA and CSIS split the task and look into it?"

"I've worked in Asia for some time but haven't come across anything like it, nevertheless I'll ask my Asian contacts to check it out," said Phil Hughes.

"And I'll see what we can find out," added Jason Brandt. "I have some good contacts in Eastern Europe. Can you give me several copies of the photograph of the dead agents?"

"I'd like some too," added Hughes.

McKay nodded his head and at the same time became conscious he had been hogging the conversation. He sat down and wrote a note to remind him to ask Sergeant Thomas to do so. There was a silence in the room and when Hugh looked up from writing his note, he saw everyone was staring at him. It was abundantly clear they all wanted him to take the role of leader. Whether he wanted it or not he had been silently but unanimously appointed the task force leader. He took a sip of water to clear his throat which had suddenly become constricted at this realization.

In his own patch, Hugh McKay was renowned for being forceful and often opinionated. His superiors put up with this, as most times he was correct. However in the presence of the members of this task force he thought of himself as being no more than junior in status. This was not false modesty. It was because he felt instinctively the case had a decidedly foreign origin and he recognized his limited experience in countries outside of North America. However his experience in working in groups had taught him the invaluable lesson of strong steady leadership. The leader did not have to be the most knowledgable person in every area but he did have to lead the parade. He was like an orchestra conductor. The excellent ones stood in front of a large group of musicians and their every movement demanded respect. And they got it.

McKay didn't feel like an invincible orchestra conductor but he had successfully lead many groups. So with smile he hoped reflected some measure of leadership he nodded his head. The others took that gesture as acceptance of his role and smiled back at him.

"Okay. Well as I see it our first task is to gather more information. We'll split assignments among us. If we are correct and this man, I'll refer to him as Mr. X, intends to inflict significant damage in America, we need the FBI to identify all major events scheduled to occur within the next six months. I believe Mr. X is far enough along in his planning to attack within that time frame. Most probably the events will either be attended by very senior leaders or be ones with a huge audience. Next we need the CIA to recheck the sources of their information. How could Mr. X, sitting in Canada, have influenced Asian sources to pass on flimsy information to Hawaii? But in the event he actually visited those Asian countries I need the Canadian police to check the passports of all such travelers. Next we need the Canadian police to check into the recent activities of all known criminal organizations. Mr. X must have used one or more of them in some way. Lastly we need CIA and CSIS to thoroughly check all their sources in nuclear countries for a missing device from their arsenals. Gentlemen, Mr. X may not be planning to use a nuclear device but it must be something equally devastating."

There were sharp intakes of breath from many around the table. Hugh had just used the word on many of their minds but the one word few were willing to utter – nuclear. He allowed the meeting to settle down before continuing.

"And I doubt he is constructing such a device on his own. But just in case I'm wrong let's be on the lookout for sales of components required to assemble one. That's about it unless someone has something to add."

An observer could quickly have noticed the respect in the eyes of all present. They had selected an excellent leader. As this newly appointed leader heard no further comments, he concluded the meeting.

"Then let's all meet here in two days and review our findings. That may not be sufficient time to get all the answers to the questions raised; however we can't afford to wait too long to reconvene. I have the feeling time is not our friend. Thereafter we will meet every two days at five o'clock for an update. Unless of course something urgent comes up: then I will call an immediate meeting. Is that acceptable to everyone?"

There was unanimous agreement.

As the meeting broke up, McKay walked over to the senior person from the Canadian Police.

"Charlie, if you'll check the passports, I'll have my boys look into the criminal organizations. I may have to call on you for assistance with the gangs in the east."

"No problem, Hugh," replied Charles Morris. "Why don't I start the boys in Toronto and Montreal looking into it? I'll have them report their findings to you. That way you can keep control over the entire process."

"That would be great, Charlie. Thanks."

"Oh by the way, Hugh, you handled that meeting masterfully. Congratulations."

McKay didn't respond overly demonstratively to this compliment. He merely nodded his head in thanks. By now his mind was fully engaged on the challenge that lay ahead. And, he was already saying a prayer that something would soon give them a lead to the identity of Mr. X. However his policeman's gut told him it was a long shot. This evil genius would most probably stay undiscovered for quite some time. He could only add another prayer that they had enough time.

Once back in his office McKay immediately barked out instructions as he entered squad room.

"I need coffee, a stenographer and Sergeant Thomas."

Johnny Thomas had anticipated Hugh's needs and was already walking to his office before McKay had finished talking.

"How did it go, boss?"

"You'll hear soon enough. Where's that stenographer?" he yelled. "Ah, there you are Sally."

"You didn't have to shout so loudly. I wasn't two streets away."

Sally O'Shaughnessy was forty five years old and already a grandmother, although one could never have guessed by looking at her smooth pale skin and lack of even one grey hair. Her slim figure may have given the appearance of a frail lady but nothing could have been further from the truth. She had a spine of steel and she was afraid of no one, as her response to McKay's belligerent request evidenced.

"So calm yourself down or you'll get my Irish dander up, Hugh McKay," she retorted as she sat down with her notepad at the ready.

A young constable rushed in with a coffee. McKay nodded his thanks.

"Close the door behind you, Mathew. Now Sally –,"

"I know, I know, this is all hush-hush. No copies are to be made and I've not to say a word to anyone."

McKay had to smile; however it wasn't one of happiness, it was a wan smile indicating how deeply concerned he was over this case.

"What would I do without you, Sally?"

"You'd be in a right old tangle."

"Okay let's get started. And Johnny, when this is typed I want you to open a case file and keep this memo and all other information we gather in that file and keep it locked in the safe in my office. Only you and I will have access to it."

"Understood, boss, but I could have Sally type it on the computer and keep it password protected along with the other entries I have."

"No, I want it in a case file."

"Okay."

Sally and Johnny exchanged amused glances. They knew McKay wasn't very computer literate and still preferred to work with paper.

Some old dogs still had trouble with new tricks.

Chapter Eight

McKay preferred to work with paper notes but the other agencies didn't. Their notes were carefully documented on computers. Naturally this type of top secret information was well protected by firewalls. They were confident their systems could never be cracked.

They were wrong! Only one of them was secure.

The planning of Mr. X which McKay had described as brilliant and meticulous was again proving to be just that. He had spies planted in several strategic locations around Canada. Of course none of them knew the real name of the person who had hired them. They had been given a generous retainer and told to look out for something specific in each of their locations. Once one of these events occurred the one who spotted it was to call the information to a designated telephone number. Each of the spies had been given a different number to call. All the numbers went to a bank of telephones in the war room of Mr. X.

The following morning he stopped to have a coffee then casually strolled to the apartment containing his war room. Along the way he periodically stopped to either tie his shoelace or to check all around him in the reflection of a shop window. Satisfied he had not been followed he entered the apartment. Instantly he saw the blinking light on a tape machine connected to one of the telephones. He listened to the message and smiled. His spy had reported a large meeting being held at a hotel in Ottawa. His next move was to change the numbers of all the telephones. Jean Mercier had taught him how to access telephone companies' main stations. One of the benefits was not only to listen in on private conversations but to change telephone numbers at will.

Once he had completed this he sat in front of a bank of computers.

"Who will provide me with the information I require," he said softly. "Why not my Canadian host?"

He utilized the special machine made by Mercier and in only two hours was into the allegedly secure computer on CSIS. It didn't take much longer to read the notes of the Ottawa meeting. He carefully scanned down the list of participants and smiled widely when he read one name. But the smile left his face when he finished reading the entire list. The second name, and by far the more important one to him, wasn't there. He swore in his native language.

"How many clues must I leave for those dunderheads? It looks like I must leave yet one more."

As he thought out what he must do, he had another idea.

"I wonder if the CIA mentioned him in their notes," he mused.

Once again he used the Mercier machine to gain access to the CIA computers. It was more difficult but he eventually did so. However he was confounded when he attempted to access the top secret files. He tried a second time and when that also failed he quickly logged off. Jean Mercier had boasted there was no one in Canada as skillful as he in computer science and only a couple in America. One of them worked for the CIA and his specially developed firewall for highest priority matters was impervious to Mercier's machine.

Nevertheless as Mr. X enjoyed his late lunch he was pleased with his work that day. Had he known the capability of a certain Edward Winfield he would not have been so sanguine. Ed Winfield was one of the two or three in America as skilled as Jean Mercier, probably even more so. His protective firewall not only protected top secret information but it alerted him whenever someone attempted to get in. As soon as he was alerted he immediately notified the deputy director who then marched straight into the director's office with Ed in tow.

"Any idea where this attack originated, Ed?" asked the director.

"I've been working on the technology to source attacks but as yet all I have is a beta test. And it hasn't been completely debugged. Sorry Director."

"That's okay, Ed, could you hazard a guess?"

"I believe it came from the States. I'm not confident of that but that's what was indicated. Certainly not from Asia, and unlikely to be from

Europe. Possibly from Central America or the northern part of South America."

"Hmm, how about Canada?"

"That's a definite possibility."

"Thanks Ed, you're a genius. Keep working on your device and let me know personally when you believe it's perfected."

"I will, Director," replied an elated young man. Compliments like that from the boss were rare and to be treasured.

When Ed had left, the deputy director looked solemnly at his boss.

"You think this is connected with the meeting in Ottawa, Jonathan, don't you?"

"Yes I do, but how in hell did someone learn of that meeting and so quickly attempt to break into our computer to retrieve the minutes. Hugh McKay was not exaggerating when he said we should be worried about the capabilities of this Mr. X. You had better inform the FBI, CSIS, the Canadian Police and Hugh McKay, not to put anything on their computers. I doubt they have anyone nearly as talented as our Ed Winfield to block this Mr. X. And call them on a secure line. Don't send anything that could be intercepted."

The message was quickly passed around. When it reached Hugh McKay, he immediately called in Johnny Thomas and triumphantly told him the news.

"See, I told you those damn things were not to be trusted."

Thomas was astounded.

"Boss you have no idea how difficult if must have been to penetrate those systems. That guy must be a genius."

"He is – and we had better find him pretty damn quick. Towards that end let's get down to the task we have to undertake by checking on our criminal friends. Get a few men and bring in the leaders for questioning."

They spent the rest of the day doing that and the results shocked them. The heads of the main gangs had disappeared some time ago and there was an obvious wafer thin uneasy truce between the gangs. Since the disappearance of their bosses, several other gangsters had vanished. Their associates believed they had been killed and the bodies sunk in the sea. Outright warfare had been avoided but it was clear it could break out at any time. One more murder and war would be declared.

Thomas had rounded up the newly appointed gang bosses but even under intense questioning they were of no help. It was apparent they had been totally shaken over the assumed murders of their bosses. Only one of them gave McKay a clue. This man was so tense over the current situation that under McKay's skillful interrogations he confided much more than gangster prudence dictated.

"My boss was tight with some guy. I never knew his name but I once saw him at the boss's home. I called there one night unannounced and caught a glimpse of the back of him. Later when I asked the boss he said this guy was giving him good information. And right enough we pulled off a few really good jobs. A week or so before the boss vanished, he called Jacques Simone and I heard him talk about this guy. That's all I know – I swear."

McKay called his opposite number in Montreal.

"Did you get anything from the gangsters at your end, Pierre?"

"Only something that blew my mind. The head of the biggest gang in Canada, Jacques Simone, seems to have vanished. We were wondering why we hadn't heard of his usual capers recently."

"Good God," exclaimed McKay. "That's what happened to a few heads of smaller gangs here. Did you question the new head of Simone's gang?"

"I certainly did but he was of little use."

"By chance, did he mention Simone having acquired a new confidant in the last year or so?"

"How did you know that? There was someone. But latterly Simone only met this man alone; others in the gang were excluded. The guy I questioned wasn't certain but he believed Simone's friend was Asian."

"Anything else to report, Pierre?"

"Sorry that's all we got, except for one more thing. Simone's driver told us he frequently took Simone to a large garage outside the city limits. We checked this and by a strange coincidence it had burned to the ground immediately after Simone's disappearance. The fire chief who investigated said it was definitely arson. The only pieces of equipment still barely identifiable were a few computers."

McKay's eyes narrowed in concentration as he hung up.

Chapter Nine

Mr. X had returned to his well furnished residence. He sat in a comfortable arm chair with his slippered feet resting on a padded footstool and his favorite drink in his hand. He was well satisfied with his work that day. His plan was on a course he believed to be unstoppable. He attempted a smile as he contemplated all he had accomplished. At least he believed he had smiled. But to anyone else observing him, it would have been more of a self indulging, mocking, sneer which hideously transformed his face into a mask of contemptuous scorn.

His effort at a smile broadened; then it erupted in a volcanic explosion of bellowing uncontrollable laughter. Spittle flowed like molten lava down his chin and his eyes bulged with this effort. His whole body shook with his uncontainable mirth. Anyone witnessing this scene could easily draw the conclusion that he was a madman - a lunatic whose place should be in a secure padded room in an asylum for the insane.

But, the mind numbing, bone chilling, soul eroding, truth, was, he was far from this. He was in fact an unusually gifted, brilliantly minded, completely sane, man. An evil fiend would more suitably describe him rather than using the unimaginative term, man: since he delighted in inflicting pain and death on people. The greater the number of his victims, the greater was his pleasure. This he did in a cold, clear, calculating manner full of maleficence, and therefore, devoid of anything even closely resembling humanity.

In the past, this terrifying devil had used his destructive talents to annihilate tens of thousands of people and had even attempted mass obliteration on a hitherto unheard of level. At that time his avaricious goal had mushroomed into millions of people. But his plan had been narrowly thwarted. Most of the world would never know how close he had come to succeeding. And he had sworn vengeance on those who had foiled his plan.

Over the past few years he had devoted his substantial faculties toward two objectives. Firstly, he planned to succeed where he had once failed, by causing the deaths of millions of people. And secondly, he had to discover the identities of those responsible for his failure and kill them. But their deaths would not be painless and quick. No – no – that would never do. He had planned a series of clues which they would eventually solve and which would lead them to discover his name. Then, knowing who they were dealing with they would undoubtedly realize they were marked for death.

Mr. X had learned enough about his quarry to understand they were not the caliber of men to be deterred from an attempt to foil his master plan even at the risk of their own lives. He would gloat at the undoubted torture they would endure as, even knowing his name, they would be hopelessly inadequate in stopping him. And he would exultantly rejoice at the pain they would suffer as even armed with any possible information they could garner, their futile efforts to avoid their own deaths and the deaths of millions of innocent people would come to naught.

His only regret was the millions to die would not live in the country he hated most. However he consoled himself by knowing the selected ones lived in the country most responsible for his past lack of success.

He had thought of every possible eventuality in his master plan, and believed all contingencies were now covered. Actually it had taken much longer that he foresaw to identify the men who brought about his downfall. But his networking skills were second to none and when combined with his recently acquired computer skills, he eventually located them. His trap for the two men most responsible for his prior failure had been meticulously laid. He took malicious gratification in the fact that just like a perfect script for a stage play it was being followed to the letter. One man was already in his trap and he was certain the other would be shortly.

He suddenly choked as thoughtlessly he poured liquor into a mouth still emitting loud laughter. That produced a substantial fit of coughing which brought him back to his senses. And made him recognize he must guard against being overconfident. Exceptional planning and meticulous execution were critical and it was satisfying to feel totally confident. But overconfidence could put paid to even the most perfect plan. His laughter died and his hideous effort at a smile returned. No, he counseled himself, he would never fall into the pit of swaggering arrogance. He was too clever for that.

Somehow it didn't penetrate even his gigantic brain he was doing just that. His arrogance was on full display and would have been obvious to anyone except himself. As if by some mystical balancing act, a modicum of doubt crept into his mind. He realized he could not feel one hundred percent certain of his plan until he had the second man in his trap. That man must have unusual skills to have foiled him once. He must neutralize him before he would be able to savor the satisfaction of mass revenge. Then he could launch his master plan with equanimity. He had never met this man but by breaking into the main army computer he had read of his exploits. They were impressive. The man was not only brave and resourceful but he appeared to have the instincts of a jungle cat. That was slightly worrying to him. Jungle cats were not to be treated lightly. That's why he must kill him first before his planned attack could be considered infallible.

"But why aren't you here? I've left enough clues to lure you from your lair." he snarled at the night and flung his liquor glass against the wall.

His body shuddered momentarily.

"Be calm," he admonished himself. "He will be here soon. It is not he who is delaying; it is the incompetence of others in not recognizing the need for him. Patience, patience, I will meet him presently."

His self counseling brought him back from the brink. There existed a mere razor thin edge between his ultra extraordinarily gifted brain, splenetically set on vengeance at any cost, and the abyss lurking on the other side of that finest of lines – an abyss of insanity.

He went over to his cabinet, brought out another glass and filled it with his special strong liquor.

'I'll clean up that mess later,' he thought as he settled back comfortably in his chair. He was completely oblivious to how close his teetering on the edge had brought him to going over into the abyss.

Chapter Ten

Like McKay, the other members of the task force had been busy. Phil Hughes had spent a long time in his hotel room on the telephone.

"I hate to think what my bill will come to," he murmured.

He had called his office in Hawaii and given his assistant a long list of tasks. However there were certain people in Asia he wished to talk to again. Although he had visited them personally and received answers to his questions, he now knew the one question not sufficiently answered and more importantly he knew how deep his questioning must go. As was his practice, he much preferred a face to face interview but if that was impossible he had to hear the tone of voice of someone he was questioning. He could detect changes in the pitch of an interviewee. Often that told him more that the answer he was given.

By three o'clock he had completed his Asian calls. He considered it an advantage to have wakened people due to the time difference. Men still groggy with sleep were less able to spin a lie quickly and convincingly. Not that he normally distrusted the sources he called, but he now had new knowledge of this Mr. X. He was a cunning character and had most certainly heavily bribed or strongly coerced people to send the messages his Hawaii office had received.

Most men have their price or breaking point.

He next checked in with his office to get the answers to the questions he had raised. Now that he had a clear picture he leaned back in his chair and whistled.

"Good God, this is almost unbelievable. How the hell did he manage to pull this off? Sorry Joseph, but I have to spoil your day."

He knew he must confirm the picture he had mentally drawn. Once again he dialed a number. This time it was to a most secret number in Tokyo. He once had headed the CIA operations in Japan and now he called the man who had worked closely with him and who had succeeded him, Joseph McNulty.

"Yes?" was the uninformative response. This line never identified itself until it recognized the caller.

"Good morning, Joseph."

"Boss, it's great to hear your voice. How are you?"

"I'm not great Joseph. I'm following up on what could turn out to be a very, very, nasty situation. Someone is planning a significant attack on America. I have been roped in as signals indicating a possible attack were received by my office. They indicated the perpetrator was in Canada. Naturally this intelligence was passed straight to Langley. They sent two young agents from our Los Angeles office to Vancouver to find out what they could. They were brutally murdered and ritually posed facing each other in a bathtub. Right now I am in Vancouver working with a joint task force."

"What can I do to assist, boss?"

McNulty had avoided any extraneous comments and had come straight to the point. He had been well trained.

"I've spent a lot of time attempting to discover the real source of the messages sent to my office. So far I have tracked three in different countries. And in each case the person who sent me the information received it either second or third hand. I've had a hell of a time tracking them back. Now hold on to your hat, Joseph. All of the messages came from you!"

"What? No way! I can categorically tell you, boss, I sent no such messages."

"I didn't for a second believe you did, Joseph. But I need you to check your outgoing secure signals"

"But boss the protocol you set up hasn't changed. No top secret message gets sent without my approval," said an agitated McNulty.

"Humor me and check, Joseph."

"Of course, boss. Give me a number and I'll call you back in ten minutes."

It was fifteen minutes before Hughes's telephone rang.

"Sorry I'm late boss but I have been raising hell. You are correct, a message from our secure computer was sent to three contacts in Asia. It read; -

'Most urgent from J. McNulty. Through trusted channels send a message to Phil Hughes in Hawaii indicating someone in Canada is planning an attack on America. Person could be in Vancouver. I repeat do not send this message yourself. Use other trusted sources once or twice removed from you. This is most secret and the maximum security must be observed.'

McNulty gave a frustrated sigh before continuing.

"Right now we have no explanation. The most likely one is someone managed to break our firewall security and put this message on our computer and had it sent. As I said I'm mad as hell this could happen. We are undertaking a detailed investigation. I'll let you know what we find. Once again my apologies, boss. I have instructed my people to inform Langley and ask for their assistance. They have a whiz kid named Ed Winfield, maybe he can help. Anything further I can do?"

"No, Joseph, it's what I anticipated. The guy we are after is incredibly gifted. If I need anything further, I'll let you know. Bye Joseph."

"Bye, boss."

It was exactly as Hughes had feared. But at least one piece of the puzzle had been completed; Mr. X was using computers to lay out his trap. Either he or someone working for him was a computer genius.

Hughes looked at his watch – almost seven o'clock. He called a few of the other task force members staying at the hotel and they agreed to meet in the bar for a cocktail then have dinner. It was almost ten when he returned to his room. He switched on the light and when it stayed dark he instantly knew he was in trouble. He quickly dived to the floor but unfortunately not quickly enough. He heard the phtt of the silencer before the bullet went right through his leg. Even before his scream of pain had stopped, a heavy object smashed into the back of his head and everything went black.

He had no idea how long he had been out. When he hazily peeped through almost closed eyelids, the first thing he noticed was the spreading pool of blood. With an immense effort he crawled to the desk and reached for the phone.

"Call emergency, I've been shot."

Everything seemed to happen at once. The alert desk clerk not only called for the ambulance, he also called the police and having seen Phil pick up his room key with friends, he called two of their rooms. They both demanded a clerk immediately go to Hughes' room with a passkey. The first friend to arrive was still in his undershorts with his shirt tail flapping behind him. Once inside the room he didn't waste time by asking questions but had the presence of mind to quickly grab a towel and tie a tight tourniquet around the bleeding leg. The police and the ambulance arrived five minutes later by which time Phil's second friend had called Hugh McKay.

A tired McKay had just arrived home and was about to enjoy a glass of wine when his phone rang. His wife, Cathy, had a look of resignation on her face when she heard it ring. It was almost as though she possessed extra sensory perception. She watched him listen intently to the message, then call his office and explain the situation to the man on duty.

"Find out which hospital he's being taken to and call me in my car," he added. Then turning to Cathy he said, "A senior member of my task force has been shot. I have to find out what happened."

She kissed him as he struggled to strap on his police revolver.

"I hope he will be all right. Call me when you can and let me know if you'll be back tonight."

The look on her lovely face told him she was totally behind him and she did recognize the magnitude of the threat he was dealing with and the strain it was putting on him.

"Bless you, sweetheart," he whispered in her ear and raced for the door.

Once at the hospital he had to wait until the doctor gave him permission to enter Hughes' room. When the doctor came out of the room, he quickly gave his diagnosis. McKay was relieved to hear the wound would not disable Hughes. It would leave a nasty scar but that would be about all.

"He is receiving a blood transfusion and has an intravenous tube to keep him hydrated. He is very weak so don't stay too long," concluded the doctor sternly.

He entered the room and saw for himself how terrible Hughes looked. In an attempt at light heartedness he said, "Well it seems you just can't keep out of trouble,"

Probably this comment was one of relief that Hughes condition was not critical. It was more an unthinking instantaneous one on his part rather than it was meant to joke with Hughes. But when he looked more closely at Hughes' ashen face, he regretted having made such a clumsy attempt at humor.

However Phil Hughes did his best to smile at his remark although it was a weak response.

"There was no need for you to come. I'll be fine," he said. But his voice was as weak as his smile had been.

"What happened?" McKay asked as he took out his notepad and pen.

"The light switch in my room had been disabled. As soon as I realized it I hit the deck, but he was too quick for me. He used a silencer and before I knew it he clobbered me. I didn't get a glimpse of him. But this was most definitely not an assassination attempt. He could easily have killed me. If not with the first shot then certainly when I was out cold. And I asked the constable who first arrived to bring me my briefcase. Everything was there; all my notes, everything. My wallet was intact therefore I didn't interrupt a burglary attempt. So the two questions I have are; why me, and not some other member of the task force? And, why only wound me?"

McKay had done some background checking on all the members of the task force and knew Hughes' reputation was that of a highly skilled and extremely brave man. The fact Hughes had not spent his time in the ambulance worrying over his leg but had thought out the situation rationally only proved his appraisal of Hughes was on the money.

"Since you have obviously been giving this a lot of thought, what's you're conclusion?"

"This was a warning. But whether it was just for me or for the task force in general, I don't know."

"I rather think it was for you, Phil. But you have to rest you've lost a lot of blood. I'll see you tomorrow morning and we can go over it once more. Okay?"

"Thanks for coming along, Hugh. Sorry to disrupt you evening. And give my apologies to your wife for dragging you out here."

That remark told McKay something else. Phil Hughes was a family man who had gone through many such disruptions to his evenings and understood what they did to family life. And further, he must have an understanding wife. One he hated to continually disappoint. It sounded very much like his own situation.

"Sleep well, Phil. Goodnight."

"You too. Goodnight, Hugh."

McKay called Cathy from his car to say he was on his way home.

"How is the man?" she asked.

"He's lost a lot of blood but there is nothing terribly serious about his wound. However he is one dedicated, brave and smart man. I'll tell you more about it when I get home. Is it too late to have some dinner? I'm famished."

"No it's not too late. I've become an expert a keeping meals hot without overcooking them. Hurry home."

McKay then called Johnny Thomas and briefed him.

"Put some men on guard at the hospital. I don't think there will be another attack but I'm not taking any chances. I'm going to visit Phil Hughes tomorrow at eight-thirty. I'd like you to join me. There is something much more significant in this attack than just a random act. We were meant to understand something by it."

"You believe it was the work of Mr. X?"

"Oh yes, it was definitely him. And the bugger was sending us a message. He's taunting us again. I have to figure out what it means. See you tomorrow, Johnny."

He abruptly hung up before his sergeant could say goodnight. Thomas could read the signs from the tension in McKay's voice. He was like a bloodhound on a trail, but the scent kept disappearing forcing him to go back and forward in desperation.

"I hope you get some sleep, boss," murmured Thomas.

But he suspected McKay would have a restless night.

As McKay drove quickly home his brow was creased in his exertion to decipher the message left by Mr. X.

"I'll get you yet you cunning bastard," he muttered as he unknowingly ran through a red light.

Chapter Eleven

The next morning McKay went over everything one more time with Phil Hughes. Johnny Thomas took everything down in his notepad.

"There's no doubt in my mind this was the work of Mr. X. And I fully agree with your assessment, Phil, he was leaving us a message. A significant one he intended one of us to correctly interpret, but I'll be damned if I can."

"I think I may have part of the answer. But since you and your sergeant are here let me start off by briefing you on how I spent my day yesterday."

Hughes related his activities in a rapid staccato fashion. Thomas wrote furiously noting all this important information.

Hughes paused to make certain Johnny had gotten everything. Then he summarized his conclusions.

"So, there are two items of criticality I take away from all of this. The first is our Mr. X is a computer genius. Of course he could have such a person working for him, but I believe he is doing this himself. The second is I don't believe he is American or Canadian. After struggling with this conundrum for most of the night I am now totally convinced his message was intended for me alone. This can only mean we have somehow been previously involved. He wants me to regret something I did to him in the past. And as I worked mostly in Asia, our paths must have crossed there. I already called Joseph McNulty in Tokyo this morning to have him review my past cases. I'll let you know if something turns up."

McKay glanced over at Johnny Thomas and saw the admiration in his eyes. Phil Hughes had been moving around in his bed as he strove to find a less painful position for his leg. No doubt this discomfort had existed all through the night. His pale, drawn, face made it obvious he was still suffering the effects of his attack but nothing would stop him from aggressively pursuing the man who was behind all this. And he would not allow his obvious pain to dissuade him from logically thinking through all the possibilities of identifying this man.

"Well, Phil, I can confirm your first point. You're one hundred percent correct in recognizing Mr. X's capabilities with computers. He attempted to break into the CIA's main computer at Langley but was foiled. However we have just received information that he managed to break into the secure one at CSIS headquarters. It was there he got information about the hotel you were using and we believe he managed to get the minutes of our first meeting in Ottawa. The bugger is staying not one, but two or three steps ahead of us. Langley issued a warning to everyone concerned not to record any further information on this case on any computer."

"Very wise, I have passed the same message to my office and I requested they give the same warning to all our Asian posts."

Once again McKay could see the respect in Johnny's eyes as he wrote everything in his notebook. He looked at his boss.

"Perhaps we should brief Mr. Hughes on our work yesterday regarding the gangs in Canada."

"Good idea, Johnny," he agreed and proceeded to do so.

Hughes was quiet for a few minutes as he mulled over the information he had been given.

"Could you do something for me?" he finally asked.

"Sure, anything, Phil."

"Have your counterpart in Montreal interview the new head of the main gang there. And ask him if his gang has been involved in any unusual importation from Asia in the past year. Probably something Simone was personally involved with."

Thomas raised his eyebrows indication he didn't see the relevance of this request. But McKay immediately did.

"I hope you're wrong, Phil. Oh God, how I hope you're mistaken. Although I was the one to raise this specter, I keep praying it just can't be. But I'll have your request checked."

"And I'll ask Joseph to do some snooping around in my bailiwick." Then noticing the perplexed look on Thomas's face, Phil Hughes explained.

"I believe it was you, Johnny, who discovered the theft of chemicals to make a bomb: not a huge one, but a bomb nevertheless. And Hugh said he believed Mr. X was planning something really big. To do so he would require a device as powerful as an atomic weapon. The theft of such a weapon would be extremely difficult, but with a sufficiently huge bribe it could be possible from one of the nations in Asia. Also, now we understand his ability with computers it adds to this possibility. It's only a hypothesis but I would like it checked."

Johnny Thomas's hand quivered as he took a note to do this.

"Okay, we had better let you rest, Phil. After tomorrow's task force meeting I'll come back to bring you up to date."

"That won't be necessary, Hugh. I'll be at the meeting. Nothing would keep me from it."

McKay was about to protest but one look at the wan, pained, yet resolutely determined face of Hughes told him it would be a futile argument. He shrugged resignedly.

"Then I'll send a car for you and see you at nine tomorrow."

As they walked to the parking lot Thomas turned to the leader he so greatly respected.

"You told me that guy was smart but gee whiz he's almost as smart as you, boss."

"Cut the smarmy crap, Johnny. You don't have to butter me up. Your appraisal is not due for another six months," he replied with a grin.

He was smiling because he knew Thomas was the last person in his squad to indulge in obsequiousness. It was just not his style.

"But I'll tell you this, Johnny," he said in a serious voice which betrayed the strain he was under. "I'm sure glad we have Phil Hughes working with us. I guessed this case had international ramifications and knew I'd be out of my depth. But with his extensive experience in that area I feel much more comfortable about our chances of catching Mr. bloody X. See you back at the office."

"I'll have all the notes typed up by Sally. On paper, and not on the computer," added Thomas with a wicked smirk.

"Get out of here you cheeky bugger," retorted McKay but couldn't keep a grin from his own face.

Johnny's arrow had struck home. His intentional jibe was aimed at slightly alleviating McKay's tension. And it did.

They had formed a good team. McKay's brilliance at solving cases often caused him to have long spells of lonely somberness as he struggled to find answers. Johnny Thomas was a fast learner and was quickly becoming a skilled investigator himself. And his impish sense of humor was a perfect offset to McKay's frequently serious demeanor. He had successfully managed to lighten McKay's mood on several past occasions. In the beginning of his assignment to McKay he had often overstepped the boundaries of sergeant to detective inspector with his rascally ill-thought out comments and had been severely reprimanded. He quickly learned although McKay was good natured he demanded his subordinates perform their duties in an excellent, thoughtful and respectful manner. Now he had learned to modulate his behavior and they interacted well.

When McKay returned to his office he was surprised to find Belinda Carson waiting for him.

"Belinda, what are you doing here?"

He hadn't intended to sound so curt and instantly regretted allowing the building tension inside of him to make him do so. His tone caused her to hesitate for several seconds, but then the dam burst and her plaintive words poured out.

"I'm sorry to arrive unannounced, DI McKay. I really do want to be useful in this case. However, my boss has made it clear he doesn't need nor wish my further involvement. Therefore my visit is completely off the record. Does that cause you a problem?"

"It's a bit awkward, Belinda. But no, it doesn't cause me a problem. I think we will need all the manpower – excuse me – peoplepower, we can muster. And off the record, I got the distinct impression your boss, Mr. Jason Brandt, is a bit of a glory seeker. Perhaps he is not always a team player. Eh?"

Belinda Carson paused before answering; this was now becoming career threatening.

"That's okay, Belinda. Your lack of an instant response tells me all I need to know. Well here's what you can do. I'm sure you have at least one contact in your office and one in Ottawa you completely trust; reliable confidants?"

Carson nodded her head, then quickly glanced around the room. McKay noticed this reaction.

"You needn't be concerned; this room is not wired to record conversations. You can speak freely."

"Yes, there are a few I can trust totally."

"Then the first thing you can do is tell me everything going on in those offices. Just in case Mr. Brandt holds back something either intentionally or not. Okay?"

"Okay. What else can I do?"

McKay thought for a minute, his brow creased in concentration and then a smile crossed his face.

"You can start dating my sergeant, Johnny Thomas!"

"That rocked Carson. Her face reddened as she sputtered, "What? I am not someone you can pass along to your sergeant on a whim!"

"Let me explain, Belinda. I require you to be kept up-to-date on the progress of this case. That's the only way you can be fully ready to be of assistance when I need you. We can't risk sending you copies of our case file which is highly restricted. And you can't keep coming to this office to be briefed without tongues wagging and that may get back to your boss. However, if you and Johnny appear to have struck up a relationship, it would account for you both meeting regularly. You see?"

The redness left her face. She stared at McKay with renewed admiration.

"You really are a smart detective. Okay, I agree. But it's just pretend, no funny stuff."

McKay stared back at her with a stern look. One that displayed he was now all business.

"If you and Johnny really want to convince others you are in a relationship you will have to kiss him now and then when people are looking. You have to fully play the part or forget it. This is not a kid's game, Belinda. There are countless lives at stake. And if you truly wish to be part of it you must do as I say."

Belinda blushed again but nodded her agreement.

"Sergeant Thomas," bellowed McKay.

When Thomas came hustling in, McKay said, "Close the door."

He did so and stood expectantly for his orders. However this was an order he could never have imagined.

"Meet your new girlfriend. You and Belinda are now officially an item."

Chapter Twelve

McKay arrived at his office at seven-thirty the following morning. Belinda Carson was already there. She was sitting close to Johnny Thomas, they were holding hands. He was pleased to see she was acting the part. He signaled them to come into his office. When the door was closed he looked at her speculatively and raised his eyebrows in a question. She didn't hesitate.

"Jason Brandt must have been given important information from Germany. He has ordered a full background check on one Klaus Schultz believed to be an expert with computers. And he is raising hell over a fictitious order from the CSIS to this Schultz. That's all I have found out so far."

"Thanks Belinda. You are doing the right thing. If Brandt brings all this out at the meeting no harm has been done. If he doesn't – well that's a different story. He picked up the telephone and called Phil Hughes' CIA partner on the task force.

"Good morning, Ronald. I need you to immediately check something for me from Langley, and I need it before our meeting starts."

"Sure, go ahead."

"Find out all you can about a German computer expert named Klaus Shultz. And what he was alleged to have shipped to the CSIS. Brief me and Phil before the meeting and I'll tell you how to handle this information during the meeting. Okay?"

"Of course, Hugh. But shouldn't you be directing this to Jason?"

"No, and I'll explain why later."

At precisely five minutes to nine the meeting convened. It had been understood by all members this task force was to be restricted to members only. Therefore they were more that a little surprised with McKay's opening words.

"I hope you don't mind, I asked my sergeant, Johnny Thomas, to attend. He has added information to our crime board as you can see and I want him to add more as you each give your reports. He is also an excellent note keeper and I would like him to have the minutes of our meeting typed and distributed for your comments before we leave. Then a final edited report will be issued. I think it best if we all sing from the same hymn sheet. I know having an extra person present contravenes the spirit of our group and if anyone disagrees I will ask Johnny to leave before we start."

The astonishment which had been on most faces immediately dissipated and was replaced with nods of agreement as they unanimously voiced their approval. They thought it an excellent idea. To all of them it was yet another manifestation they had picked the right man to lead them. He knew when it was appropriate to bend rules.

"Let's start with the report from the FBI."

He nodded to the senior of the two agents, Larry Douglas.

"We checked for major events within a six months period as requested. Unfortunately there is one such event in New York, Washington, Atlanta, Miami, Dallas, Los Angeles, San Francisco, Denver and Chicago. However the only ones to be attended by senior members of the Administration are in Los Angeles and Chicago. Therefore If you want me to check further I would give those two top priority."

"Thanks, once we have heard all reports we can assign further tasks." All at the meeting were impressed as Johnny Thomas had already pinned a card on the board with the names of the locations.

"What did CSIS find out?"

"There was nothing in particular. I checked my sources in both mainland Europe and East Europe, nothing of note was reported."

There was a look of initial astonishment on Ronald Coleman's face from which he quickly recovered. This was a contradiction of the information he had discovered and passed to Hughes and McKay before the meeting. McKay gave him the slightest of nods as a signal for him to do exactly what he had been told.

"Okay, thanks Jason. Now I'll pass the floor to one of the most stubborn men in our group, Phil Hughes. Despite his injury he insisted on being here."

The looks on the faces around the table were a mixture of admiration and concern.

'This man ought not to be here, he is too ill,' was the common thought.

Phil reiterated the account he had given Hugh in the hospital.

"To conclude, this Mr. X either is a brilliant computer whiz or has someone working for him who is. I suspect the former as he shows tendencies of being a lone wolf. I talked to our best computer expert in Langley and he explained how Mr. X could have gotten into our system in Tokyo to send out those messages to three Asian countries. I was told it could only have been done by the most exceptionally gifted person. In addition we believe Mr. X attempted to penetrate our secure computer in Langley. Fortunately he was unable to do so. I asked our expert if he could trace other such attempts and it was revealed Mr. X did get into the computer of CSIS. That's how he got the names of all who attended our meeting in Ottawa and the name of the hotel where I was staying. I'll repeat the warning passed along to all our organizations. Put nothing on a computer regarding this case."

"Let's be certain we all heed that warning," added McKay for emphasis. "Anything further to report, Phil?"

"Yes, CIA checked all nuclear nations in Asia. We requested they check their arsenals. Not unexpectedly we received frosty responses, along the lines their arsenals were intact and it was none of our business anyway. We were most pointed in our request of one nation. We knew a highly placed general connected to their nuclear program had died in a traffic accident. The terse response was, of course, it was standard procedure in such a case to make a thorough check. When we attempted to suggest a physical count may be useful we were icily told their computer records were intact."

"Perhaps you'll explain why a traffic accident aroused your suspicion, Phil."

"We know if such a highly placed officer was to be murdered or appear to have committed suicide, it would trigger an alarm and a physical count would have been taken. However an apparently innocent traffic accident would only call for a computer check. And Mr. X has proved he has the capability of manipulating computer systems. I have my people in that country digging into the details of that traffic accident. I'll let you know what we find."

"So gentlemen, we must take it as a possibility a nuclear device has been stolen," concluded a deeply concerned McKay.

When the gasps of horror had died down, he continued.

"To further strengthen this possibility let me tell you what we found in checking into all the major gangs in Canada. In doing so we were surprised to discover the head of the biggest gang in Canada had disappeared. And we learned this man, Jacques Simone, had been using a possibly Asian man as a confidant. Furthermore we got Simone's replacement to admit a secret cargo container was picked up somewhere in Asia and was personally brought through all formalities in Vancouver by Simone. He was able to so as his gang has control over many of the workers on the docks. We have no idea where that container went."

There was a moments silence while all this new information sunk in. Then one of the FBI agents addressed McKay.

"But how on earth could anyone breach the security of national computer systems? Surely they must have the most elaborate protection devices possible?"

"I'll ask Ronald Coleman to explain."

"We believe there are only a handful of enormously talented computer experts in the world. We have one of them in Langley. He says the person who pulled this off would need two of the rarest pieces of equipment. One would be a random routing message transfer device. In layman's terms this device can transfer a computer message to any number of locations around the world so that a normal computer expert could not identify its original source. This device was conceived in Germany and to the best of our knowledge only five were built: all allegedly for government security agencies. Then the German developer, named Shultz, got greedy and tried to market it to important criminal organizations. He was caught and is now in a high security German prison. We talked to German National Security who got the information out of Schultz that the fifth was allegedly commissioned by Canadian Security but it never arrived. I don't believe you have such a device do you Jason?"

Jason Brandt of CSIS did not reply immediately.

"That is a matter for CSIS and is information I am not at liberty to divulge," he finally said.

"We are attempting to prevent a madman from possibly detonating a nuclear device which would kill tens of millions of people," snapped McKay. "I would advise you to tell us all you know and I would remind you our prime minister said all Canadian agencies must fully cooperate. If you continue to obstruct this investigation, Mr. Brandt, I will have to inform the prime minister."

Brandt blanched at this and attempted to cover his gaff.

"Oh well, forgive me, I suppose it's all right to confirm we do *not* have such a device."

All the other members of the task force had noted McKay's use of 'Mr. Brandt' and not 'Jason' as a clear indication he did not trust him. Coleman continued with his commentary.

"It must therefore be assumed it was Mr. X who broke into your system, Jason, to place this order. And if you don't have it we must also assume he does."

An enraged McKay attempted to control his wrath before speaking again.

"When I asked you earlier, *Mr. Brandt*, if you had anything further to report you said, 'No'. You should have reported this matter. And I also find it strange given your avowed excellent contacts throughout Europe that your German contact didn't mention the imprisonment of this highly dangerous man."

The inference in his voice made it abundantly obvious to all he did not believe Brandt.

"If he did I must have thought it inconsequential and missed its importance. My apologies."

Once again they all knew Brandt had been caught withholding information. Knowing his conversation with his German contact could be checked he had been forced to come up with a lame lie.

After an embarrassing moment the junior of the two FBI men, Jim Parker, spoke, addressing his question to Coleman.

"You mentioned there were two rare pieces of equipment, what was the second?"

"To break into all of these security systems one would have to discover the security phrase or password. And as these are normally changed on a regular basis, sometimes as frequently as daily, that would be an impossible task to do manually. Our computer expert remembers being at a conference and meeting a Canadian named Mercier who was brilliant. He let it slip one night in the bar he was working on just such a device. We tried through our sources and those of CSIS to find him but he seems to have vanished. It was rumored he was working for some shady characters. Maybe he crossed them and they disposed of him."

"Wait a minute," interrupted McKay. "When I was checking on Jacques Simone I was told he had a large garage he used for some purpose but it was destroyed by fire. It was determined it was an arson job. The only things the investigators managed to identify in the ruins were pieces of computer equipment. And the fire occurred immediately after the disappearance of Simone. I'll bet my bottom dollar this Mercier was working with Simone and somehow Mr. X knew of his special equipment including the German piece and he stole them after disposing of Mercier and his garage. That's how he managed to crack all the systems around the world, except the one at Langley. And, gentlemen, by attempting to infiltrate Langley, he made his first mistake. It led us to the knowledge of his computer skills. This man believes he is infallible. His hubris will be his undoing."

That thought had just been digested by the group when Phil Hughes spoke.

"You were to check the Canadian Immigration Service looking for a passport that had visited several Asian countries recently. Did you find anything, Hugh?"

"No, nothing. But that doesn't rule out the possibility of his having more than one passport. Excellent fakes are produced these days in several countries. Having several he could drive over the border to America and simply show one of his passports. Then he could leave America on another and travel to several Asian countries. But given his extraordinary computer skills he would not need to leave Canada, he could do everything from here."

All this time Thomas had been posting notes. McKay stood to review the board.

"We have put together a pretty compelling story as to the events until now. But we are no closer to identifying Mr. X!" he exclaimed in exasperation.

"There's one other thing," said FBI Special Agent, Larry Douglas. "We tried but couldn't find the significance of the positioning of the bodies in the bathtub. Did anyone have any better luck?"

The universal response was 'No'.

"As Hugh mentioned," he continued, "It must have been a message. I'm certain it is an important clue," he averred as he stood and spread all the photographs taken at the scene in front of him. "Why the hell place the bodies fully clothed and facing each other," he mused. "And why put the man's bloody hand on the shoulder of the woman, leaving that awful handprint on her white blouse?"

He shook his head in bewilderment, and was about to sit down when he heard the rasping voice of Phil Hughes.

"Show me that photograph," he hissed.

Everyone stared at him. His hand shook violently as he grasped the photograph. His entire body swayed precariously and his eyes seemed to want to pop from his head. Sweat pored from his face and his voice almost deserted him. They had to strain their ears to hear his strangled words.

"Oh no! Sweet Jesus no! It can't be him! We all thought he was dead."

The silence in the room was deafening.

"Phil, are you all right? What is it?" asked a deeply concerned McKay.

"I know who did this. I know his name," he managed to croak before collapsing in his chair and passing out.

Chapter Thirteen

It had been the combination of this devastatingly traumatic discovery and his previous loss of blood that caused him to faint.

"Get the doctor, and call an ambulance," McKay barked to Thomas.

Hugh had been sufficiently concerned over Phil's insistence on attending the meeting he had asked Thomas to have a doctor stand by in an outer office. His prescience paid off and the doctor quickly arrived.

"Stand well back!" the doctor ordered as the natural inclination of all present was to congregate around Hughes in a protective semicircle. "Get me a cushion and help me get him on the floor. And you're all still too close. Please leave the room while I attend to Mr. Hughes They all left except McKay.

The doctor was about to protest but instead quickly turned his attention to Hughes. He listened carefully at his heart and felt his pulse.

"His pulse is racing, he should never have left the hospital," he cried out, glaring at McKay before opening his bag and taking out a pellet of smelling salts.

He broke this under Hughes' nose and his eyes fluttered open. At first he was totally confused then his bleary eyes cleared and he focused on the doctor's face. Almost at the same instant he sought out McKay and attempted to get up. The doctor restrained him but he pushed the doctor away.

"This is critical, let me up," he demanded.

Once again the doctor gave McKay an accusatory glare. McKay shrugged.

"This is a matter of vital national importance. I'm afraid I must ask you to leave, doctor. Please wait outside. I promise he will be with you in ten minutes."

When he had gone and the door firmly closed Hughes took several sips of water before starting.

"The man's name is Ma Guan-lui. He is Chinese from Hunan and was an acolyte of Mao. During that regime he was directly responsible for the deaths of thousands of people. His nickname is Red Hand. He got that name at the end of WW11 when he personally slaughtered twelve captured Japanese soldiers being held in a hotel. He had them locked in separate rooms and went from room to room killing them one at a time. As he descended the stairs after the killings he slapped his blood soaked hand against the white wall leaving a bloody handprint. So you see the positioning of the bodies in the bathtub was of no consequence only the man's hand was."

"Oh my God, that's why he put that handprint on the woman's blouse. He was leaving you a message," exclaimed McKay.

"That must be correct," confirmed Hughes. "And he shot me in the leg as another message. He could easily have killed me as revenge for my part in stopping his heinous plan."

"What plan?" asked McKay.

"I can't go into all the details but several years ago he came within a cat's whisker of starting a nuclear war."

One could have heard the proverbial pin drop. McKay's heart rate was racing and he felt certain its thumping was echoing around the room. He finally regained control of his emotions and redirected his attention to his wounded colleague.

"You have to get checked out at the hospital right away, Phil. But, your news is so staggering if you feel you can hold on for another minute please tell me as much as you can."

"Ma is a manipulating genius. There are no other words for him. He is a true genius, believe me. He single handedly convinced a group of right wing Chinese generals to steal nuclear missiles and be prepared to use them. He even had other Asian country leaders hoodwinked into abetting him. He completely disappeared after his failed attempt. But we all believed the Chinese had caught and executed him."

"That sounds more like the plot of a horror movie than reality. It's almost impossible to believe it's true."

"I'm afraid it is. And it would have worked but for the exceptional bravery and intelligence of one man. And that's why Red Hand did not kill me. He wants me to bring that man here to help stop him. Knowing Ma, he will be supremely confident in his ability to kill both of us as revenge before launching his attack on America. This man delights in killing as many people as possible."

As he spoke it was apparent he was in considerable pain. His leg had begun to bleed and he swayed in his chair.

"Thanks for this invaluable information, Phil but now you must get some rest. I'll visit you in the hospital once we are finished here," said a concerned McKay.

"There's one more thing. He is slimly built and about five feet nine inches tall and walks with a definite limp, due to a club foot. He also has a pink scar on his chin. But he has been known to grow a beard to hide this mark."

"Thanks, Phil, now you really must go."

He quickly called in the doctor and the ambulance arrived soon after.

As the others filed back into the room Johnny was given instructions and he quickly departed.

"I will write some of the valuable information Phil gave me on a couple of cards and pin them on the board."

Once again there was silence in the room as everyone studied the board.

"Well we certainly have made progress," said one member of the group.

"Yes, but at what price?" mused McKay. "I have sent Johnny to greatly reinforce the guard we have at the hospital. I don't need to tell you that the life of Phil Hughes is in constant danger. And we are dealing with a criminal the likes of whom we have never seen. Johnny will be back shortly and will take any further notes we may have. Are there any comments on how we should proceed?"

"Well the obvious first step is to inform the heads of our organizations of the identity and description of Ma Guan-lui. But from the way you asked that question, I gather you do not wish an all out search for this man. Am I right?" asked Coleman, the colleague of Hughes at the CIA.

"That's exactly what I was thinking," confirmed McKay. "Ah, here's Sergeant Thomas. Just in time to take notes. I have to believe Ma has several disguises and he may even have a way of mitigating his limp. I also believe he has set up recording machines tuned into all our radio bands. So in addition to breaking into our computer systems he will be listening in to our broadcasts. If we were to put out an all points bulletin he would simply vanish into the wind."

"We just can't sit on our hands, we have to go after him," protested Jim Parker.

"I agree, but it must be done subtly. Let me propose this for your consideration. First, let's assume he is still here in Vancouver. I'll pull together a small team of my best men to go over the stories of the local gangs with a fine tooth comb. The ostensible reason will be an investigation of their missing leaders. I will ask Pierre in Montreal to do the same with Simone's gang. My team here will also grill the leaders of the dock workers, giving the disappearance of Simone as the reason. Under no circumstance will any of the police mention the name or the description of Ma. If we shake the bushes hard enough something may fall out."

"And what's the second thing?" asked the bright Coleman.

"We ask the FBI to pick a couple of their very best men and check out the sites of the identified large meetings to be held soon. Once again I must stress no name or description of Ma is to be given. I'm certain they will be skilled enough to question the right people regarding anyone having been there in the last six months and displaying an inordinate interest in the meetings or the buildings. They should also be checking any building suitable to hide a shipping container. They'll know what to do."

"Is there a third thing?" persisted Coleman.

"Since you're full of questions, I'll give you the third task," responded McKay with a smile. The others chuckled.

"Have your people, in the Asian country where the general was killed, do their best to identify all major weapons in the arsenal. Not just nuclear ones but any that could kill significant numbers of people. And have your sources in the other nuclear countries check for similar weapons. And before you ask - I do have a fourth task."

This time the chuckles were louder. It was more of a tension release mechanism than a response to a joke.

"I want the Canadian police to check with all relevant foreign delegations in Canada for visa applications issued recently. If there is a planned major attack I don't believe our Mr. Ma will stay around to be caught. He probably plans to travel to a non-extradition country. That's all from me. Anyone have something to add?"

There were shakes of the head. This time there were no chuckles but the eyes of the members reflected the high respect for the man they had chosen to lead them.

"Then before I leave to visit Phil, I'll ask all of us to stay here until Johnny gets the minutes typed. However for absolute security reasons I don't want the minutes distributed. I do want all of you to sign them indicating they are correct."

Sensing uneasiness at this he quickly continued.

"Believe me, this is not a sign of a lack of trust. However, the more copies issued, the greater the possibility of an inadvertent leak. Perhaps I am being paranoid over security and if I am, I apologize."

Perhaps slightly reluctantly, everyone agreed.

Thomas took his cue and quickly left the room. Sally was in an office nearby standing at the ready.

"I'll leave you now. I'm anxious to check on Phil."

"Some of us would like to visit Phil, but if you think it would be too much for him we'll just ask you to give him our best wishes," said Coleman.

"I think it would be best if I go alone. Phil mentioned a man who had previously foiled Red Hand. I could tell from his attitude he didn't wish to mention his name. I'm guessing he was struggling with whether or not to involve him as it could lead to his death. However I must know if this man could be our best bet to foil Ma once again. I don't like putting Phil under pressure but it is incumbent on all of us to do whatever it takes if we are to save the lives of millions."

There were nods of agreement around the table. Their faces were set in grim expressions. The pressure of the magnitude of this case and the recognition that time was running out fast, was obviously getting to them.

Johnny handed him the first draft of the minutes as he rushed out the door.

Chapter Fourteen

McKay noticed the four plain clothes men strategically positioned around the entrance to the hospital. He didn't greet them verbally but gave the briefest of nods. He was also pleased to see the three men in the vestibule. When he got off the elevator at the fourth floor he recognized two women police dressed as nurses and the man polishing the floor was one of his. Outside Phil's room stood three uniformed policemen. He smiled his approval. You wanted at least one obvious show of security at this location.

"How are you feeling?" he asked as he entered the room.

This was more of a general greeting than a question. One look at Hughes told him he was a sick man.

"Oh, I'm much better," responded Hughes crossing his fingers under the blanket at this lie. "The doctor believes it was the sudden rush of blood in my system at recognizing Red Hand which caused me to faint. But I really feel so much better now. Let me just get dressed then we can get back to work at your office. There's a lot to do now."

"Easy, Phil. Everything that can be done has been set in motion. Here, I brought you a copy of the minutes. It will make good bedtime reading. If your recovery is as good as you think, the doctor will release you tomorrow. But you had better behave tonight. Okay?"

"Okay, I promise."

McKay wasn't one hundred percent certain he believed him, so he played his trump card.

"If you don't, I'll call your wife. I managed to get your home telephone number."

"Ouch! That's a really low blow. I thought we were friends."

"We are. And in many ways we are alike. So I tried to think what I would do in your position. Most probably I would try to get out of bed. The only person who would stop me would be my wife. Ergo, my threat to you is the same."

Hughes grinned at him.

"Maybe we are too much alike," he said.

The grin left his face as he studied McKay. He saw a shadow come over his face and knew he had something serious to discuss.

"Go ahead – lay it on me."

"Just like you, Phil, I am not afraid to admit I am scared out of my mind over this case. Red Hand is way out of the league of criminals I have ever dealt with. And I am terrified I get it wrong. Oh, I know we have the full backing of the FBI, the CIA and the CSIS. Yet I still feel uneasy."

"And you want me to call on my friend to help. Even though Ma has made it abundantly clear he wants to kill both him and me."

"Even at such a high risk, my answer is yes. I'm sorry, Phil, but I can leave no stone unturned in this case. But with all the resources I mentioned I need to know exactly what your friend can do that they can't. Or at the very least if he has advice to offer."

The look of desperation on McKay's face visibly demonstrated the stressful dilemma he felt. Hughes held out his hand to shake McKay's.

"I feel the same way, Hugh. I'll make a deal with you. Get me out of this hospital tomorrow and I'll arrange a CIA plane to fly us to Hawaii and we will both talk to him. This type of thing cannot be done over the phone. He is one of the finest men I have ever met; and his bravery and hunting skills are the best I have ever heard of. He utilized those skills to become the most talented leader of Special Forces in Vietnam. But I'll give you a complete briefing tomorrow on the plane. After you meet him I believe you will understand why I have undying faith in him. And why I know he will bring that something special to our quest, should he agree to assist us."

McKay screwed up his eyes as he stared into those of Hughes.

"You know, Phil, if I didn't know you better I could believe you didn't completely trust me and that's why you are not prepared to give me all his details now. Maybe you think I would jump the gun and call your friend now. Eh?"

Hughes feigned a look of astonished innocence before replying.

"Let's just say we do have many things in common. And just like you I believe in a little insurance. *Eh*?"

His 'eh' was his best imitation of Canadian idiom. McKay had to smile.

"I'll call for you at nine o'clock and come with my bag packed."

Just before ten the following morning they were strapped in their seats and the jet raced down the runway. Once airborne the flight attendant served coffee.

"Breakfast will be ready in ten minutes," she said with a smile.

"Thanks for coming, Hugh, and for not pursuing my friend's name. I know you could easily have gone over my head to Langley and they would have given you all they had on him."

McKay nodded.

"But then I wouldn't get this first class ride to Hawaii. I hope the CIA serves mai tais on this plane" he said with a smile.

"If not I promise to buy you one in Honolulu."

He didn't wait for breakfast to be served but started immediately with his story.

"The man we will visit is Colonel Philip Melville, one of the most decorated soldiers of the Vietnam conflict. I called him to expect our visit."

McKay's face showed his initial concern at this information.

"Don't worry, Hugh, I didn't mention the reason. But he's smart enough to understand a face to face meeting is not good news. Now to get on with my story. Several years ago I got wind of something strange going on in Vietnam and Japan. It worried me sufficiently to have me call on a highly placed general I knew to ask him to recommend his best man to investigate. That man turned out to be Philip Melville. He agreed to help and went to Vietnam, by that time occupied by the communists, and began to unravel a heinous plot. It finally led to China where he succeeded in stopping rogue generals in the process of sending nuclear missiles to North Korea. Red Hand was behind this plot. He had personally convinced the leadership in North Korea that the missiles were non-nuclear and were to be fired at the South. However in reality he had sent his own technicians in readiness to launch the missiles. Not to South Korea - but one to Tokyo and the other to Osaka. To destroy the country he hated most."

"But surely America would have discovered they were Chinese missiles and retaliated."

"Ah, but that was the brilliance of his plan. The rogue Chinese generals had massed their troops ready to invade South Korea, and the rest of South East Asia. They would aver this nuclear attack was taken by disaffected elements in their army who had now been uncovered and executed. And they would stoutly claim they had only taken over almost all of Asia to protect themselves against a possibly rash American retaliatory invasion of China. They would strongly petition the United Nations to mediate a peaceful solution."

"Was the Chinese leadership involved in all of this?"

"No, they were in the dark. But Red Hand had surmised that when presented with a 'fait accompli', most of the leadership would see this as the realization of China's dream of becoming a world leader. Red Hand had calculated, probably correctly, the United Nations would strongly urge America not to retaliate with a nuclear attack. And while the debate raged at the United Nations, China would strengthen her control over all of Asia. And with Japan decimated, China would become even more powerful than the United States!"

McKay whistled. His face had turned a pasty white.

"And this Colonel Philip Melville prevented all this from happening?" he asked in a hushed voice.

"Yes he did. He uncovered the plot. Once Philip informed me, I petitioned my director to have the president immediately intervene. Disastrously, when the director did, he was over-ruled by senior State Department personnel who said our information was too outlandish to be credible. Despite our protests, both he and I were unable to make Washington believe it to be true. So Philip had to act on his own - without authority."

"How the hell did he manage that?"

"Ah, here's our breakfast. I'll tell you the rest when we've eaten."

McKay was not to be put off so easily. After his first bite of toast he voiced his protest.

"You can't leave me dangling over a plate of scrambled eggs and bacon not knowing how the whole damned world was saved from devastation."

Hughes stuffed a generous amount of his breakfast in his mouth before relenting.

"Very well," he said resignedly as he ruefully eyed the rest of his breakfast which would soon become cold. "As I said, Philip was persuaded to undertake the very dangerous mission of travelling to Vietnam. His task was to discover why a very prominent person, named Nguyen, who had always been a vigorous anti-communist, was now broadcasting strongly pro-communist messages to the Vietnamese people. Philip was accompanied by his wife, Mei Li. Did I mention she is Vietnamese?"

"No, you didn't," responded McKay tersely, wanting him to get on with the story.

"Well she is, and she had known Nguyen since childhood. She knew he had to have been coerced into making these broadcasts. To shorten the story, Philip rescued Nguyen and his family. In doing so he learned what the Nguyens had overheard in tripartite meetings between the president of Vietnam, the son of the president of North Korea and a Chinese delegation led by a man with a decided limp."

"Red Hand!" interjected McKay.

"Correct. He had masterminded the broadcasts having Nguyen claim America was preparing to invade Vietnam. The invasion would be spearheaded by troops based in South Korea. And as I said previously, he had convinced the son of the North Korean leader he could give him non-nuclear bombs to launch at the south and he guaranteed China would assist him in following up this attack with an invasion force. Allegedly, all of this was supposed to be in support of their soon-to-be-invaded brothers in Vietnam."

"What a plot," exclaimed McKay. "Then instead of launching non-nuclear missiles at South Korea, he would actually fire nuclear ones to essentially wipe out most of Japan."

"Precisely. So Philip first went to Hong Kong then infiltrated into China. There he picked up the trail of Red Hand and succeeded in persuading a top Chinese leader of the plot. The whole thing was stopped just in time but although the rogue generals were executed, Red Hand escaped."

"Wow, he must be some guy, this Philip Melville!"

"He is. And now if you don't mind, since you ruined my breakfast, I'll order a muffin to go with another cup of hot coffee!"

Chapter Fifteen

The jet touched down at Hickam Air Force Base where a SUV with tinted windows awaited. They were driven directly to the Melville residence. On the way Hughes gave McKay a warning.

"You must not be fooled by the beautiful and seemingly delicate, Mrs. Melville. Mei Li is not a person to be underestimated. She is an outspoken, strong-willed, and influential partner of Philip. So beware! Once she realizes why you are here she will attack with the ferocity of a protective she bear."

The van drew up at the door of the residence and they were met by Mei Li and Philip. She wrapped her arms around Hughes in a warm greeting. As soon as she released him, she shot a worried glance at her husband. Philip had also noted the cause of her concern. Their friend, Phil Hughes, did not look well.

McKay studied this lovely lady while this was happening and was certain Hughes had overstated his warning. She was charming during the introductions and her invitation into her home where she had prepared coffee, home-made cookies and slices of pineapple. However once they were seated he happened to glance at her again and her look could have turned him to stone.

'Wow! Phil was right. I guess I'm in trouble. They must have deduced why I'm here,' he thought.

When coffee had been served, Mei Li wasted no time in attacking McKay.

"You're here to ask my husband to put his life in danger! Aren't you?"

"To be fair, Mei Li, it was my idea to visit Philip. Hugh is in charge of a case which could have the most terrifying consequences."

He turned his gaze toward Philip. He almost didn't have to say anything. Philip Melville could read the look of dread in his face.

"I'm terribly afraid Red Hand has resurfaced. We all hoped he had finally been captured by the Chinese and killed. Unfortunately he is very much alive."

Mei Li's hand flew to her mouth as a gasp of horror escaped her lips. Philip's face was impassive.

"Where is he and what's he up to?"

"I'll let DI McKay tell you."

Hugh covered everything in a succinct manner.

"Colonel Melville, I've handled some truly gruesome cases. But I have never in my entire career been so frightened. Mrs. Melville, despite what you think, I didn't come here expecting your husband to join my task force. But what I desperately need is advice. And I'm hoping you can help me in any way possible, Colonel Melville."

Mei Li was a good judge of character. Not as perceptive as her unusually talented husband, but good nevertheless. She saw the utter anguish on the face of McKay and heard it in his voice. Almost as a token of forgiveness she put a slice of pineapple on his plate first, before serving the others. Philip also clearly recognized McKay's agonizing plight.

"First of all DI McKay, My name is Philip. You can dispense with the title colonel and my wife is Mei Li. And you can be assured I will answer any questions you may have and if I can offer advice it will be given freely. You see, there is no one I'd like to bring to justice more than that maniacal person."

The cloud of friction dissipated somewhat. Phil Hughes helped himself to a cookie and sipped his coffee. Mei Li could still become hostile if she sensed her husband was in jeopardy, but for the moment there was calm. However McKay's next words were about to change all that.

"I would be remiss if I didn't say Red Hand has made it abundantly clear he intends to kill Phil Hughes. The only reason he didn't when he had the chance was he wants to bring you, Philip, into the battle and do the same to you. He did this by shooting Phil Hughes in the leg. Phil lost a lot of blood and I am eternally grateful to him for making this long trip to bring me here, when he definitely must be suffering considerable pain."

There was a sharp intake of breath from Mei Li. Initially it was shock that her friend had been shot. Quickly that became anger at her husband being the target of a deadly assassin, and this man, McKay, having the temerity to involve him.

Her flashing eyes transmitted this message to Hugh.

He didn't blink, but stared back into her eyes. His own blue gray eyes transmitted their own message. He was a desperate man attempting to save millions of innocent people.

"I always do my best to be truthful, Mei Li; even if it is painful. Lies always catch up with you sooner or later."

The anger died from Mei Li's eyes but was replaced with deep concern. Hughes read the signs and breathed a sigh of relief. Hugh McKay had gone up in Mei Li's estimation.

"But I'm still not certain what I can do to help. Since you know the identity of the terrorist, surely this has been reduced to a manhunt. And you have the Canadian Police and the FBI. Between them they have the best resources for such a task. In addition you have the CSIS and the CIA. I don't see what I can add," said Philip.

The thoughtful McKay had anticipated this response and had an answer.

"There are two ways you can assist. First you have matched wits with this man. Instinctively you understand his tactics better than anyone. And secondly, he is conducting this crime like a military operation. He has thought of all the likely contingencies. It is possible your military training is exactly what we need to figure out his future moves. Already we have seen his deceptive feints draw us down one road while he attacks somewhere else. I feel in my bones he will employ other diversionary tactics and I fear we may be fooled. The future ones could be the vital ones."

"Please leave him alone, he has not been well," pleaded Mei Li.

"What's wrong, Philip?" asked an instantly worried Hughes, forgetting his own illness.

"It's nothing. I've just been off my food. Nothing to worry about."

All eyes spun instantly as they heard a muffled moan come from Mei Li. Those of Hughes and McKay were filled with deep concern but the eyes of Melville only showed understanding. He knew exactly why Mei Li was so upset.

"Dear God, you sensed this didn't you Philip? That's why you have been so out of sorts. You sensed it and it has been gnawing at you. You didn't know exactly what it was but you sensed danger."

"Most probably," responded Philip.

McKay and Hughes were acting as though they were at a tennis match. Their heads swiveled from Mei Li to Philip, back to Mei Li and again to Philip. McKay glanced at Hughes and saw his mouth was open wide. It was only then he recognized his was too.

"What's going on?" rasped Hughes.

"As Mei Li said, a few weeks ago I began feeling a bit unwell. It was nothing physical but something was troubling me. It has gradually been becoming more acute. It was the same feeling I would get when I was on patrol in the jungles of Vietnam. I could sense the enemy was near before we met up with them. I guess I must have known danger was getting close to me, but until you told me that Red Hand was alive, I had no idea of the source. Now I know."

McKay became conscious they were all staring at him.

"Mr. McKay, would you please stop drooling on my tablecloth," said Mei Li softly.

McKay realized his mouth had gaped open again and embarrassedly wiped his chin with his handkerchief.

"I'm sorry," he mumbled. "This is almost unbelievable."

"It happens to be some sort of gift I possess," explained Philip. "It's why I managed to survive all those years in Vietnam. But I feel much better now. You see, Hugh, the greatest fear a soldier on patrol has, is the unknown. Once the enemy is located his training kicks in and he knows what to do. And now that I know about Red Hand, let's get down to discussing how I can be of assistance."

Instinctively he looked at his wife who had stiffened with worry. He moved closer to her and held her tightly.

"We both know how fiendish he is, don't we Mei Li?"

She nodded silently.

"What I can't understand is why he has waited so long. Knowing his ego there must have been a white hot, all consuming, fire, burning inside him caused by his past failure. Undoubtedly he will have blamed Phil and me for that defeat. But he could have come after us some time ago. Why now? It must indicate he has a plan of massive proportions and he has finally acquired all the necessary tools to carry it out. Having taken years to do so I'm afraid his blazing vengeance is directed not only at us, but also at America. This time I can't let him live; the only way to stop him is to kill him. Do you understand, sweetheart?"

She nodded her head as tears rolled down her cheeks and she clung to Philip. But a few seconds later she brushed away the tears and McKay saw the steel spine of Mei Li. She straightened up and turned to Hughes.

"How long are you staying in Hawaii, Phil?"

"Only four hours. And I would like to see my wife for at least one of those."

"Very well. I'll clear the dining table. You can work there. And I'll make more coffee."

After clearing the table and before she left she looked directly at her husband for what seemed like an eternity to McKay. In truth it was no longer than about ten seconds. But that look left a searing impression that chilled his very soul. It was a mixture of love and deep concern and even perhaps of warning - and – most definitely - of fear.

Red Hand could have that effect on people.

Chapter Sixteen

Philip gave her a reassuring smile before opening a drawer and taking out three legal size paper pads and a variety of pencils and pens. He placed these on the table and asked the two men to be seated.

"To start, I would like both of you to once again go over everything about the case so far. And please do not skip anything, not the slightest detail."

Just by observing his calm but determined demeanor McKay instantly knew why this man had been so successful a leader of troops. He had assumed complete command without being officious. He took notes as the two went through everything. They were so absorbed they didn't seem to notice Mei Li placing large mugs of coffee beside them along with sandwiches. She sat next to her husband but did not interrupt. When they finished, Philip stared at his notes in silence as though he was burning every detail into his memory.

"Thank you Mei Li," said Hughes as he sipped his coffee.

Melville did not take his eyes from his notes but stretched out his hand to touch Mei Li's arm as a gesture of his appreciation for the coffee. At last he looked up and straight at McKay.

"I believe you're correct in assuming he is handling this like a precise military operation. Therefore, you must find out who is working with him."

"But we believe he is working alone. Anyone who has worked with him has been killed."

"That may be, but as a commander he can't do everything. He must have acquired a cadre of completely loyal soldiers. Whether he controls them with money or fear, I don't know; probably a mixture of both. Most likely they have no idea what his overall plan is. They merely do as he instructs. I would guess he has recruited about four of five, no more. I would suggest you have your department once again interview the current leaders of criminal gangs and find out if some of their best members have left. They probably don't know their men defected to Ma. Most likely they believe the men were murdered in the initial warfare following their past leaders' disappearance. If possible, get photographs and recheck the pharmacies you first interviewed. Perhaps Hsieh was not the only one looking for chemicals."

McKay hastily wrote down this instruction.

"You see, in addition to using the gangs to lead him to Simone, Ma was assessing their members to carefully select his recruits."

Hughes nodded his understanding, and McKay realized they had not pursued this avenue of investigation.

"One other thing and you may have already considered this, do a thorough check on every member of your task force."

Both McKay and Hughes were startled at this advice and their faces clearly showed it.

"But, Philip, every man on the task force will have been thoroughly vetted by his organization. They are above reproach."

"I'm not referring to a background check conducted some time ago. I mean something that may have occurred since they joined your task force. I don't wish to malign your members; however, you must recognize Red Hand will do anything to keep information on the task force's activities flowing to him. And as you have effectively sealed off his ability to get this by prohibiting anything being recorded on a computer, his only recourse is to get information directly from someone on the task force. Information is the life blood of his operation. He must learn how close you are to uncovering him. The moment he gets a whiff you are closing in, he will disappear. Probably to the bomb's location; and then it will be too late to save lives. Never underestimate the lengths this fiend will go to in getting information. This will include kidnapping members' families. You must both be vigilant during your task force meetings for signs a member is under duress. I am certain you know what to look for. Those signs include a person not participating in discussions; excessive fidgeting; taking an unusual amount of notes; and, not making eye contact when being talked to."

"I see," responded an understanding but very unhappy McKay. Having a traitor on the task force was too repugnant to contemplate.

"Also if his computer installation is as powerful as you indicated, he has the capability to record phone conversations. Instruct all concerned not to pass important information over their regular phone. You need someone to install protective devices on newly dedicated lines. I am not sufficiently knowledgable to advise you on this. You need an expert."

"We have just the man at Langley. I'll call them immediately and have Ed Winfield dispatched to Vancouver to take care of that. Do you think your home phone has been tapped?"

"Possibly, to be safe don't use it to call Langley."

"If you'll excuse me I'll use the phone in the CIA car outside to call Langley's secure line. I'll have Ed Winfield instruct my office here how to secure their line, and ask them to do the same for yours. If you would like to come with me, Hugh, you can brief Ed on whom to contact in your office to accomplish this."

This was Phil's way of leaving Mei Li and Philip alone. He knew they would want to talk. Once they had left, Mei Li clung close to Philip. He had a solemn look on his face.

"I know it's scary, darling, but I beat him once, and I can do it again. Anyway we have no choice. He knows about me and will come after me. I have to get him. Now listen to me, Mei Li. I can't concentrate on this mission if I am constantly worrying about you. I want you to go and stay with your uncle in Hong Kong. If you stay here Red Hand may resort to attempting to harm you or kidnap you in order to get to me. That's the way his mind works. Your uncle will hire security for you in Hong Kong,"

She immediately began to protest but he put his finger to her lips.

"I know you would want to be with me but if I am to help catch this evil fiend, I must go to Vancouver. I'll go under his radar and stay away from places he will be watching like police headquarters and the hotel where Phil is staying. But I must be up-to-the-minute on all that is happening. You have to trust my judgment on this, please darling."

She knew he was right. He was always right on missions like this. With a disconsolate nod of her head she indicated her agreement. That didn't stop tears from flowing again.

"Will you call me each day? I need to know you are safe," pleaded Mei Li.

"I promise. But try not to worry too much. I couldn't be working with a better person than Phil. You know that don't you?"

"Yes, I trust Phil implicitly."

"And when he told me he was bringing DI McKay, I quizzed him about him. Phil said he was the smartest detective he has ever known. That's something coming from a spy like Phil. So I shall be working with a good team. We'll get this bastard."

He hugged her close. He didn't want his insightful wife to study his face too closely. He understood perfectly that catching Red Hand would be the most difficult of tasks. She was wiping away her tears when the men returned. McKay could guess what had been said, not in detail but his instincts told him Philip would join him in Vancouver. He immediately began thinking where to keep him and quickly came up with a solution while Hughes was talking.

"George Melton from my office will be here later this afternoon to take care of your phone," said Hughes. "Ed Winfield is briefing him now on how to protect the phone in my office. George will be working with a guy he knows in the phone company to accomplish all this. Now is there anything further we should cover before I visit my wife?"

"Only one thing. Can you send a CIA plane to pick me up the day after tomorrow and take me to Vancouver? And can you find a place for me to stay?"

"I've already thought of that, Philip," said McKay. You'll be met at the airport by Belinda Carson of the Canadian Security Intelligence Service. She'll take you to a safe house. You should stay away from hotels and our offices. We'll conduct our meetings in the safe house. You mustn't be known to be in Vancouver. Your wife would never forgive me if I allowed that to happen. And I'll make certain you have secure communication to be able to regularly contact her wherever she may be."

Mei Li could not keep a look of astonishment from her face.

She thought, 'How on earth could this man have deduced Philip would go to Vancouver? And how did he know she would not remain in Hawaii.'

"I told you so. He's good," whispered Philip in her ear.

"I'll arrange for a plane to be at Hickam at seven o'clock," confirmed Hughes. "Now if you'll excuse me I'd like to see my wife."

"Why don't you stay with us until Phil is ready," suggested Mei Li to McKay. "I'm certain Philip and I would like to get to know you better."

Both Phil and Philip were delighted at this suggestion. It was apparent Mei Li had decided she could trust this detective to take good care of her husband.

This was a trust she gave to very few people.

Chapter Seventeen

Philip's recommendation to check all relevant telephones was excellent advice - but unfortunately it came too late!

When Jason Brandt returned to the CSIS office following the second task force meeting he immediately called his boss, Jeremy Mason. He wanted to report the proceedings, but he also wanted to complain over the treatment he had received at the hands of Hugh McKay.

"I was only trying to protect the integrity of our office by keeping certain things confidential. He didn't have to make such a big deal about it."

Brandt knew word of the events would eventually get back to Mason. He wanted to get his side of the story in first, hoping for a compassionate understanding. That didn't happen.

"You were an ass to hold back on that information," responded an unsympathetic boss. "You haven't protected our integrity, Jason; you've succeeded in making us look guilty of not fully cooperating. I'll have to seriously consider whether you can continue to adequately represent us on the task force."

Without a further word he hung up.

That really stung Brandt. He sat in his chair staring into space with all of his hidden insecurities aflame. They continued to burn all afternoon. Finally he decided to leave the office early and headed straight for one of his favorite bars. After three martinis he went home and heated up a packaged meal in his microwave. While doing so he had two more vodkas. By now he had decided his future definitely did not reside at CSIS. He picked up the telephone and dialed a long series of numbers.

"Ya, who is this?" asked a guttural voice.

"Hello, Herman, it is Jason."

"Jason, good to hear from you. It's been a long time. What can I do for you?"

Herman Friedrich had moved with his parents from Germany to Brazil when he was fourteen years old. His mother was German but his father, Fritz, had actually been born in Canada of German immigrants. At the insistence of his wife, Fritz moved to Germany after their marriage. Herman's father was a shady character involved in several illegal actions. He received a tip the authorities were about to pounce and quickly decided to relocate to Brazil.

Herman had been a clever boy but more importantly a big, strong boy who soon learned the advantages of bullying his Brazilian schoolmates. Therefore it was not surprising to note when he left school at eighteen, he was already the leader of a gang. The apple doesn't fall far from the tree. The gang soon became involved in drugs, burglaries and petty thefts from stores. However Herman was an astute boy. He very soon came to understand a few policemen were not above accepting money to overlook crimes. Even more astutely he managed to find a corrupt lieutenant who, for the right price, was willing to instruct his men not to arrest Herman's gang.

By the age of twenty two, Herman was not only rich but he had formed his own company. Officially it was an import/export company. This neatly covered his nefarious activities. Smuggling was by far the most profitable one with drug importation being the major activity. He was twenty five when he came to the notice of Fernando Diaz, a Peruvian villain who specialized in supplying arms to several terrorist groups throughout South America. Herman accommodated Diaz by smuggling in a few weapons into Brazil then redistributing them to other countries. Nothing was on a major scale but sufficient to make them both considerable profits.

By now Herman was attracting the attention of highly placed law officers. He had successfully managed to avoid arrest but the cost of doing so was becoming prohibitive. To protect the fortune he had amassed he gave serious consideration to putting illegal activities behind him. He could easily afford to do so as his legal import/export business was quite profitable. Furthermore, due to his wealth, he had moved up in society and enjoyed the party life. It was at one such party he met a member of the Canadian Embassy, one Jason Brandt. They began a friendship and enjoyed having a good time. Much of the cost of this fell to the criminal and not the diplomat. The friendship resulted in the bright Herman deducing Jason was more than an Economic Secretary. He suspected his true work was in the field of espionage. A fact he tucked away for some possible future benefit. At the same time Jason had become aware of his friend's infamous activities.

It was about this time Diaz came to Herman with the deal of a lifetime. Terrorism was ramping up in some countries and he had been commissioned to supply a huge amount of armaments to several groups. Diaz found a source in North America. The problem was importing such an enormous amount of arms. Herman saw this as being his ticket out of crime. One last throw of the dice could set him up for life.

He wracked his brains for a solution and it came to him one night as he and Jason were partying. If Diaz could get the arms over the American border into Canada, could Jason bring the shipment into Brazil under diplomatic coverage designated as Canadian food aid to the poor? There was no need for Jason to know the true contents of the containers and Herman would take care of everything on the docks. The payoff for Jason would be seventy five thousand dollars. That proved to be too big an incentive for him to pass up and the deal was done.

It was six months after the deal when Jason was reassigned to Canada. And now, Herman's business was one hundred percent legitimate and he gave his friend an alternative to his new posting by offering him a position in his company. But Jason had globe-trotted enough and longed to return to Canada.

But tonight as he called Herman, Brandt had decided it may be time to accept the previous offer.

"I think I may have had enough of diplomatic life and wondered if your offer of a position in your company was still available?"

"Of course my friend, anytime. And if it is necessary, I have a contact who can arrange a new identity complete with passport, birth certificate, driver's license. The completed works," said the still astute Herman, sensing Jason was in trouble.

"I'll think about it for a few days and give you a call."

"Give it serious thought my friend, and call me anytime. Ciao, Jason.

"Ciao," replied a wavering Brandt.

"Ciao, to you too," cried out an elated, Ma Guan-lui, after listening to the tape of his tap on Brandt's phone. "I've got you now!"

Red Hand had been furious when he discovered he could no longer get information about the task force from the computers he had infiltrated. He guessed the minutes of meetings were now heavily censored and probably handed out in printed form only. And he had to know what the task force knew about him. Now he had that resource.

The day after Brandt called Brazil, he was sitting at his desk when he and a colleague were ordered to go straight to another room for a conference call with Jeremy Mason in Ottawa.

"We've had a catastrophe. Somehow someone has managed to penetrate our secure computer system and stolen five hundred thousand US dollars from our accounts. I have informed our State Department but not the police. This is money we had reserved in a slush fund for espionage purposes. Special auditors from State will be here shortly to check over everything. There will also be two auditors visiting you. Give them your full cooperation."

That day was frenetic as everything came under review. Brandt was glad to leave the office that night and stopped at another of his favorite bars for a few drinks. He has just started on his second when someone on his left bumped into him. He turned to remonstrate with the offender but he had quickly moved away. This so occupied him he didn't notice the man on his right slip something into his drink. He had intended ordering a third but after his second his head was swimming. He stared uncomprehendingly at his empty glass. Two drinks never affected him this way. It must have been the pressure at work and the fact he had skipped lunch. As he stepped unsteadily out into the street, a burly Chinese thrust a piece of paper in his hand.

"Call this number, it is very important."

Brandt's first thought was to contact the duty officer at CSIS; so he hurried home as quickly as his drugged state allowed. Once there he studied the message. He had to read it twice before understanding it. The message told him to call a number and give the account number of LRT 726839 and the security code of Archangel. Still under the influence of his doctored drink he had to read it a third time. Then the thought struck him this could be a message from Herman. He decided not to call the duty officer. This was just the type of foolishness Herman would get up to.

He didn't recognize the country code but dialed it nonetheless.

"Good evening and welcome to the Regal Bank," said the charming voice of a young lady. "May I have you account number?"

"Excuse me, but where are you located?" he asked in a puzzled and somewhat slurred voice.

There was a moment's hesitation before the lady answered.

"In Grand Cayman, of course, sir. May I have your account number?" she repeated.

He stared at the paper and finally gave the number typed on it.

"Thank you, and am I speaking to Mr. Jason Brandt?"

"Yes, this is he," he answered in a stunned voice as his fuzzy brain sought to comprehend what was happening.

"And may I have your password?"

"Archangel."

"Excellent. Then as you instructed I can confirm the account has a balance of five hundred thousand US dollars and is now activated. However as you also instructed funds may not be withdrawn until you give the new password."

"New password?"

"Yes sir, as per your instructions the password 'archangel' was only to confirm the account but you insisted the new password must be used to utilize the account's proceeds. Isn't that correct, Mr. Brandt?"

Still completely confused all he could think of saying was, "Yes."

He hung up the phone and stared at it in a trance for a full minute. When it rang he almost fell out of his chair with fright.

"Good evening, Mr. Brandt," purred the silky voice of Red Hand. "Congratulations on your new found wealth. Now listen carefully; you have two choices. Either go to jail for life for the theft of Canadian secret funds. Something I can ensure with one call. No one would believe a mysterious benefactor stole that money and deposited in an account you opened in Grand Cayman. Would they? Or, your more reasonable choice is to work with me. It will not be onerous work. All you have to do is keep me informed of the deliberations of the task force. Have you a pen and paper handy?"

"Yes," replied the even more dazed Canadian.

"Good then write down this number and call me at precisely seven o'clock tomorrow morning when you are fully sober. Now please repeat the telephone number to me and the time you are to call."

His handwriting was askew and he had trouble reading it.

"No, the third number is five not four. Now read it to me again. Good. Now go to sleep, Jason."

Brandt just managed to hang up the receiver before his head dropped on the desk and he fell into a deep sleep.

Chapter Eighteen

Brandt wakened at five-thirty, fully clothed and still sitting by the phone. At first he thought it may all have been a dream but then he saw the scrawled number he had written. Instantly a surge of panic swept over him. He had been craftily cornered. He knew the man who called him last night was right. No one would believe someone had robbed the CSIS and put the money in his account. Or would they? He needed time to calm his nerves and to think. He started coffee and while it was percolating he took a shower.

"Damn," he swore after his first gulp of coffee. He was trapped. If he told his story to security at CSIS they would check with Jeremy Mason who would say he had reason to severely admonish him. Then security would check his phone log and find out he had called someone in Brazil. The cards were stacked against him. He waited until seven o'clock before dialing the number he had been given.

"Good morning, Jason. I trust you slept well."

"Who the hell are you?"

No sooner had he asked the question when the answer came rocketing into his brain.

"You're Mr. X aren't you?"

"My name is unimportant. By now you realize you must do as I say. However I am not an unreasonable employer. I will only require your services for a short time. If your first report to me is satisfactory, I will add another five hundred thousand dollars to your account. At the end of our relationship I will double that amount, and, I will give you the password to access all that lovely money. As there is no extradition treaty between Canada and Brazil, you can live the rest of your life in luxury. I will contact you tonight to find out when the next task force meeting will be held. Goodbye."

The line went dead. Brandt thought for several minutes then decided he would negotiate with his adversary. He would demand an interim payment in cash, say fifty thousand. He picked up the phone and dialed the number.

"You have reached a number that does not exist. Please check your number and try again," intoned the automated message. He tried again thinking he had misread the number. He got the same result. He quickly dialed the operator to say there had been a mistake.

"I'm sorry sir there is no mistake. There is no such number."

"I'm telling you there is. I just dialed it a few minutes ago."

"Please hold."

It only took twenty seconds before the operator was back on the line.

"I checked and there have been no calls made from your line today. And I can definitely confirm the number you gave me in not a listed number. Is there anything further I can assist you with?"

"No thanks," he said softly as despondency settled over him like a heavy black cloak.

Instantly he knew Mr. X had the computing power to infiltrate the telephone company's system. He felt walls closing in all around him.

"You son of a bitch," he screamed vehemently.

Then his brain began engaging and he calmed down.

"Think, Jason, think. There must be a way out of this mess."

Nothing came to mind as he finished his coffee. He dressed, skipped breakfast and headed to work.

Fortunately the office was still in turmoil over the missing funds and he had time to sit quietly in his office and consider his dilemma. His first attempt at a solution was to have CSIS security tap his telephone to hear the next contact from Mr. X. But he quickly rejected that idea. Uncomfortable questions would be raised as to why he wished this and he would be forced back to attempting to explain how the missing funds wound up in an account the bank would say he personally opened.

His second solution was only a partial one. He would tape record the next phone call. Exactly how he would use the recording required further thought. At least he felt some comfort with the first step. As he had several meetings to attend he couldn't give the second step further serious thought.

That evening he avoided drinking and sat by his phone with a tape recorder at the ready. His nerves were jangling but he still resisted the urge to have a drink to steady them. He must keep his wits about him. He was so intent on the expected call he let out a yell of alarm when his doorbell rang. He sat transfixed for almost a minute before rushing to the door. Nobody was there. It was then he saw the piece of paper on his doorstep.

It read, 'Go to the nearest public telephone and dial this number – 629 – 7227. And do it now!'

For several seconds his mind was numb. Obviously Mr. X had decided calling his home number was too dangerous. Most probably he had divined all Brandt's possible reactions to his first message.

'This man is clever. I had better not underestimate him,' he thought as he put on his jacket before leaving his apartment.

Unfortunately he completely ignored the advice he had just given himself as he didn't do a thorough job of checking his surroundings before stepping into the telephone booth. He dialed the number and heard the same mellifluous voice.

"Thank you for being so prompt, Jason. I am certain you will have spent most of the day in a futile endeavor to think of a plan to frustrate my hold over you. You will soon discover I will always be one step ahead of you. Now when is the next meeting of the task force?"

"Before I tell you, I need some money. I must make arrangements to leave Canada once our relationship is over. Let's say fifty thousand dollars."

"Not only won't you get your money, but if you attempt another foolish action you will not live."

"What do you mean by foolish action?" gasped Brandt.

"You were followed to the phone booth and while we have been talking a friend has reported you have been recording our call. Please turn round and give him the recorder."

Brandt slowly turned and his face paled. He vaguely recognized the expressionless face of the burly Chinese as the man who had given him the note outside the bar. What he definitively did recognize, was the large pistol fitted with a silencer pointed right at him. The man held this in his right hand while holding out his left. Brandt meekly gave him the tape recorder. It was only them he noticed another Chinese holding a portable telephone to his ear. He turned back and put the receiver to his ear.

"That is much better, Jason," purred Red Hand.

Then the purring tone changed to a raging high pitched screech.

"If you ever try something like that again, I will keep my promise to kill you!"

This so terrified Brandt his only response was to nod his head. Then he realized what he was doing.

"I understand," he mumbled as he trembled with fear.

"Now, when is the next meeting?"

"The day after tomorrow."

"Good. Now tell me is anyone else to attend other than the members?"

"Not that I have been told."

"I see."

Brandt may have been scared almost out of his wits but he still detected a note of disappointment in Red Hand's voice.

"One last thing, I want a copy of the minutes of the last meeting. Tomorrow morning at exactly seven o'clock you will hand them to a man standing on your doorstep."

"I can't do that."

Before he could explain the screeching tone returned.

"You will do what you are told!"

"I can't. I don't have a copy. There was only the original and it was kept by McKay."

"Clever man. Then you will write out all you remember and give that to my man tomorrow."

"I understand."

"Goodnight, Jason."

The line went dead. Guessing the result would be the same as his last effort to reestablish contact with Mr. X, yet out of curiosity and desperation, Brandt dialed the number again.

"You have reached a number that does not exist. Please check your number and try again," responded the disembodied voice.

He replaced the receiver and began walking home. This time he checked several times to see if he was being followed. But he spotted no one. Once inside his apartment he immediately sought out the vodka bottle.

He had a large one and sat in a comfortable chair to think. Strangely, he realized he no longer felt afraid. After a few minutes of analysis he came to the conclusion this was because, for the first time, he believed he had an element of control. Mr. X had no idea what had been discussed at the task force meeting therefore he could not refute anything he would write.

"How can I use this to my advantage?" he wondered out loud.

Not waiting for an answer to come to him, he had another large vodka.

Chapter Nineteen

It was late when Hughes and McKay arrived in Vancouver. Phil was clearly showing the strain of two long flights. Hugh had been deeply worried over his health. But true to his indomitable spirit he put on a good face as he descended from the plane.

They were met at the airport by Sergeant Thomas. McKay looked surprised as he had not told him of his trip.

"What are you doing here, Johnny?"

"A fellow called Ed Winfield arrived today from Langley. After we danced around for a bit we finally recognized we were working on the same problem and began sharing information. While he began the process of checking all our phones, I updated our crime board with a few things he mentioned. He told me Phil Hughes was arriving from Hawaii and I guessed you were with him. Your car is here, boss, but I wondered if you had anything you wanted me to start on tonight?"

"Thanks anyway, Johnny, but everything can wait until tomorrow. Oh no, that's not true. Please ask your sweetheart to be in my office at nine in the morning."

Hughes looked at both of them in puzzlement.

"We've had a long day, Phil. I'll explain that tomorrow. I'll send a car for you at eight-thirty if that's okay?"

"Sure."

"And, Johnny, could you drop Phil at his hotel?"

"No problem, boss. See you tomorrow."

That night, comforted with the knowledge of Philip Melville's future assistance, he slept sounder than he had since the whole affair began. He awoke refreshed and ready for action.

"Anything of particular note to report?" he asked Thomas when they met at eight o'clock.

"No boss. I was hoping you would have something for me. Like, what were you doing in Hawaii yesterday and who did you see?"

"Not yet, Johnny. It's still too early to discuss. I can only tell you I made significant progress."

Thomas made a face.

"I would rather you had said nothing than that. Now you have me agitated wondering what's going on," he replied in exasperation. "And why do you want to see Belinda?"

"Sorry Johnny – keep wondering," McKay said with a smile.

"You do remember there's a law against inhumane torture in Canada, don't you?"

"Listen Johnny, I believe I've found the one man who can help us in finding Red Hand. But until I'm ready to brief the task force, I can't tell you. And I'm not even going to brief them yet."

"Okay boss. I'll not pester you further."

"Now there are several things I want you to do."

Thomas perked up at that and took out his notebook.

"I want you to personally re-interview the new bosses of the local gangs. I have reason to believe that valuable members of the gangs have disappeared and have actually been recruited by Red Hand. If you can verify that, and get photographs of them, we will be much closer to finding out where he is hiding. You understand how sensitive this is? If I am correct and word gets out we are after them, it is probable it will reach the ears Red Hand. You know what he will do then. We need to track his new recruits and maybe – just maybe – they will lead us to him. So your questioning has to be most sensitive."

Thomas nodded his head and his eyes shone at being assigned this highly important task.

"Also contact Pierre in Montreal and have him do the same thing. Make sure you stress the need for the utmost care. Got it?"

"You can rely on me, boss."

"Good, and make sure you spend some lovey-dovey time with Belinda before bringing her into my office."

"Huh, anyone with only one eye would see I spend so much time on this job I have no time for romance," he snorted and left.

Phil Hughes arrived just before nine and settled down with a coffee.

"I've got some initial news from Ed Winfield. But before that what's all this about Johnny's girlfriend?"

"Her name is Belinda Carson and she works at CSIS. She was the first person to come along when I asked for an agent following the discovery of the bodies of your CIA agents."

"Oh yes, I remember. She was at the first meeting of all the agencies in the hotel in Ottawa."

"That's right. Her boss Jason Brandt lost no time in telling her he didn't require her services. That upset her and she requested I keep her on the case. I am doing so in a clandestine manner as I don't have much faith in Brandt. Her job is to keep me informed of all information emanating out of CSIS. You saw how Brandt attempted to hold back important intelligence at our last meeting."

"You really took him to task over that."

"I was furious. So I accepted Belinda's offer to help. To be effective she must be kept up-to-date with everything. Johnny Thomas will see to that. As a cover for the reason she will visit this office so frequently, I concocted the story that she and Johnny are romantically involved. They are doing their best to act out this charade."

"You are a devious devil, aren't you?"

"If I am, then maybe I'll apply for a job with you lot," he said with a grin.

"Talking of my lot, as you disdainfully referred to my agency, Ed has discovered Philip was right and telephones have been tapped into. There is no problem at Langley or FBI headquarters. He knows they are secure. This morning he is working with the telephone company to install protective devices here in Canada, including at the hotel rooms of task force members. We didn't have much time together this morning but he did say there was something odd with one of the lines he had checked; and he needed more time to investigate. He should be here later and can give us an update."

"Excellent. Ah here's Belinda."

Johnny and Belinda entered the office and introductions were made.

"Okay, Johnny, you can get on with the challenge I gave you."

He waited until Thomas had gone and the door was closed.

"Belinda you said you really wanted to help and you have already proved that. Now I have another demanding task for you. One that is vital to our pursuit of Red Hand. I don't believe it will be dangerous but if I am wrong and word somehow leaks, I must tell you it could be life threatening."

Hughes was impressed by the courage of this young woman. Her face paled but her voice was unwavering. He was even more impressed by her words.

"I joined CSIS to serve the people of Canada. I requested to be involved in this case because the lives of so many people are at stake. Whether the lives at risk are Canadian or American is not the important factor. They are innocent people who do not deserve to die. Tell me what I can do and I'll do my best."

"Have you been briefed on the shooting of Phil."

"Yes I have."

"He could have been murdered but Red Hand wanted him alive. He is hoping Phil will call another man to assist us. Red Hand wants to kill both of them before launching his devastating attack on America. He wants to do so because they were deeply involved in foiling his last attempt at mass murder. The other man he seeks has agreed to assist us but his presence here must be kept a closely guarded secret. If you agree I want him to stay at your home. Phil and I will meet with him there. I don't want to use a safe house of ours or of CSIS. I'm afraid Red Hand is too clever and may discover it. The danger is, if he does somehow find out this man is staying with you he will attack with a vengeance and you could wind up being collateral damage."

Hughes had kept looking at this young woman as McKay spoke. He felt anyone would wither under his unvarnished warning. Particularly, if that someone was familiar with Red Hand's cunning and remorseless appetite for killing. He was astounded at her reaction. He could sense by the change in her eyes she must have winced inside, but her voice remained steady.

"I have a spare room in my apartment and he is welcome to it."

McKay was equally amazed. He had anticipated an initial reluctance once Belinda knew her life could be at risk. He sat silently for a while then rose, went over to her, and shook her hand.

"Thank you, Belinda. The man's name is Colonel Philip Melville. He will arrive tomorrow morning on a CIA plane. I'd like you to be there to meet him. We'll arrange for a car to pick you up; one with tinted windows. One more thing, Belinda. A man from Langley – an even greater expert with computers than Red Hand – will be along to your apartment tonight to install a special telephone line: one that cannot be invaded. Please use it whenever you have to urgently contact me. Keep your present line in case friends call you, but as a precaution let most of your calls go to your recording machine before answering."

"Why do I need to do that?"

"Probably I'm being too paranoid. But maybe Red Hand has managed to get the names of all agents at CSIS as he did break into their computer. If he did and found out your telephone was protected he would become suspicious. If he calls your regular line and finds nothing unusual then all should be well."

"I've said it before; you're some detective, Hugh. Okay, I'd better get to work. Colonel Melville will be the first one to use the secure line to be installed tonight. Most probably, he will call you tomorrow to let you know he arrived safely; and to get an update from you."

She turned as she was about to leave.

"It was nice to meet you Mr. Hughes," she said then closed the door.

"Wow! She's quite an agent. Do you think CSIS would be offended if I tried to recruit her?"

"Keep your hands off. Canada needs all the talent we have. But you're right; Belinda is proving to be a great talent."

Chapter Twenty

It had been Hugh McKay's experience that police work was the proverbial feast or famine. Either one had no major case and the hours seemed to drag past or something big was in hand and there were not enough hours in the day. Today proved to be the latter.

Following his meeting with Belinda, telephone men had arrived to install the security devices. Later Superintendent Larson wanted an update. Three other members of the task force called concerning the next day's scheduled meeting. They had ideas to be put on the agenda and each of them took up over half an hour. Then he had to spend considerable time preparing his notes for the meeting. Part of that time was in debate with Phil Hughes deciding if he should mention the impending arrival of Philip Melville. Then he and Phil reviewed possible activities for Philip. It was six o'clock before he finally caught his breath; and then Johnny Thomas arrived to brief him on his interviews. And just as he and Hughes sat down with Johnny, an excited Ed Winfield burst into his office.

McKay had to make an immediate executive decision and he did.

"This looks like being a late night, so, Johnny, first things first. Order in Chinese food from Wei Tong's and have someone prepare a plentiful supply of coffee. And let's treat ourselves, have a few beers brought in with the food. I have the dreaded task of telling Cathy I shall miss dinner yet again."

When all that was settled, Ed Winfield was asked to report.

"Firstly the telephone company has been most co-operative and *all* the phones have been secured."

He had been told never to mention the new line in Belinda's apartment. He merely placed a bit more emphasis on the word all. Both Hughes and McKay got the message.

"The telephone company also supplied records of all calls going into and emanating from all those lines. I checked those meticulously and there were no unusual calls, except one, which I will come to in a moment. Then I dug deeper into those records by using a device invented at our labs in Langley. Obviously it had never been seen up here. It was a bit awkward not allowing the local phone company to discover how it worked. However in the end they saw it was a security issue and didn't push for too many explanations."

"What type of device is it? Or do you feel uncomfortable telling me?" asked McKay.

"No, not at all! My instruction, which came straight from the director, was to keep nothing back from you and your task force. It recreates a log of any call erased from the system. I won't go into the technical details but it is a very sophisticated piece of equipment. Once again everything was in order except for that same line where I had noticed the previous anomaly."

"Okay, Ed, now that you have us holding our breath in suspense, for God's sake tell us whose it is," demanded Hughes.

"It belongs to Jason Brandt."

There was a sharp intake of breath from Hughes as he looked at McKay. Hugh didn't say anything. It was almost as though he anticipated this answer. He simply waited for Winfield to continue.

"The first unusual call was made to Brazil. I tracked it and he called the home of a Herman Friedrich. Without consulting you, Phil, I took the liberty of contacting our office in Rio, and asked them to look into this guy. It didn't take long to get a reply. He and Brandt had been drinking buddies when Brandt was stationed in Brazil. Actually drinking buddies is not a precise term. They both attended a lot of the same high society parties and, on occasion, went nightclubbing together. Friedrich had been quite a notorious gangster but seems to now only concentrate on his legitimate export/import business. Our guys in Brazil knew all this as they had been following his activities. He was reputed to be involved in smuggling drugs and guns - some from the United States. But Friedrich seemed to have several highly placed local officials in his pocket and charges were never brought against him."

"Do you want all this put on the crime board, boss?" asked Johnny who had been furiously taking notes."

"Not yet, Johnny. Let's hear the rest of Ed's report."

"The second part relates to my use of our erased call interceptor device. The next night Brandt placed a call to the Regal Bank in Grand Cayman."

"In Grand Cayman," echoed Hughes.

"Yes, and once again without consulting you, Phil, I asked Langley to look into this."

"Well done, Ed. When do they think they will have a reply?"

"Perhaps tomorrow."

"That might be optimistic, those banks are very secretive. We shall see. Anyway, go on, Ed."

"Immediately after that call, Brandt received a call. It was from a recently issued number which was immediately discontinued. This could only be done with a very powerful computer system and by someone with considerable skill. Probably it was done by the same person who broke into the CSIS computer."

"Red Hand," interjected McKay.

"Who?" asked Winfield.

"The villain we're after," was the only explanation given by Hughes.

"Did you track the location of that call?" asked McKay eagerly.

"No, that's not possible. Only a number, and as I said, he skillfully expunged it from the system. The following morning Brandt called another number and once again at the end of the call the number was expunged. Then Brandt tried the same number but found it was discontinued. He then called the operator. I managed to talk to the operator who took that call and she remembered a caller insisting the number was active, claiming he had just used it."

"You said the person who did all this must be unusually skillful, Ed. How many people would you guess have these skills in Canada?"

"There's only one person I know of who could do this. His name is Jean Mercier. I met him at a conference. He is very good."

"He is also very dead," said McKay. "The only one left is Red Hand. He must be the one in contact with Brandt. The only question is, is Brandt working with him willingly or is he being coerced?"

"What about tomorrow's meeting? Do you still want Brandt to attend?"

"Until we get some further proof we must let him attend. What we desperately need, and we require it now, is that information from the bank in Grand Cayman."

A hesitant Winfield raised his hand. McKay raised his eyebrows and slightly moved his head backwards as an invitation for him to speak.

"If I can use one of your computers and you promise not to ask questions which could land me in jail, maybe I can get an answer," he volunteered.

"Do it, Ed. You have my authority. Any fallout will be on my shoulders," responded Hughes immediately.

"I'll take you to a room where you won't be disturbed and give you my computer," offered Thomas.

When Johnny returned he was asked to give his report on gang interviews.

"Being cognizant of the strict warning you gave me, boss, to be extremely careful in my questioning, I told each of the new gang leaders we suspected the person who bumped off their previous boss had fled. And that person was most likely a gang member who was paid a large sum to commit this assassination. Therefore I wanted every detail of any of their members who has disappeared. I got seven names. Four bodies have been found and their deaths are attributed to the initial warfare that broke out after the top men were presumable killed. Of the other three only two fitted the profile of people Red Hand would be interested in. They were smart, big and ruthless. I got a detailed description of both with their names and a photo of one of them. The third person was described as a young kid with not too many brains, so we ruled him out."

"Well done, Johnny," said a delighted McKay. "How about Pierre in Montreal?

"He used the same story and came up with one possibility. Again we have his name and a detailed description but no photo. I have two of our very best men out showing the photo to the pharmacies. They also have a sketch of the other two drawn by our artist from the descriptions we were given."

"Excellent work, Sergeant," added Hughes enthusiastically.

"Go easy on the compliments. Next thing he'll be asking for a raise," said McKay with a broad smile.

But there was no doubt about the pride in his voice.

"Well, now that you bring up the subject, boss, I could use the extra money. Don't forget, thanks to you, I've got a sweetheart now!" added the irrepressible Thomas.

"I'll take care of you, Johnny," promised McKay.

Before the repartee could continue there was a loud rap on the door. Dinner had arrived. They were ravenous and began eating immediately. The food was delicious and was being washed down with good Canadian ale. Hughes was enjoying it when he suddenly remembered Winfield.

"We had better leave some for Ed," he said guiltily.

"Did someone mention my name?" said Ed, as he walked into the room.

"Any luck?" demanded Hughes in a gruffer tone than he intended. Yet another sign of the increased tension everyone felt.

"Yes sir, a ton of it. It seems the sum of five hundred thousand dollars was deposited to an account in the name of Jason Brandt."

Thomas let out a long whistle.

"That seals the deal," he exalted.

"Maybe not," demurred Winfield. I tried to trace the source of the money but couldn't. Unfortunately Johnny's computer is nowhere near powerful enough to do so. But I tapped into my computer in Langley and we should have an answer in a few minutes. What I did succeed in learning was, the funds appeared to come through two different countries before landing in the Grand Cayman. However that was not the end of the trail. There were other countries involved. I could only track two countries on Johnny's computer. I'm certain my computer at Langley will provide the final answer. So unless your Jason Brandt is a computer expert, I don't believe he deposited the funds. It is true the records in Grand Cayman indicate he deposited the funds: but with a rather peculiar caveat. A password was set up only to verify the funds had been deposited. However, a second password is required before the funds can be accessed. The first password has been utilized, but not the second."

"What's the likely explanation, Ed?" asked Hughes.

"My best guess is someone other than Brandt set up this account but is holding up access until Brandt delivers something. The money is a carrot to do someone's bidding. Maybe Brandt is to kill someone."

That brought down a curtain of silence as everyone pondered this new situation. It was broken when Winfield spoke.

"Anyone mind if I have some dinner? I skipped breakfast and lunch today."

"Sorry, Ed, help yourself," said McKay, his mind still wrestling with this information.

They were still quiet three minutes later when they heard a loud ding coming from outside McKay's office.

"Ah, that's the answer," said Winfield as he rushed out of the room; his mouth full of noodles.

He returned in less than two minutes.

"This is astounding. The half-a-million dollars was routed through seven banks in seven countries. But it originated in Canada. And you'll never guess the source."

"Just tell us, Ed," demanded Hughes, his impatience being obvious.

"It was stolen from a fund held at the Canadian Security Intelligence Service. So it could have been Brandt after all."

"No, I don't believe so," mused Hughes. "I bet this fund was separate from normal bank accounts – a special fund. And if so only the head of CSIS would have the entry password. Even if Brandt was unusually skillful enough to discover the password and route the transfer through seven countries, why would he lock himself out of the funds by using a second password?"

"I agree," chimed in McKay. "Someone stealing that amount of money would first have an escape plan to some safe country. And, he would immediately take that escape route and live on his loot. He would not hang around. No, the only person we have come across capable of such a plan is Red Hand. This is all his work. And I doubt he was recruiting Brandt as an assassin. He has already proved he is capable of such a task himself. There can only be one thing Red Hand desperately wants and does not already have. And that thing will eventually only be known by the task force."

He stared at Hughes who had already come to the same conclusion.

"He wants to know if my friend is coming here to Vancouver. Then he can plan both our deaths and get on with his ultimate goal of devastating mass murder."

"Who are you talking about?"

The question shot out of Johnny's mouth in an uncontrollably loud voice. Phil's response was terse.

"The only man on this earth feared by Red Hand!"

Chapter Twenty One

"Ed, do you have Jeremy Mason's home number in Ottawa, and is it now a secure line?"

"Yes and yes," responded Winfield. "Here it is."

"Would you and Johnny wait outside while I make this call? Sorry but Jeremy Mason's reaction should be held confidential. Only he can give permission to have this known to a wider circle."

When they left McKay asked Hughes to listen in on an extension then dialed the number.

"Hello."

"Jeremy, this is Hugh McKay."

"Oh, hello, Hugh. What can I do for you?"

"You do know your telephone line is now a secure one, don't you?"

"Yes, the telephone company completed its work this afternoon."

"I have Phil Hughes on the other line."

"Hi, Jeremy."

"Hello, Phil. I must say this is beginning to sound quite ominous."

"Listen carefully, Jeremy. This is very important and I require you to be absolutely honest with me."

"Of course, DI McKay."

That formal response indicated he was on high alert and more than a little miffed at the questioning of his honesty.

"Has CSIS had a large sum of money stolen? Half a million dollars to be exact?"

Mason had braced himself for a difficult question following McKay's initial comments. But not for this. Air escaped from his lungs like the sound of a high pressure gas pipe being pierced. He struggled for control of his voice.

"Why would you ask a question like that?"

"Please, just answer."

"Yes, we have had that amount stolen. How did *you* find out?"

"I think it best if we meet tomorrow morning to discuss this."

"I would be happy to meet with you but I *insist* you tell me all you know – *now*! This is a matter of the highest national security. *I cannot wait until tomorrow.*"

McKay told him the whole story.

"This is unbelievable. Why did he pick on Brandt?"

"By chance did he complain about my treatment of him at the last task force meeting?"

"Yes, and I told him he deserved it. And further, I was thinking of replacing him on the task force due to his stupid actions."

"I see. Well the combination of my rebukes and your comments caused him to call a friend in Brazil: a man with a criminal past. Brandt must have been seriously thinking of going there to live. And Red Hand taped that call. That gave him the opportunity he desired, to blackmail someone on the task force to get information. The question is what do we do now? Obviously he can't stay on the task force and we have a meeting tomorrow. I can have him arrested and held for questioning to find out how much damage he has done."

"No, Hugh, this is a matter of National Security. Whether coerced or not he did not come to us with this situation which tells me he must have considered getting his hands on the stolen money. I will have State Security arrest him tonight and keep him safely locked up. We will get the full story out of him then decide what to do. Meantime, with your permission, I will take his place on the task force."

"You would be most welcome, Jeremy. You do realize I must brief the task force on this matter. Don't you?"

"Yes that's inevitable. I can only ask the members to keep this as restricted as possible until we have time to consider our next move."

"Agreed. I'll see you tomorrow, Jeremy."

"I may be a little late. I believe the first plane arrives at 8.30 am."

"We'll wait for you as this will be the first item on the agenda."

"Excuse the interruption but there is one other possibility," said Hughes. "We could keep Brandt on the task force and feed him false information. Undoubtedly he would pass this along to Red Hand. We may be able to lay a trap that way."

"The difficulty with that is we would have to call a secret meeting of all the other task force members to tell them. Otherwise this false information would be spread to the FBI and CIA. And, I believe Red Hand may see through this trap and that's a risk we cannot afford to take. We need time to find Ma, and any action which tips him off to our planning may persuade him to move up his timetable for whatever catastrophic arrangement he has prepared."

"Good points," agreed Hughes.

After only a few moments reflection he continued.

"There is one other thing we can do. And I want to mention it while Jeremy is on the line."

"Go on," said McKay.

"Red Hand will expect a report on tomorrow's meeting from Brandt. He will send a message to him telling him how to make this report. When he doesn't get a response he will probably send one of his men to check Brandt's apartment. Once he knows Brandt is not there he will suspect we have discovered Brandt's treachery. However he will also have to consider the possibility of Brandt having left the country. He knows Brandt has been in contact with his friend in Brazil, therefore he will check the manifests of flights. But he is not the only genius with computers. Ed Winfield is even more skilled. He works at Langley, Jeremy, and he is here assisting us. I will have him enter Brandt's name on the manifest of a flight leaving tonight for Brazil. Admittedly it is no guarantee it will fool Red Hand."

"That's an excellent idea," said Mason. "It may, or it may not, do the trick, but there is no downside to it. At the very least it will sow a seed of doubt in his mind."

"I'm certainly glad to have such a devious espionage mind working with me," rejoined McKay, smiling broadly at Hughes.

"And as a second thought, I'll arrange a private jet from Canada's fleet to fly me to Vancouver tomorrow. That way I can make your meeting by nine o'clock. And of more importance, I can take Brandt back to Ottawa without going through a public airport," added Mason. "Now if you'll excuse me I must get State Security to arrest Brandt immediately and hold him for me. Then I have to inform the Prime Minister. See you both tomorrow."

Once having hung up, McKay and Hughes sat looking at each other for a minute. Each pondering what had transpired. Finally Hughes spoke.

"I don't envy Jeremy. His conversation with his Prime Minister will not be a pleasant one. To have one's top espionage service damaged in such a way is a severe blow. Undoubtedly it will lead to the commissioning of a full, but secret, review."

"You don't think this will prevent Jeremy attending the task force meeting, do you?"

"No, I don't. While Brandt's case is an embarrassment, the threat posed by Red Hand is of such importance it will take precedence. And, for many years, and through several prime ministers, Jeremy Mason has served his country very well. His position will not be at risk. He will feel this deception by Brandt more deeply than anyone."

"At least we've stopped another source of information to Red Hand. Let's call Ed and Johnny back in and have a beer. Then we should call it a night."

Phil Hughes nodded his agreement before advancing a concluding comment.

"We've got quite a way to go to catch this bastard; however, we can count it a blessing we now have Philip Melville on our side. And after tonight I believe we can chalk up one more point for the good guys."

Chapter Twenty Two

Belinda Carson had taken considerable care in selecting her wardrobe. Definitely nothing flashy that would attract attention but stylish enough to demonstrate she was a confident and competent agent. Having been made painfully aware of the absolute criticality of her task, she couldn't help feeling a bit less than completely confident. With a final look in the mirror, she stepped gingerly out of her apartment.

The SUV with the dark tinted windows was waiting. The driver stood by the open door. He was over six feet tall and had the lithe muscular build of a quarterback. She was pretty sure, as a trained CIA agent, he would have checked out the street; nevertheless she took her time to stare intently in both directions. During her indoctrination she had been drilled in both the techniques of following people and the methods of spotting a tail. Satisfied she walked unhurriedly towards the van, but did not enter.

"Good morning, Miss Carson," said the driver.

"Good morning, er, ….. What's your name?"

"Sam."

"As in Uncle Sam?"

"No, it's really Sam," he replied with a chuckle.

"Well it's nice to meet you, Sam. Have you had your coffee yet?

"Yes, Miss Carson."

"Could you stand another?"

"Always."

"There's an outstanding coffee shop on the corner. I'm going to have one. I'll get you one too. How do you take it?"

"That's okay miss, I'll get them."

"No. I insist. I doubt your true profession is driving and I have found it wise always to be on good terms with agents --- particularly ones sent to guard you."

The agent smiled and nodded his head.

"Thank you, Miss. I'll have it black with two sugars."

She brought back two large coffees, two enormous muffins and a handful of napkins.

"These blueberry muffins are to die for. I'll try not to get crumbs all over your spotless van."

The SUV moved effortlessly into the stream of traffic. Belinda sat back and munched happily on her muffin, drank about a quarter of her latte before speaking again.

"Be careful not to lose your buddy in the traffic."

Sam's head rocked slightly then he grinned.

"You don't miss much do you Miss?"

"I try not to. But really, Sam, a black SUV and a black Ford sedan also with tinted windows. I think I would feel safer in my old Alpha Romeo and certainly much less conspicuous."

"Most probably, Miss Carson, but I bet your little Italian car is not bullet proof."

It was her turn to rock her head.

"You got me there, Sam. I'll stop being a smartass and enjoy the ride. How's the muffin?"

"Absolutely delicious."

"I briefly thought of giving your friend in the Ford a coffee and a muffin but that would really have been acting like a smartass."

Sam roared with laughter.

"I would love to have seen old Harvey's face if you had done that."

Then she looked in the driver's mirror and noticed his face turn serious.

"What is it, Sam?"

"I feel a bit guilty by accepting the coffee as a surety of protecting you. To be honest, the instruction I was given was to protect the passenger we are to pick up at the airport. And to do so at all cost. Your safety wasn't mentioned."

"Oh, I see."

"In fact Senior Agent Hughes told me in graphic, explicit, terms what he would do to my anatomy if anything bad happened to that man."

Sam's body gave an involuntary shudder.

"That bad, eh?"

"And I don't think he was kidding. I don't know Senior Agent Hughes but I have certainly heard of him. And he doesn't make idle threats. On the other hand he is known to be absolutely fair. And true to his nature, when he finished threatening me, he smiled, held out his hand, and gave me a hundred dollar bill. He told me to get the best dinner I could find after successfully completing this task."

"Well I have only met him a couple of times but he gave me the impression of being a very competent and determined man. If I were to choose sides I would want to be on his side. Conversely I would really hate having him for an enemy. So let's you and I make a deal, Sam. Nothing must go wrong with this mission. Eh?"

"That's a deal, Miss."

"How long have you been an agent, Sam?"

"One year, seven months and three days."

"But who's counting, eh? Is it really that bad?"

"No Miss, it really is that good. And that's the truth."

"And before you became an agent?"

"I served in the US Marine Corp."

"See much action?"

"More than I would have liked. I lost a good many friends in 'Nam."

Carson had the sensitivity to not pursue that. Such memories could be extremely painful. She sat quietly until they reached the private airport.

"I'll check on the plane's progress, Miss. Would you like to wait inside the arrival building?"

"Yes, I think I will."

Instead of going straight in, she stopped at the black Ford and tapped on the driver's window.

The occupant was not the person she expected to see. Sam had referred to him as 'old Henry' but it was a pink cheeked twenty-two-year-old who sat there.

"Sorry you didn't get a muffin, Henry," was all she said, leaving him looking mystified.

It seemed her fictitious love affair with Johnny Thomas had affected her. Some of his impish humor had rubbed off on her.

They didn't have long to wait. Fifteen minutes later the sleek, silver aircraft swooped down to a perfect landing. It taxied to within thirty yards of the arrival building and Sam and Henry drove their cars close to the plane.

The aircraft door opened and a tall, handsome, blond haired man strode down the steps. His blue-eyed gaze professionally swept the area as he descended. Sam opened the passenger door as Belinda walked quickly forward.

"Welcome to Vancouver, Colonel Melville," she cried out piercingly to be heard over the noise of aircraft engines.

The man quickly looked around to see if anyone was within earshot. Instantly Belinda realized her gaffe by calling out his name so loudly. She wished the ground would open up and swallow her. Her face was still bright scarlet with shame as she came close and apologized.

"I think we are okay," he said. "It's Miss Carson isn't it?"

Before she could reply she heard this unidentifiable sound from behind her. It seemed like a cross between a moan and a cheer. She whirled around to see Sam hunched over and clinging to the door of the car as though he was about to collapse. His body shook and his bulging eyes were fixed on the passenger.

As if a magician waved a magic wand to change the scene, Sam shot into a rigid stance of attention and his arm snapped up to a perfect salute. He rattled off his name, his old rank and unit in which he served. Belinda had never seen eyes shine so brightly. It was as though a powerful light was emanating from Sam's eyes. But there was no mistaking the look in those eyes. It was pure adulation.

Philip was not in uniform but he came to attention and returned the salute. Still Sam's arm did not fall. His perfect salute remained. Finally Philip said, "Stand easy, Sergeant Wilkins. I believe we met once. In Da Lat, wasn't it? You had just completed a very successful mission."

Belinda Carson wasn't conscious of her gaping mouth.

'How could this man possibly remember Sam out of the hundreds of soldiers he had met?' was the thought that raced through her mind.

"Yes, Major, sorry Sir, - Colonel."

"Well it certainly is a pleasure to meet an old comrade. Your first greeting was appropriate, I was a major in those days," said Philip as he held out his hand.

Sam appeared to have lost the ability to move. He stood nonplussed at the fact a colonel would offer him his hand. A colonel he had only briefly met. A colonel whose name was known throughout all of the American fighting forces in Vietnam. A revered hero. Philip extended his hand further and at last Sam grasped it. Then Philip wrapped his other hand around their handshake.

"It's very good to see you, Sergeant Wilkins and from the bottom of my heart, thank you for your service."

A few teardrops welled up in Sam's eyes as he seemed reluctant to let go of Philip's hand. Belinda only became aware of her undignified gaping mouth as she tasted the salt from her own tears.

Philip put his arm around Sam.

"I have a favor to ask you, Sergeant."

Sam struggled to come to rigid attention again, but Philip held him firmly.

"Anything, Sir! *Anything at all.*"

"I am on a dangerous classified mission. I cannot afford to have anyone know I am here. Please never mention you saw me. Not to your wife if you are married. Not to your confessor if you are religious. To no one. Is that understood, Sergeant?"

"Yes, Sir!"

And let's not show our past by saluting or coming to attention or by addressing me as sir. I want to appear just an ordinary man. Can you do that, Sam?"

Sam didn't know how to reply without using the term colonel or sir, so he nodded his head vigorously.

This was the proudest day in the life of Sam Wilkins.

Chapter Twenty Three

The black SUV pulled up outside Belinda's apartment. Sam leapt out to open the passenger door. Instinctively he stood at attention; however, as Philip alighted Sam caught himself just in time to prevent a salute. Military training is a difficult habit to break. Philip recognized this and smiled an acknowledgement.

"Thanks, Sam, Maybe I'll see you again."

"I have been assigned to you, ----," blurted out Sam then suddenly stopped as he struggled to find a way to address his hero without using colonel or sir.

Melville saw his dilemma. He put a hand on Sam's shoulder.

"Sam, I appreciate your help but if this is going to work you have to call me Philip. And you must lose this SUV. Get something less conspicuous. Also get rid of our escort in the Ford."

"You can use my Alpha Romeo," offered Belinda with a knowing grin at Sam.

"Thanks, but those little cars are not too comfortable for tall men like Sam and me. I'm sure the CIA can supply a roomy sedan. Something old and a bit beat up but with power. Now how do I get in touch with you, Sam?"

He was handed a card.

"Good, do you think you could be back here with the right type of car in an hour and a half?"

"Yes, S--, Philip."

"See you then."

"I'll help you with the luggage – Philip."

Sam had noticed the trouble the pilots experienced in loading Philip's luggage into the SUV. He had two suitcases. One was a large standard soft-sided type. It was the other that created the problem. It was a large dark gray metallic case. However the sides were not made of the usual flexible light weight metal. They were reinforced heavy duty metal. He recognized that type of case. Special Forces used them to transport their weapons. Such men did not borrow weapons. They always carried their own.

"Thanks, Sam. But be careful with the gray one – it's heavy."

"Oh, I already know that. But I think I can manage it if you take the other one."

Sam did manage it, but only just. It was really heavy. He was perspiring profusely when he got it to the apartment door.

"Thanks, Sam, I'll see you later."

Once inside the apartment Belinda tentatively asked the question troubling her.

"Should you be going out? I mean is it safe?"

"I'm not Sherlock Holmes, Belinda. I can't solve mysteries by smoking a pipe and sitting in an armchair," he answered with a smile.

"Is there anything I can do?"

"Yes, look up the telephone book and get a list of Chinese restaurants. I am looking for Hunanese restaurants. But if you can't find any with that particular cuisine, look for smaller Chinese restaurants. Definitely not the ritzy ones that cater to tourists."

She nodded her head she knew exactly what he meant. Red Hand and his recruits would prefer authentic Chinese cooking, not the food doctored to suit westerners.

"And if you'll show me my room and the bathroom, I'll unpack then take a shower. One more thing, Belinda, could you nip out and get me black hair dye. Ma Guan-lui may have managed to get a photo of me from an army database. You may have thought me a little scruffy when we met at the airport. I haven't shaved for two days. Black hair, some facial hair and a few other things I brought with me, should make an adequate disguise."

The drug store was close by and Belinda returned in fifteen minutes. Philip was dressing.

"I left your dye in the bathroom," she called out. "I'll check the telephone book for restaurants."

"Thanks."

She had written down the names and addresses of five restaurants when the bedroom door opened.

She dropped her pencil.

The man coming out of the bedroom had black hair, but his face was not the tanned one of Philip Melville, it was an awful, sickly, pasty white one. And the posture was not the erect one she had known. His back was bent and he had a most noticeable paunch which even his stained floppy shirt couldn't hide. His baggy trousers and down at the heel shoes completed his wardrobe.

"My God," she gasped.

"Not too bad. What do you think?"

"I would never have recognized you. How did you manage all that?"

"Before leaving Honolulu, I visited a friend who produces TV shows and told him I was going to a fancy dress party as a homeless person. He had his wardrobe mistress fix me up."

He lifted up his shirt to show the pillow strapped around his body.

"But your face?"

"A special cream she gave me, it dries in a few minutes after application and it is difficult to rub off. It's certainly better than the trick used by some soldiers to dodge patrol duty. They would swallow gunpowder. If they could avoid throwing up, their skin would turn deathly white within two hours."

The horrified look on her face told him he had better not continue his story and detail the consequences those soldiers suffered for their attempted subterfuge.

"How are you getting along?" he asked her to change the subject.

"Chinese restaurants are popular here. I am avoiding the large ads. They are probably the touristy ones. I have a few more pages to go."

"Do you mind if I call Phil Hughes?"

"Not at all. Use the black telephone. It has been specially adapted by the CIA. The white one is my regular one but I must be careful in using it."

She explained McKay's warning.

"Smart man. Do you have a safe number for Phil?"

"Yes," she responded and handed him a card. "There was a task force meeting today. I guess he will still be in Hugh McKay's office. That number is also on the card."

Philip talked with Hughes for several minutes before Hughes brought up the subject that was troubling him.

"What are you up to, asking Wilkins to get a beat up car and pick you up tonight?"

"To paraphrase an old adage – you can take the man out of the Special Forces but you can't take the Special Forces out of the man. I could never sleep until I had reconnoitered this area. I need to know everything about it. Where Red Hand would set up an ambush if he discovered me. And which routes I would use to escape if I were to be attacked."

"That sounds like a fisherman's tale to me."

"If you don't want to send me a car, I'll go out on foot. I thought it would be safer in an unidentifiable car, and, with a good man like Sam."

"Oh, Okay. But I still don't believe your story. Be careful, Philip. By the way, you were right in assuming Red Hand had recruited a few gangsters. We believe he has three."

"Do you have photographs of them?"

"One. But we have an artist's sketches of the other two."

"Good work. Oh and, Phil?"

"Yes? What else do you want?"

"Send along the photo and the sketches with Sam."

"Philip," exclaimed an exasperated Hughes. "I told you to be careful."

"I only want to be able to identify these men in case I should see them lurking about."

"A likely story. You can't kid a kidder."

"Hold on a minute, my friend. It was you and Hugh McKay who came to me. You have to let me assist you in the way I know best. Otherwise I may as well go home to the pleasant sunshine of Honolulu."

Melville didn't speak in a threatening tone. It was only a gentle admonishment to Hughes. He got the message. He also knew Philip Melville would not rest until Ma Guan-lui was caught.

"Excuse me, Philip. I am a bit wound up over this bastard. I apologize. But I still know you're up to something! Hugh and I will come around and see you tomorrow morning at nine. We can give you a complete briefing then. And equally important, you can give us a briefing on *your* activities!"

"Good night, Phil."

"Sleep well after your *reconnoitering.*"

"That didn't sound like an altogether friendly conversation," opined Belinda.

"Oh, it was fine, just two very good friends expressing concern for each other's health."

"I see," said an unconvinced Carson. "I've finished. Now I'm marking their locations on this map."

"Very good," replied a highly pleased Melville. "May I keep this map?"

"Of course I bought it for you. I also have a gun if you require it."

"No thanks. I brought my own weapons. Could you do me one other favor, Belinda?"

"Sure."

"I see you have a printer/copier. Sam should be here in a few minutes. Go downstairs and ask him for the photo and sketches he brought for me. Bring them up here and make two additional copies of each. One you should keep for yourself and the other is for Sam. They are the men recruited by Red Hand. Memorize their faces and keep a sharp look out for them. Oh, and tell Sam not to be surprised by my new look."

Sam was early and Belinda returned quickly to the apartment. She made the copies and sat down to study hers.

"I hope you bring back some delicious Chinese food for dinner," she called out as he was leaving.

He waved an acknowledgment.

She hurried to the window eager to see the result of her mischief. It appeared the proximity to Johnny Thomas had caused some of his personality to actually rub off on her. She had deliberately disregarded his instruction and had not told Sam to expect the disguised Philip. She chuckled as Sam robustly waved away the approaching homeless person. Even after he attempted to explain to Sam, the big CIA man moved threateningly towards him. Philip must have spoken in a commanding voice because Sam took two steps backwards and stared at the man. Then he came to full attention completely forgetting the previous warning given to him to act casually.

Before getting into the passenger seat next to Sam, Philip looked up at the window where he knew Belinda would be watching, and vigorously shook his fist.

Belinda collapsed in a chair. Her laughter echoed loudly around the apartment. Abruptly her laughter died. Her little joke had been fun. But now those two soldiers were going into dangerous territory. She knew instinctively Philip Melville was not merely reconnoitering. He was looking for trouble. Worse still – he hoped to find it.

An icy tingle ran down her spine.

Chapter Twenty Four

Philip had visited six restaurants. He was not surprised to learn that of these six 'Chinese' restaurants, one was run by Koreans and another by Vietnamese. He didn't waste time there. Their patrons were all Asians but not a single Chinese among them. He stood in the doorways of the other four begging for money, and carefully scrutinizing the customers. And in every case he was eventually chased away by a knife waving chef or owner.

The seventh was less threatening. In fact the chef gave him food as an enticement to leave.

"At least I've got dinner for Belinda," he said to a worried Sam. He had been afraid Philip would really be attacked.

As in Asian culture the number eight proved to be a lucky one. There was no doubt the burly Chinese patron who brushed past him at the doorway was the one in the photograph. And to Philip's delight he spoke Cantonese, a dialect of which he had quite a good understanding. The man asked for his usual, which turned out to be three Cantonese dishes. This was definitely unusual since the restaurant had a large sign proclaiming it served only the best Sichuan food - a completely different cuisine from the significantly blander Cantonese. But one look at the fear and resignation on the face of the owner told Philip he must have been bullied into providing these special dishes in the past. He went back to Sam.

"Take this food back to Belinda. There's no point in letting it get cold. Then go home. I'll call you tomorrow."

"But sir, I've been instructed to stay with you," replied Sam, once again forgetting the instruction not to be formal.

"This guy came on foot, Sam. I'll have no problem tailing him. He'll be here for at least forty-five minutes. And I'm certain he is not going to visit Red Hand tonight. He has only ordered food for himself and intends eating it here. All I'll learn tonight is where he lives, not where Red Hand lives."

"But I have the strictest orders," pleaded Sam.

"I am countermanding those orders. Don't force me to be formal with this request, Sergeant Wilkins."

This was said in a manner which struck home to Sam's military training. He knew he was in a bind. But he also knew he could never argue with Colonel Melville. He would much rather face the wrath of his CIA superior. Reluctantly he nodded his head.

"Very good, Col----, Philip."

"Thanks Sam, you're a good man. And don't worry; I'll clear it all tomorrow with Phil Hughes."

As he had promised, Philip followed the man to his apartment building in a poorer section of the city. In fact he was so close behind him he hid underneath the staircase to get the number of his apartment. This he carefully noted on his map. Then he called a number permanently logged on his portable phone by the CIA.

"Hello."

"Ed, this is Philip Melville. Do you recognize the name?"

"Of course I do, Colonel. What can I do for you?"

"Can you find the telephone number of this apartment?"

He gave Ed the location.

"Do you want it right away?"

"That's not necessary, Ed. Perhaps you'd call me later tonight."

"Will do."

Once again he consulted his map. Belinda's apartment was about two miles away. He had to walk as he knew no cab driver would stop for a dirty homeless person. On the way back he bought a hamburger for his dinner. In this fast food store located in such a poor district, they were accustomed to serving underprivileged customers. However, the sight of the dirty, disheveled Philip caused one employee to nervously stand next to the telephone, obviously ready to call the police.

'Hmm, this disguise is too realistic. If I use it again I had better come with a sandwich,' he thought.

At about the time he was walking back to Belinda's, Red Hand was giving one of his other men a message over the telephone. This man spoke good English and carefully wrote down the instruction. It was addressed to Jason Brandt and was to be slipped under his door.

'Have a full report prepared and leave it on your doorstep at precisely seven o'clock tomorrow morning.'

Ma Guan-lui was a meticulously careful man. He would not use the telephone to call Brandt again, nor would he have him use a public telephone. He understood the psyche of a man in Brandt's position. He would be frenziedly and relentlessly searching for a way out of his predicament. Ma knew it was advisable to be wary of a cornered animal. They were totally unpredictable.

Although he had specified collection of his greatly desired information at seven, his man had been instructed to collect the report at seven-forty-five and bring it to a specific location in a busy Asian shopping area. Red Hand usually met his men somewhere in this area. None of his men had ever visited any of his three homes. And the exact location of meetings was changed each time. That way no unusually observant person would have a reason to remember him by having seen him more than once.

Satisfied with his preparations, he played his stereo, as he sipped his special maotai, the strong fermented liquor from Guizhou province. He fully anticipated tomorrow's report would inform him of the arrival of his long hated Colonel Melville. His mind warmed at this possibility. Killing always gave him great satisfaction.

He began thinking of the many ways he could kill Hughes and Melville. He was on his third maotai, when he fantasized Melville may even bring his wife with him. That would be a special pleasure. He could torture Mrs. Melville in front of the colonel's eyes before killing them both. Then he would dispatch Hughes with an equally brutal and slow death.

With these delicious thoughts as a warm blanket of contentment he drifted off to sleep.

Chapter Twenty Five

"Oh, thank God you're safe," cried out Belinda when Philip arrived at her apartment. "Phil Hughes has called three times frantically asking if you had returned. You are to call him right away!"

"Did you enjoy your dinner?" asked Philip.

Belinda stared at him in total incomprehension.

"How can you ask an inconsequential question like that when you have been taunting death by playing with fire?"

"Belinda, I was doing no such thing. I merely found out where one of Red Hand's men lives. Nothing more! It was a piece of cake. Talking of cake, do you have any ice cream or cookies – something sweet? I had a disgustingly greasy burger and it is still sitting uncomfortably in my stomach."

By the way her eyes bulged at his nonchalant attitude he thought she was about to have a fit of epilepsy. He grabbed her by the shoulders.

"Belinda, Belinda, you must calm down. I was never at the slightest risk."

She finally did manage to calm herself a little and sat down in an armchair. But her body still twitched with pent up concern.

"I suppose having gone through as many missions as you have in Vietnam, this was nothing to you. The fact you could have been discovered by Red Hand and killed, probably never entered you mind. This may have been unexceptional and ordinary to you but you'll have to excuse me if I seem rattled. I have only gone through some basic training when joining CSIS. Other than that I have been sitting behind a desk. I have never really faced any danger, and if I did I'm certain I couldn't do it in your dispassionate manner. It all seems so ---," her voice trailed off as she sought the right word. "So – *unreal!*"

Now her voice was rising again, and for the first time Melville realized the strain she was under. He now clearly recognized she took the assignment McKay had given her of having him stay at her apartment, very, very seriously. She had taken this assignment as a deep personal challenge and was now displaying signs that she had also assumed this role involved being his protector. He sat in front of her and took her hands in his.

"In 'Nam we often made bad jokes just to relieve the tension. So If I appeared to be cavalier it was only habit. But in all truth there was little danger tonight. However I appreciate your concern but please don't get too worked up. I assure you I can handle myself. And by the way, I do not believe you would wilt in the face of danger. You would do okay. Anyway I don't want you to take any risks, leave the dangerous stuff to me. Now, seriously, Belinda, ---"

His comments helped soothe her concern; however, his last words caused her just relaxed body to tense immediately, and she leant forward onto the very edge of her chair expecting information of great importance.

"Do you or don't you have any ice cream?"

There were several seconds of silence. Then she couldn't help herself. She burst out laughing. Maybe it was the release of the tension she had felt. She gave him a look as though she could happily throw something at him.

"Yes, I'll get it for you. Meantime, please call Phil Hughes, his number is by the phone."

"Yes, ma'am," he replied with a smile and gave her a mock salute.

He was pleased to see her grin and return the salute. It indicated she was back on an even keel. He dialed the number.

"Hello Phil, you requested I call you."

"You're damn right I did. Where the hell have you been? I almost had a heart attack in Beijing, the last time you decided to hunt for Red Hand. Are you trying to give me one now?"

"Your heart is as sound as a bell, Phil. And as I was explaining to Belinda, there was never any danger tonight. I simply found out where one of his men lives. Ed is getting the telephone number. Have you a pencil and paper handy?"

"Yes."

"Then give this address to Hugh. Have him assign one of his very best men to tail this guy. I'm almost certain Red Hand won't allow anyone to know where he lives, therefore if the guy I tailed is to meet with him, it will be in a public place. And Phil, it would be ideal if Hugh could send an Asian detective. That public place may well be in the Chinatown area. Now get some sleep and rest that heart of yours. Goodnight."

"See you tomorrow at nine, you deceitful bugger."

Phil Hughes had a smile on his face as he hung up. He *knew* Philip Melville was as far from deceitful to his friends as anyone could possibly be. He *knew* Philip could take care of himself. He *knew* he didn't have to worry about him. He *knew* he had the best possible man on his side looking for Red Hand. It had been the build up of anxiety over the last week which had caused him to overreact. Hearing Philip's calm, almost cheerful, voice gave him the hope they would ultimately track down Ma Guan-lui. With a huge sigh he yawned. He *knew* he would sleep well tonight.

Belinda gave Philip a large bowl with one scoop of vanilla ice cream and one of chocolate. Once he was seated she then produced from behind her back four ginger cookies.

"You're a treasure, Belinda. Thank you."

He ate slowly enjoying every mouthful. And as if by some telepathic message he sensed he too would sleep well tonight.

But not until he called Hong Kong; a call which lasted forty minutes. Mei Li was not as easy to convince as Phil Hughes that he was being careful and not taking any undue risks. She knew him all too well. But deep in her heart she fully appreciated the danger posed to many, many people in addition to both her and her husband by this evil demon, Red Hand. And also deep in that heart she was glad it was her beloved Philip who would do everything in his power to stop him. There was absolutely no one else in whom she had such faith.

Next morning Philip sat at Belinda's dining table enjoying coffee and a large blueberry muffin.

"This is delicious. I'll have to watch my weight. Ice cream and cookies and now this muffin," he joked.

It was eight-forty-five and he was happily relishing his second coffee. But across the city, on a street corner in Chinatown, someone was decidedly unhappy.

"I carefully watched his apartment from six-thirty. At seven, he left no note on his doorstep. At eight I rang the doorbell but there was no answer. He could not have gotten past me. However just to be sure, on the way here I took the liberty of calling his office from a public telephone so my call could not be traced," he said full of pride in his acuity. "And I was told he was not there."

Red Hand's head flooded with mixed emotions. He had spent long hours in the training of his recruits; teaching them to use prudent initiative. He was pleased this one had taken some initiative but disquieted he had not recognized the attendant risks. He should never have rung Brandt's doorbell nor should he have telephoned his office. Such calls could be traced, even those from public telephone booths. It could give away his location. But he consoled himself with the thought it was highly unlikely the receptionist would have initiated such a trace. Brandt was under no suspicion and as yet would not be considered permanently absent. Despite this he knew his recruit required more training.

While he had no reason to believe there would be serious adverse consequences of the man's actions, the overriding emotion he experienced was rage. His normally pallor facial appearance was now bright red. He strode up and down the street for several minutes before regaining control of his emotions. He realized if he yelled and screamed as every fiber in his being truly wished he would attract attention. It looked as though he had lost his one way into the inner workings of the task force.

"Go home. I will contact you later," he said abruptly to his recruit.

The man walked away filled with disappointment and confusion. He had hoped for praise in using his initiative and wanted to know if he was the cause of his boss's displeasure. However one look at the face of Ma was sufficient to tell him not to pursue this matter.

Ma surreptitiously scanned the area. Satisfied there was no danger, he hurried to the apartment he referred to as his war room. He must find Brandt. His first task was to call the CSIS office using an untraceable line. He put on his best English accent.

"Good morning. May I speak to Jason Brandt?"

"May I tell him who is calling and the nature of your call?"

This receptionist was well trained in her work in a spy office. She had come on duty at eight-thirty. The one who had earlier spoken to the recruit was a junior in the typing pool.

"This is Archie Glover. We were to meet for lunch but I'm afraid I will have to cancel and I would like to explain to Jason personally."

"I regret to say Mr. Brandt is not available at the moment. May I have your number and I'll ask him to call you?"

"That's all right. I'm calling from the airport and my plane is about to leave. I'll call him at home tonight. Please be kind enough to tell him I called and give him my apologies."

He hung up and quickly erased the number he had used. He was disappointed he could not elicit better information. He sat with his brow furrowed in concentration.

"There are only two possibilities," he murmured. "Either he has left the country or he has been found out and arrested."

The latter would cause a great deal of worry. But he soothed his concern over this possibility as he muttered to himself.

"No, I don't think so. I left no trace of our conversations. Everything was planned perfectly," he said with supreme egotistical confidence. "He must have left the country."

But that likelihood made his rage boil over once more. He strode around the room using every swearword in his extensive vocabulary.

"I must find him!" he fulminated. "When I do, I can arrange for a suitable punishment."

By that he meant a way of killing Brandt. He continued to stride around until he was calm enough to begin his search. Then, he sat at his computer and checked airline departures. After fifteen minutes he detected a Mr. Jason Brandt had departed Vancouver to Miami with a connection to Sao Paulo. He checked the Miami flight and noted a Mr. Brandt had boarded a flight that was about to leave.

"Just to be sure, I'll check the immigration computer at Sao Paulo after the flight lands," he said with a trace of doubt still in his voice.

He, above all others, knew the potential of a skilled person manipulating airline computers. Meantime he began the task of again checking the information he had on the other members of the task force. He had to find another weak link.

He was half way through this exercise and so far had no success when yet again his anger and frustration erupted. He grabbed a vase from a desk and smashed it against a wall. Even in his state of frenzy his brain must have been working because he had selected the least expensive object in the room. Even so, this uncharacteristic action reminded him of his shattering a glass in his other apartment. Even under stress he had always managed to keep a cool head which enabled him to find solutions to seemingly insurmountable problems. That was one of his trademark talents.

'Why am I giving way to such fits of uncontrolled fury,' he wondered. Like a lightning bolt a possible explanation hit his brain.

"It must be I sense the presence of Melville. He must be here or on his way," he cried out.

His body shuddered at the thought. Quickly, with characteristic arrogance, he put his quite violent reaction down to the fact it was his *pleasure* at the thought of having his nemesis so close. His psyche would never allow the thought of being worried at Melville being on his trail. No it was definitely his pleasure at such an occurrence. It would now allow him to begin seriously planning the precise details of his revenge on Melville and Hughes.

After only a few seconds basking in this ray of conceited sunshine, a dark cloud began insidiously creeping into his thoughts. And for the first time the previously unthinkable occurred to him.

His exquisite planning may not be going quite as well as it was intended.

'Is it even remotely possible Melville could be a greater problem than anticipated?'

Chapter Twenty Six

The car driven by Sam went around the block before dropping Phil Hughes two blocks from Belinda's apartment at eight-fifty. It then circled the area once again as both Sam and McKay closely scrutinized every yard before finally dropping McKay off at eight-fifty-six. They arrived together at exactly nine o'clock. They were surprised to see Belinda until she explained she had already called her office saying she was sick and would not be in for a few days. She thought she ought not to attempt being more specific than that until it became clearer if her services would be required in the near future.

"Coffee and muffins are on the dining table. I'll leave you to your discussions. I shall be in my bedroom should you need me."

"Thanks Belinda. Not just for breakfast – for everything you're doing," said Hugh McKay. "And you were smart to take a few days off. Things are heating up and we may need you."

"That goes for me too," added Hughes. "I'm only sorry your guest is proving to be so troublesome. Perhaps you could chain him to his bed. Then we would always know where he is."

He stared at Philip as he spoke.

"Oh, oh. Better put cotton wool in your ears, Belinda. I don't want you to hear me cry as I get beaten up," responded Philip with a wide smile.

She was laughing as she closed her bedroom door. The three men sat at the table.

Phil Hughes had to get something off his chest.

"Okay, we've had our conversation about your actions last night. And I agree you must do some things your way, but a little advance notice wouldn't go amiss. Then I don't have to worry about you."

"Point taken. I can only promise to try. But both of you have to understand when I have been in battle I've been used to taking the lead with my men and to giving orders, not to taking them. And when I see an opportunity to harm the enemy I automatically take it. But I will try to keep you better informed."

"That's all we ask," said McKay. "Anyway, I can't be the one to criticize you for acting on your own," he added with a wry smile. "I'm guilty of the same trait, as my boss will gladly tell you."

"Well before I forget, I'll be going out again tonight. There are several other Chinese restaurants I didn't visit. I don't believe I will locate Ma Guan-lui but I may find another of his men. And you shouldn't worry; my disguise is pretty good as Sam no doubt told you."

"He did," confirmed Hughes. "Why do you say you don't expect to locate Ma?"

"Firstly we do not have a photo or a sketch of him. I'm certain he has, in the past, bought food from some of the restaurants. But he would certainly be disguised. And I am sure he has mastered the technique of walking short distances in a way his limp is not noticeable. He would probably walk slowly to do so. And I am also sure he had not gone to any Chinese restaurant in the past two weeks. He is a very careful character."

"What else have you thought of?" asked McKay.

"I assume you have put a man to watch the fellow I followed last night?"

"Of course. The gangster's real name is Lim Wan Choon. He rented his apartment under a false name. My very best *Asian* detective, as you specified, has the duty of keeping an eye on him."

"Good. He had better be really talented. If Ma gets even a sniff that his man has been made, he will kill him. And we won't find the body!"

"Ed Winfield attempted to get Lim's telephone number, but couldn't. Ed deduced Red Hand must have enhanced his software program to continually change his men's telephone numbers after each time they are used. I asked him if he could try to put a trace on any of the phones to get an instantaneous reading on Red hand's source," said Hughes.

"What did he say?"

"He laughed at me and proceeded to explain in technical terms why this was impossible. I still don't understand, but, reluctantly, I believe Ed to be correct," said Phil regretfully. "We had hoped Ed would be able to catch Red Hand calling Lim and track Red Hand's location. Hugh had a squad of men standing at the ready to move at a moment's notice. But obviously we have abandoned that plan."

"Well at least you have a detective watching Lim. Will you keep me up to date on anything he finds out?" requested Philip.

"Sure. And anyway I think we should keep in touch by the secure telephone every night. We can't risk coming here all the time."

"Agreed," said Philip. Then he lowered his voice. "And it would be wise to assign another of your best men to keep an eye on this place. Not for my safely, for Belinda's."

"I have already done so," replied McKay.

Hughes appeared somewhat shocked at this. He had not been told. But Melville only nodded his head. He had developed a high regard for this Canadian detective.

"Great, now please bring me up to date on your activities."

McKay proceeded to do so by relating everything about Brandt; including the fact that Ed Winfield was poised to gain access to the immigration computer in Sao Paulo and add Brandt's name to the list of arrivals.

"Also I have called in detectives from other cities. I will assign one to each of the members of the task force. My reason will be clear when we update you on our activities."

"Ah, I see. Now that Brandt is no longer available to him, you suspect Red Hand will go after someone else. And he may use abduction and torture if he is desperate enough."

"Exactly."

"May I make a suggestion?"

"By all means."

"When will the flight Brandt is supposed to have taken arrive in Sao Paulo?"

"Around five-thirty our time. Why?"

Ma will assume we have been smart enough to find out Brandt has left the country. And he will believe either we will have sent someone from the local CIA office to check arrivals or CSIS has. He will know we can't ask the Brazilian authorities to intervene as we have no extradition treaty with them. Once we have confirmed Brandt's arrival, he will expect us to heighten security on the remainder of the task force. So as from tonight the men you assign to this should not attempt to hide themselves. In fact they should make it obvious they are bodyguards. Not only will it provide security but it will reinforce Ma's opinion that Brandt is in fact in Brazil."

"I will have to request Jeremy Mason to send someone to Sao Paulo. And not to attempt to conceal this action," said Hughes suddenly.

McKay looked perplexed at this but once again Melville understood.

"Why?" asked McKay.

"If one of our CIA people fled to Brazil, we would do two things. We would snatch him at the airport and we would send an interrogator to find out why he had left. If Red Hand discovers CSIS has sent someone to Brazil, he will be convinced Brandt has been taken into custody there," explained Hughes.

"And it has one more benefit," said Philip. "Ma is not the type of person to accept Brandt's escape. His ego will not allow this to happen. He will begin searching for an assassin in Sao Paolo and put out a contract on Brandt. However, if he believes Brandt is in either CIA of CSIS custody he will not waste his time in doing so."

"But how do we ensure Red Hand learns CSIS has sent someone to Brazil?"

"That's not too difficult. I will have Ed Winfield temporarily remove the security device from Jeremy's phone. He will then send an urgent and frantic call to his people in Sao Paulo telling them to grab Brandt and to wait for an interrogator to arrive."

Hugh McKay's head was spinning at this Byzantine labyrinth.

"And you really think this guy, Red Hand, will fall for all this?"

"Oh yes," replied Philip. "He is a past master at this sort of thing. This is the way his mind works. It will all appear normal to him."

"This all seems so complicated and confusing. And I thought detective work was difficult enough."

"Obfuscation is a regular part of our tradecraft, Hugh," said Phil Hughes.

Hugh McKay was still doubtful. Nevertheless he was eternally grateful he had the benefit of espionage experts.

"Now for the sixty four thousand dollar question. When and how do we let Red Hand know I am here? We can't wait too long."

"I have been giving that some thought," said McKay. "If we did wait a bit longer, Red Hand may get impatient and decide to move ahead with his plan to attack America. If he made that decision, he would undoubtedly want to kill Phil immediately and hope to get you later. No matter what we do, I think you had better move out of the hotel, Phil. You can stay with Johnny Thomas."

"That sounds like an excellent idea," concurred Philip.

"All right, so long as Johnny doesn't object."

"I've already mentioned it to him and he would be delighted to assist."

Once again, Philip admired this man's ability to think ahead.

"Anyway, I don't think it will take our Mr. Ma much longer to find that Philip is no longer at home. I would bet he has used his gangster contacts to have their nefarious friends in Honolulu post a watch outside of Philip's house. Any day now he should receive a report that there has been no sight of occupancy for some time. He will believe Philip has come here."

"Perhaps we can deceive him," mused Hughes.

"How?"

"I have spent some time with Ed Winfield trying to better understand all that can be done by a computer expert. And relating to Philip leaving Honolulu, Ed told me a real expert can insert a name into all the airline computers at a particular airport. When that name appears on a passenger list it will be flagged on the expert's computer."

"Good God," exclaimed McKay. "Is nothing safe nowadays from prying eyes?"

"Not much, if one is as skilled as Ed and Red Hand. You remember at the second meeting of the task force, Hugh, the FBI suggested of all the big events to take place in the States, the most likely one to be targeted by Red Hand would be either in Chicago or Los Angeles."

"Yes it was based on the presence of very senior administration figures attending, maybe even the president."

"Well I bet a report on that meeting was passed from Brandt to Red Hand. So, if Ed were to show Philip leaving Honolulu for Chicago, maybe Red Hand would believe we had decided it was the most likely target and we sent Philip there. To add to that, now it has been decided I should leave the hotel, Ed could show me departing on a flight to Chicago."

"The only fly in that ointment is if Ma intends a target other than Chicago. Then he would be faced with the dilemma of deciding whether to go to Chicago first, to take care of Phil and me, or immediately proceed with his planned attack. If it would be the latter we would have inadvertently pushed up his schedule. And at a time when we have no idea where the ultimate target is."

"What do you suggest, then?" asked Hughes.

"Let's wait for another day. By that time I may have been lucky to locate one or both of Red Hand's other men. We will also have a report from the man tailing Lim. And, the FBI should have a report on their findings in checking out both Chicago and Los Angeles."

"Okay, I agree," said McKay.

"If we don't get good intel from these sources I can play my final card," said Philip.

"And what's that?" asked McKay.

There was so much caution in his voice, it was apparent he was almost afraid of the answer.

"I will flush out Red Hand by snatching either Lim or another of his men. That will be a clear signal I am here and I am hot on his trail. He will have no option to speed up his schedule. However I fully expect the prize of dispatching Phil and me first will be irresistible. He will come at us with everything he has. When you force an enemy to radically change a well thought out plan, they tend to make mistakes."

"There are a lot of 'ifs' in that scenario," said McKay softly as he stared intently at Philip.

"Yes there are. Let's hope we don't have to play that card."

"I hope you're not intending to remove one of those 'ifs' by somehow letting Ma know where you are staying."

Although Philip had increasingly admired McKay, he was shocked he seemed able to read his mind. He shrugged noncommittally.

That caused Hughes to shudder with trepidation.

Chapter Twenty Seven

McKay and Hughes left at eleven o'clock.

"Did you have a worthwhile meeting?" asked the ever curious Belinda.

"I would say on the whole, -- yes."

She was a perceptive agent and sensed there was something further he wanted to say.

"I need some assistance but I certainly don't want to get you into trouble."

"It's a bit late for me to be concerned about getting into trouble," she responded with a rueful grin.

"I don't mean with CSIS, I mean with Hugh McKay," he said.

That wiped the smile from her face.

"I won't do anything to undermine Hugh," she said determinedly.

"I know. I only need a few things for a job. I promise you Hugh will not be affected. However if he knew what I planned he may be tempted to assist or even try to stop me."

"And you believe you can pull off this job, whatever it may be, without police assistance?"

"It would be better that way."

"Why don't you tell me what you want and let me be the judge of whether or not it would harm Hugh McKay's ability to do his job? That's the best I can offer."

"Okay, that's fair. I need to contact a really good forger; I want a fake driver's license. Also I need to buy some special clothes. In your work at CSIS you must have come across a forger. Or you will know someone in your office that could help."

"So far I don't see a problem but tell me what you plan."

He hesitated then poured two cups of coffee and motioned for her to sit at the dining table.

"Hugh did excellent work in discovering the top gangster in Canada, Jacques Simone, was involved in smuggling a container into Vancouver. A container originating from somewhere in Asia. We believe it held a bomb of some type."

"Yes, I know about that."

"However Hugh's men could find out nothing further. I want to take a crack at that. If we could discover the location of that container this whole situation would be defused."

"And how do you propose to do that?"

"Disguised as a dockworker with Chinese features, I will pose as the brother of Hsieh, the pock marked Chinese who was pulled out of the bay."

"I still don't see how that will help you find the container."

In addition to my disguise, I'll need some fisherman's clothing. Also a driver's license as an ID; and whatever pass is required to get me into the docks. I'll tell dockworkers I'm looking into the murder of my brother. Before his death he told me he had just received an offer of a very high paying job. He had been recruited to do a job involving Jacques Simone. He was to be one of the men smuggling in a container."

"And you hope someone will drop an unintentional bit of information. Maybe someone involved in the smuggling?"

"You catch on fast, Belinda."

"You do realize if you do find such a person he is more likely to inform a higher authority in this smuggling racket. And that could get you killed."

"That is a possibility. But I can take care of myself and I will go armed."

"You can't smuggle a gun onto the docks. There is a detection device everyone must pass."

"It only detects metal. My weapon will pass without a problem. And it's better if you don't ask me too many more questions."

"This really gives me a problem. Hugh McKay would be furious at me if he found out and may even take me off the case."

She sat with a worried frown on her face and involuntarily wringing her hands.

"Let's just forget I asked you, Belinda. I don't want you impaled on the horns of a dilemma."

"You are crafty. You know I can't just forget you told me all this. And you know how much I want to be of some assistance in foiling this fiend's plan to kill millions of innocent people. Those horns you mentioned are really digging into me. Oh, all right. God save me, I'll help you."

"Thanks, Belinda. We have to hurry. Sam will come back here after taking Hugh and Phil back to police headquarters. The first thing is to find suitable clothing. I'll take my make-up kit with me and put it on in your car after we purchase the clothes. Then get me to the forger. Do you know one?"

"Of course. In my business we learn of most of the criminals who can be used in international activities. We don't have them all arrested as they can always be a useful source of information. Let's go."

It only took two hours to acquire the requisite forged documents and to transform Philip into a Chinese fisherman from Vancouver. Even Belinda was impressed and was beginning to believe this could just work. As instructed she dropped this fisherman close to the docks and returned home.

Philip got on the docks without a problem. But once inside he received careful stares from men who didn't recognize him. He made his way to the dock thought to be the one that imported the container. Here the stares were not merely curious, they were hostile. He approached a group just finishing their sandwich and soup lunches. He did so using the slightly swaying gait of a man used to being on heavy seas.

"Me looking for information on my brother. He work here and was murdered. Police no give me any help. He big man and face got many holes in it. You know him? He work for man called Simone."

Philip spoke quite a lot of Cantonese and was fluent in Vietnamese. Therefore he had no trouble in speaking English with an oriental accent.

"Nah, nah, we don't know your brother. No Chinks work here," rasped the man who apparently was the leader.

Philip could tell the mention of Simone struck a chord with many of the men and the leader had jumped in to cut off further conversation. He uttered several phrases in Cantonese to show his frustration. Then bowed slightly and moved away.

The second cluster of men he approached had watched him talking to the first group and they were ready to also send him packing. He repeated his speech, this time with more urgency and several 'pleases' and bows. One man waved him away, but a young man blurted out to his companion, "There were no chinks that night."

The man next to him gave him a kick to shut him up. The young man did so but couldn't help staring at one of the warehouses. It was emblazoned with the logo of American International.

Philip walked away slowly muttering to himself in Vietnamese. He was much better in this language than Cantonese, and his fluency completely convinced those watching that he was indeed Asian. Not that any of them could tell the difference between Vietnamese and any Chinese dialect.

He went around a corner and stopped. He waited until the men walked back to the ship they were unloading and then quickly went over to the warehouse. He looked through a side window and was not surprised to see it was empty. All the containers from the last shipment would have been dispatched. Still he couldn't help feeling a little disappointed. He had harbored a faint hope one container would still be stored there. With nothing further to be learned he took a taxi back to Belinda's apartment. But before hailing a taxi he removed his facial disguise. He didn't want the detective watching the apartment to take defensive action.

From experience he knew men who had been assigned a long boring stakeout often acted too quickly towards a suspect entering the place he was observing.

And sometimes they did so with deadly force!

Chapter Twenty Eight

Philip alighted from the taxi about a block from the apartment. And to his immense relief he saw Sam parked about a block in the opposite direction. Philip had already spotted the man in the dark blue sedan on the opposite side of the street. The car was unobtrusively parked in a row of cars. He believed him to be Hugh's detective and knew he would have been made aware of the homeless disguise he had used but no one in the police force knew of his present disguise.

Philip was correct in his identification. Detective Sergeant Black had eleven years experience in the police force. He had been selected for this important task as he had, on several occasions, completed successful stakeouts. Many policemen detested stakeouts as most proved fruitless. David Black had mastered the technique of occupying his mind during the long hours yet keeping alert. Oftentimes he wished he had not. Stakeouts were still eternal bores for most of the time. In addition to his record of success he was still young, in his mid-thirties, and was strongly built.

Philip's concern was that the detective would be worried by his fisherman's outfit and rush to intercept him, thus giving himself away should there be unseen and unfriendly eyes on the apartment. His hope was Sam would also be concerned and get out his car to stop him. Once Sam looked past his fisherman's clothes and recognized his face, all would be well. Philip was certain the detective knew Sam was CIA and his tension would dissipate at Sam's recognition.

The moment Sam noticed the fisherman he got out of his car, but halted his approach once he finally focused on Philip's face. He curbed his astonishment at Philip's garb and after a curt nod of recognition, returned to his car. And at seeing this, as Philip had surmised, Detective Sergeant

Black, who was then half way out of his car, quickly closed the door, sat back in his seat, and relaxed.

Belinda was enormously relieved to see him and immediately wanted to know all that had transpired.

"Tell you what; you can listen to my call to Phil Hughes giving him a complete report. Then I don't have to say it twice."

He dialed the number using the secure phone with Belinda sitting next to him, her ear close to the receiver.

"What have you been up to since we left the apartment?" demanded the perceptive Hughes."

Philip only had to tell of his disguise and intentions before Belinda heard the explosion from the other end of the call.

"What? Of all the dumb, idiotic, things to do. Do you have a death wish?"

"Calm yourself, Phil. It worked a treat. I was totally accepted as Hsieh's brother. Now here's what I found out."

He recounted his meetings at the dock.

"Have Ed use his computer to check the last arrival of an American International freighter from Asia. He may even get a manifest identifying the consignees. The warehouse is so large it has the capability of loading containers onto trailers and having semis haul them out. Even if Ed could find destinations of the various trucks, I doubt the container we are interested in went far if it had an American international logo on its side. I would bet it didn't. Most likely it was an unmarked container."

"I agree with that. Ma wouldn't make such a simple mistake."

"However, even if Ed can't track destinations, he should be able to check the quantity of containers leaving the docks against the ship's manifest. They should tally except for one – the one we are looking for. And there just may be a driver identified for each truck. We may be lucky and get the driver's license number and name. There must have been some identification indicating the driver was the correct person to take control of the container once it passed through customs."

"You don't sound too confident, Philip. And I would tend to concur with your feeling. It all depends how many people had to be bribed both on the docks and at the customs. But it's worth a shot. When we talk tonight I'll let you know what we find. And, --- Philip?"

"Yes?"

"I apologize for my earlier outburst. That was exceptional work. And a job an undercover agent or policeman could never have done. I'll brief Hugh. Talk to you later."

"I didn't understand Phil's last comment," said Belinda. "Why couldn't a very good agent or policeman have done what you did today?"

"It's the same situation regarding going to the restaurants I visited, Belinda. Full time criminals, and people who have bent the law sufficiently to be afraid of the consequences, have an almost sixth sense of law officials. Some claim they can smell a law officer. But I believe the real reason is it is just too difficult for a law officer to lower himself down to the level of criminals. No matter how hard they try, they often finally give themselves away by exuding an air of authority. Sometimes it's the way they walk, sometimes it's the language they use, but most often it's the look in their eyes. Some agents and police *can* manage to fool the bad guys: the ones who are extremely good actors. But there aren't many."

Belinda nodded her understanding.

"Thanks, I'll try to remember that if the occasion arises."

"First you have to get your head in the right place. In such a role you are a low life. And you must convince yourself of that and your lack of worth. Then, there's the golden rule. You must never, never, *never,* make eye contact with your prey. Got it?"

"Yes, I intellectually understand it, but I'm not sure I could pass the test in a real live situation."

"I think you'd be able to pull it off. But I hope you don't have to come up against that situation too often."

Late in the afternoon Philip reemerged from the apartment. Once again, he had donned his homeless man disguise.

"Where to now, Philip?" asked Sam.

"I have a few more restaurants to check out. Here's the list."

"Don't you think some of our agents or DI McKay's men could do this?"

Melville smiled to himself. He didn't want to go through all this again.

"Possibly," he said non-committally. "But right now it gives me something to do."

"But, I have been thinking about this," persisted Sam. "And it occurred to me this is rather a hit or miss approach. I mean, you could stay outside a restaurant for an hour, and five minutes after you leave, your man may show up. Couldn't a plain clothed policeman show the photo and sketches at the restaurants and ask if they are known to have been there?"

Philip sighed.

"What you say is perfectly true, Sam. My method is far from perfect. However you have to understand most Chinese restaurant owners are leery of the police. They will know a few of their customers are gang members or perhaps even men with long police records. And they will definitely know the brutal consequences of being discovered as a snitch. The last thing they want is to get involved. And believe me anyone asking direct questions and showing sketches will immediately be identified as a policeman. Worse still if they do recognize one of the men, they will warn him the next time he comes into the restaurant, out of a sense of self preservation. Then Red Hand would know what we are up to. That's why I can't risk doing as you say."

"Oh, I see. Okay let's get going to the first address."

This time it was the fifth restaurant which yielded a result. Once again Philip followed the man and sent a report to Johnny Thomas who said he would get on it straight away. He had initially asked for Hugh but was told the task force meeting was still in progress. So he decided to again visit some of the previous night's restaurants in case the third man showed up. Philip recognized it was a risk going back a second time but decided it was an acceptable one. He knew he could not go back a third time. That would raise too many suspicions. But these second visits proved fruitless.

He said goodnight to Sam at nine-thirty. Once again Belinda had been unable to control her anxiety and was highly relieved to see him.

"Hugh McKay has called four times," she burst out before greetings were exchanged. "He must speak to you urgently."

"I'll just have a quick shower to clean off all this dirt."

"I think you had better call him now. He really insisted you do so the very second you returned. He sounded really, really, agitated."

This gave Philip a sinking feeling in his gut. He sensed that something was terribly wrong. With his heart full of trepidation he picked up the phone and dialed Hugh's secure contact number.

Chapter Twenty Nine

"What's the problem, Hugh?" he asked peremptorily.

"I hate telling you this, Philip, but after today's meeting I was taken aside by Superintendent Larson and ordered to be in his office first thing tomorrow morning. And he has further ordered me to bring Phil and you."

This message was relayed over the speaker phone with Phil Hughes in attendance.

"And I said to you, Hugh, Larson can order all he wants but he has no authority over me," interjected Phil heatedly. "Doesn't he recognize his office may be under surveillance by Ma's men? And if they catch a glimpse of you, Philip, your life won't be worth ten cents; not to mention mine. So I told Hugh to tell his boss to take a hike."

"Obviously I tried that but he said he was coming under increasing pressure to end this thing quickly. He didn't say from whom, but when he mentioned the chief of police and a high ranking member of the prime minister's office would be there it became clear. Obviously Canada doesn't wish to be known as the country which failed to prevent the deaths of millions of American lives. Equally obviously the PM is becoming edgy and he wants to impress on the task force the need for immediate action. I know the risks of such a meeting, so let's put on our thinking caps and look for a compromise. And for the record, I don't think everyone meeting in Belinda's apartment would be a good idea. We have managed to keep that location secret so far but it could easily become compromised if some high ranking official rolls up in a large car sporting the Canadian flag."

"Well I intend calling my director at Langley. He can put a stop to this madness," retorted a still fuming Hughes.

"Hold on, Phil," interceded Philip, "let's just think about this for a minute. I don't blame the prime minister for being nervous and for wishing us to act quicker. However instead of having someone from his office and the chief of police fly here to give us that message, why don't we go there. I'm sure Superintendent Larson could arrange a plane. And it would be more secure for us to travel to Ottawa. Perhaps we could even suggest the prime minister himself attend."

"Say, that's not a bad idea," agreed Hughes. "And if he's not happy with our progress so far, he can do the damn job himself! Philip and I can go back to the delightful weather in Hawaii."

His anger and sarcasm indicated his extreme frustration.

"Phil if you don't cool down by the time of our meeting, you'll probably say something you'll regret. Then in a fit of pique you may indeed run off to your idyllic island, but you could get me fired or even thrown in jail," said McKay.

"Don't worry, I'll send you a cake with a hacksaw blade inside," cracked Hughes.

By his tone, Hugh recognized Phil's spike of anger had settled down a bit but had not totally diminished.

"Well if we're agreed I'll contact the superintendent and suggest Philip's idea."

"Go ahead."

"I'll call you back when I have an answer, Philip. And when I do, I'll give you an update on our meeting. Meantime I'll throw this irate CIA agent into a cold shower."

In the background Philip heard Hughes laugh and knew he was back on an even keel. He hung up and headed for a shower too. When he finished, he returned to the living room dressed in his pajamas and a robe.

"I don't suppose you have eaten tonight and you'll expect me to prepare a meal," exclaimed Belinda with feigned exasperation.

"A sandwich would be great," responded Philip somewhat sheepishly.

"Well, how would wiener schnitzel and spaetzle do?"

The look of astonishment on Melville's face made her laugh out loud.

"It's not a big deal. The veal is breaded and ready to be fried and the spaetzle is from a packet and only requires heating in the microwave. Why don't you open this bottle of Pinot Grigio and the dinner will be ready in fifteen minutes."

He had just finished his delicious dinner when the phone rang.

"We're all set. Larson thought your idea splendid as did the bigwigs in Ottawa. Phil and I will pick you up at six tomorrow morning two blocks north of the apartment," said McKay. "And rather than taking the time tonight, I'll brief you on today's meeting once we're on the plane."

"Roger that," replied Philip. "See you then."

Next morning Sam pulled up at one minute to six. This time he had the SUV to more comfortably accommodate all the passengers. The back door of was already open and Philip quickly jumped in. This was quite a feat as he had four coffees and four blueberry muffins in his hands. He passed them out as Sam skillfully picked his way through traffic while all the time scanning the rear view mirror for any sign of a tail.

"We're clear," he announced after seven minutes and gratefully took a sip of the hot coffee.

Hughes was digesting a large mouthful of muffin when he remembered something. He swallowed the last morsel.

"By the way, the guy you followed yesterday is a Yong Chen Onn. Hugh has posted someone to tail him when he goes out. Again Ed told me we can't get a listening device on his phone. Anyway good work. We've tracked two, only one to go."

Philip was happy to hear this but was mainly eager to hear about yesterday's meeting. But knew he had to curb his curiosity until they were airborne. Not that they didn't trust Sam but the task force information had to remain as closely guarded a secret as possible. However, he showed his impatience for news, as, even before the plane's wheels were up, he turned to face McKay with arched eyebrows. He didn't have to say anything. McKay got the message loud and clear

"Okay, okay, Philip. Keep your shirt on. Here's the good news. The FBI found out there was a man asking questions at the convention center in Chicago. He was Asian and walked with a limp."

"When was this?"

"Four weeks ago. And he was specifically interested in the convention which begins in ten days, and is to be attended by several senior administration figures. Furthermore, although it has not been officially announced, the FBI confirmed the president intends to make a brief appearance."

"And was this information relayed to the prime minister before your meeting yesterday?"

"Yes, as soon as it was received. That was yesterday morning at eight o'clock; one hour before our meeting began. And as you have no doubt already deduced this can only be the reason why today's meeting was called."

"And presumably the president has been asked to cancel his intended attendance."

"He has."

"And his senior administration personnel?"

"We don't have any information on them. Larson said it would be discussed at our meeting today."

Philip sat silently staring out of the window as he mulled over this information, After ten minutes, McKay was about to say something but Hughes put his hand on his arm to stop him. After another five minutes Philip turned his attention back to McKay.

"Anything else of importance come out of yesterday's meeting?"

"Only that the FBI found nothing suspicious concerning the meeting to be held in Los Angeles. Agents are very carefully conducting searches of the area surrounding the Chicago convention center."

"Hmm," was the only response from Philip who then returned to staring out of the window. He stayed that way, deep in thought, until they landed in Ottawa.

The meeting was held in a conference room in the prime minister's building. Attending were the prime minister's chief of staff, Michael Strang; the chief of police, Harold Simmons; his deputy Christopher Johnson; Jeremy Mason of the CSIS; and Superintendent Larson.

Coffee and cookies had been laid out on a sideboard. The members had just begun serving themselves when Strang spoke.

"If we are all *quite ready*, we can begin," he said in a punctilious manner. A tone which did not please anyone there.

When everyone was seated, Strang stood, paused a few seconds for dramatic effect, and then opened the meeting.

"I am Michael Strang, the prime minister's chief of staff."

He had not allowed time for any other introduction. Apparently he was so full of self importance he felt it only necessary to introduce himself.

"The PM is extremely worried over the current situation. And *I* completely concur. He wishes DI McKay's assurance this thug, Red Hand, will be arrested shortly. The information on the Chicago convention only gives us ten days. We demand to know the current status. What do you have to say, McKay?"

'Oh, oh, this smug bastard is about to get both barrels from Hugh,' thought Larson as was about to stand to intervene.

Before he could do so, McKay quickly stood and with remarkable restraint, responded.

"As of this date we have no information of his whereabouts. However thanks to the good work of Colonel Melville we have located two of his men. They are under surveillance twenty four hours a day and it can only be a matter of time until one of them leads us to him."

Johnson, the deputy to the chief of police was a huge man. Well over six feet tall, with extremely broad shoulders, and a massive body which gave the impression of wanting to burst out of his uniform at any second. He was renowned for his impatience; but to be fair, this had on many occasions led him to successfully conclude several cases. But at hearing Hugh speak, this character trait could not avoid rising rapidly to the surface.

"Damn it all to hell. If you know the whereabouts of these men bring them in immediately. What are you waiting for McKay? Between Jeremy and me we can sweat the truth out of them. We'll have all the information required to have this Chinese locked up in a day."

His forceful tone caused an immediate tension in the room. This was aggravated by the braying Strang.

"I must say I agree. What we need is action and not sitting around hoping for the best."

The tense atmosphere was broken by the soft voice of Philip.

"That would be a disastrous thing to do."

"What? Who the hell are you?" Johnson demanded.

As Strang had begun the meeting so peremptorily and had not shown the courtesy of introductions, Johnson had erroneously assumed Philip was another CIA agent, a lackey of Phil Hughes. Earlier Hugh McKay had indeed shown great restraint but now his internal rage was about to explode. With tremendous self discipline he did not scream out a reply. However although not a scream his voice had a quality which no one could mistake for anything other than suppressed fury. He glared at Johnson and Strang in turn.

"This is Colonel Philip Melville. The most decorated leader of United States Special Forces in Vietnam: and the man who went undercover and tracked down Red Hand several years ago in China. Colonel Melville foiled a plot of Red Hand's to annihilate tens of millions of people. That mission is one of the most highly classified in America. Therefore I am not at liberty to say anything further. Anyway that's all I know. That's correct isn't it Phil?"

He looked at Hughes for agreement.

"Yes it is. I am Phil Hughes, the Regional Director of the CIA for South East Asia. I worked with Colonel Melville on the mission Hugh mentioned. And I can tell you it was only his brilliance which averted a disaster of untold proportions. He is the only man I know of with the skills to catch Ma Guan-lui, the man referred to as Red Hand. *You had better listen to him.*"

He emphasized the last sentence in a threatening tone as he stared unwaveringly into the eyes of Johnson.

"I still say we bring in his men. That's a certain way to get them to give up Red Hand's location."

This time Johnson felt less adamant, he was obviously impressed with Philip's credentials. But he was still unwilling to give up his tried and true past methods as he stood to respond. His boss interrupted before Johnson could speak further. Harold Simmons was a highly esteemed man due to the quality of service he had given to his country. This respect came from his superior, his peers and importantly from his men. This was in contrast to Johnson who was feared by his men much more than respected.

"Colonel Melville, it is indeed an honor to meet you. Your reputation has even made its way all the way north to me."

He said this with a smile.

"But tell me, why would you say bringing in his men would be a mistake?" he asked in a gentlemanly manner.

"Sir, this man trusts no one. And when he is through using someone to aid him, he kills him. While he is still using someone he weaves a web that connects that person to him constantly - a one way connection. And just like a cunning spider whenever that web has the slightest tremble he moves in for the kill. To protect himself, he always stays in the shadows leaving no trace of his location. It's the reason he was able to stay below my government's radar for so long. Therefore I am certain his men have no knowledge of his whereabouts. And just as he had in Beijing, I am equally certain he has more than one location in Vancouver. If you were to bring in even one of his men, he would know this immediately and disappear, killing as many of his associates as possible before doing so."

"Well that would be good wouldn't it?" said Strang. "It would eliminate the danger if he went to ground."

He felt very self assured his analysis was correct.

"I'm afraid not. You see, just as he did in China he will have already set up a network in the location of the bomb. They are ready to move at a moment's notice. I'm not sure if his presence is required at that location or not. If not, it would mean he could detonate the bomb with one phone call. And bringing in his men could trigger that phone call."

Johnson was sometimes irascible, occasionally rude, often impatient, but he was not stupid. His eyes lost their aggressive look and he nodded his understanding towards Philip. Simmons also understood and it was he who spoke next.

"I see. Then our idea was not a good one. Thank you for explaining the thinking of the man we are after. I can only agree with Mr. Hughes that we are fortunate to have you working with us. Tell me, Colonel Melville, do you believe he would telephone his instructions for detonation and not wish to do so in person?"

Philip looked at Simmons with renewed respect. This man had good intuition and knew the correct question to ask.

"I believe he would prefer to detonate the bomb personally and would only give telephone instructions as a last resort."

"Why do you conclude that?" asked Jeremy Mason.

"There are three reasons. First and foremost is pride. This is his plan and he will wish to execute it himself. Second is certainty. He will always have the nagging suspicion his accomplices may give in to humane feelings and decide not to kill millions of people. Third is security. Once he uses his accomplices to move the bomb from its present hiding place and put it in his selected location he will have no further use for them and will kill them."

The coldness of Philip's logic was chilling and caused several in the room to shiver.

"Then what do you suggest we do, Philip?"

This was the cue for Johnson's streak of impatience to once again become evident.

"If we have not located them with the present FBI search, then on the day of the convention we'll have every available FBI agent surround the Chicago convention center. And we will have the Chicago police check every person and vehicle going into the center. The obvious presence of the uniformed police will most likely scare away the attackers. And the large number of undercover FBI men will look out for a vehicle or a person turning away from the center. We'll trap them that way."

There were nods of agreement from several around the table. Taking this as his cue to reassert his authority over the meeting, Strang again spoke in his haughty manner.

"Then that's settled. We can bring this meeting to a close. I will personally brief the prime minister."

This apparent consensus was blasted into smithereens by Philip's next statement.

"He's not going to Chicago!"

Chapter Thirty

The cacophony of voices could not have been louder if an actual bomb had exploded in the room.

When it gradually subsided, it was Strang who spoke.

"How can you say that with any certainty? Was it not researched and discovered the two most likely near term large conventions were to be held in Los Angeles and Chicago?"

"Yes," replied Philip softly.

"And, did not the FBI, after a thorough investigation, discover an Asian man walking with a limp had been asking probing questions about the Chicago convention?"

"Yes."

"And does not this Chinese man, Red Hand, walk with a decided limp?"

"Yes."

"Then in the name of God, man, how can you say the bomb will not be exploded in Chicago?"

Strang's voice had risen to almost a shout. Even McKay and Hughes were staring at Philip in disbelief.

"Because it's just too pat. It doesn't fit Ma's devious mind."

"But Philip," said Hughes, "the FBI didn't just find this out by asking the first person. It took a great deal of digging to discover it. Whoever it was went to enormous lengths to cover his tracks."

"Of course he did. That was part of his plan. But believe me, if Ma Guan-lui had actually wished to truly cover his tracks, no one would have discovered a thing. He is much too talented for that. Remember he is a master of disguise. The least he would do is not let it be seen he is Chinese.

And as I believe I told you before, it's not terribly difficult to avoid limping for short periods at a time. No, my friends, we were meant to find this supposed piece of evidence. It was a plant!"

"If it's not to be Chicago, does that mean it will be Los Angeles?" asked Jeremy Mason.

"Possibly, but I doubt it. You see Ma would have checked all the upcoming conventions just as we did. And I believe he would have avoided them as being too obvious. Undoubtedly he went to Chicago to lay a false trail. A trail he hoped would require the FBI to search for quite some time before uncovering. That's his genius. And if we did catch on to his trick, he would hope by not leaving any clues in Los Angeles we might assume it was the target. I have to admit that Los Angeles presents a juicy target for a nuclear attack; however in my gut I feel he is going somewhere else."

"But where?" demanded a confused Strang, struggling to keep his confusion out of his voice.

"I don't know. I was hoping we might get a lead following my investigation at the docks. But both the FBI and Hugh's people are still looking into that. If we could track the container we would find Red Hand."

"What's the status on that, DI McKay?" asked Simmons.

"We do know it was an unmarked container and it was cleared through customs by a Chinese who also drove the rig out of the docks. We interrogated the gate keeper and he identified the photograph of Hsieh – the Chinese who was found drowned in the bay. This is another example of Philip's point regarding Red Hand's method of covering his tracks once he has no further use for someone. FBI agents are tracking the bank accounts of all the customs officers. If I may I will call them for an update."

"Please do," commanded Simmons.

McKay was only on the phone for a few minutes.

"They found one customs officer who had an unusual deposit to his account of five thousand dollars."

"Is he still alive?" asked Philip hesitantly.

"Yes."

"Then he will be of no use to us," he said dejectedly.

The others looked expectantly at McKay hoping Melville was wrong.

"You're right Philip. He will have been bribed by Hsieh. Ma would have delegated this so as to not be identified."

One could almost feel a tremendous sense of disappointment settle over the room. It was eased a little by the next words from McKay.

"We are still collecting the tapes from every security camera in the area. We know this is an unmarked container on a rig. It shouldn't be too hard to track it."

Philip didn't share the easing of disappointment. He knew the container would not be found. The best he could hope for would be to discover where its terrible cargo was switched to another container. This was a long shot but it was the only shot he had.

"I think we had better get back to Vancouver and follow up on this possible lead," he said firmly.

"But what do I tell the prime minister?" asked Strang plaintively; for once letting down his mask of superiority.

"May I suggest I come with you, Michael? Together we can recount today's meeting and assure him everything possible is being done. We can also explain that precipitous action in terms of pulling in Red Hand's accomplices could have disastrous consequences," said Harold Simmons.

And although his comment was phrased in a gentlemanly question, everyone saw it as a command.

"I will of course brief my director. And he will certainly inform the president. I feel confident the director will suggest the president calls the prime minister to indicate he agrees with our actions," added Phil Hughes.

He was not only a talented senior member of the CIA but he clearly understood how politicians thought. Michael Strang was nothing if not a competent politician and he immediately grasped the significance of Phil's comment. Two political leaders sharing a common point of view lessened the responsibility of each of them. He almost smiled at this solution.

"Very well, but keep me fully up-to-date on progress," he commanded austerely as his mask of superiority again took over his countenance.

"One second," interjected the sharp Jeremy Mason. I'm sure the White House must currently be concerned over senior administration figures attending the Chicago convention."

"It was hurriedly decided by my director not to announce their cancellation," responded Hughes. "It would have given Red Hand a warning, if in fact Chicago was the target. Obviously as the president's attendance had not been announced it was safe to cancel his appearance. However the director wanted to wait until after our meeting today before deciding on the correct course of action for other officials."

"That was smart," said Philip.

"Then I think it obvious you can let them attend the conference," said Strang in a condescending tone. Implying others may not be as astute as he.

"No, just the opposite," contradicted Philip. "They should cancel their attendance and say it was due to some other important urgent matter. That will indicate we have decided Chicago is indeed the identified target. Ultimately it may not fool Red Hand, but he will be wondering whether or not we truly believe he intends attacking Chicago. And the more uncertainty we can put in his mind the better it is for us."

Strang's only response was a slight shake of his head. He just couldn't keep up with the machinations of the situation. All the devious moves of Red Hand seemed to be offset by Philip's warrior's intuition. This game of chess was at a level well beyond Strang's experience. However his ego could not allow him to acknowledge this.

"Well that seemed rather apparent," he said airily and marched out of the room.

But the looks of admiration for Philip, in the eyes of the intelligent Simmons and Mason, were quickly recognized by McKay and Hughes.

"May I ask you to stay a moment gentlemen?" asked Simmons after checking the door to ensure Strang was well beyond hearing distance.

"Some of you may know Harold Beaumont was the original chief of staff to the prime minister. Unfortunately he passed away six month's ago. It is not generally known but a very senior Member of Parliament in the PM's party begged him to take on a junior MP from the party; who just happened to be his nephew. That junior member is Michael Strang. Unfortunately he has a rather high opinion of himself as you will have observed. That's why I will go with him to brief the PM. Just to be certain the true outcome of our meeting is presented. Please keep this information confidential. However I wanted you to be certain the PM will receive a true recount of today and I will ensure he understands the particular importance of your experience, Colonel Melville. Now if you will excuse me I must catch up with Strang."

When he had gone the others looked at each other silently. They merely nodded their appreciation of Simmons intervention. They all left the office feeling a little better.

As they rode in the car back to the airport Hugh McKay offered his own silent prayer of thanks for having the assistance of a certain Colonel Philip Melville.

Chapter Thirty One

It was dark when they landed back in Vancouver. Sam was waiting for them.

"Where to, Philip?" he asked.

McKay quickly glanced at Hughes with a smile on his lips. Phil answered his silent comment with a slight shrug of his shoulders. It was apparent to both of them that although Sam was employed by the CIA, his primary allegiance was to his hero. Melville didn't seem to notice this exchange.

"Drop me off at the apartment then I guess Hugh and Phil will be going to police headquarters. Right Hugh?"

"Right, I have to check on the progress in tracking that container."

"And I had better get on the horn to Langley. I'll have to inform the director of all that transpired in Ottawa," said Phil. Then turning to look at Philip with his eyebrows arched in a suspicious manner, he asked, "And what mischief will you get up to tonight?"

"There's nothing to do until Hugh tells me about the container. So I'll just do some thinking."

Sam either did not hear him or more probably didn't believe him, because he asked, "What time do you want me to come back to the apartment, Philip?"

"Not tonight, Sam. I'll see you tomorrow morning. And make sure you bring our beat up car and not this fancy wagon."

Sam just grinned; he had already figured out which vehicle Philip would want.

"What time?"

"That depends on Hugh's information. I'll call you."

"Roger that," responded Sam and drove off to police headquarters.

"Which telephone can I use?" Phil asked Hugh, once they were inside the building.

"Use the one in Johnny's office. It's the only other secure line besides mine."

"Thanks, see you a bit later."

McKay then called for Thomas.

"I've told Phil Hughes to use the secure line in your office."

"No problem, boss."

"Come into my office and I'll brief you on today's meeting. It was a beauty."

Thomas sat goggle eyed as he listened.

"Wow. Thank heavens we have Colonel Melville."

"Amen to that, Johnny. Now let's go the incident room. You can tell me the latest on tracking the container."

Once there and with mugs of coffee in their hands, Thomas began.

"The security camera at the docks caught the direction the semi turned out of the gate. We then checked the tapes from other traffic cameras and discovered it passed over the border into USA and took Route Five. I have requested the FBI to check traffic cameras along Route Five."

He nodded to a corner of the room where agent Jim Parker was on the phone. McKay waited until he had finished his call then sat down beside him.

"Anything, Jim?"

"I'm working with FBI headquarters. All traffic camera tapes are being looked at by local FBI agents and copies are being air dispatched to headquarters. They have the best lab equipment should we need special analyses. Let's go over to the large board on the wall and I'll explain the situation.

He stopped in front of a large map of the west coast of America.

"If we attempted to check the tapes of traffic cams through every small town along Route Five it would take an eternity. Therefore, we issued an instruction to check every hundred miles or so. We caught the semi trailer here, entering Bellingham."

He used a pen to point to the location.

"And again entering Mount Vernon here, and again entering Everett here. Then we jumped to the major location of Seattle. But no trace of it."

"Damn, he must have turned off," cried out McKay in frustration.

"Hold your horses, Hugh. That was my first thought, too. Then I asked our people to check the traffic cam coming out of Everett, and guess what?"

"No trace of it."

"Right."

"Could he have headed east on Route Two and into the Cascade Mountains?"

"Possible, but unlikely. Driving a semi trailer across the Cascades would be no easy task. Why do that when he could stick to main highways? No, I'm betting the cunning bugger transferred the container to another semi trailer somewhere in Everett. I instructed the agent in Everett to make copies of the last tapes of the sighting of the container as it entered Everett, along with all tapes showing traffic exiting Everett; and to send those copies to headquarters. I have just requested headquarters to make blow ups of the container as it entered Everett and look for it leaving on a different rig."

"If it has noticeable markings, like dents or scratches, you can track the container and not the semi. Is that it?"

"On the nose. The analysis from the lab should be complete by morning"

"Great work, Jim."

"There's only one snag," interrupted Johnny. "What if they had the capability of transferring the bomb into another container loaded on a new semi?"

"Then we're screwed," answered Parker.

"I don't think they would take the time to transfer the bomb," said McKay. "If, as we suspect, it is a nuclear bomb, and it was shipped from somewhere in Asia, It must have been very securely bolted to the inside of the container. I recognize it would not explode without a triggering device, but they wouldn't want it damaged by being unbolted and tossed around inside a container. Anyway let's hope I'm right. I'll see you first thing tomorrow morning, Jim."

"What now, boss?" asked Thomas.

"I'll have to brief the other members of the Task force, then I'm going home to see my wife and hopefully get some dinner. I want you to go to see your *girlfriend* and brief Philip and her on the status of the container. Then get some sleep. See you bright and early tomorrow."

Usually, even after a hard day, High McKay enjoyed his drive home. The thought of seeing his lovely wife, Cathy, and the anticipation of one of her perfectly cooked dinners, drove all of that day's problems out of this mind.

But not tonight.

This case was consuming his every waking moment like no other had done before. He constantly fretted over the possibility he may have missed some important clue. His extensive experience with criminals of all types made it seem inconceivable any villain could be so utterly omnipotent. His mind raced over all details yet again. There must be a weak link in this man's capability. There always was.

Fortunately for McKay, his car appeared to know the way home – and to get there without an accident. He was still engrossed in the mysteries of Red Hand and was surprised at realizing he was home. The front door opened to reveal Cathy standing there to greet him, never had there been a more welcome sight.

"Ah, so you've remembered you have a home."

McKay chuckled despite his tiredness.

"Yes I remembered. And how are you my bonnie lass?"

Cathy wore a broad smile on her face when she had greeted him in jest. However his reply in his Scottish accent, wiped it from her face. Any time he reverted to this accent meant things were not going well.

"What's wrong, Hugh?"

"Oh, it's just this case. We're up against the most brilliant mind in criminal history. And every time I think we are getting close, the devious bugger slips away. No, that's too pessimistic. Philip Melville *is* getting us closer. Oh, pay no attention to my rambling, my love. I'm so tired, I can't even think straight."

"Well I've got a lovely dinner for you. Have a cocktail then sit down at the table. What you need it a quiet night and a good sleep."

Good wives know their husbands well; and tonight, as usual, she was correct.

The next morning he felt much better and was in the office at six-thirty.

He marched straight into the incidence room where Jim Parker was waiting for him.

"Did you get it?"

"Yes and no," responded a bleary-eyed and somewhat deflated Parker.

The observant McKay noted the several empty coffee carafes and the large wastepaper basket chock full of polystyrene coffee cups. This combined with the crumpled open neck shirt (the tie had long been discarded) told him what had happened. Nevertheless he asked the question.

"Isn't that the same shirt you wore yesterday, Jim?"

"Yeah, I stayed up all night keeping in touch with headquarters. They completed the trace of the container at four this morning. I was right; the rig was switched in Everett."

There was no elation in his voice; only tiredness.

"We began tracking the new rig and verified it entered Tacoma and on to Portland."

"That's good, Jim. Why so downcast?"

"Then we got ambitious and went straight to San Francisco. No sign of the rig. They must have switched again. Dammit! Now we are backtracking and are currently checking Eugene, Oregon. I'll give you a call when we reestablish contact."

"Why don't you take a rest, Jim? We can get someone else to sit in for you."

"No way, Hugh. I'm going to track that damned container."

McKay knew better than to argue with a dedicated professional. He had been in similar situations. Once a lawman gets his teeth into a mission, he feels he owns it, and won't give it up to anyone else. You'd have more luck taking a juicy bone from a hungry Doberman.

At midday Hugh received the welcome news the FBI had located the container once again. It had been transferred to another semi trailer and this one had been spotted crossing into California. The message was given to him by Senior Agent Larry Douglas.

"I have taken over from Jim Parker, although I had to pull rank and order him to sleep for a while. Jeez, Hugh, you've no idea how stubborn that son-of-a-gun can be!"

Hugh McKay wasn't fooled by his outburst. He could see the pride in the eyes of Douglas.

"I'm not even certain he obeyed my order. I rather suspect it was a case of being unable to keep his eyes open any longer. He finished all the coffee in your office and all that he subsequently ordered in. There may not be any coffee left in all of Vancouver."

Chapter Thirty Two

Later in the afternoon, McKay was shocked to see Michael Strang walk in to police headquarters.

"What are you doing here?" he demanded ungraciously.

This was his territory and he felt no obligation to be overly respectful of Strang's position. He certainly had no regard for Strang.

"The prime minister and I felt it appropriate for me to be on the scene as things are moving ahead at a better pace. The tracking of the container is obviously the key to this entire affair. I will attend all your meetings here and therefore be in a position to relay up-to-the-minute information to the PM."

McKay saw through this charade. It was patently obvious Strang wanted to be closely associated with the operation now he believed it could come to a successful conclusion. In this way he intended to spin a story that he was integral to its triumph. Personal aggrandizement was the goal of many politicians.

"Now, if you don't mind, give me the latest situation," requested Strang.

He made this request sound like an order.

"I have an important telephone call to make, but my sergeant will brief you."

He called in Johnny Thomas.

"Sergeant Thomas, this *gentleman* is Mr. Michael Strang, the prime minister's chief of staff. Please give him a briefing on the current situation."

Johnny clearly got the message. The emphasis on 'gentleman' told him his boss had no respect for this man no matter what his position. Yet McKay was required to keep him fully informed.

"Certainly sir," he replied.

The look in his eyes told McKay he understood the situation.

"If you would follow me, Mr. Strang," he said and led him to his office.

Hugh's important call was to Philip. He wanted to bring him up to date on the tracking of the container.

"I'm afraid he's not here," said Belinda. "After your telephone call late yesterday afternoon, he spent the rest of the day sitting thinking and writing in his notebook. He said you would most likely call and asked me to give you a message. He said he couldn't think clearly enough in a confined space so he went for a walk to get some fresh air."

"Oh my God, will he never stop taking risks?" exclaimed McKay rhetorically. "I thought we asked you to chain him to his bed?"

"I will attempt most things you request of me, Hugh; but tackling Colonel Melville is not one of them," she laughed as she replied.

"Yes, he is a bit of a monster, isn't he? Ask him to call me when he returns, Belinda."

"Roger that," she replied, using Philip's military acknowledgement.

McKay smiled as he put down the receiver. But fifteen minutes later his facial expression bore that of a worried frown. Looking out of his office window into the squad room he saw Johnny Thomas and Sally O'Shaughnessy involved in highly animated conversation. She was waving her hands frenetically in a manner he knew all too well. Something or someone had really got her dander up. He walked out of his office and asked what was going on.

"That obnoxious, pompous, bugger threw me out of my office," she sputtered.

"Who did?"

"Strang," answered Johnny.

"Why?"

"He wanted to use my phone and demanded I leave as it was a highly confidential matter involving national security. The stupid idiot – he only had to ask me politely and of course I would have understood and complied. But no – everything he does is of the utmost importance and he wants everyone to know how critical his needs are and you have to jump at once to his every command. He may be calling his bookie for all I know."

That brought an instant grin to Johnny's face. It appealed to his impish sense of humor.

But a look of horror came over McKay.

"Oh, no! That imbecilic bastard couldn't be ----."

Without completing his sentence he rushed into Sally's office slamming the door behind him so violently that the entire office wall partition shook. Strang looked up in alarm before quickly continuing his conversation.

"Excuse me, PM, but I have just been rudely interrupted."

He put his hand over the receiver.

"Get out McKay, this is a highly confidential conversation," he shouted.

McKay had not stopped his rapid forward motion. He came around the side of the desk grasped Strang by the knot of his tie, jerked him out of the chair and violently banged him against a filing cabinet. The telephone immediately fell out of Strang's grasp and clattered against the desk. McKay temporarily released Strang and retrieved the phone.

"Sorry, Prime Minister, this is DI McKay and this line Strang has been using is not a secure one."

"What? - the blasted idiot!"

"I will call you back in about half-an-hour. I must find out what damage has been done and remedy it."

"Thank you, DI McKay."

Hugh turned back to face the wide-eyed, terrified, Strang and grabbed him by the throat. Outside, several others had joined Sally and Johnny to gawk at this sight through the office windows.

"Now Strang, exactly what did you say to the PM?"

McKay seemed to have temporarily forgotten he was almost throttling Strang until he finally allowed his ears to hear the choking noises emanating from his restricted airway. He quickly released his grip on Strang's throat. Strang took several seconds while he wheezed and gasped before answering.

"That is none of your business. I told you it was a privileged conversation. And you will be lucky to only be demoted to a beat-walking policeman after I report your unwarranted, vicious, attack; you moron."

"Listen to me carefully, you supercilious bastard, perhaps your ears were blocked when I was speaking to the PM. I just said this is not a secure line, therefore, if you have given the PM critical information on our current state of knowledge, there is a chance Red Hand will have recorded it."

McKay's voice then dropped to little more than a whisper – a whisper full of venomous threat.

"Now, for the last time, *tell me precisely what you said to the PM*."

Strang saw the unmistakable menace in McKay's eyes. His knees buckled and his body involuntarily shuddered with fear. Then he noticed for the first time, the crowd standing outside the office. They couldn't hear but they obviously were keen to watch. He straightened his tie and attempted to stand as erect as possible. He quickly and wisely decided to relent and answer the question. He would take care of McKay later when he gave a biased, skewed, report to Chief Constable Simmons. Right now he had to focus all his attention on avoiding severe bodily harm at the hands of the enraged McKay.

"If you must know, I only passed along the information Sergeant Thomas had given me on the latest news we have regarding the container. I fail to see what possible use that could be to this Red Hand at this stage."

He said this in a haughty tone as his air of superiority returned.

"Anything else?" demanded McKay.

"No, nothing, before you barged in like a lunatic."

"Are you certain?"

McKay stepped even closer. The look in his eyes of dire consequences if he didn't get the truth again caused Strang to quiver. More importantly it brought something further to his memory.

"Well there was only one other point. However it is so insignificant I didn't mention it to you. I informed the PM we could be extremely proud of the role being played by CSIS. Even down to the minor detail that one of our young female agents, Miss Belinda Carson, had graciously agreed to grant accommodation to this Colonel Melville chap."

If someone had lobbed a hand grenade into the office, it could not have had a greater impact on McKay. For an instant he was stunned. He stood stock still as though unable to react. Then he uttered the most blood curling scream as a blanket of red mist came over him: a mist caused by a mixture of unadulterated rage and dread.

He seized Strang by the lapels of his jacket and banged him against the filing cabinets.

"You stupid bastard – you useless stupid bastard!" he yelled at the top of his lungs.

He continued to hammer him repeatedly against the cabinets. Now the gawks on the faces of the crowd outside turned to terror. They could now clearly hear McKay's agonizing cries of horror and Strang's woeful shrieks of pain. Johnny Thomas reacted instantly, rushing into the office and putting his arms around McKay.

"Boss, boss, you'll kill him!"

McKay's mist cleared and he released Strang.

"Not yet, but I might later. Quick Johnny, call DS Black and tell him Philip's location at the apartment has been compromised. And send reinforcements over there immediately!"

He ran back to his own office, snatched up the phone with the secure line and frantically dialed Philip's number.

Once again it was Belinda who answered.

"Belinda," he gasped. "Is Philip there?"

"I was just about to take a shower. Can't a girl get any personal time?" she joked.

"Belinda! *Is he there*?"

His voice had risen to a level which immediately erased her jocular mood.

"No, Hugh, he came back from his walk, put on one of his disguises and left for your office. He's wearing a false beard and moustache and thick glasses. He should be there soon as Sam was outside in the car. He said it was a slight risk coming to your office; however, he wanted to be inside your incident room to get the latest briefing on the tracking of the container. He said he had some ideas. You sound upset, Hugh. Is there a problem?"

"Oh thank God," he sighed.

Then realizing his tone must have caused Belinda to be concerned he quickly improvised.

"There's nothing to worry about, my dear. I was only concerned over his habit of leaving without notice and walking about in the streets," he lied. "Go have your shower. I'll see Philip when he gets here."

He hung up the phone leaving a confused Belinda. She did not for a second believe his flimsy excuse. Something was terribly wrong but there was nothing she could do about it. She walked into the bathroom.

Back at headquarters McKay ran back to Sally's office, but Strang was no longer there

"Where'd he go?" he demanded of Johnny.

"As soon as you released him, he left here like a cat with its tail on fire. All he said as he left was, 'Bloody amateur theatrics. All this cloak and dagger stuff has warped McKay's tiny mind.' I suspect it was a feeble effort to restore his dignity."

"Damn, I wish I had caught him before he bolted."

"I'm glad you didn't, boss. I really thought you were going to choke him to death."

"Hopefully I would have stopped before that; but, at least, I could have broken a few bones. I bet he came on one of the PM's jets and he's most probably rushing to the airport now. When he gets to Ottawa he'll be complaining about me. Not to worry. I don't regret a thing – except not being able to really hurt him!"

With that, he again ran back to his office, closed the door and called the prime minister. He gave a truthful, unvarnished account of all he had done.

"Don't trouble yourself, DI McKay. It's more my fault than yours. I should never have hired the sniveling toady. I'll deal with it. I hope no irreparable damage has been done."

"As do I, Prime Minister."

He sat back in his chair trying to catch his breath after all his running around. There was a knock on his door. He looked up and was surprised to see Thomas. Normally Johnny breezed into his office without knocking. This time he hadn't rushed in as he had never seen McKay so angry and so out of control. It deeply worried him. Not that his boss would ever strike him – or had he so lost his senses – he would?

'No never in a month of Sundays,' he thought.

Just then he looked up to see McKay waving him in. He entered and produced a mug of coffee from behind his back.

"I thought you could use this, boss."

Thomas could read the gratitude in McKay's eyes and was instantly relieved.

"Thanks, Johnny. I certainly could. Oh and tell the front desk Philip will arrive wearing a false beard and moustache. They should show him up here right away."

Thomas was smart enough not to linger. He knew McKay would like a little time to restore his normally balanced senses.

McKay took a little sip of coffee. He couldn't take much as his chest was heaving. This was partially caused by the thought of what he nearly did to Strang, but mainly due to the thought of anything untoward happening to Philip. By the time he had finished his coffee he had consoled himself with the reflection it was highly unlikely Red Hand would have been listening in at the very moment Strang had called.

"No, no, that would be a million to one shot," he muttered.

But he was wrong!

Chapter Thirty Three

One of the improvements Ma Guan-lui had made to Jean Mercier's programs had been on the telephone tracking system. To Mercier it had been child's play to break into a known telephone number and listen in on the conversation. Equally easy for him had been devising the capability of remotely posting listening devices on certain lines which would record any calls from that line made at any time. It was Ma's genius to recognize it may be as beneficial to reverse that order. He had decided it to be equally useful to insert a remote recording device not only on any outgoing call, but also on any incoming call. And to have a signal sent to his computer when this occurred.

His careful planning has been thwarted with the arrival of Ed Winfield and his particular genius. Important telephone lines had been made secure in a manner Ma could not circumvent. However, Ed's precautions had not been taken on all lines, only on the most important lines.

The prime minister had three telephones on his desk. The red one had the same technology as that of the similar phone of the desk of the president of the USA. It rapidly changed coding sequences making it impossible to break into. This red phone was used to call heads of states and the most senior military personnel. Then there was a green telephone. It had been made secure by CSIS and was used to make important calls within Canada. The third phone was white and used for all other calls. CSIS had bristled at Ed's suggestion he be allowed to use his technology to make the green one safe. They regarded their own expertise sufficient for security. And it was, for almost every situation, but not quite good enough to protect against Ma Guan-lui.

Regrettably, when he called from Sally's phone, Strang had not taken even the most basic of precautions. He did not call the green telephone; instead he called the number he most often used - the white phone.

Ma's computer lit up with this call. If Strang had used McKay's or Thomas' phone all would have been well. Ma would still have received a warning light on his computer but would have been unable to listen in. On its own, even Strang's stupidity would have posed no imminent danger. As, it would have required quite some time for an alerted Ma to contact his men, instruct them to take action, and for them to assemble then drive to the apartment. Meantime McKay would have immediately alerted CIA operatives and policemen to race to the apartment. They would have arrived well before Ma's men.

Sadly, Lady Luck was sitting on Ma's shoulder that day and not on McKay's.

In anticipation of having Hughes and/or Melville within striking distance, Ma had devised options to extract his revenge. His least favorite was killing them with a high powered rifle. His favorite, by far, was to capture them, then having the luxury of time, to torture them mercilessly. He intended to do so for several hours before finally killing them. One part of such a plan was the use of a snatch and grab technique in capturing his targets. For this he would use his acolytes. They had memorized the faces of both targets from photographs acquired by Ma from computer records.

The technique was simple. Once locating one of his prey, he would send his men to race to wherever he may be. Eventualities for an inside a building snatch were imbued in them. Obviously an 'on-the-street' situation was favored. He had given his men dart guns. The darts were coated with a rapidly acting drug. The target would then be bundled into a specially fitted van stolen from the gas company seven months ago. It was very roomy and the engine had been enhanced making it capable of high speed. Inside, along with some of the gas company's equipment, three uniforms were hung.

Lee was the leader of the trio. He was by far the smartest which was probably why he had not been traced by Philip. He was a very cautious man. Also he had been appointed as the driver. He possessed the best driving skills and had been raised in Vancouver. He knew all the streets including the back roads. Lim and Yong were to be the snatchers.

He had rehearsed his men on several occasions using himself as the target. It had taken time but they were now proficient. To keep their proficiency and alertness, at a high level, he held periodic dummy runs. On these occasions he did not use a target. He merely sent them out in the van then timed them from the moment he called until they reached the designated location. During these runs he was constantly in touch with them on a car radio.

Being the perfectionist he was, he had added one other element to his planning. Foreseeing the possibility (although he thought it remote) one or more of his men may be under surveillance he devised an escape route for each of them. The apartments they occupied were not chosen at random. They were on the top floor. Each had a fire escape at the back window. This led not only down but also to the roof. There a broad plank of wood was hidden. It could reach the neighboring apartment building's roof. And a second plank could reach yet another apartment roof. From there a fire escape led down to the ground. Once there they would use a back alley to emerge to the street, far from their own apartment building.

As Lady Luck would have it, one of these dummy runs was in progress when Strang called the prime minister. And it was close to the apartment. From receiving the signal on his computer to finding out Belinda's address took Ma only twenty seconds. His call to the van redirected it virtually instantly.

"Lee, this is not an exercise. Melville is at the following address. Go quickly!"

One of the instructions drilled into Lee was never to drive so recklessly as to attract police. Therefore, although he pushed the van to slightly over the speed limit whenever possible, he still had to maneuver through one patch of heavy traffic. Still, it only took eight minutes to reach Belinda's apartment. The two Chinese, wearing gas company overalls, entered the apartment building with Lim carrying a tool box. This was noted by the watching policeman. DS Black decided it would be wise to check out the van.

He showed his warrant card and asked Lee for identification. He smiled in an accommodating fashion and produced expertly forged documents; a gas company employee card and driver's license.

"Would you like to see the inside of the van?"

"Sure."

Lee opened the back door.

"Looks okay," said Black. "Do you have a work order?"

"It was an emergency call from apartment 4C. It sounded like an old man. I don't think it will take long. If there's a leak we'll turn off the gas at the main, but often it's a simple matter of an elderly person forgetting to light a cooking ring he had turned on."

Lee shrugged his shoulders. His part training and part ad libbing was perfect. Black returned to his car. By this time Yong had quietly picked the lock of the apartment and Lim had taken the two dart guns out of the tool box. He also took out a pistol fitted with a silencer.

"What's that for?" hissed Yong. "The boss said no guns."

"I know what he said, but I'm not about to get shot if we run into a problem. We were warned this man could be very dangerous," said the nervous Lim.

Now that they faced the real thing he was scared.

Belinda had just finished drying her hair when she heard a noise in the hallway. She opened the door of the bathroom dressed in her robe and still clutching the hairdryer. She stepped out as far as the hairdryer cord would allow, with the bright bathroom lights behind her.

The panicky Lim only saw a figure coming out of the bathroom with what looked like a gun in his hand. He was sure it was Melville. With no second thought he fired his silenced gun twice. Belinda crumpled to the floor.

Yong smacked Lim on the side of the head as he rushed past him.

"You stupid fool, you've killed him."

He turned over the body.

"It's not him, it's a woman! He can't be here or he would have heard her fall. Better be certain, check the other rooms."

Lim did as he was told.

"No one here," he confirmed "But there's a man's clothing in one bedroom. Let's go! He may be on his way back and if he finds us here he will kill us," hissed the now thoroughly terrified Lim.

They avoided the elevator and raced down the stairway. They got in the van quickly. Lee looked at them quizzically. They were supposed to bring Melville.

"What happened?"

"He wasn't there, get going," cried out the perspiring Lim.

Lee drove away as quickly as he thought safe so as not to arouse the suspicion of the policeman. He kept looking at Black's car in his mirror until they turned a corner. Then he put his foot down.

They had traveled less than a mile when the phone rang.

"Give me a status report," barked Ma.

"He wasn't there," said Yong.

His wavering voice betrayed him and instantly put Ma on alert.

"*Tell me what happened!*" he demanded.

"There was a woman and she appeared to have a gun. Lim shot her."

"With the dart gun?"

"No, with his pistol; she's dead."

"Put Lee on the phone."

"Lee here, sir."

"After dropping the other two, get rid of the van. I don't want it ever to be found. Understood?"

"Yes, sir."

"And stand by tonight for my call. I shall want to see you later. Now put Lim on the phone."

"Y-y-yes, b-b-boss?" stammered Lim.

"Mistakes happen, Lim. We will have success next time. It was not your fault. Do you hear me?"

This was said in an almost gentle tone; not one Lim had expected to hear. It had taken every ounce of Ma's self control to master it. With every fiber in his being he had wanted to scream abuse at the dunderhead.

"Yes, boss. Thank you. I promise I will do better next time," replied the enormously relieved Lim.

"Good. Now listen carefully, I don't want the others to hear, they may become jealous. When you get back to your apartment wait for my call. I have another important job for you. You are the one with the greatest skills for this job. Remember say nothing to the others."

Lim's chest swelled with pride. When he was dropped off, he rushed up to the roof of the escape apartment building, and used the various planks to arrive at his own apartment. When the telephone rang, he ran to it eagerly. He was given instructions to meet Ma at four o'clock.

No one ever saw Lim again.

Chapter Thirty Four

The gas company van had only just driven out of his sight when his phone rang. DS Black listened in horror to the message from Johnny Thomas. Despite all of his checking he now knew the gas company men had been imposters. Quickly he gave this information and the van's license plate number to Johnny. Then he ran as fast as his legs would carry him to Belinda's apartment. The open door confirmed his worst fears. He drew his pistol and cautiously entered. The sight of the young woman with blood still coming from the bullet wounds sickened him. He knew it would be in vain but his training made him check for a pulse.

There was none.

Black had seen a few dead bodies in his time on the force; however, this was the first time it was someone he had been sent to guard. He felt sick. It wasn't the sight of blood, it was a feeling he had let Belinda down. Even in this moment of personal distress, his policeman's brain told him time was of the essence and he must focus on what was now required. The first step was to thoroughly search the apartment looking for any clues the murderers may have left. The only obvious one was they hadn't picked up their shell casings. He didn't touch them; that would be the job of the forensics team. It was now time to call in the terrible news.

Johnny sat nonplussed for several seconds almost unable to process the information. Then he sprang into action. He put out an all points bulletin on the van; he called the medical examiner to go to the apartment; then the thing he dreaded most; he told his boss the news.

"I've asked Angela Rossini to go to Belinda's apartment. I'll take a forensics team and get over there. I'll give you a full report as soon as I can."

"Hold on, I'm coming with you," was McKay's instinctive reaction.

"No, boss, you can't. You have to handle things from this end. You must inform CSIS, Phil Hughes and perhaps other members of the task force. The prime minister should be told as this was all the fault of that bastard Strang. And --- you have to tell Philip."

McKay looked at the distraught Thomas through his own damp eyes. The million to one shot had occurred and it pained his heart massively.

"Yes, you're right. Thanks Johnny. Call me as soon as you can."

He sat back in his chair and in his mind's eye saw every detail of Belinda's beautiful face.

"I'm so sorry for getting you into this, my dear," he mumbled.

Finally and with considerable mental effort he picked up the phone and began making his calls. He was completing his third when he was conscious of a stranger standing in the doorway. He stared at the man until the penny dropped and he recognized Philip.

"Hi, Hugh how ---."

Philip's voice trailed off. He was about to ask Hugh how he was when his attention was drawn to McKay's anguished face.

"What is it? What's happened?"

In a voice full of emotion he told Philip the whole story.

Colonel Philip Melville had lost men in battle. He had never become inured to such tragedies but had learned the hard lesson of the necessity of going on. He had been taught, in spite of the loss, his duty now lay in protecting the men who still served under him. And if he allowed his grief to interfere with that duty more men would die. But this was different. This was the assassination of a lovely, dedicated, young lady. And a killing he couldn't understand. It appeared obvious assassins had been sent to kill him. But why kill Belinda? Unconsciously he spoke that question out loud.

"I don't know, Philip. Johnny has taken a team to the scene. Maybe we'll have an answer when he has concluded his investigation. If you'll excuse me there are more people to be informed."

"Hugh, the only way to avenge Belinda's death is to kill that bastard Ma. No matter how deeply we may mourn her, nothing must stand in the way of doing this. Agreed?"

"Agreed!"

"Go ahead and make your calls. In the meantime I'd like someone to brief me on the tracking of the container."

Once again, unconsciously, Colonel Philip Melville had assumed a leader's role and was issuing orders.

McKay called in Larry Douglas and introduced the men. When they left for the incident room he returned to his task of informing people. When he had finished, he again sat back thinking of Belinda. Then Philip's words came back to him and he knew he had been correct. The only way to avenge her was to get Red Hand. There would be time for mourning later. He walked quickly to join Douglas and Melville.

"I've just brought Philip up to speed. After confirming the container crossed into California, we searched traffic cams around Los Angeles with no luck, then we did so around San Francisco, but again no luck. So we must assume yet another switch has been made. We are going back along Route Five in an attempt to locate it. However, since you ruled out Chicago as the target it appears it must be Los Angeles, Route Five runs straight into it."

There was a short period of silence as the others mulled over this statement.

"I don't think so," said Philip at last. "Do me a favor, Larry and check traffic cameras here."

He stabbed his finger on a spot on the map. Douglas let out a gasp of surprise.

"But Reno would mean he has changed direction and is heading east straight towards Chicago. And you ruled that out."

"Please check it for me," was all Philip said.

"Okay," replied Douglas resignedly, as he reached for the telephone. "We have an office in Reno and as it is a somewhat remote city, the access and egress will be simple to check. I should have an answer within the hour."

"What are you thinking, Philip?"

"Somehow Los Angeles doesn't seem right to me. It's too spread out. Maybe I'm wrong, but let's wait for the result of Larry's checking."

McKay was quiet as they walked back to his office.

"Where's Phil?" asked Melville.

"After I gave him the news about Belinda he said he had to call his director in Langley. Phil believes this could possibly be a worrisome sign of impatience on Ma's part. And, if so, it could be indicating zero hour is very close."

"That's a possibility but I don't think it's likely."

"Why not?"

Almost certainly Ma was not present at the apartment; he would have sent his men to get me. And I am equally certain no one was to be killed, one of them must have made a mistake. You see, Ma wants the pleasure of killing me personally and doing so very slowly. Of course if my hypothesis is incorrect, and Ma was there, then Phil is correct and things will start to move very quickly. But I just can't see him making such a blunder."

"He would not have been the only one. We did too. I've called in my men who were to watch Lim's and Yong's apartments. I want to know how the hell those two Chinese got out without being seen."

His tone of voice indicated his extreme anger. Undoubtedly it was more than partly due to his own feeling of guilt over Belinda's death. They lapsed into a morose silence. Fortunately they didn't have to wait long before Larry Douglas burst into the room.

"By God, you were right, Philip. The semi was caught on a traffic cam going into Reno. But not leaving it. They must have changed rigs yet again!"

Philip was quiet for a moment as he thought this over. Then the answer came to him.

"Did the container have any particular mark which first aided you in its initial identification?"

"Why, yes. There was quite a large gash along one side."

"Well you can stop looking for it."

Both McKay and Douglas stared at him waiting for an explanation.

"The bastard has been toying with us again. He had that gash put there deliberately to test and tease the FBI. He hoped you would see it and ultimately track it to Reno. Once in Reno he transferred the container to the inside of an inconspicuous van; most likely a moving company's van. You will get no further sightings of that container."

"That may be an educated guess, Philip," said Douglas. "You can't possible know it is a fact."

"Oh, but I do. I'm positive of it. I know Ma. He will have had enough fun tormenting us by the time we discovered Reno. After reaching Reno he wanted to be sure his container went directly and undetected to his target city. You see, by Reno he believed we should have been able to deduce his real target. In fact he wanted us to do so."

"He wanted us to know his plan?" cried out McKay in disbelief.

"Only as a final contingency," replied Philip.

"I don't understand," said a still perplexed McKay.

"His plan and passionate desire was to kill Phil and me in Vancouver. But his fastidious compulsion for contingency upon contingency compelled him to contemplate that may not be possible. So he left sufficient clues to lead us to his target. That way he intended us to be vaporized by his nuclear explosion. His clues are goading us to follow him east."

"So you now believe the target is Chicago, do you?" asked Douglas

"No, Larry, not Chicago, his target is the largest, most densely inhabited, city in America."

"Oh, no!" cried out Douglas.

"Yes -- he intends detonating his bomb in New York."

Chapter Thirty Five

That afternoon and evening proved to be eventful.

Firstly the detective sent to watch Lim arrived in McKay's office.

"You better have a good story," barked McKay, his anger still evident.

"I have, boss. Somebody was pretty damn smart to devise this escape," he replied without any sign of fear at McKay's ire.

McKay picked good people who had strong backbones. They seldom made mistakes but when they did, they readily admitted to them and learned from them.

"To find out how they eluded us, my partner and I decided to use the old trick of one of us dressing up as a mailman hoping to gain entry and study the apartments of the Chinese. I did that and rang the doorbell of Yong's apartment. I had a package with Yong's apartment number on it, but bearing the name of a tenant from the floor below. But he peeked out behind a half closed door and only glanced at the package. Then he quickly sent me on my way with a few choice words. I didn't get the opportunity to see anything inside the apartment. But when I did the same thing at Lim's apartment there was no answer, even after I banged on the door several times. So I picked the lock and went inside. I discovered the back window leading to the fire escape was unlocked. So I went up to the roof. After a good look round I noticed an imprint in the dirt on the parapet. That's when I saw a broad plank of wood on the next apartment's roof. We checked that roof and found the same thing leading to a third roof. When we went back and carefully checked the apartment next to Yong's we found the same thing. That's how they evaded us. I left my partner to guard Yong and I came here to report."

"Crafty buggers. Okay, now get another two men and cover both ways out of the apartments."

"Right, boss."

Next, Johnny Thomas arrived a little later and made his report to McKay, Hughes and Melville.

"I am convinced it was all a horrible mistake. The men were obviously sent to capture you, Philip. That alone would have made them nervous. They picked the lock and came cautiously into the apartment. Either Belinda heard a noise or coincidentally came out of the bathroom at that time. I believe it must have been the former. She was drying her hair and still had the dryer in her hand when she opened the bathroom door. The lights inside the bathroom are very bright; some of them are heat lamps. The men would only have seen the outline of a figure against the bright background. They may have thought it to be you, Philip. And the hairdryer was most probably mistaken for a gun. In their nervous condition I'm guessing they shot the figure without attempting to find out who it really was."

"Surely they could have distinguished the difference in height between Belinda and Philip if nothing else," said Hughes.

"That would be true if they had taken a moment to think. But I agree with Johnny, they would have been more than a little frightened at the thought of tackling Philip. And in a split second one of them was so scared he fired," concluded McKay.

"I tend to agree," added Philip. "And it only confirms my belief that Ma was not there. He would never have made such a mistake. Now the question is what will Ma do? Will his strong desire to kill Phil and me keep him here a bit longer? Or will he do as I suspect and abandon that move and move up his timetable to head for New York?"

"New York?" echoed Thomas. "When did we find out it was New York?"

"Go talk to Larry Douglas; he'll bring you up to date."

Sensing the three wished to talk in private, Thomas turned to leave the office.

"That was a good report, Johnny. Very insightful. You'll soon be as good a detective as your boss," said Philip.

"Never," replied Thomas with political correctness. "Oh, I should tell you I had your things packed. Both suitcases are in my office. I know you won't be staying at the apartment again."

"Good thinking, Johnny. And good detective work. You're getting so good I had better look out for my job," added McKay.

And although Johnny's heart was still heavy at the loss of Belinda, he left the office with his head held high.

McKay picked up the telephone.

"Who are you calling now?" asked Philip.

"My wife, you will be staying with me from now on."

"Well what do you think, gentlemen?" asked Hughes when McKay finished his call.

"I think it's time to call another meeting of the task force. I've already missed one. And I think you had better attend, Philip. As to Red Hand's next move, I'll leave that up to Philip to answer. The bugger is just too unpredictable to me."

They both looked at Philip who had been silent as he gave this matter thought. At last he spoke.

"We must always remember he is consumed by a blazing vengeance to settle accounts with Phil and me. That fire will never be extinguished until he succeeds. Therefore, although he has laid out a contingency plan leading to New York, he may linger here -- unless --."

He lapsed back into thought. Finally McKay could bear it no longer.

"Unless what?"

"Unless he gets another setback."

"Like what?" asked Hughes.

"I don't know. I'll have to think it over. Meantime, have you heard anything about the visa search you commissioned, Hugh?"

"Our initial check revealed nothing in the name of Ma. But I had the passport service check again. This time for any visa issued to an Asian by a country with no extradition treaty with Canada or America. But damn it, with everything that's been going on, I haven't followed up on that. I'll call now."

While he was on the phone Phil, not wishing to disturb him, whispered a question to Philip.

"You think if we discovered Ma has used another name to get a visa and we had that visa rescinded, it would be enough of a setback to cause him to abandon Vancouver?"

"Definitely."

"Well let's hope we get a hit."

He stopped talking as McKay ended his call.

"I had no idea there were so many countries with non-extradition situations. Of course those countries declared their sovereign rights and refused to give us a list of visa applicants. So it has required our CSIS people doing a little illegal midnight searching. Luckily they have a couple of expert burglars. But this is taking too much time and we are getting too many names. So far we have eighty four. However the good news is my contact in the passport office is a smart man. He had given those names to the police in relevant towns and cities. They are conducting a check at each given address. Also that intelligent passport officer got the name of your associate on the task force, Phil and has requested the CIA to do the same in America. Now I know neither the CSIS on the CIA has a charter to conduct domestic missions. But this can absolutely be construed as a matter of the very highest national security. If we do avoid the killing of millions of people, I don't think either government will create too much of a brouhaha."

Hughes rolled his eyes and rubbed his neck as though feeling for a hangman's noose. No one was above the law.

"In for a penny in for a pound," he said resignedly. "I believe that is the appropriate English expression."

"Let's just say we have another hopeful sign and leave it at that," added Philip.

Someone else thought he saw a hopeful sign that evening. Michael Strang was delighted to see Commissioner Simmons waiting for him as he descended the steps from the plane. He had used the plane's radio to send a message to Simmons indicating he had to see him immediately. He would waste no time in boiling McKay in oil. Little did he know the prime minister had already been in contact with Simmons and briefed him on all that had occurred.

"Commissioner, how glad I am to see you. You will hardly believe the treatment I suffered at the hands of DI McKay. When I tell you the details you will agree it is cause for dismissal and arrest. The man is a raving lunatic."

Strang was puzzled at the commissioner's apparent lack of response. His face retained a stony look.

"It's not Hugh McKay who will lose his position. This letter is from the prime minister, you have been sacked. And, I am placing you under arrest for the cause of the death of an agent of the CSIS. There may well be other charges relating to giving away state secrets."

He turned to the two officers behind him.

"Read this man his rights and throw him in jail."

Strang's mouth opened and closed like a fish out of water, but no sound came out. He was utterly speechless with confused shock and fright.

Another person was suffering shock that night.

Ma Guan-lui was taking stock of his position. The idiotic Lim had bungled things so badly it had upset his perfect planning. After disposing of him he had returned to his apartment and called Lee. By far the smartest of the three he had retained, Lee could be relied on for the task he had in mind. But Lee did not answer the call.

'He must be out to dinner,' thought Ma.

But later when he had tried unsuccessfully three more times he was worried. So worried he went to Lee's apartment. There was no answer to his knock so he used the spare key he had and went inside. There were no clothes or any other of Lee's things in the apartment. The smart Lee had sensed things were coming apart and knew instinctively he and Yong would suffer the same fate as Lim. If not now, then soon. He had suspected such an ending a week ago and already thought out an escape plan: after disposing of the van had put it into effect.

Ma was furious as he thought of his next move. Not even his strong liquor soothed his anger. With Lim dead and Lee gone he only had Yong and he was not up to the tasks he had in mind. There was no way of capturing Melville and Hughes unless he and Yong attempted to do so. And that was too risky. They would be too heavily guarded from now on.

That only left him with his least favored choice for the deaths of his adversaries - a rifle shot. But it had to be soon. By now they should have discovered his target location. He had left enough clues even for the FBI. An organization he held in low esteem. There was no alternative; he had to leave for New York. He had already arranged transportation which he believed would be difficult to trace. Not that he cared too much. Once in New York he was sure he was safe. His transportation consisted of a private plane to Toronto and from there he had already bribed a pilot working for a freight company with regular flights to the New York area.

All his meticulous planning had been working perfectly only to be upset except by the actions of that dumb fool, Lim.

Not for the first time, a liquor glass smashed against a wall.

Chapter Thirty Six

At nine o'clock the next morning the task force convened. Hugh's boss, Sven Larson, was invited to attend.

Despite their initial protests of excessive security, Hughes and Melville arrived at the police headquarters wearing Kevlar flack jackets and helmets and surrounded by bodyguards.

McKay was taking no chances.

There was general unease within the task force as each of the new facts was revealed by McKay. This was somewhat alleviated after Philip Melville was introduced and his role in uncovering Red Hand's plot explained.

"Both the president and the prime minister have been told we believe the planned attack is imminent," concluded McKay somberly. "Larry, bring us up-to-date on the precautions taken so far."

"The FBI with the assistance of US Army specialists has begun a bomb search of all high value targets in the city. And, of necessity, the New York Police Department has been informed. They too are on the lookout for anything suspicious, and are monitoring all entrances to the city; train stations, airports, tunnels and bridges."

"But where is this guy, Red Hand? And should we still be expending resources looking for him here in Vancouver?" asked Jeremy Mason.

The answers are, we don't know, and yes," responded Phil Hughes. "As you all know he has the strongest desire to kill Philip Melville and me. That's why we arrived here in full body armor and under heavy guard. Ma probably hopes for an opportunity to use a sniper's rifle. However Philip and I believe once he sees our protection he will pull up stakes and head for New York."

"With all the entrance checks Larry told us about, surely he'll find it almost impossible to get there," said Coleman, the CIA agent. "Also with all the NYPD on the streets he can't move a container with a large gash on its side from its hiding place to its target."

Philip spoke for the first time.

"He'll get there all right. He has anticipated all the precautions we have taken and has it all worked out. Remember he is a master of disguise. We will not be able to identify him. As for the container we won't find that, the bomb is already in place."

That caused an immediate communal gasp then a chorus of questions rang out.

"Let me explain," said Philip rising to his feet. "Let's just review what he has accomplished with his immaculate planning.

First, he acquires the most sophisticated computer capability in the world, after befriending Simone, the head of the biggest gang in Canada.

Second, he steals a nuclear bomb from an Asian country. Then he has it shipped all the way from Asia to Vancouver using the services of Simone to clear it from the docks.

Third, he breaks into a highly secure CIA computer in Hawaii to send mysterious messages from three Asian sources indicating there is a plot based in Vancouver to attack America.

Fourth, he kills the heads of several Canadian gangs including Simone. Their bodies are never found.

Fifth, he sends men to acquire materials necessary to make a small bomb leaving a trail for us to follow after one man, Hsieh, conveniently turns up drowned.

Sixth, he calculates the CIA will send agents to check the Vancouver tip. It's important to recognize his genius in completing all the first five steps *before* they arrive. He then unfeelingly assassinates them leaving the clue of the bloody handprint on the woman's white blouse. He calculates that sign will draw Phil Hughes and me to Vancouver. After killing them he coolly waits six hours before leaving the hotel during the morning rush.

Seventh, he breaks into another secure computer system, this time belonging to the CSIS and learns of the task force, the names of its members and where they are staying. Then unhappy I am not among them, he shoots Phil in the leg to finally draw me in.

Eighth, he uses a brilliantly conceived financial plot to trap Jason Brandt into revealing our plans.

Ninth, he has already discovered the locations of all large conventions or meetings to take place in America over the next several months. And he has left a false trail for us to discover of an Asian man with a limp checking out the meeting site in Chicago.

Tenth, he lays another trail we will eventually uncover by marking the container holding the bomb with a fresh large scrape on its side."

Philip paused for breath and a sip of water.

"This man is a vengeful, heinous, brutal, unfeeling, killing machine. Yet we must admit he has an astonishingly brilliant mind, capable of all these things. Even though one of his greatest wishes is to get revenge on Phil and me, his primary goal is to wreak havoc on America. In his warped mind it bears the principal blame for his failure in killing tens of millions of Japanese. So having done all I mentioned, can anyone here doubt he has not used his gifted brain to figure out a way into New York without being detected? Or that he has left it to the last minute to move a marked container through the streets of New York? No – the bomb is in place."

"Then what the hell do we do?" demanded Superintendent Larson.

There was silence, but all eyes were on Philip. He rose once again.

"Even if all the people Larry mentioned do a thorough job, I seriously doubt they will find him. He will only be found if we manage to outthink him."

"How do you propose we do that?" asked Larry Douglas, a bit aggrieved at Philip's apparent dismissal of all the precautions he had put in place."

"I meant no affront, Larry. All I was implying was Ma will have thought of all of them. Nevertheless should he, or one of the men he undoubtedly is using in New York, make the slightest slip, your net will catch him. We have to use our brains to figure out the point of attack. I'm guessing it will not be an obvious one like the Empire State Building or Rockefeller Center, nevertheless all such locations must be thoroughly checked. Just eliminating them is of great help."

"I see," responded Douglas, his feelings assuaged.

"If you're correct and the nuclear bomb is in place, why did Ma acquire the chemicals to build a smaller bomb, or bombs?" asked the intelligent Mason.

"I must admit that still troubles me. I have no idea. Anyway I gave you all the bad news. There is a little good news," continued Philip.

One could feel the tension rise in the room as people leaned forward in their seats in anticipation.

"First, we had the services of Ed Winfield from Langley. His genius neutralized much of Ma's computer capability; particularly his ability to manipulate the telephone system.

Second, using that genius, we caught Brandt and convinced Ma he had fled to Brazil.

Third, we tracked down two of his men and put them under surveillance.

Fourth, even with the greatest serendipity, Ma's attempt to capture me failed. It pains me that a beautiful and talented young lady was killed in that attempt."

He paused to take another sip of water and all could feel his anguish.

"Following that attempt we have now discovered one of his men, Lim, has disappeared, presumable killed by the unforgiving and merciless Ma. And Hugh sent his men this morning to pick up the other, named Yong.

Fifth, we are still pursuing the possibility Ma has applied for a visa to a country with no extradition treaty with either America or Canada. If we can discover such a visa being issued we can narrow down the search for the exit location he has chosen to leave the country."

"But that would be after detonating the bomb. Catching him after he had killed millions of people would be a Pyrrhic victory," said Jeremy Mason.

"That would be true. But being a bit more optimistic; should we discover the bomb and have it disarmed, we could use the visa information to prevent him leaving."

That didn't appear to appease Mason. Like everyone else he couldn't stop thinking of the horror of a nuclear explosion in New York.

"At any rate the first four items I mentioned have somewhat dislocated Ma's perfect planning. We must remember there is a razor thin edge between Ma's egotistical genius and madness. I don't know about you, but I find it hard to imagine any sane man would kill millions of innocent people. Yet that is precisely what Ma intends. If we can disrupt one more aspect of his plan it may push him over the edge. And then he will act irrationally and we'll get him. But I have to admit I'm still puzzled over Hsieh buying all those chemicals. As Ma has a nuclear bomb, what does he want with a smaller one?"

"Well what's our next move?" asked Larson.

"I estimate Ma will either have seen Phil and me arrive this morning or he will see us leave. The tight security we have will annoy him enormously. He will be forced to face the exasperating reality his chance of killing us in Vancouver has evaporated. When he does, he will leave for New York. And we should do the same. Larry, can you arrange a secure location in New York for those who wish to travel? Also transportation, and a place to meet over there?"

"Can do."

"Thanks Larry, oh, one more thing. NYPD should run checks on gang members there, particularly those from Chinatown. Ma will have recruited men to initially store the container and to have the bomb moved to its location. Without a doubt those men will receive the same fate as others he has used. When their work is done he will kill them. It wouldn't do any harm for NYPD to spread the word that anyone who has recently worked for a Chinese with a scar on his chin and a limp now has a contract placed on his life. We may be able to shake someone loose."

"Good idea. When do you want to travel?"

"It will take a little time for you to set everything up. Let's say early evening today."

"No problem. Will those wishing to travel see me after the meeting?"

"Okay that's all. I'll see some of you on the east coast And please, those of you who are religious – say a prayer."

The meeting broke up and Hughes and Melville joined McKay in his office.

"What do we do between now and this evening?" asked Hugh.

"Phil and I need to travel somewhere with all our security in order to be seen by Ma. That's if he hasn't already seen us."

"It can't be a busy public place. Ma could blend in with the crowd and that would be too dangerous for us," said Hughes.

"Once he sees us leave here with all our security, I don't think he will follow. Nevertheless I agree a public place is an unnecessary risk," responded Philip.

It only took another few seconds for him to address a question to Hugh.

"Do you think Cathy could arrange lunch for us?" he asked with a smile.

Hugh McKay could only marvel at this soldier's total calmness in the face of pending danger.

However behind Philip's smile of apparent serenity his brain was searching out all possible perils. His experience as an exceptional military leader had taught him the vital importance of never transmitting his concerns to his men. That would spread uncertainty through his command as rapidly as a plague.

Notwithstanding the short notice, Cathy had prepared an excellent lunch. It helped ease the tension all the men felt. They had finished desert and were enjoying a coffee when the telephone rang. It was Johnny Thomas. Hugh put him on the speaker box.

"Boss turn on the TV, there has been a terrific explosion in an apartment block in a poorer part of town. If you plan to be driving, stay away from that area."

Philip slapped his knee.

"Now I know why Ma had Hsieh buy those chemicals. He has destroyed his entire computer set up."

"Now the chase is really on," intoned an apprehensive McKay.

They were on their second cup of coffee when the phone again rang. McKay answered it.

"It's me again, boss. A John Staley called from the office of Phil Hughes. He must speak to him urgently."

Phil's hand shook a little as he dialed the number. John wouldn't call him unless it was a burning issue. The others in the room could hear the worry in his voice when he asked a series of staccato questions.

"Hello John, what's up?" *What?* When? How bad is it? What's the prognosis? Are you certain? Which hospital? What's the number? And the name and number of the doctor? I appreciated the call, John. I'll be in touch later."

Hughes hung up the phone and slumped against the counter. Philip ran over to him.

"What is it, Phil?"

"It's my wife Anne, She has suffered a heart attack."

"Oh, no."

"However the doctor said it was a mild one and she'll recover quickly. He said it was more of a warning and medication will most likely prevent it becoming a serious problem. As a precaution, they are keeping her in hospital under observation for a few days."

Philip stared over at McKay, who recognized it as a signal he wanted to be alone with Hughes. McKay ushered his wife into the kitchen.

"I know what you are about to say, Philip, but I have been assured Anne will be fine. She is getting the best care possible. My job is to stay here and catch Ma."

"Phil, Phil, you are *not* going to stay here. We now have Ma on the run. We'll get him. Right now your place is with Anne."

Hughes shook his head in disagreement. Philip grasped his head between his strong hands.

"This is what you will do. You will call the doctor to get the full story. That will ease your mind a bit. Then you will call Anne. And then you will get your ass on a plane to Honolulu. Nothing is more essential to Anne, than to have your moral support at this time. I know her, she is a resilient woman, but she will have been scared by this attack. She needs you, Phil."

Hughes was about to object but Philip continued to hold his head and stared deep into his eyes.

"Please, Phil, no argument. In your heart you know what I say is true. Believe me I understand your devotion to finding this bomb and saving millions of lives; and how much you want to put a bullet in Ma's head. Allow me the privilege of doing it for you."

"But Philip I feel I am deserting my post. As a soldier you should understand that emotion."

"I do, Phil, I do. However if we were serving in the army and this arose, I would order you to do the exactly the same thing. There is no human way you could avoid constantly worrying about Anne if you stayed here. No way. You would rip up your guts being torn between worrying about your duty here and your duty to be with your wife in Honolulu. As one of my dearest friends, I am begging you, Phil. Go home."

Hughes lowered his head. His reply was spoken in the faintest of whispers.

"Okay, Philip."

Chapter Thirty Seven

The task force arrived in New York in the wee hours of the next morning. They were met at a private terminal in JFK airport by a series of SUV's, all with black tinted windows. The SUV's left at three minute intervals for a location in Queens. It was not prudent to leave at the same time and travel in a conspicuous convoy. Philip and Hugh alighted from their SUV in an alley at the back of a four story building. The front entrance bore the faded sign, Kelly's Boarding House. Larry Douglas had traveled in the previous SUV and was waiting for them.

Inside at the front desk sat a matronly lady with grey hair. She had a register in front of her but didn't request they sign in. A janitor in blue overalls mopped the floor lethargically. Two guests sat at a table drinking coffee.

"We'll wait for the other two vans then I can give all of you a run down on our '*guest house*'."

Douglas led them up a slightly dirty stairway and along a dimly lit corridor with a threadbare carpet. Philip studied the corridor and finally noticed the carefully concealed cameras. At the end of the corridor they entered room number 110.

Inside was a well lit, beautifully oak paneled, large meeting room. The furnishings were of high quality. A bar was situated along one wall and had a large selection of liquor; beer; and freshly made coffee, available. Three of the task force members were seated around the table with their drinks. As soon as everyone had arrived, Douglas stood to speak.

"This is an FBI safe house. We also use it as a covert command center while conducting operations in the New York area. We own the two buildings on either side of this 'guest house'. Downstairs you will have seen four of our agents. The lady at the desk is actually thirty-five years old and her register is kept up-to-date every morning with fictitious names. Anyone wandering in off the street would be met with an apologetic smile and told the boarding house was full. Should there be any trouble, although we never have had any, the lady is as well qualified in martial arts and marksmanship as any of the other three male agents in the lobby. The two floors above us have well appointed rooms. I am certain you will find them comfortable. Each room has a secure telephone. But I should tell you all calls are logged. Also you will find a computer in your room. It also is secure, but again usage is logged. Next to this room is our communication center with the latest equipment capable of contacting almost any spot on the planet. It is manned 24/7 and should you have need to use it, our agents on duty will be happy to assist. At the ends of each of the corridors above us are steel doors which lead to the adjacent buildings, where we have more agents. We also have special rooms for interrogation and for incarceration. I guess that's about all for now."

"Thanks for your briefing, Larry. This is certainly some place. Now, I suggest we get some sleep and meet here tomorrow morning at eight," said McKay.

Douglas raised his hand for attention and stood.

"One more thing I should have mentioned, you will find the dining area on the ground floor. Agents will be there to guide you. And we have agents posted at the stairs on every floor and at the elevators. And, Hugh, I took photographs of every item on Johnny's board in your incident room. I will have them posted on a board here by tomorrow morning, along with a large scale map of central Manhattan."

"That's very thoughtful, Larry, thanks again."

The members sat chatting while finishing their drinks. McKay nodded to Douglas and Melville to join him in a corner of the room.

"On the plane, I was going over a few things and it seemed obvious Ma would have left Vancouver a bit before the bomb blast in the apartment block. I am guessing he most probably had a private plane take him somewhere in Canada. And from there he will have made plans to cross the border. To get to a private field in Vancouver or its surroundings, he would need transportation. And bearing in mind all you said, Philip, about Ma always killing his associates when he was through with them, there would be nobody to drive him to the plane. It's possible he had a car; however, it is also possible he took a taxi. Being well disguised he may have felt comfortable doing so. I'm going to call Johnny and ask him to check every cab company looking for one of them picking up a fare near the bombed building. It's a long shot but I believe it worth a try. What do you think?"

"I think it's a very good idea. I was also doing some thinking on the plane and it occurred to me the bombing of his apartment was definitely part of his longer term plan. But the apparent killing of Lim, added to you picking up Yong, will have upset his plans. I have been waiting for some incident or incidents to push him off center and create a little uncertainty in him. The abrupt bombing of his hideaway may be just such an incident. It tells me he is now a man being hurried more than he had anticipated. And in that condition he is more apt to make mistakes," concluded Philip.

"If you will excuse me I'll find my room and call Johnny right away."

"I'll take you next door to the communications center and you can call Johnny immediately. That will save a little time. And I'll give you a number he can call you back on."

"Just before you go Larry, I would like to call my wife in Hong Kong. Will that be okay?"

"Sure, Philip, call wherever you like."

Their leaving coincided with the others deciding to do likewise.

Some would have a restless night. Others would use sleeping pills to get through the night.

It was six o'clock in the morning when McKay's telephone rang. He had been in a deep pill induced sleep. He checked his watch twice first thinking it had been his alarm. But he had set that for six-thirty.

"Hello," he mumbled into the receiver.

"I thought you might be awake, boss," said Thomas.

"Well I wasn't," grumped McKay.

"At least you got some sleep. I haven't been to bed yet. Anyway here's the news. You were right as usual; I tracked a taxi cab that picked up an elderly man a block from the apartment that blew up. He was bent over with age and had to walk with a cane. The taxi driver remembered him because he thought it strange such an old man should have such a heavy suitcase. Especially as he walked with a limp."

"*Well done Johnny!*" cried out McKay, shaking off his slumber and becoming instantly alert. Where'd he go?"

"He went to a small airfield outside the city. I went there and the dispatcher clearly remembered the old man. He was on a private plane logged to fly to Buttonville Municipal Airport. That's about twenty miles outside of Toronto. I had air traffic control check on the flight. It arrived in Toronto at five-forty-five in the afternoon. I called Buttonville and asked for the pilot but as he's not scheduled to return to Vancouver until tomorrow morning, he had apparently gone to a motel. I have requested Toronto police to look for him at hotels and motels and asked them to check on all flights leaving the Toronto area for New York. I gave them a description of the man we are seeking. They asked my name and rank and weren't very impressed by me only being a sergeant. They told me they were already short staffed and would get around to my request whenever time permitted."

"Snotty buggers. I'll call them right away. Give me the name and the telephone number of the person you spoke to."

"No need, boss. They have been jumping through hoops to oblige."

"How'd you manage that?"

"I said this was a top priority request from Superintendent Sven Larson's office and a matter of the highest national security. I added if they wanted further validation they should call Commissioner Simmons directly, or, call the prime minister's office. And when they did they should mention it concerned Operation Red Hand. Then I asked for the name of the person to whom I was speaking and the name of his superior officer. I said I was certain Commissioner Simmons would be interested."

"By God that was inspired work, Johnny. Well done! Have they gotten back to you yet?"

"Oh, yes. They didn't totally believe me so they checked with the commissioner's office. They must have gotten an earful because they have been bending over backwards to cooperate. Initially they contacted all airports in the Toronto area regarding any flights to New York, but were told there had been none last night. They found no trace of the pilot at any hotel or motel. So if he wasn't staying with a friend or relative --?"

"Red Hand has found him a permanent resting place."

"That's my thought, boss. But there's more. Toronto police weren't happy with the news of no aircraft flying last night, so they sent one of their best detectives out to inquire. After twenty minutes of intensive grilling, the airport manager said, "There's nothing more I can say. Arrest me if you like but no plane left for New York."

The manager was close to exhaustion so the detective turned to leave. He had his hand on the door knob when the man said in a low voice.

"Hold on a minute, there was a special flight last night. But it went to New Jersey. Is that of any interest?"

"It turned out, a cargo consisting of avionics and instruments manufactured in Canada, was rush air freighted to Morristown, New Jersey. It left at six-thirty. The cargo had previously been checked by US Customs in Toronto therefore there was no delay in the take off. That flight arrived in Morristown at eight-thirty. I checked all local taxi services and limo companies and wouldn't you know – a limo picked up an elegantly dressed gentleman with a heavy suitcase at Morristown airport. Yet another disguise used by Red Hand. No one can find the pilot of the plane. And – the limo company has lost contact with its driver."

"Wow, we're really on his trail now, Johnny. Fantastic work! I've got to go. I'll have the FBI search for that limo. If you get anything further, give me a call."

Johnny Thomas was left tired but pleased with the telephone receiver still clutched in his hand. It was three-fifteen in the morning in Vancouver. Duty demanded he stay at the police station in case further information was called in. He looked around his small office.

"Oh, well, I guess I'm sleeping on the carpet."

Hugh McKay raced out of his room and cried out to the agent on duty at the head of the stairs.

"Quick! Quick! Which room is Larry Douglas's"

The agent stared at him strangely. It was only then Hugh McKay realized he was naked.

Chapter Thirty Eight

The eight o'clock meeting had an electric atmosphere. Over breakfast, most of the members had heard of Red Hand's entrance into America. Hugh McKay went quickly over the details for the few who were too late for breakfast and hadn't heard. Larry Douglas entered the room. He had been on the phone to an agent in New Jersey receiving an update. Everyone looked at him expectantly.

"The limo was found at a diner frequented by truck drivers a few miles away from the Lincoln Tunnel. The driver was found dead, stuffed in the trunk of the car. We believe Red Hand either hitched a ride or hid in a truck and is now in the city. He probably hid as we have no information of a missing truck driver. This man seems to kill frequently and mercilessly."

"He takes great pleasure in it. He is entirely without remorse," added Philip.

"Why don't you outline what you think our next moves should be, Philip?" suggested McKay.

"A thorough search has been made of all obvious high target locations with no success. However I believe we must assume the bomb is in Manhattan. Thanks to the excellent work of the FBI it was discovered a moving van was stolen two weeks ago. That's how the bomb was transported into New York. There is no point in looking for the van; it will have been well hidden. And as for the driver – well you know Ma's methods of rewarding people for their services. However the van is no longer important as the bomb has undoubtedly been moved to its final location. It's anyone's guess how long we have. However, I believe we have a day or two. I say this because my gut tells me, if it is at all possible, Ma will have one more shot at taking out Phil and me. His hatred is that strong."

"But he can have no idea of our location. I can guarantee this place is absolutely safe," avowed Douglas.

"I believe that, Larry. Therefore, if he does want one more chance he must lure us to a spot where he is set up and waiting."

"How is that possible?" asked Sven Larson who, while not an official member of the task force had asked to be allowed to come with them. Like all good policemen, he couldn't just drop a case. He wanted to be close to Hugh McKay's side to offer any possible assistance.

"Possibly like some of you, I didn't get much sleep last night. I kept thinking of just the question you raised, Sven. And I have a possible answer. But first, tell us Larry, I requested NYPD to check all its sources in Chinatown. I'm certain that's where Ma would first look to recruit men to assist in positioning the bomb. Did they have any luck?"

"I'm afraid not. They know all the gangs there, but nobody is talking. And the snitches they have know nothing. They're probably too low down the pecking order to be trusted with anything significant."

"That's what I suspected. But to get back to your question, Sven, Ma would deduce I would first look in Chinatown to discover his new accomplices. I suspect he is holed up there somewhere waiting for me to appear."

"That is too spooky. You really believe he can read your mind?" asked Jeremy Mason incredulously.

"I told you tracking Ma would be more of a mind game than anything else. We have to outthink him and never, never, to underestimate him. But in this game we now have one slight advantage. He has been hurried by events in Vancouver. And men in a rush often make mistakes. So, although I am guessing he is hoping we will go to Chinatown, we won't."

"It wouldn't do any good anyway," stated Douglas. "As I told you, the Chinese won't talk."

"Right, but If I asked you to take one more crack at it, who would you go to?"

"Well the obvious answer is to the head of the biggest gang. But he is the toughest nut to crack. He is believed to be behind some of the boldest and most lucrative crimes; however NYPD have never been able to pin anything on him."

Douglas consulted his notebook.

"His name is Chua Ming Kee. And he uses as his cover being the owner of an antique shop. In fact it is an excellent front, as, upon investigation of his tax returns, NYPD found it to be quite a profitable business."

"The thought that came to me last night is, he must either know something or, be able to get answers we need. And if I were Ma Guan-lui, I would be holed up close to Chua's place of business expecting me to call."

"So what do we do?"

"It's time to take the gloves off. The lives of tens of millions of people are at stake and Ma won't wait too much longer. Here's what I want you to do."

Larry Douglas listened carefully and more than a little disbelievingly, shook his head.

"I could lose my badge over this. The FBI doesn't break the law. But what the hell - as you say, it's only my career versus the lives of millions. I'll call for the dossier you want, then we'll swing into action."

"Before you leave could you once again ask NYPD to put all their officers on the highest alert? I know we have requested this, but there can be nothing quite as valuable to us as a good cop spotting something unusual."

"Will do."

The dossier was transmitted to the communications room within fifteen minutes. It contained all Philip had hoped.

"Time to move, Larry," he said resolutely.

Within an hour a blindfolded and handcuffed Chua Ming Kee was led from the alley at the back of the safe house, through the back door and into one of the interrogation rooms. He was thrust into a chair at a table with a telephone on it. Once the blindfold and the handcuffs were removed he studied the bare, green painted, room which had a mirror on the wall opposite him. Realizing what was about to happen he waved mockingly at the mirror knowing people were watching him. This was not the first time he had been questioned and he felt no fear whatsoever.

The door opened and two men entered. He glanced at Hugh McKay who stood to one side and his confidence increased. He could smell a cop a mile away. But when he studied the man who sat down opposite him, his heart skipped a beat. He was no cop. His entire bearing was different. And his tall frame with broad shoulders was a little intimidating. But it was the flinty look in his steely blue eyes which caused his fearlessness to waver for a few seconds. However he recovered his composure and with his best fearless sneering grin he addressed this man.

"Well - kidnapping is a new technique for you cops."

Philip stared at him for several seconds before pulling a dossier hidden on his lap and slamming it on the table. The noise was so loud it caused Chua to involuntarily twitch. Philip continued to stare into Chua's eyes for a while before speaking. Chua had undergone many questioning sessions but never one with man like this one, and his confidence slipped a little.

"I will ask you a few questions and you had better be truthful."

Now Chua's confidence returned. This line had been tried on him many times before.

"I want my lawyer and until he gets here you can go to hell."

The next thing that happened caused him to slightly wet his pants. The man pulled out a gun, slammed it on the table, and screamed at him in Cantonese.

"You'll be the one going to hell, Chua."

It was not the tone of voice that caused Chua's fearfulness as much as the increased flintiness in this man's eyes. For a reason he couldn't quite define, Chua was starting to believe he could be in terrible danger. Then he regained his senses and remembered people were watching from behind the mirror. His instincts told him he would not be shot in front of witnesses. At least that's how he handled his killings.

"I said go to hell."

Philip ignored his comment.

"A man rented a room close to your shop - a room with a clear view of your front door. Probably he used one of the two or three gang members he recently recruited, to actually rent the room. He intends using that room for an assassination. After killing his intended target, he plans to explode a bomb in Manhattan – *a nuclear bomb!*"

Chua blinked at this but then came to the conclusion it was some type of new trick. He pretended to pick a piece of lint from his sleeve to indicate he was unconcerned. Philip missed none of the signs.

"He required the services of his recruits to place the bomb. Now that the bomb is in place, I would guess he has disposed of his recruits. I need information and I need it now. You know all that goes on in Chinatown, so tell me everything you know about this man."

Chua's sneer returned.

"You expect me to believe that fairy story. I told you where to go. And don't think you can threaten me with that gun. You won't use it. There are too many witnesses."

"I told you a nuclear explosion will occur. So what if I kill you first. It really doesn't matter; you'll be dead either way."

"Hah!" spat out Chua.

"And so will your wife; your daughter and - your grandson."

"Hah," reiterated Chua scornfully.

"Oh, I see. You believe we have no grounds on which to prosecute you and you will be set free. Then, just to be absolutely sure, you will take you family away from New York to a safe place."

Before Chua could repeat his retort, Philip leant across the table. His face came close to Chua's.

"I know how important it is to Chinese to protect their lineage. Your grandson means everything to you. But your lineage is about to be melted in that nuclear attack."

This time Chua definitely flinched.

"You can't protect them. They have been taken into *'protective custody'* by agents; they cannot get out of the city. They will be melted by the blast, like all of us."

Now Chua looked distinctly uncomfortable. There was something about this man that deeply troubled him.

"You cops always try to bluff," he blustered.

"If that's what you believe – there's the telephone. Call them."

Chua sat for almost a minute while he weighed up all this man had said. Then, reluctantly, he dialed his home number. A maid answered.

"Let me speak to my wife," he demanded in Cantonese.

"Your wife is out. She went with a man. He showed her a badge and led her away. She appeared upset, sir."

Now his concern intensified and he quickly dialed his daughter's number. Again a maid answered and her response was even more terrifying.

"She and your grandson left with two men in a big black car with black windows."

He replaced the receiver with a thud and stared with hostility at Philip.

"You can't go around kidnapping people," he screeched in a loud voice.

"Listen very closely to me, Chua. I don't want to die, you don't want to die and you wife, daughter, and grandson don't want to die. But we all will unless you help me. The man who rented your room and who has planted a bomb is a highly talented lunatic. He worked for Mao, and is responsible for the deaths of untold numbers of Chinese. He relishes killing. A few years ago he had a plan to kill many more Asians but was stopped by American forces. As a result of this failure, he plans to take his revenge on America by exploding this bomb. I want three things from you. First I want to know if a stranger rented the room I mentioned."

Chua caved.

"Yes, opposite my store - number forty six, apartment 2A."

Philip nodded to the mirror and Douglas hurried out to send his men.

"Good. Now check with your other gang chiefs and find out if some of their best men have disappeared."

Chua reached for the telephone and frantically began dialing numbers. On the third try his golden face turned an awful pasty white. He didn't have to say anything to Philip. He held up three fingers indicating the number of men recruited.

"Ask him if he saw a Chinese with a limp talking to his men."

Chua did so, then dumbly nodded his response.

"Now ask him if he knows where that man is."

"He doesn't know," he replied in a shaking voice and hung up.

"Now tell me the truth, do you know where this man is?"

"No, no, I swear I don't."

Philip sighed in disappointment, believing him.

"I want you to send out all the men you can, looking for this man. In addition to his limp he has a pink scar on his chin. But he often wears a disguise. Any information can be called in to you at this number."

Once again Chua reached for the phone and began barking out orders.

Philip's shoulders sagged as he left the room with Hugh.

"Have someone stay in the room with him. We're going to keep him here," he instructed the FBI agent at the door.

The task force gathered in the meeting room waiting for a report from Douglas's men. When it came they all felt a sense of gloom.

"The apartment was empty. I'm guessing Red Hand saw us pick up Chua and fled. He left a high powered rifle in the apartment. You were right, Philip, he was waiting for you."

"That can only mean there is nothing stopping him from detonating the bomb soon," said Mason.

"It depends on the type of trigger," said Philip. "The older type used by a third world country usually requires manual intervention."

"What does that mean exactly," asked Larson.

"It means the timing mechanism has to be set manually. Ma will have to go to its location and set the timer. And he has to allow sufficient time to escape. Which means, hopefully, the earliest it can go off is at least five or six hours from now."

"Larry," intervened McKay, "you had better have several teams of demolition experts posted throughout the city. When we find it we may only have a matter of minutes to defuse it."

His request seemed to indicate he was confident the bomb would be found.

If so, it was a confidence not shared by the majority in the room.

Chapter Thirty Nine

Paddy O'Neil was a sturdily built man with a friendly, freckled, face and red hair. His blue eyes normally had a happy glint. All these traits made him popular on his beat in central Manhattan. However, this likeable policeman could be very, very, tough should the occasion arise.

In fact, he was a trained killer.

Paddy's father had been, of course, Irish. But his mother had been Scottish. And to complicate his heritage further he was born and raised in London. His catholic father had wanted him to develop an Irish accent. He would forever speak to him using language like – begorrah and bejeebers. His protestant mother wished he would develop a Scottish brogue and spoke to him using terms like – dinnae be daft and dae as yer telt. Needless to say Paddy's upbringing was complicated. Yet somehow he managed to juggle his parents' different wishes.

Nowhere was this success more evident than in his character. He was a strong lad not only physically but mentally. He retained his father's sense of humor and his mother's crafty intelligence. While all this may have appeared to be a recipe for disaster, it wasn't. Despite their religious differences his parents loved each other deeply and his home was a happy one.

As soon as he was old enough he decided to solve the dilemma of his parents' different wishes by speaking exactly like all the other kids in school. To the eternal dismay of both parents he spoke with a decidedly English accent. And when he was eighteen he did another thing which greatly distressed them. Instead of going to university he joined the army. Based on his outstanding scholastic record in high school, his parents had assumed he would go on to university. His choice not only disappointed them, it worried them. Although Paddy was a strong young man, the army could be a dangerous profession. Their disquietude was further heightened when after only a few months, Paddy applied for, and was accepted in the Paratroop Regiment. The paratroopers were among the toughest men in the British military. They were given extensive commando training including killing an enemy, and often had to use this training as they tended to be sent into the most dangerous situations.

It was almost exactly a year after joining the regiment when both his parents were killed in a car accident.

Paddy has been raised in a Christian home, although admittedly a divided one. He needed to find some solace, but was uncertain which church to turn to. The catholic one his father believed in or the protestant one of his mother. He decided his first step would be to consult the regiment pastor, who happened to be Anglican. The pastor proved to be extraordinarily kind and helpful. A few weeks later Paddy opted to join the Anglican Church. He felt it a fair compromise between his parents' religions.

Upon the completion of his tour of duty, he made a life changing decision. There really was nothing for him back in London, so he chose to start over in a new country. He selected America and when he discovered the quickest way to become an American citizen was to serve in the military, he enrolled. It did not take long for his paratrooper service to become known and he was transferred to Special Forces. Here he served with distinction.

Upon leaving the military he had many ribbons and medals on his uniform. With all of this he had no trouble being accepted into the New York Police Department. In fact the admitting officer questioned him on the wisdom of his choice. He surely could have found a better paying job than merely walking a beat. But Paddy had thought it out carefully and had two objectives in mind. First he decided after experiencing so much bloodshed, a quiet life where he could help people was just what he needed. Secondly, and of great importance, it would afford him the opportunity to attend college at night. He now had a thirst for greater knowledge.

He ruefully recalled the vigorous debate he had with his parents as they attempted to persuade him to enroll in university and not the army. But, as a teenager he believed he knew better than his parents. Now he vividly remembered his mother's last words on that debate.

"One of life's great mysteries is the older one becomes, the smarter one's parents become."

At the time he had thought it rather silly. As he started his first night school class, he realized his parents had suddenly become very smart.

It didn't take Paddy long to appreciate he had only achieved one of his aims. He was doing well at night school and enjoying it immensely; but being a cop in New York was far from a quiet life. Nevertheless he was happy. He did help many members of the public and with his military training found it relatively easy to handle the several bad guys he encountered, for which he received several commendations.

Not long after joining the NYPD he sought out a church to join. Being faithful to his parents' Christian ways, yet also to being true to the compromise denomination he had selected, he joined an Anglican church in Manhattan.

As he passed on his beat, he greatly admired the grandeur of St. Bartholomew's. It was this initial attraction which led him to join. Yet he had only attended for a little over a month when he sought an audience with Father Mitchell.

"I have to be honest with you Father; I feel a bit awkward in this congregation. Many of them are so rich. Can you recommend a more appropriate church for me to attend?"

"Is that so, Paddy? Have a cup of coffee and tell me all about yourself."

When he had finished, Father Mitchell sat forward in his chair.

"You are a very self-effacing young man, Paddy. You have served two countries with distinction, and you have put yourself in harm's way in the course of doing your duty. Furthermore you have been wounded a few times in doing so. And now you are taking care of the people of our city by serving in the NYPD. It is true we have quite a few parishioners with lots of money but there are very few who are as *'rich'* as you. Remember our Lord doesn't put wealth above goodness. We, at St. Bartholomew, are honored to have you as a member of our church."

Paddy hung his head at such praise.

"Tell you what; I'll introduce you to another member of my staff, Father Diaz. He also came from a humble background being born in

Nicaragua. He knows quite a bit about sacrifice. I know he is supporting members of his family but he is a very private person and doesn't wish to talk about it. I think you two would get along famously."

That proved to be true and over the course of the next year, as their friendship deepened, Father Diaz took him into his confidence and told him of his problems. He was supporting his mother who was suffering with a heart problem. Also his younger sister was undergoing medical treatment. During their subsequent meetings, it was obvious to Paddy Diaz didn't want to continually talk about his family's problems. It was too painful a subject.

Therefore he was surprised at their last meeting when Father Diaz did raise the subject. Paddy thought it strange that for a man who had always internalized his problems, he seemed eager to talk about them.

"My mother has now deteriorated to where she is in urgent need of a heart transplant. And if that is not bad enough, my sister has been diagnosed with a severe kidney condition."

Paddy had always respected his friend's feelings of privacy. He was loath to intrude, but felt compelled to do so on this occasion.

"Why not go to the bishop. I'm sure the church would help you."

Father Diaz smiled wanly.

"Paddy, you have no idea the fortune it would take to help them. You see it's not just the cost, it's the wait time. There is such a long wait list; I'm afraid my poor mother and sister will be with God before then."

"There must be something that can be done."

"No, I'm afraid not - at least not legally."

"What do you mean?"

"Please never mention this. I was told by a fellow Nicaraguan of a country in South America which specializes in such operations. It has doctors trained at the best hospitals in America."

"Well then, ask the church for the money and go there."

Diaz had the same weak smile on his face.

"There are two reasons, my friend. First, although the cost of such operations in America is astronomical, the cost there is two or three times as great."

"How could that be?"

"It's the only reason those skilled doctors choose to live and practice there. They are becoming very rich."

"What's the second reason?"

"It's linked to the first. And it is against all my religious beliefs. They have jails full of alleged criminals, who are charged with crimes against the State. In reality they have probably only spoken out against the dictator who runs the country. And those types of prisoners are invariably executed. The doctors test prisoners about to be executed for matches with patients waiting for organ transplants."

"Oh, no!"

"Yes, those doctors have a high rate of success with their patients. I am told they receive patients from all over the world. Of course all of them are extremely rich."

"I don't want to seem morbid, but it may be the gruesome truth their patients' needs are first determined, and then they seek out prisoners who are a match and have them executed."

"That has occurred to me too. So even if I won the lottery, how could I, a priest, take my family there?"

He began crying.

"I'm so sorry, Father."

Father Diaz dried his eyes then stared intensely at Paddy, who had the oddest feeling his eyes were trying to tell him something his voice could never utter. Diaz hung his head and Paddy had to strain his ears to make out his next words.

"The truth is Paddy, if I did win the lottery at a time when my mother and sister were close to dying, I don't know if my faith would prevail over my desire to save them."

He began crying again.

Paddy O'Neil could only look on helplessly. But the weird feeling he had experienced as the eyes of Father Diaz bored into his was to stay with him.

In the days that followed he often wondered if Father Diaz had been trying to tell him something or was he only looking for understanding.

'No, not understanding,' he thought.

'More like absolution!'

Chapter Forty

It had been three weeks since Paddy had his talk with Father Diaz. He felt remorseful he had not sought him out to have another chat. However preparation for final exams had taken up all of his spare time. Taking the exams was stressful enough, but now he must await the results. That was even more stressful.

Today, all thoughts of exams had been banished from his mind. As he walked his beat, the warnings by his commander still rang in his ears. He had issued a high alert situation and impressed upon his men they must be especially watchful and immediately report anything unusual, no matter how insignificant it may appear. His military training told him this was no ordinary warning. Something big was feared. Perhaps it may even be a terrorist group. He had faced a few of them in his overseas service in the Special Forces. And when he had, a prayer never did do any harm. As he approached St. Bart's he thought it may again be useful to nip in and quickly pray.

However once at the entrance, he hesitated. Maybe he ought to continue his beat and offer a silent prayer. He stood there debating for a minute before deciding it would be okay to go in. Also it would give him the opportunity to say a few words with his friend, Father Diaz, whom he hadn't seen for three weeks.

Twenty yards away an old man walking with the aid of a cane eyed up this strongly built policeman and cautiously moved another thirty yards further down the sidewalk.

Standing outside the church, Paddy experienced the feeling of wondrous awe he always had when admiring the Bysantine style architecture. And once inside, even in the somewhat dim light, the high arches and magnificent stained glass windows only augmented his sense of wonder. He rapidly moved to a pew, knelt down and was praying when he was startled by a voice.

"Is that you, Paddy?"

He looked up to see Father Mitchell.

"Yes Father, it's me. I just wanted to say a quick prayer."

"Good for you, my boy. Prayer is excellent for the soul."

"That it is Father. But why are you on duty at this time of day. I thought I might see Father Diaz."

"You know it's the strangest thing. Father Diaz didn't show up a few days ago. However Father Davidson saw him last night but again he didn't show today. Worried he may be ill, I sent a messenger round to his place this morning. But he and his family had gone."

"That's not like him, not to report for duty."

"Indeed not," he said pensively; but then changed the subject.

"You caught me about to indulge in a sin," he said with a mischievous smile on his face."

Paddy looked up in complete surprise. Then the cleric produced a cigarette from behind his back.

"I'm only going outside for a smoke," he confessed. "And while I'm out I intend to use my new gadget, a portable phone. I'm about to call Father Davidson to come and relieve me. It really is a nuisance being short handed now that Father Diaz has gone."

"That's the second time you've said gone, Father. Did you mean they were out for the day?"

"No, no. Paddy, I really meant gone. The messenger I sent spoke to a neighbor who told him the entire family was seen with packed suitcases taking a taxi to the airport. I can only think there must have been some family emergency. I must say I found it most unusual of him not to inform me."

"That is unusual, Father, But if you'll excuse me I must get back to my beat," said Paddy quickly, as he suddenly remembered the importance of his instructions to be on high alert.

"Of course, my son, God be with you."

"And with you, Father."

Paddy marched out into the bright sunlight and proceeded for a block before turning the corner.

The old man watched him leave; relieved he had not spent more time in the church. Then he saw the cleric come out and light his cigarette. He decided it would be wiser to let the policeman get further away on his beat. He would wait for another half-an-hour before returning to the church.

After turning off Park Avenue, Paddy had not gone a hundred yards when he abruptly stopped. He had the strongest feeling that something was terribly wrong. Everything about his last meeting with Father Diaz came vividly back to mind. Father Diaz had told him how conflicted he would be if he suddenly came into enough money to take his family to the doctors in that South American country. And now he had hastily left for the airport. Like a thunderbolt striking him, Paddy instantaneously recognized the key was that odd look in the Father's eyes. His eyes were trying to tell him something. No not tell, they had been pleading for understanding. No, that wasn't the word he had previously thought of – not understanding – it had been - absolution. Father Diaz had been in a tug-of-war between his faith and the needs of his family – and his family had won. He had done something terrible to earn a huge amount of money and was on his way to get the transplanted organs his family required to live.

Paddy turned and raced back to the church.

Father Mitchell was just finishing his cigarette and stared in amazement at the policeman rushing towards him.

"In the name of heaven, what's the matter, Paddy?"

"Father, when did you last see Father Diaz?"

"As I already told you, about three days ago."

"At what time did Father Davidson see him?"

"What's all this about, my son? You sound very upset."

"Let's go inside, Father. Now – please listen to me very carefully. This could very well be a matter of the highest importance. Tell me what time Father Davidson saw him."

"He had been working late on a sermon, I believe it was close to midnight when he was about to leave. That's when he came across Father Diaz. He must have startled him because he said Father Diaz looked very alarmed."

"And what was Father Diaz doing?"

"Well, I guess he was leaving too."

"Where was Father Diaz standing - precisely?"

"Look here, Paddy, you're getting me very worried by all these questions. What is this all about?"

"Sorry, Father, this is too urgent to go into detailed explanations. Where was Father Diaz standing?"

"I really don't know, but I just spoke to Father Davidson. Let me call him back."

Father Mitchell listened carefully to Father Davidson's explanation. He had become very anxious over Paddy's line of questioning and the urgency in his voice, and wanted to get every word Father Davidson uttered absolutely correct.

"Thank you Father Davidson, I'll see you soon," he said concluding the call.

He pointed to a door.

"It was just there."

"Where does that door lead, Father?"

"It's not an exit. It only leads to the crypt."

"Is it kept locked?"

"Yes, the key is kept in the office."

"Please Father, this could be critical, hurry and get the key. I have to inspect the crypt right away."

"But, ---," Father Mitchell began to protest.

"Father, this could be a very serious matter. Please – go quickly."

As Father Mitchell walked rapidly towards the office, Paddy called his station.

"This is O'Neil. I am at St. Bartholomew's church on East 50th and Park Avenue. At the briefing this morning every patrolman was told to look out for anything unusual. I may have something to report. I need another five minutes to verify. But be ready to respond quickly."

Father Mitchell came hurrying back and unlocked the door and switched on the lights. They were barely adequate. Paddy led the way using his powerful flashlight and with his gun drawn which greatly offended the cleric. As they went carefully down the spiral staircase Paddy whispered to him.

"Is it possible to gain permission to be laid to rest here?"

"It is a highly spiritual place. Special dispensation must be granted by the Archbishop after being petitioned by the Bishop. It only happens in the rarest of cases."

When they reached the last steps, Paddy motioned for Father Mitchell to stay on the stairs. He shone his flashlight around and kept his gun leveled.

"I wish you would put that gun away. The church is no place for firearms, Officer O'Neil."

"Shh!" responded Paddy noting the formal nature of the reprimand he had received.

"Look there, Father. See all the footprints on the dust on the floor. Several men have been down here recently."

His flashlight focused on a coffin lying on top of another.

"Is that normal to stack one coffin on another?"

"Oh dear God! I have never seen that coffin before. It has never been sanctioned and it certainly should not be placed on top of another sarcophagus."

"Carefully now, Father, let's go back up the stairs."

"But I have to investigate that coffin. It's very important that I do. This must be immediately reported to the Archdiocese," protested an agitated cleric.

"No, Father, I must call in a forensic team to do the investigation. We mustn't disturb anything. This could be a major crime scene."

"You don't think someone had been murdered and left here, do you?"

Officer O'Neil smiled grimly.

"I don't know, Father, but you and I should not play detectives. Let the experts check. Now, as carefully as you can, but as quickly as you can, let's go back upstairs."

Once back in the church Paddy called his station again.

"This is O'Neil."

Before he could go any further his commander spoke.

"O'Neil you are on a patched line with the FBI. Tell us clearly what you saw."

"There is a highly suspicious coffin in the crypt of St. Bart's, sir. It should not be there. And there are several fresh footprints on the floor. This coffin appears to have been put there in the last several days."

"Officer O'Neil, this is Special Agent Douglas of the FBI. Have you opened the coffin?"

"No, sir! Father Mitchell and I stayed on the staircase. I surveyed the crypt with my flashlight but didn't want to go further in case we contaminated the scene."

"Excellent. A team will arrive there in a few minutes. Meet them at the door to the church."

"Roger that, sir."

Douglas who was in the communications center, gave urgent instructions to the team closest to Park Avenue. Then he spoke again to Paddy's superior.

"You have a smart man there, Commander. None of my business but he seems to be too good to be pounding a beat."

"He is, Special Agent Douglas. I've tried to promote him but he refuses to accept."

"Why is that?"

"He says he can help more people by doing what he does."

"Intelligent and caring. That's a rare combination Commander. Thanks for your help. I have to go now."

He rushed to inform the others.

"This could be the break we have been praying for."

"Larry, can you get in touch with the team you sent?" asked Philip.

"Of course."

"This is very important, Larry. Ask them not to use sirens. When they get there, they should do their best not to disturb the scene. That means only one man, stepping carefully, should approach the coffin. If it is the bomb and the timer is running, call in the bomb squad and have the area evacuated. If the timer is not running, don't touch the bomb. They should leave the crypt. Then the leader should ask the priest if there are any priest's robes in the office. If so take them. Then everyone should leave as quietly as possible and park a few blocks away.

"I see, you want to lay a trap for Red Hand going into the church."

"Exactly!"

"I'll tell the team to park a block east of the church on 51st Street."

Chapter Forty One

It seemed like an eternity but, in reality, it was only twenty minutes before the team called in a report. During that time several things took place. Firstly Douglas ordered a car to take Melville, McKay and himself to the scene of the action. And before leaving the safe house, Douglas instructed three teams to join the first team on 51st Street. That pleased Philip. One never knew how many men would be required for a mission. Better to have too many than too few. But then he gave a second instruction to another team he had standing by to move to the opposite side of East 51st Street from the church.

"What are you doing, cancel that order. Ma is too clever not to spot them," cried out a distressed Melville.

"Don't worry, Philip. We have practiced this maneuver several times and nobody has ever suspected. Trust me on this. You'll see," replied a confident Douglas.

In Vietnam, Philip Melville had never assumed he was smarter than everyone in his squad. Each man had special skills Philip admired. Consequently he often consulted his team before going on a mission. His one cardinal rule had been never to leave any doubt in the minds of his men that he was in charge. The last decision would be his and his alone. Consultation was one thing, but only he could determine the optimum tactic for a mission. It had been a winning strategy.

Now he had to face the fact he had not yet consulted with members of the task force. He had issued some orders. However he had to admit he had not yet formed the next moves beyond having someone dressed as a priest be somewhere inside St. Bartholomew's. He had intended to consult with the others in the car on the way toward the church. Douglas had jumped the gun by ordering in a surveillance team. Faced with a 'fait accompli' he decided to go along for the moment. Anyway from what he had witnessed of Larry Douglas, he was a highly competent agent. His confidence was affirmed when the car Douglas had ordered drew up in the alley behind the safe house. It wasn't exactly dilapidated, but its appearance was not far from it. Definitely not the way one would expect an FBI car to look.

Once in the car he was again pleased by the throaty sound of the powerful engine as it sped away.

"I don't think we can finalize a plan until we reach the team on 51st Street and get advice from Father Mitchell on the layout of St. Bart's. Obviously I would like at least one man to be inside the church. But I want him to be hidden. The priest's garments are meant only to be a backup should something go wrong and Ma spots him. Any other ideas?"

"We should check all local airports including private ones for today's scheduled flights. If this is the real thing, Ma will want to be as far away from the city as possible," said McKay.

"You're right, Hugh. That's part of our standard dragnet procedure when we are pursuing high target criminals. All possible exits from a location must be secured. In this case it means all bridges, tunnels, heliports, airports, train stations, bus stations and piers."

Philip lowered his head to hide his smile. Once again Larry Douglas was doing exactly what he would have done.

"My men are taking along a portable computer. It's now standard practice in the FBI. They will access a floor plan of St. Bart's on it. That along with Father Mitchell's advice will give you the hiding place you want, Philip," concluded Douglas

"Great, now we have to decide who is going in. It can't be a member of the task force. Ma may well have used his computer to pull up photographs of everyone from various records."

"I have just the man," said Douglas. "His name is Andrews and he is a member of one of the teams on its way. I have used him on many situations like this. He is just under six feet tall and slimly built. However his build disguises the fact he is strongly muscled and an expert in martial arts. Even better, in college he acted in plays and can assume identities quite readily."

He reached for the car radio.

"You *are* well prepared, Larry," said Philip as his admiration of this man increased even further. Any other good news? I'm beginning to feel much better about this operation."

"One additional thing is worth mentioning. We can keep in radio contact at all times. In the past we learned the hard lesson of ear buds and wires giving away our men. Also the ringing of an incoming call ruined many a covert operation. Now we have a radio strapped to the chest which uses a vibrator as the signal. Whenever a man gets this signal, he pulls his ear bud and microphone from his pocket to communicate. But he only does this if his coast is clear. That way he doesn't give away his position if a target is close by."

"Ingenious," said McKay. "I'll have to get a batch of those."

Just then the car radio buzzed and the FBI team in the church reported tersely.

"The timer is not running. We are about to retrieve the robes you requested and leave the church. We will await your further instructions."

"Understood, will be with you shortly. Have Andrews put on the priest's outfit." responded Douglas equally briefly.

Philip approved of such messages. He had drilled this into his men in Vietnam. 'Brevity saves lives' was one of his mottos. In the jungle a few missions failed due to someone staying on the radio too long and being eventually overheard. You could never always be certain of the proximity of the enemy. KISS was a well known military acronym for Keep It Simple Stupid. Philip added Keep It Short Stupid.

Their car slowed to a cruising speed as they approached the church. Opposite the main entrance a hippie was completing the set up of his electric guitar. The tall gangly man wore a floral shirt and faded bell bottomed jeans which were not long enough to reach his bare ankles and badly scuffed sandals. His face was either weather beaten or rather dirty. It was difficult to tell with his straggly beard. His long hair was kept away from his face with a red headband. As he adjusted his amplifier it emitted a loud screech. His female companion, who sang to his accompaniment, and was similarly dressed, cursed him as she plugged her ears with her fingers. He shrugged an apology then laid down his hat for tips and began playing.

"What do you think of my team now, Philip?"

"Those are your lookouts?"

"The best in the business; and both excellent shots, particularly Evelyn. If anyone cuts up rough she can be really nasty. Believe me you do not want to get on her bad side."

"I'm impressed, Larry. No one would ever suspect them of being FBI. But do they have a description of Red Hand.?"

"Yes, and they have been told he will most probably be disguised. So they are to report anyone going into the church. You probably saw they are on the corner and not directly opposite the front door. They will have been briefed on the location of any side doors to the church. From their position they can keep watch on several doors."

Philip nodded his approval. He would have expected no less from his own men.

They pulled up behind the other FBI car on 51st Street. It was only then Douglas pointed out the other three cars. They were not as beat up as the one they were in. They were three year old models with a few dents and dings and city dirty: perfect camouflage. Philip and Douglas walked casually to the car where Andrews was sitting. They leaned through the open windows and were shown the floor plan of St. Bartholomew on the portable computer. Andrews had already consulted Father Mitchell and selected a recommended location to hide. After a careful study of the floor plan, Philip agreed.

"We haven't yet finalized our tactics, Andrews. So get in position and await further instructions," commanded Douglas.

Andrews nodded and left.

Both men were surprised by a voice behind them.

"The name's O'Neil. I'm the one who called this in. I think it best if I get back on my beat otherwise it may look suspicious. I'll keep as close to the church as possible without being obvious. Do you have any specific instructions for me?"

Philip and Douglas turned to see the broad frame of Paddy.

"Yes, can you keep your radio on the FBI channel in case we need you urgently?" asked Philip.

"I've already coordinated with the agents in the car and done that, sir."

"Excellent. The main thing is crowd control. If shooting starts we don't want innocent bystanders caught in the crossfire."

"Roger that, sir."

Philip looked up in surprise at his response.

"I was a British paratrooper and also served in Special Forces here in the States, Colonel. You are well known to anyone who has served in that branch."

Philip stuck out his hand.

"I'm very pleased we have you here, Officer O'Neil. We may need you for other duties given your training. If so we'll contact you on the radio."

"Yes, sir!" replied Paddy and walked off to continue his beat.

"He's a good man," said Douglas. "I've already complimented his actions to his commander. I should have known he was one of yours by the calm manner with which he has handled this highly dangerous situation."

"It's good to have him," agreed Philip. "Let's get back to your car and decide on our next steps."

Suddenly Douglas's radio began vibrating. He pulled his ear bud from his pocket and held it so both he and Philip could hear. It was the 'hippie' reporting.

"Go ahead, this is Douglas."

"Everyone take cover, a suspicious vehicle is cruising the area. Dark gray Volvo sedan with mud covering its license plates. Can only identify first letter H and last two numbers 37

Chapter Forty Two

Douglas and Melville ran quickly back to their car almost dragging Father Mitchell with them. They couldn't all fit comfortably into the car so the driver had to leave for another car.

"Get your hippie on the radio," commanded Philip. His order indicated he was now on a full war alert.

"I'm here," responded the hippie.

"How many times has that car passed by? And how many passengers?" asked Philip.

"Identify yourself," was the curt response.

Philip's voice was not known to the hippie.

"This is Douglas. That was Colonel Melville who is a leader in this investigation."

"Sorry, sir. I didn't recognize the voice. It just made its third pass. The windows aren't tinted but they are dirty so it's difficult to be sure. I could only identify one in addition to the driver."

"Thank you, and no apology required. You did exactly the correct thing by requesting identification," answered Philip.

Then he drew his finger over his throat to have the radio contact discontinued. He sat in deep thought for almost thirty seconds. To the others it seemed like thirty minutes. Each was conscious of how precious time was, yet unwilling to interrupt his thoughts. When he finally spoke it was with a sigh of disappointment.

"That's not him. It's a decoy."

"How can you possibly know that?" burst out Father Mitchell.

Then realizing he should not be interrupting a police matter, he put his hand over his mouth and apologized.

Philip shrugged indication no harm had been done, but his cold stare left no doubt Mitchell was not to do so again. He was now a leader in full battle mode, and one not accustomed to interruptions.

"Red Hand would never give away his position so obviously," he responded brusquely.

Father Mitchell squirmed in his seat. He desperately wanted to ask who this Red Hand was. Only a few people could keep this priest quiet. Not even his Bishop. His Archbishop, – certainly – and, this scary colonel with the penetrating blue eyes.

"But even if he didn't suspect we knew about the church, wouldn't he check it out thoroughly before going in?" persisted Douglas.

"Most certainly, but not that way. A car driving slowly past the church three times is a very high risk situation. Someone could easily have noticed it: a policeman on the beat, a hippie playing his guitar, or even a priest being outside for a smoke."

Father Mitchell flinched at this.

"He would use a better way to reconnoiter and check out the lay of the land. Remember Red Hand has to make a speedy getaway. Most likely to a private airport where he has a plane waiting. And should there be any unintentional meeting inside the church, such as bumping into a priest while he retrieves the crypt key from the office, an alarm would be raised. And he can't afford the slightest delay. He has to set the timer and exit quickly. He has no intention of being a martyr and being vaporized like everyone else. He must have time to get off this island of Manhattan."

At the word 'vaporized' Father Mitchell forgot all about the warning eyes of Melville.

"Vaporized? What do you mean by that?"

"Sorry, Father, perhaps we should have mentioned. That bomb in your crypt is a nuclear one."

"Then we must warn everyone in the city. There must be an evacuation. I must tell the Mayor's office. He must have that bomb moved away from my church. Let me out!"

He reached for the door but it was locked.

"Stay exactly where you are, Father!"

The strident tone in Philip's voice again froze Father Mitchell in his seat.

"We have the best expert team nearby ready to disarm that bomb; it will not be allowed to explode. Our present challenge is only to catch the perpetrator of this crime. Any issued warnings would only drive him into hiding and I fear he would one day return with an equally heinous scheme. Can you understand that, Father?"

"Yes. But are you certain your team can defuse this bomb?"

"As head of the FBI forces involved, I can give you that assurance, Father," said Douglas. "Now please sit back and do not interrupt again. We have critical work to do."

Duly chastened, Mitchell sat back; however, his face reflected the grave concerns he still harbored. No one doubted he would bolt at the first opportunity.

"What's our play?" asked McKay.

"We need more eyes close to the church. Larry, position a few of your best men close to the side doors. They must be as inconspicuous as possible, preferably hidden. And tell Andrews if anyone enters the Church office for the crypt key he must be stopped. Only injured if possible but definitely stopped. He should use a silencer. And alert your hippie watchers to be ready to move in at a second's notice."

Douglas immediately transferred those instructions.

"Anything else?" he asked.

"Ask Officer O'Neil if he has seen that Volvo."

Paddy O'Neil's voice came over the radio.

"It looked suspicious from the first time I saw it. The second time it passed me I pretended to be reprimanding a bunch of kids. Anyone inside only saw my back and would have thought I was only doing my duty. Thereafter I kept a sharp eye out for it and when, for the third time, I saw the tip of its hood start to come around a corner, I hid in a doorway. They didn't spot me."

"Good man," said Philip. "If you can, stay out of sight but be ready to assist in the church in case we need you."

"Roger that," responded O'Neil and rang off.

Douglas nodded his head in yet another affirmation of the esteem in which he held Paddy O'Neil.

"Father, are you certain you have told us of all the ways into the church?" asked Philip.

"I believe after twelve years service at St. Bartholomew, I should know there is no other," replied Father Mitchell in a stiff, huffy, voice.

Apparently he was still smarting from his earlier treatment.

"Thank you, Father, that's very useful," said Philip ingratiatingly.

He wanted to ameliorate Mitchell's feelings of anger. At this vital stage, the last thing he needed was to have to worry about him attempting to flee. He must fully focus on the job at hand.

That was the exact thought of someone else. The old man who had watched Mitchell light his cigarette had returned. He studied the avenue. The hippies were performing but getting little in the way of tips.

'Little wonder,' he thought.

The girl's caterwauling assaulted the ears. Even though it was partially drowned out by the excesses of the guitar's amplifier, it still offended. He tried to put the noise out of his mind

'Focus your attention,' he counseled himself.

He did this, and satisfied all was in order, he walked around the corner and spoke into his lapel microphone. He sent the same message to two different locations.

"Go now!"

Despite Philip's best efforts to keep all his concentration on the current situation an undefined uncertainty troubled his mind. Try as he might he just couldn't give it an identity. Yet he had the strongest feeling the jigsaw puzzle was not complete. He had a nagging impression there had to be a few other pieces. Something told him this operation was not of the caliber he normally attributed to Red Hand. His style was often convoluted but always immaculate.

'Have I missed something?' he wondered.

Try as he might nothing came to mind. He shook his head trying either to dislodge the thought or bring it into the light.

"You look troubled, Philip. What is it?" asked McKay.

He was beginning to better understand Philip and recognized the facial signs of his dilemma.

"Oh something is at the back of my mind but I can't seem to focus on it."

"I know the feeling. But it will come back if it's important."

"Probably."

Just at that second, the thought was forced from his mind by the hippie's urgent radio message.

"The Volvo has stopped twenty yards from the church."

"Is anyone getting out?" demanded Douglas.

"Negative."

"Keep us informed."

"Wait a minute. The driver is helping someone out of the car. It's a woman. They must be going to the church!"

'Standby, everyone. It's about to go down!" cried out Douglas.

Chapter Forty Three

Exactly twenty four days prior to all this happening, the school bell rang at the end of the day at an exclusive private boys' school in Vancouver. The children poured out noisily. As usual, one of them was met by two unsmiling Chinese men each of whom kept one hand inside a bulging jacket. They kept a constant three hundred and sixty degree watch as they escorted the boy to a waiting large car with its engine running. On the dashboard ledge was an automatic pistol. It was always kept in plain sight as a warning to anyone who may attempt to harm the boy. It was only when the two men opened the back door they noticed the head of the driver was slumped over the steering wheel. They gaped for only an instant. But that was long enough for the back of their heads to be blown off.

Ma had arranged this kidnapping. It was the ten year old son of Lee Khoo Ming, the now leading gangster in Vancouver. Lee had a non-listed, secure telephone number he used only for the most important of his gang's business. Acquiring that number had been child's play for Ma.

"Yes," barked Lee, annoyed at being called at this particular time. He was always impatient to see his beloved son and learn of his day at school.

"Listen carefully, Lee. I have your son. He will be returned shortly after you do exactly what I say."

"How much?" demanded Lee woodenly.

It was not uncommon for such kidnappings to occur to rich Chinese families. The gangster code mandated that after a ransom was paid the child would never again be kidnapped.

"I don't want money, just information."

That shook Lee. After a moment's thought he wondered if this really was a kidnapper.

"I don't believe you have my boy," he bluffed.

The sound of his son's crying voice convinced him.

"What is it you want?"

"Get me the name of the very best safe cracker in the Chinese gangs in New York" demanded Ma.

"I'm not sure I can so that," whined Lee.

"Oh, in that case, don't worry. I'm sorry to have troubled you."

"Then you'll return my son," cried the relieved Lee, hardly able to believe his luck.

"Of course I will," purred Ma. Then his voice rose to a shriek, "*In tiny pieces!* You have twenty four hours to get me a name and the exact contact details. Also I want to know everything about this man. Every ten minutes after that time your son will lose a digit. And after an hour he will lose his head. I will call you in exactly twenty four hours."

Red Hand didn't wait that long. He knew he didn't have to. It was eighteen hours later when he called again.

"Do you have my information?"

"Yes, yes. I have it. Is my son okay?"

"He is in excellent health. Now give me the information I requested."

Lee quickly complied.

"Now please release my boy."

"After I have verified the details you gave me."

"But, but ---."

The line had gone dead.

Ma dialed the number he had been given, and received a frosty reception.

"Who the hell are you? And how did you get this number?"

"I am a friend of Lee Khoo Ming."

"Never heard of him."

"He mentioned you would say that. He said I should say the word Primrose."

"Primrose, huh. That's a common word in a flower shop. But I don't sell flowers."

"That is the correct response, Mr. Tan Chin Chye. My final word is Orchid."

"Who are you? And what do you want?"

The voice was still gruff but unlike previous responses it was now more accommodating.

"I shall be in your city three days from today and will call you at exactly four o'clock. Then we can agree where to meet. I promise you will find the subject intriguing and very profitable, Mr. Tan. Or, as your intimate friends call you, Light Fingers Chye."

Tan had only time to gasp before the line went dead. He immediately called the telephone company to find out the source of his caller. However to his utter amazement he was told no call had been placed to his number. After his astonishment came fear. He called his best two bodyguards and told them to be at his home in three days at quarter-to-four. While he was contacting his men, Ma called a not very reputable, but effective private detective in New York. The man he would use would fulfill his needs and thereafter would disappear.

The next day on a cold rainy day, an old man alighted from a flight at JFK airport. Red Hand was again using his favorite disguise. He took a taxi to Chinatown where he checked into an old style boarding house. He had come early as he had preparations to make.

On the appointed day at exactly four o'clock, Tan's secure telephone rang.

"Good afternoon, Mr. Tan. I would like you to come to room 15 at the following address. Of course you may bring your two favorite bodyguards, but only those two. And please do not attempt to bring them into the room. That would have unfortunate consequences. One may stand outside the boarding house and the other outside my room. Your place of business is only a ten minute walk away. I shall expect you at that time."

The line went dead before Tan could respond. He had thought a great deal since receiving the first call. The fact that someone could get his number and somehow erase the call from the telephone company's log so quickly, indicated he was dealing with a very intelligent person. Perhaps even more than intelligent, this man could very well be dangerous. And his caller knowing he always traveled with two bodyguards was even more troubling. He decided to play along; at least for the moment. However as an extra precaution he had added three more bodyguards to his contingent. He called them in and gave them instructions.

It had taken ten minutes to reach the boarding house; exactly as the stranger had said. Three of his men were hidden in doorways and as ordered he left one at the entrance. He stopped at the desk to check who was in Room 15. The landlady wasn't there which put him on guard. He whispered to the man at the entrance to alert the other three to be ready for instant action. Then he checked the register. A Mr. Shue from Los Angeles was the occupant. He climbed stairs to room 15. The bodyguard drew his revolver ready for trouble as Tan knocked on the door. There was no answer, so he knocked again; this time louder.

Everything seemed to happen in a blur of motion. The door opposite room 15 was flung open. The man standing there used a silencer to shoot the bodyguard in the arm, then the silenced gun was spun around and the bodyguard knocked out with its butt. By the time Tan could focus he found the hot muzzle of the silenced gun in his gaping mouth.

"That was extremely foolish. I thought I would be dealing with a professional, not a bumbling amateur."

He took Tan's gaggling sounds as an attempt at an apology and removed the gun from his mouth.

"Now, Light Fingers Chye, tell your man at the door to fetch his bleeding companion and have him seen to. Then have those thoroughly incompetent three others remove themselves from across the street and go home. If any of your men attempts to heroically rescue you, he will die shortly after you. Do you understand?"

A badly shaken Tan could only nod his head before doing precisely as he had been told. Ma ushered Tan into room 15 and had him sit at the table. He poured Chinese tea into a cup and offered it to Tan. If Tan had been scared before, he was now more terrified than he had ever been in his life.

This stranger was acting as though this was a social meeting between friends and showing no signs of concern over having shot a man. Tan accepted the offer but the teacup rattled so violently in the saucer, he had to put it on the table.

"Be calm, my dear Tan. No harm will come to you, if you, -- *do everything I ask at precisely the time I specify.*"

The last words were hissed so menacingly that Tan had to request a visit to the toilet. This was granted but he had to leave the door open. Tan was a burglar; one who avoided injurious harm. He never carried a weapon and would have readily surrendered if trapped by an armed policeman. But he had never been caught. His skill at cracking safes was legendary; however, he only undertook assignments after personally checking every detail. If there was the slightest doubt in his mind of anything less than a successful outcome he walked away from the job.

Tan returned to the table and was able to sip tea without spilling it. A commendably achievement since his insides had turned to jelly. Ma placed a map of central Manhattan on the table.

"Of course you know this store," said Ma pointing to the map.

"That's Tiffany's. It's impossible to crack unless it were to be an armed raid."

Then he rattled off a remarkable listing of the security involved. Ma was impressed.

"And you also know this store," he said again pointing.

Once again Tan knew all the details of its security. Now Ma knew he had the right man. Tan had meticulously identified the security setups of all the major targets in Manhattan.

"But do you know this store?"

"Yes, but the owner never leaves his most valuable merchandise in the store at night. He has some excellent pieces but they are taken by armored truck to the security company's warehouse at the end of each day's business. The area is not terribly secure. I could break into it with very little trouble."

"But do you know its basic security system?"

"Oh yes. Like all jewelry stores it has a silent alarm system that can be activated by a switch under the counter. And he has a rather outmoded safe where he keeps the rest of his merchandise overnight."

Tan had become more at ease as he displayed his expert knowledge. No one could avoid being impressed. He was even feeling much safer.

"Good. Here's what I want you to do. You will recruit the services of a third rate burglar. One who is not averse to committing armed robbery. You will convince him you intend expanding your business and need a partner. He will be exultant at being chosen. You will put him through a two week training program. Then you will identify the target and for a week you will school him in the tactics to use in robbing this store in daytime. Those tactics will include you informing him how you will cut the power to the security alarm. Is this understood?"

"I understand the words but I have to tell you it is not worth the risk. I said the store has a few good pieces but a broad daylight robbery carries too much danger. There are so many variables."

"I have considered all those variables. Tell me, do you know such a third rate burglar?"

"Yes, there are several. Only the younger ones are prepared to use guns. They are more reckless. However I do know an excellent candidate."

"I shall want you to be ready to move in a week or so after the training is completed. You and your assistant must be ready to move at an hour's notice. Now here is the most important part. You will have your burglar carry a small case into the store; one which I will supply. Tell him it is lined with special velvet so that the stolen merchandise will not be scratched. And – this is critical – he must not open it until you enter the store. Once he has secured everything you will come in and place the jewels in the case."

Tan's head was now spinning.

"This is all too complicated. If you want those jewels just let him take them. No risk to you and none to me."

"But I don't want the jewels," said Ma. "I only need a little diversion. A few blocks away I will be stealing a much, much, more valuable prize."

Tan wracked his brains to think what it might be. Then he remembered the great collection of foreign art to be displayed at a nearby gallery.

"You don't mean --?"

"Shh, better not to guess."

"But how can you be certain this minor jewelry theft will raise such a monumental alarm as to distract all law agencies?"

"There are two reasons. First you will *not* cut the power to the jewelry store alarm. And second, inside the case will be a small explosive devise. Oh you need not worry. It will only have the effect of several Chinese firecrackers. And you will activate it by a remote switch. You only have to be a few yards away to be completely safe. Although it will not do much damage it will make a lot of noise. The silent alarm inside the store and the small devise will cause enough distraction for me to achieve my goal."

Tan's mouth fell open. He thought this man crazy.

"I shall contact you and supply the case and the remote activator the day of the robbery. As I said you must be ready at a moment's notice."

Tan's recent sense of security was vanishing rapidly. His brain began thinking of ways to extricate himself from this situation. As though he read his mind, Ma stared into Tan's eyes.

"As a precaution one of my men will be with you."

Tan lowered his gaze. This new information may make it more difficult but he would still think of a way to get out of this situation. Then Ma played his trump card. He drew a photograph from his pocket. It had been taken by the unfortunate private detective.

"As you have witnessed I have many men at my disposal in this city," he bluffed. "One of them knows every detail of this young lady's life. She hopes to graduate next year and attend a most illustrious college. She has rather a lovely face. It would be a pity to have to attend that college with forty or fifty stitches in her face."

Tears sprang into Tan's eyes as he gazed at his daughter's photograph. He knew this man would not hesitate to carry out his threat. He now felt completely helpless. He nodded his head.

"I shall be ready."

The man who would accompany Tan was the third gangster Ma had recruited. The other two had received the usual treatment of those no longer of use to Red Hand. This one had been told he had only three further minor assignments to do before receiving his reward for all services. The reward was not in cash. He had been shown two gold bars. He could hardly believe his eyes. He wasn't exactly certain of the value of the gold but he knew they would be worth much more than he ever dreamed of owning. He would live in luxury for the rest of his life. The first task was simple, steal a police car radio. The second was equally simple, steal an inconspicuous car, leave the radio inside and park the car in a parking garage Ma had specified. Then give the parking ticket to Ma. The third even simpler; when notified deliver a case and a small device to Tan and stay with him to make sure he stood outside the designated jewelry store at the appointed time.

Gold bars danced in front of the gangster's eyes. He couldn't stop thinking about his luck. He spent hours dreaming of his future life.

Some life!

Chapter Forty Four

The message, "Go now" was the signal for the man and the woman to get out of the Volvo and stand exactly fifteen seconds before moving very quickly towards the church.

Outside the jewelry store the same message of "Go now" had been transmitted to Tan. He immediately waved the young burglar to enter the store. He and his guard stood a few yards away from the front door to keep an eye on things. Tan's instruction was to wait exactly thirty seconds then enter the store and once inside press the button to detonate the small explosive device.

As the man and the woman almost ran towards the church, the hippie yelled into his radio.

"They're making a run for the church."

"Everyone go now, stop them!" screamed Douglas.

Federal agents appeared from every direction racing towards the church. The hippie agent and his partner sprinted across Park Avenue. In her haste Evelyn didn't pay sufficient attention to the traffic and a car hit her.

"I'll be okay. Go ahead and get them," she shouted.

The hippie hesitated for only a second then raced on. He caught up with the man and woman just as two other agents did. All three had their guns drawn. They grabbed the couple who stared in amazement and fear at the agents.

KABOOM

Ma had lied to Tan and the supposed very small explosive device was anything but. He had used half of the chemicals Hsieh had obtained to build a bomb as powerful as the one used to destroy his apartment in

Vancouver. The effect was devastating. Everyone inside the shop, Tan and his guard, and many people in the street were instantly killed. Red Hand had not planned this massacre merely for its own sake or to just kill the two remaining people who could identify him; it was a distraction. A distraction which could not only be heard at St. Barts, but could almost be felt.

The noise was so loud it slowed everything to a halt outside the church. Instinctively the agents crouched low to the ground until they could identify the location of the bomb. Even the agent guarding the side door came out of hiding to see what was going on. He was passed by three other agents rushing towards the front of the church.

The old man walking with the aid of a cane, smiled when he heard the explosion. His diversion was loud enough to create a major distraction. He had carefully planned this to draw away any policemen who might be in the vicinity of St Bartholomew's. This would give him the opportunity to set the timer on the bomb inside the church. The smile was wiped from his face when he saw the running agents and the one who had quickly returned to his hiding place.

"No, no," he involuntarily roared.

This couldn't be happening. His planning had been meticulous as usual. How the hell did these men, undoubtedly FBI agents, come to be here? There was only one answer.

"Melville!"

He spat the name out loud with the utmost venom. Then, coming to his senses, he turned around and hobbled back down the street.

The agent heard the loud voice although he couldn't make out the words. He peeked out and saw an old man scurrying away.

"I don't blame you old timer. Run for safety," he muttered.

Red Hand's brain was in overdrive. He must come up with a plan. It would only be a matter of seconds before his other distraction was uncovered. The man and woman had been recruited by his third gangster, the one now lying scattered over the inside of the jewelry store. Their purpose was to sidetrack the attention of any policeman not drawn to the blast or any priest who may be inside the church. It was a contingency plan. One he was sure would not be necessary but his brain was always thinking of the minutest potential problem. He had used his gangster to recruit them so that if by some unthinkable occurrence they were questioned, they could not identify him.

Now the unthinkable had happened and he cursed Philip Melville so violently he felt a pain in his chest. That's when the idea came to him. He took out his portable phone and dialed 911.

"Which service do you require?"

"Ambulance and hurry!"

"What's the problem?"

"A man has collapsed and is lying on the sidewalk. I don't think he's dead but he must be close. I can hardly hear any breathing."

"Where is this?"

"On Lexington Avenue near 53rd street. Hurry!"

There was a momentary pause.

"An ambulance is on its way. Please stay there to assist. What is your name sir?"

Ma hung up.

"Hello, hello."

But Ma was on his way to assume his pose. As he walked quickly through the panicky throng of people he surreptitiously discarded his disguise and cane.

Outside St. Bartholomew's another crowd of people was also in panic. Hearing the tremendous blast was sufficient to terrify anyone. But in addition to that, to witness the significant number of FBI agents racing to surround a man and woman was frightening. However, human nature being what it is, the fear was mixed with intense curiosity. As the crowd surged forward to get a better view of the couple who had been thrust to the ground and handcuffed, the FBI found itself involved in crowd control. An even more important concern for the FBI was the injury to one of its team. Evelyn was still prostrate on the ground with traffic backed up all around her.

Philip gave instructions to Douglas.

"Get a team to disarm the bomb and remove it. We can be certain Ma did not anticipate all this chaos. I'm sure he wasn't expecting the FBI to be here and he will have fled the scene. I'm afraid we have missed him. We can't do anything further here. Larry, let's get the two suspects to the safe house for interrogation and bring all your men who had eyes on the church for a debriefing. If we're lucky we may be able to salvage some useful intel from this mess."

Saying he wanted all these things done was one thing, but having them done was quite another matter. With an increasing crowd and blocked traffic it would be quite a task. Lucky for them Paddy O'Neil arrived on the scene and was succinctly briefed by Philip. Douglas and Melville listened as he swung into action. He immediately used his portable phone to call the police control center.

"This is a national security matter. I understand there has been an explosion not far from where I'm now standing. I'm outside St. Bart's with the FBI. We have a bad situation here. It may involve a massively powerful bomb. It is imperative we clear the street to allow the bomb squad to get here. We must have ten officers to assist in crowd and traffic control. We need them now!"

He turned to Philip.

"I'll handle this, sir. You should go. I know you have to move quickly."

Philip gave a nod of thanks. As he had been trained to do, this ex-military man was demonstrating his ability to remain calm and efficient in the face of turmoil.

"I have an injured agent in the street, Officer O'Neil. An ambulance has been called but may have trouble reaching her," said a worried Douglas.

"I'll take care of that too. You go ahead."

Without wasting another second Paddy pushed the crowd back, then began directing the traffic to clear a way for the ambulance and bomb squad. It was only when he saw a man bending over the injured agent that he left this task to rush to the stricken agent.

"Move away, sir," he said stridently to the hippie.

"I'm agent Hudson," replied the hippie showing his badge.

"Sorry, sir."

"Hudson, get in one of the cars. We need you," called out Douglas.

The hippie hesitated. This was his partner.

"It's okay, agent Hudson, I'll take good care of her. I promise," said Paddy in a soft voice.

Hudson looked into the face of the strong young officer and was reassured this was a man who kept his promises. He ran to one of the waiting cars. Paddy went over to Evelyn.

"What happened?"

"It was my fault, I was in such a rush to apprehend the suspects, I didn't see a car come from behind a bus. It's my hip and leg. Hurts like hell."

"I'm not going to attempt to move you. That may do more damage. But let me put my jacket under your head. I'll stay here with you until the ambulance arrives to make sure it can get through the traffic to reach you."

"Thanks, Officer O'Neil," she said gratefully after reading his name on his badge.

The urgency in Paddy's voice when he called the control center had done the trick. Within a few minutes policemen were arriving. He directed them to move people a block away and to have the jammed traffic clear lanes for the ambulance. When it arrived he gave his final instruction to his fellow policemen.

"I'm going with the lady to the hospital. Clear all the traffic. The bomb squad is on the way. And then take cover."

Once the door was closed, the ambulance moved away slowly. The two attendants shooed Paddy out of the way as they got to work. They hooked her up to an IV.

"What's that," she asked stridently.

"Only a pain killer."

Then they began removing her jeans but saw the pain it was causing her.

"I think it will be easier on you if we cut them away," said one of the medics.

They were just about finished when they noticed she had removed her pistol from the back of her jeans and now held it in her hand.

The startled medics let out cries of surprise. Paddy moved forward to check on the cause.

"You're not a medic, Officer O'Neil. Turn your head away," she barked out.

Paddy blushed and did as he was told. The attendants eyed one another. This woman liked to give orders.

"You don't need that gun. Let me put it with you jeans," one said.

"An agent must keep her weapon with her at all times while on duty – regulations."

"We can't treat you while you are waving that gun around," protested the other.

"Oh, okay, give it to the police officer to hold for me. But tell him not to look round."

When this upsetting task was accomplished, one attendant gently moved her leg and she let out a scream.

"Give me back my weapon, O'Neil" she commanded.

The attendants paled. But she was grinning.

"Only a joke, but that really hurt."

"Looks like it could be a fractured femur," he said.

"Could be. Let's have a look at the hip. It's badly bruised."

"You don't think it's broken," asked an anxious agent.

"Can't be certain until we take x-rays. But I don't intend poking around. I'll leave that to the doctor."

"Are you afraid I'll shoot you," asked a smiling agent.

"Yes, I am deathly scared," he replied, but he was grinning too. "No, it's just that there is no need to cause you any further discomfort. Better to wait for the x-rays.

Just then the ambulance driver gave a single toot of his klaxon.

"No need to worry, folks, I was just greeting a fellow ambulance driver. We have a bunch of ambulances going to that explosion. But Jacky is on his way to a possible heart attack on Lexington. The old hospital will sure be busy today," he drawled in his Texas accent.

"You didn't have to come with me," said the injured agent to Paddy once she was under a blanket. "Shouldn't you have stayed at the scene?"

"We had plenty officers to take care of things there. And yes I had to make sure you were well taken care of. A certain colonel is involved in this operation and he would never forgive me if I didn't."

"Are you so afraid of him?" she asked incredulously, as she eyed his large frame.

"No, miss I am in awe of him. He would never do me harm. It's just I could never let him down."

"I don't understand. I don't know him and he doesn't know me. I work for the FBI not the army. And you are a policeman. How would you be letting him down?"

"I was in the paratroop regiment in Britain and the Special Forces here in America. He is one of the most revered officers ever to serve in the Special Forces. I know what he expects of me."

"Even though you're now a civilian?"

"Yes miss. He is on a mission and it is something big. I can only assure you if he is involved, he is in charge. Not the FBI or CIA or the NYPD. Therefore as you were obviously a part of this mission, he will want a full report on your injuries."

"You really believe a man I don't even know will be so concerned over me?"

"Most definitely. You see, miss, we never leave a fallen comrade on the battlefield."

Agent Evelyn Pearson's eyes began to close. The pain medicine the ambulance attendant had given her was beginning to take effect. One attendant had listened with growing interest to the conversation. He shook his head in wonder. He had served in the army.

"This colonel I would really like to meet."

Chapter Forty Five

The man and woman were interrogated separately. Their stories were essentially the same but with sufficient slight differences to convince the interrogators they had not been rehearsed.

Douglas had interviewed the man with Philip in attendance. When he was brought into the interrogation room the man immediately assumed a belligerent attitude. He had been brought here with a hood over his head and he was frightened. However in his street smart way he figured a good offense was better than an adequate defense.

"Who the hell are you? And what right have you got dragging me in here? And where the hell am I? I ain't seen no lawyer yet. You must be a cop, probably a detective since you ain't wearing no uniform. I wasn't stealing that car, and you can't prove I was. I want a lawyer or I ain't saying no more. So there!"

Douglas walked up to him and stared balefully into his eyes.

"Sit down," he barked.

The man's braggadocio was slipping away from him. Yet he still held a little in reserve. That was until the looming figure of the big, blue eyed, man also came very close to him.

"My friend asked you to sit. I suggest you do so. *Now!*"

The man completely crumpled at that and he hurried towards the chair. With no preamble, Douglas began his questioning.

"What were you doing at the church?"

"We wis hired to go there and told what to do. I wis to drive around the block three times then stop near the main doors at precisely eleven o'clock. Then we wis to stand on the sidewalk for fifteen seconds then walk as quickly as we could to the church."

"And what were you to do once inside?"

"Sit in a pew for three minutes then leave."

"That's all?"

Yes sir, that's all. We didn't break any law did we? I mean I ain't going to jail, am I?"

"We'll see about that. But I can promise you this; you will end up in jail, and for a long, long time, if I find you've been lying to me."

"I ain't lying, honest."

"Who hired you, was it a Chinese man?"

"Yes sir, it sure was."

"Was he slim, about five feet nine and walk with a limp?"

The man looked puzzled.

"No, sir. He wis a big guy; maybe over six feet and he didn't have no limp."

"Are you certain about that?"

"Yes, sir. I'm about five eleven and he wis a bit bigger than me."

"Why'd you do this?"

Again the man looked puzzled.

"Well, for the money, of course."

"How much?"

"Five hundred each up front and another thousand each when we finished. Your guys took my five hundred when they searched me. I'll get it back, won't I?"

"We'll see."

"Where did this Chinese pick you up?"

"At the homeless shelter in Brooklyn. Just after breakfast. That'd be about nine o'clock."

"How did he select you?"

"He asked the lady in charge, Mary, for someone who could drive. Said he wanted a driver for the day. And when he gets me outside the shelter he asks me to get a woman to go with me. That's when he told me about the money."

"And whose car is it."

Again a puzzled look as though it was a stupid question.

"Well, his, of course. You don't think I got a car do you?"

"Then what?"

"Well I asks Lizzie to come with me and tells her the price and naturally she says yes. It's then I thought the game was up. He asks me for my driver's license. Well mine expired nine years ago. But he didn't seem to mind. Just wanted to know I really could drive."

"And then?"

"He drives us to the Battery on the south of Manhattan. Then he sits in the back and asks me to drive around for a bit. Once he sees I really can drive, we park. He gets out a map and shows me where to go. Piece of cake really. And then he gives us each five hundred dollars. *Five hundred dollars! Can you believe that?* Of course now that you cops have spoiled things I doubt we'll get our thousand dollars."

"And what were you to do after the church?"

"Leave the car outside the shelter and leave the keys under the visor. If he wis satisfied he would bring us the thousand dollars tomorrow. Course Lizzie believed him but not me," he said with a knowing look. "But who cares, we already got five hundred."

A worried look came over his face.

"You don't think the five hundred is fake money, do you?"

They ignored his question. Philip sat down next to Douglas and leaned over close to the man.

"Just think how stupid your story sounds. A man you have never seen before lets you use his car to drive around Manhattan, sit in a church, and then leave it outside your shelter. He doesn't tell you why. You don't bother to ask. And he pays you for this. And you expect us to believe you?"

"Look mister, I didn't care what he wanted me to do. He gave me five hundred dollars. I'd do anything for that. I'd even jump off the Brooklyn Bridge. Well – maybe I wouldn't do that. But I don't intend upsettin' this guy by pokin' my nose where it don't belong. I wanted that five hundred smackers. And whether you want to believe me or not, that's the truth."

They believed him and returned him, complaining loudly, to a cell.

Hugh McKay and a female agent interviewed the woman and got more or less the same story. Money conquers all: particularly when you don't have any. You do what you're asked and keep your mouth shut.

Larry Douglas, Hugh McKay and Philip then began debriefing all the agents who had eyes on the church. They did so one at a time. It was getting close to four o'clock in the afternoon when they realized they were hungry and stopped for a very late lunch. They were almost finished when an agent came in.

"Excuse me, Special Agent Douglas, but there's a policeman on the phone who demands to speak to you."

"He wouldn't happen to be Officer O'Neil, would he?" asked Philip.

"Yes, that's the man."

"Switch the call in here," commanded Douglas.

"What's up, Paddy?" he asked.

He listened for a few minutes asking only one question.

"Thank you very much on behalf of Agent Pearson and the entire FBI. I much appreciate all you have done."

He replaced the phone and turned to smile at his companions

"It seems our indefatigable Paddy O'Neil not only made Evelyn Pearson as comfortable as he could while she was lying on the street, but went with the ambulance to Presbyterian Hospitable. She has been thoroughly examined and x-rayed. She has several cuts and bruises. Her hip is the most severely bruised area. Her femur is cracked but not broken. It will heal with time; nevertheless, as a precaution against further damage the doctor put the leg in a cast. Now that she has come out of the administered pain killing drug, she is raising hell over the cast. Claims it will keep her from her job. That's Evelyn for you. When I asked him why he decided to go to the hospital, he said to ask you Philip."

Philip Melville smiled.

"We never leave a comrade on the battlefield."

McKay had heard this said before but had never fully appreciated its substantive meaning to soldiers. However the look on Philip's face when he heard of Paddy's actions spoke volumes. The Special Forces had a bond which was immutable.

They quickly finished lunch and continued with the interviews. Nothing of any consequence was learned until they came to Agent Johansson at seven o'clock.

"I was assigned to watch a side door from a hiding place. No one approached the door. That's about all I can tell you, sir."

"So nothing unusual such as someone loitering near the door?" asked Hugh McKay.

"No sir. Everything was quiet. Except, of course, for the explosion. What a blast. I guess we learned it was a jeweler's store. And it killed twelve people. I thought it may have been the bomb in the church at first. I must say that was worrying."

The blast had the same effect on every agent they had interviewed. They had thought, 'This may be it. I'm about to die in a nuclear explosion.' However to their credit they did their jobs.

"And you stayed hidden all the time, watching the side door?" persisted McKay.

"Yes, sir. Well - when I heard the explosion I did take a peek outside to see if I was needed. But a few of our guys ran past me towards the church so I stayed at my post."

"Good," said Douglas and was prepared to end the interview, when one more question occurred to him.

"Did you see anyone other than the agents when you peeked outside?"

"There were only a few people. As in most cases of panic they didn't seem to know which way to run."

"Define few for me," asked McKay.

Somehow this apparently innocuous question sparked an increased interest on the part of Philip. He could not have defined why, yet his heart began to beat faster. He sat forward in his chair. McKay noticed this and thought, 'It seems the hunter has caught the scent of something'.

"Five," replied Johansson. "Two young women, a boy, a middle aged man and an old man. I didn't have time to take a detailed look at them. If it was necessary I doubt I could pick them out of a lineup."

"That's okay, I don't believe that will be necessary."

Douglas was proud of his agent. In the midst of a chaotic scenario and with only a peek, he had been able to itemize the people on the street.

Johansson smiled wryly as he recollected the scene.

"I had just gone back into my hiding place when I heard someone yell out. I thought it might be a cry for help, so I looked out once more. But it was only the old man. He was speeding away as quickly as he could walk. I thought he might fall but his cane kept him upright as he almost broke into a trot. Poor old guy."

Philip's sudden increased interest boiled over.

"Was this old man Asian?"

Hugh McKay recognized the intense tone of Philip's voice. He was definitely on to something. Unconsciously he sat bolt upright and held his breath as he waited for the answer.

"I couldn't tell. His back was to me by that time."

"Think carefully, Agent Johansson. Did he have a limp?"

"Why yes. It was noticeable as he rushed away."

"It was him," shouted out Philip, unable to contain himself.

"It was Red Hand!"

Chapter Forty Six

Douglas was nonplussed. Johansson was confused.

"You mean that old man was the one we were after?"

"I'm afraid it was," replied Philip. "He was heading to the side door, when he saw the agents racing towards the church and you come out of hiding. That's why he turned around and was going away from you. He didn't want you to see his face. And the cunning bastard still had the presence of mind to keep up the pretense of being an old man. Your suspicions would have been aroused if he had dropped his cane and ran."

"I was within twenty yards of him," moaned a distraught Johansson.

"There was no way for you to know. No one could have known," said Philip soothingly.

Douglas was already on the phone.

"I want reports from all points of exit from Manhattan. Our man was spotted attempting to approach the church. He is on the run. Have everyone intensify their surveillance. And check all CCTV's in the vicinity of the church."

Then he called the police control center.

"Our target was spotted at the church but escaped. He is on the run. Please have your men check in their areas for a recently rented or purchased apartment by a Chinese bearing the description previously given to you. By recent I mean within the last year."

He sat back in his chair with a sigh. Then he noted the distressed look on the face of Johansson.

"That's all Johansson, you may go. But you mustn't blame yourself. As Colonel Melville said, there was no way to know. In fact your keen observation has given us important information."

Johansson left still feeling badly. Douglas's words of praise had not made him feel any better.

Philip wasted no time.

"Let's put it together. It's now obvious Ma did not expect us to be at the church. His meticulous planning was knocked into a cocked hat by the insightful work of Officer Paddy O'Neil. He planned a diversion with the explosion at the jewelry store. It was meant to draw all police to the scene and away from the church. I wouldn't be surprised if one of the victims turns out to be his last recruit - the Chinese who hired the man and woman to go the church. They didn't know it but their real job was to distract any other policeman who may have lingered close to the church or any priest who may have been inside it. He intended to enter the side door and set the timer. I have no idea how he intended to get away. But you can bet it was carefully planned. I am guessing he had transportation lined up to get to Mexico and from there to a South American country."

"Well right now he's a hunted animal. And a hunted animal usually goes to ground. You're right to have apartments checked Larry. I doubt he would use a hotel, unless it was a flop house of some type. It still may be worth checking, particularly in the Chinatown area," added McKay.

Douglas went straight to the phone and issued instructions.

"I'm making the assumption Ma will now be so focused on escaping he will give up his rabid intention to kill both you guys. Even thought he won't know Phil has returned home. Am I right in that, Philip?" asked McKay.

"I believe so Hugh. He would only change his priority if he believed escape was impossible; and knowing him that is not even worth considering. He will have thought out every contingency. That's how his mind works."

"Hold on just a second," exclaimed McKay as a thought suddenly struck him.

He paused as he searched for the right words. Then they came pouring out.

"What you said about his planning is undoubtedly true, Philip. But maybe we're looking at this the wrong way. Go back to the comment you made about Paddy O'Neil. You said he knocked Ma's plans into a cocked hat. That being so, it may just be the case he no longer has a plan. All his painstaking efforts over a long period are now in total disarray. His contingencies were based on a successful nuclear explosion. But that's gone. So what does he do now?"

He stopped to take a breath.

"He's thinking on his feet. Making it up as he goes along; one step at a time," he postulated.

"Exactly," agreed Douglas. "And what does that lead to?"

"He's apt to make mistakes," interjected Philip. "By God, you're right, Hugh."

"Great – but being right – where does that get me? It doesn't lead to a solution," bemoaned McKay.

"I always said we had to outthink this bastard. So let's think like he would. We are on an island with exits guarded and observers on high alert. The police are combing neighborhoods looking for us. What would we do?"

"Like I said about any intelligent hunted animal, it goes to ground. Ma will stay hidden for a while then make a bolt for it. It's only then will he revert to one of his contingencies," said McKay.

"But how long will he wait?" mused Douglas.

"I imagine the mayor of New York has many of the same problems as our mayor in Vancouver. Once he's informed there no longer exists a threat of a nuclear explosion, he's going to give in to the impatient outcries of his citizens. They won't put up with every mode of transportation being held up as each one is searched for this man. He'll lift the searches to let traffic flow normally. That's when he'll go," averred Hugh McKay sorrowfully.

"We can't let him escape! We can't! We were so damned close," said an exasperated Philip. "Okay let's say the traffic checking is lifted. Ma will know we will keep men posted at every exit. What type of transportation will he attempt to use?"

"It'll be easier to rule out the ones he won't use," suggested Douglas. "And we shouldn't forget between FBI Headquarters, CIA Langley and the vast capability of NSA in Maryland we have people monitoring surveillance cameras at all public transportation boarding areas."

"That's a good point, Larry. Let's write those on the board," added McKay.

"Well that rules out major airports, ferries, buses, subways, trains, helicopters; and we have issued an alert to private airports. We will receive information on all passengers before any aircraft is permitted to take off," said Douglas "He can use one of his disguises but he will still look Asian. That's in our favor."

"Maybe he can or maybe he can't," said a pensive Philip.

"Can or can't what?" asked a perplexed Douglas.

"Use a disguise. Going back to something Hugh said. He's on the run. My guess is that wherever he was staying he will abandon it and not go back. He may be afraid our dragnet will have found that location. We found the apartment he rented from Chua. We found the bomb. If he doesn't go back to his hiding place he will be without his disguises. Of course he can buy others but that means going outside. If our earlier hypothesis holds water, he will have gone to ground and will stay hidden for at least the next day or two."

"Let's get back to ways out of Manhattan," said the dogged McKay.

"Okay, we have requested all taxi and limo companies to alert us should an Asian man ask to be taken off the island. However we have to admit money talks. We can only hope they comply," said Douglas. "Of course there still remains a private car or a fast boat. I would put my money on one of those and more probably a car."

There were tired nods of agreement. The tiredness was brought on, not so much by the efforts of the day, but by the disappointment at missing Ma and consequent dissipation of adrenaline.

"I think we should call it a day," said McKay. "I don't know about you fellows but after our late lunch, I'm not too hungry. But I could certainly use a drink."

That met with unanimous approval. Douglas called for ice and a few snacks to be sent to the meeting room. As if his mind had been read the door opened and agents brought in ice, potato chips, pretzels, cheese and crackers.

They were halfway through their first drink when an agent burst in.

"Colonel Melville, the prisoner Chua wants to see you urgently."

They all slammed their glasses on the table and raced to Chua's room.

"What is it?" demanded a breathless Philip.

"One of my men has found the apartment where your Chinese has been living. It is in an old boarding house, room 15. He is registered under the name of Shue. Here is the address. My men are standing guard in case Shue returns. Now can I leave?"

"Maybe tomorrow. Meantime we have located the bomb. You and your family are safe. But I want you to stay here until we have checked your information."

"Then why can't I leave tonight?"

"Because tomorrow you will tell me the information you are still holding back."

With that they rushed out leaving Chua with a wondering look on his face.

"That one's too damned smart," he muttered in Cantonese.

It didn't take long to travel to Chinatown. The sirens on their cars blared loudly clearing the way. Two of Chua's men stood outside room 15 looking decidedly smug. Like their boss they had little regard for officers of the law. The Chinese lived by their own laws.

"Did Shue come back?" demanded Douglas, ignoring their looks.

The men stared blankly at him as though they didn't speak English.

Philip repeated the question in Cantonese and then added.

"Don't try to kid me you don't speak English. If you do you will be sharing a cell with Chua for a long time. Is that what you want?"

"No sir," said one of them. "Sorry, I didn't quite understand the other gentleman's question," he lied in perfect English. "No one has returned. The landlady has not seen him all day. But a few of his things are still in the room. We touched nothing, sir."

Philip turned to one of the accompanying agents.

"Don't let these two leave. If they try to go, shoot them – in the balls!"

The Chinese fell back against the corridor wall with the smug looks now replaced with ones of fear. This man not only spoke their tongue but also used Chinese threats.

Once inside the room, Douglas and McKay began a thorough search.

"A few clothes, that's all. We'll bag them for analysis but I don't expect much," said Douglas. "I'll leave two men just in case he returns. But I doubt it. He hasn't left anything of real value. No computer, mobile telephone or cash."

"Any sign of his disguises?" asked Philip.

"No, they're gone too."

"Damnation."

On the way back to the safe house, Philip was quiet for most of the journey. Suddenly he said to Douglas, "Can you call ahead and ask Agent Johansson to be available?"

"Sure, but why?"

"I have one more question for him."

Then he lapsed back into silence until they reached the safe house. Upon arriving he bounded up the stairs to the meeting room where Johansson was waiting.

"Agent Johansson. The old man you saw. Was he carrying anything?"

"Why yes, sir – a suitcase – and it looked heavy. That's why he was struggling so much to move quickly."

"Damn, damn, damn."

"Sir?" said a startled Johansson.

"Oh, nothing. That'll be all, agent. Thank you."

When Johansson had left it was Hugh McKay who spoke.

"He was carrying all he required to stay on the run, including all his money. That kind of blows away our hope Ma would be without resources. He can still be very dangerous and elusive."

"That's right Hugh. But he still has to be laying low somewhere. Maybe something will turn up tomorrow."

"Let's hope so," said McKay. "Anyone for that drink we almost had earlier?"

"If you'll excuse me, I had better check in with my team," said Douglas.

"How about you, Philip?" asked McKay.

"I'll join you for a quick one. After that I should call Mei Li, and then get an early night. Maybe something will come to me during the night. I doubt I'll get much sleep."

"Do you want a sleeping pill?" offered McKay.

"No thanks, Hugh. I often do my best thinking in the dark. It's a bad habit I picked up in 'Nam."

If Philip hoped to do some serious thinking that night, he was not the only one. In a hospital bed in Presbyterian Hospital someone else had the same thought.

Ma Guan-lui knew it would soon be time to make his move.

Chapter Forty Seven

When the ambulance arrived, he was lying on the sidewalk feigning unconsciousness, but he still clutched his securely locked suitcase firmly in his hand. He was carefully loaded into the ambulance. Once they were moving, he fluttered his eyes open.

"Where am I? What happened?"

"There is no need to worry, sir. You were found lying on the street, unconscious."

"Where are you taking me?"

"To a hospital for a check up. Everything will be all right. Now let's give you a brief examination."

"If you think that's necessary," he responded with a false weak voice.

"It's our normal procedure. We can pass along our findings to the hospital. But first a few questions. What happened exactly?"

"I don't know. I was walking to the hotel and the next thing I know I was with you. I suppose I must have fainted."

"What is your name, sir?"

"Wong," he said and reached for the fictitious Canadian passport in his pocket. The passport showed an address in Toronto.

He closed his eyes as though indicating this effort had been too much for him.

Ma had learned many things during his time serving in the Red Brigade of Mao. Much time had been devoted to teaching comrades to survive interrogation after capture. One of those tricks was to artificially speed up one's heart rate to simulate a condition close to death. This was intended to have the enemy postpone further torture for fear of killing the subject before extracting essential information. This bought time. And time was a critical element in capture. It delayed the infliction of pain, perhaps for quite a long time. And it gave one's own troops the opportunity for rescue.

Now he used that well learned technique, as the attendant went through his usual check list.

"My God, look at his heart rate," exclaimed a worried attendant. "Call ahead and have an emergency unit waiting."

"Do you have relatives in the city, Mr. Wong?"

He kept his eyes closed pretending to have lapsed back into unconsciousness. This was a necessary part of his act. It avoided the need to answer further questions.

When they arrived at the hospital he had slowed his heart rate considerably. The waiting hospital staff quickly transferred him to a gurney. Almost immediately he attempted to get off the gurney.

"I'm sorry to have troubled you but I feel perfectly all right now. I must get to the Hilton Hotel to meet my son. He is arriving from Hong Kong."

"I'm sorry sir," said the waiting physician. "But you were very sick. We need to run a few checks before releasing you."

"If you believe that is wise," he relented. "But may I use your telephone to leave a message for my son?"

"Of course, sir. Please sit in this wheel chair and our attendant will take you to a phone."

He dialed a series of numbers but cunningly cut off the connection. After speaking into the dead phone he hung up.

"My son has not yet arrived. It was suggested I call the airline. May I make one more call?"

"Certainly."

He used the same trick.

"It seems my son's flight was delayed and will not arrive until tomorrow. But really I feel quite well. Perhaps I should leave."

"I would strongly advise against that. You had better stay the night. We can keep you under observation. If all is well tomorrow you may leave. Obviously we have no right to keep you here. But if you choose to leave you must sign a waiver."

"If you truly believe I should stay, doctor, it would be foolish of me to refuse."

The face of Ma Guan-lui was solemn but inside he was a very happy man.

Everything was going according to his improvised plan.

He was taken to a private room on the fourth floor. When a male nurse attempted to undress him he insisted on doing so himself.

"Very well, Mr. Wong. Here is a gown and socks. You can change in the bathroom then I'll hang your clothes in the wardrobe. I'm going to get some things to check your vital statistics. I shall be back in a few minutes. By the time he came back, Ma was already in bed with his clothes neatly hung.

"My, that was quick. Now I just have to check your blood pressure, your heart rate and your oxygen level."

Ma artificially elevated his heart rate but not to a very high level. The nurse marked everything down on a record sheet clipped to a board, which was then left hanging at the bottom of his bed.

"Hmm, your heart rate is still high. A doctor will be by later to have a look at you. Meantime you should just rest. Here's a menu card, simply tick your choices for dinner tonight. I'll be back a bit later to collect it. Would you like the television on?"

"Yes, please. To a news channel."

The news was full of the explosion. From the description of the number of deaths and where the victims had been standing, he knew he had achieved his objective of killing the two men who knew him. That was the only thing that pleased him. After about two years of careful planning he had failed to detonate his bomb. He clenched his teeth to prevent a scream of frustration spilling out of his mouth.

'I will be back, Melville, and you will surely die,' he thought as his eyes blazed with a fury which burned down deep inside him.

He slammed his hand on the bed.

"Take control of yourself, Guan-lui," he muttered. His heart was racing and this time he had not surreptitiously induced it. He took a few deep breaths to regain control of his emotions and then began thinking about his next moves.

He still had to escape from the hospital and get out of the country. Escaping from the hospital would certainly not be a problem. It was simply a matter of timing. Probably around one in the morning would be the best time, but not tomorrow; he would spend another day in hospital to let things settle down. Then he would have to retrieve the stolen car from the parking garage and drive out of Manhattan. That shouldn't be a problem; he still had a few disguises in his suitcase. He would drive to the Carolinas and from there take a bus to a Texas border town and then across into Mexico. It should be quite simple. And he still had a suitcase stacked with lots and lots of money and several gold bars. If necessary, bribery would present no difficulty.

Then, of course, he still had the fortune he had purloined and stashed in foreign banks; all easy to access with his portable computer. When he had finally settled in another country he was confident he could once again build a highly sophisticated computer set up. He would be without the two specialist items he had stolen from Jean Mercier in Canada. Nevertheless it would be adequate to once again plot his revenge on America and specifically Melville and Hughes.

'This time I'll travel to Honolulu and take care of them first,' he mused.

He congratulated himself on his quick-thinking initiative to be admitted to hospital. It was the last place the FBI would dream of looking for him. And it would give him time to further develop his plans. But that could wait until tomorrow. He had all day to do so.

About an hour later a doctor came to see him. Ma performed his trick and slightly raised his heart rate. After concluding his examination the doctor looked a little concerned.

"Have you recently been worried about anything in particular, Mr. Wong?"

"No doctor, however I have been very excited over the prospect of seeing my son again. It has been three years. He is flying in from Hong Kong tomorrow night."

"That could be the reason your heart rate is still high, Mr. Wong. There doesn't seem to be any other reason. But just to be sure I'm going to have some blood drawn for analysis and have you put on a vitamin IV. I'll check on you in the morning. Perhaps a good night's sleep will do you good. It often does when someone is overexcited."

After a surprisingly good dinner, Ma read the evening newspaper then watched some television. At ten o'clock a lady nurse came to check on him.

"My name is Lilly and I will be your night nurse. If you need anything just press this call buzzer. If at any time you want to sleep and not be disturbed press this button. It lights up a message outside you door which reads, do not disturb."

She then produced a hypodermic needle.

"What's that for?"

"Don't worry I'm not going to stick you with it. It's only your vitamins which I'll inject into you IV fluid."

"Oh, I see."

"Remember if you should require anything don't hesitate to call me, Mr. Wong."

What nurse Lilly hadn't told him was, the hypodermic not only contained vitamins but also a sleeping solution. Shortly afterwards, he began feeling drowsy. Before dropping off he once again rejoiced in the thought, 'Everything is going according to my new plan.'

But he was wrong.

Chapter Forty Eight

Ma wakened abruptly. Automatically he looked at the bedside clock – three-twenty-four. Sweat was beaded on his forehead. He had dreamt he was in the church crypt when the bomb exploded. And in his nightmare he could actually see pieces of his body fly in all directions. The most lurid and vivid part of his dream was he was holding his club foot. His fingers were touching it.

Fingers *were* touching it! Not his – Nurse Lilly's.

In his nightmare he had tossed and turned, throwing off his blanket and sheet. Even his socks had come off. He must have cried out because the nurse had hurried in to check on him. She saw his club foot and was attempting to put his sock back on.

"You poor dear, you've had a bad dream. I'll get you a wet towel. You know, Mr. Wong, you should have told us about your foot. I'll tape your sock on to prevent it coming off again. And I'll put a note in your file so the doctor will know."

Once she had reorganized his bedding she left to fetch the wet towel. He lay there with his mind working furiously. Most probably his foot would create no problem; however, he knew his description would have been widely circulated by the police as a matter of the highest priority. There was a remote possibility this notification could have reached the hospital security. And however remote, it was something he could not ignore. To have failed to explode the bomb was a searing debacle which would plague his mind for a long time. His road to fulfill his blazing vengeance had been blocked. Blisteringly disappointing as this was; to also be caught was totally unimaginable suffering. He knew what had to be done. He pretended to have fallen back asleep when she returned. She gently washed his sweaty face, checked his IV, switched off his overhead light and left quietly.

He waited forty minutes then crept out of bed. He looked for the supply room and found it was only fifteen yards from his room. He cautiously entered and soon discovered all he required. A pair of rubber gloves; a linen trolley; a sheet; and the location of the dirty linen chute to the laundry. Calmly he put on the gloves took the trolley and the sheet to his room then rang for the nurse, keeping his light off.

"Yes, Mr. Wong?" called out Lilly as she reached for the light.

She didn't make it. He had been behind the door. Although he had a slender build, his hands and arms were strong and his vast killing expertise included snapping necks. Hers broke quite easily. Almost casually he stuffed her body into the linen trolley, covered her with a sheet, wheeled her to the supply closet and unceremoniously pushed her down the dirty linen chute.

With an unruffled demeanor he found his chart at her desk and continuing to wear the rubber gloves to avoid leaving fingerprints, removed the note concerning his foot. Back in his room he locked the gloves in his suitcase. He had no intention of discarding them in a waste basket. There was always the off chance the police may search waste baskets. And cautiousness was a rule he always adhered to.

Once in bed the killing had the usual effect on him. It made him lust for more. The flame of his vengeance was rekindled as he lay there imagining all the ways he could kill Melville and Hughes.

With these delicious thoughts, he drifted off to sleep.

It was after five before Nurse Lilly's presence was missed. The night supervisor notified security but Lilly could not be found. A little after eight as the laundry was coming into full swing, a Haitian worker had to struggle mightily to pull out the unusually heavy cart at the bottom of the chute. He tossed a mound of blankets, sheets, night gowns, towels and socks, into the washing machine. Ultimately his hands found Nurse Lilly.

His scream of terror startled the other laundry workers. They all came running and stood transfixed at the sight of the body. At last one had the presence of mind to call security.

Security guards arrived quickly and instantly decided this was a job for the police homicide department.

Detectives Malone and Jackson were dispatched along with the medical examiner and a forensics team. Once the cause of death had been established the questioning of staff began. This took a long time and proved disappointingly fruitless. They then interviewed the patients resident on the floor, two of whom were questioned in the physical therapy room.

"We are still missing one," Malone said to one of the nurses on duty.

"Oh, that's Mr. Wong. He was brought in with a dangerously high heart rate. We are keeping him under observation. He is exercising by walking around the ward. He is probably on the other side at the moment."

They caught up with Mr. Wong as he came around the corner accompanied by a nurse. They eyed this slimly built Asian man walking very slowly with the aid of a borrowed cane, and were ready to dismiss him instantly. Nevertheless duty demanded they ask the obligatory questions. They received the same answer they had gotten from every other patient. He had been asleep all night and neither saw nor heard anything.

"Time for a coffee and a sandwich, Charlie," said Detective Malone dispiritedly after glancing at his watch.

"Sure thing, Joe, let's go the cafeteria. First I'll call in and give the boss the bad news."

He dialed a number.

"Forensics came up with zilch and we've discovered nothing. I've faxed over a list of everyone we've interviewed. Someone should run a check on them. Yeah that's all. What? Really? Okay you're the boss."

"What is it?" asked Jackson.

"He wants us to wait and interview the night shift when they report."

"Oh great."

That day was Paddy's day off. Not exactly positive why, and rather self-consciously, he went to the flower shop in Presbyterian Hospital and bought a large bouquet. As he walked along the hallway a voice yelled out to him.

"Oh, you shouldn't have, Paddy. That's so nice of you. I didn't know you cared so much."

Paddy turned to see the grinning face of Detective Joe Malone.

"Hi, Joe, hello Charlie. What are you guys doing here?"

"Well some kid lost his roller skates and we were sent to find them," said Jackson.

"Ask a silly question and you get a silly answer. Okay a homicide – but here in the hospital?"

"Yup. A nurse had her neck broken."

"Where was this?"

"Well we found her in the laundry room. But she worked on the fourth floor. That's not where your girlfriend is, is it?" asked Malone

"No, and she's not my girlfriend."

"Yeah, yeah," said Jackson derisively. "Want to join us for a coffee and a bite to eat?"

"I'll join you once I leave off these flowers."

"Well don't take too long with your goodbyes, we only have about five hours to spare," teased Malone.

The detectives went on their way chuckling. Malone and Jackson were two of the best detectives on the squad. Their joking was a way of handling the often gruesome nature of their work. Any death was a tragedy but some of the victims they investigated were so badly mutilated it took a strong stomach not to throw up. It had taken a long time for this pair of detectives to become sufficiently hardened to the point they could do their job without becoming overly distressed. Some crimes still left them nauseated but not to the point of throwing up. Away from the crime scenes humor was one way of remaining sane.

They had an enviable record of solving crimes. Paddy had worked with them on a few occasions and respected their ability. In turn the detectives had seen enough of Paddy at work to have the highest regard for his dedication and capability.

Paddy took the elevator to the third floor and walked hesitantly towards Agent Pearson's room. This was a man who had faced death on several occasions yet now he was more than a little apprehensive about visiting a lady. He took a deep breath and entered her room.

"Don't you ever knock?" demanded Pearson as she quickly arranged her gown and pulled the sheet up to her chin.

"I'm—m, s--sorry," stammered Paddy. "The door was open. I only wanted to see how you were – and to give you these."

He held out the flowers.

Evelyn Pearson was embarrassed.

"They're beautiful. Thank you, Officer O'Neil. I really didn't mean to bark at you. Working in the FBI with all those men who believe they're so macho, and trying to hold my own, has made me attempt to be tougher than they are. I'm afraid it had given me the reputation of being a hard case. Sometimes I forget I am also a lady. Will you please forgive me?"

She flashed such a lovely smile that Paddy felt his face redden.

"Oh don't mention it. It must be a difficult job, Agent Pearson."

"And this damned cast isn't improving my attitude. It itches like blazes. It's driving me crazy. They gave me this."

She held up a long stick which had a little wooden hand at the end.

"One of the nurses said in Japan it's called a grandson's hand. But I've spent much of this morning trying to maneuver it to reach down this cast. I think I've just about got it."

She abruptly stopped talking.

"Oh, here I am going on about a little thing like this and leaving you holding those lovely flowers. I'll get the nurse to put then in a vase."

When the nurse had relieved Paddy of the flowers he stood tongue-tied. He didn't quite know what to say or do.

"Well, good luck, Agent Pearson. I suppose I should go now."

"I don't know you first name, Officer O'Neil. Mine is Evelyn."

"It's Paddy."

"Could you stay for a little while, Paddy? It would be nice to have someone to talk to."

Paddy felt his face redden again.

"Okay, sure."

He could have kicked himself at this inarticulate response. It wasn't that he was overly intimidated by this self confessed hard case; he merely didn't know what they could have in common to talk about.

He pulled up a chair closer to her bed and to his astonishment he found he had no difficulty talking to her. In fact twenty minutes seemed to pass in a flash. That's when the nurse returned.

"It's time for you walk, Evelyn. As this is an all women's ward, I suggest your gentleman friend comes back later. Our gowns tie at the back and you don't want him to see your pretty little tush waddling along the ward, Do you?"

This time it was Evelyn's turn to blush.

"Sorry, Paddy. I have to do this. I hope to get out of here soon and they won't release me until I can prove I'm mobile. Could you come back some time?"

"Actually I can join a couple of detectives I know. They are in the cafeteria. Maybe I could come back in an hour."

"No, that won't do," said the nurse. "After the walk it will be lunch time and we don't allow non-family members back in until three o'clock."

"Okay I'll come back then if that's all right, Evelyn."

"Great, I'll see you then."

But she didn't stop there; her FBI mind had been intrigued by something Paddy said.

"Detectives? What are they doing here?"

Her question was curt. In the blink of an eye, she had changed back to Agent Pearson of the FBI."

"A nurse was murdered last night. Haven't you heard?"

"No, I haven't. That's terrible. I'll get the details from my nurse while I walk."

There was another blink of the eye and she returned to Evelyn. She reached out and touched Paddy's hand.

"Thanks again for the flowers, Paddy. I'll see you later then?"

Paddy wasn't sure his feet were touching the ground as he made his way to the cafeteria. He felt like he was walking on air.

Chapter Forty Nine

That was the antithesis of the feeling experienced that morning by Philip. He hadn't slept at all and to his dismay he had no flash of insightfulness during the night. Worse still the FBI had uncovered no sign of Red Hand.

With the threat of a nuclear attack avoided, the task force had disbanded and the other members had returned to their home bases. All had received messages of congratulations and gratitude from the president and the prime minister. That left Philip with only McKay and Douglas at the breakfast table. The conversation was stilted and desultory.

"Maybe we'll get a break today," said McKay without much conviction.

"It had better be today," responded Philip disconsolately.

His hunter's instinct told him Ma was still in Manhattan. He believed Red Hand would wait for a day two at the most, then make a run for it. And he would have a plan.

Larry Douglas interrupted his thoughts.

"I still believe his most likely way out is by car. As you probably know one must pay at bridges and tunnels to enter Manhattan but not to leave. That makes it difficult to spot a suspect. However, in collaboration with NYPD, we have men with binoculars posted at every exit point. I have also issued orders to strengthen the searches at all points of entry into Mexico."

"Very good, Larry."

Douglas rose to leave.

"I'll just check in with my team,"

This was nothing more to do than to hope for good news. Waiting around was the most frustrating part of any manhunt. Before leaving he turned again to Philip.

"Oh, by the way, what do you want us to do with the gangster, Chua, Philip?"

"Hell, I had forgotten him. I'll see him now. I have one more question for him then he can go."

"Mind if I tag along?" asked McKay.

"Not at all."

Chua was in a grumpy mood. Quite apart from being held overnight, scrambled eggs and bacon was not his idea of a Chinese breakfast.

"Can I get out of here now?" he demanded churlishly.

"After you tell me exactly what you have been holding back from me."

"I told you everything I know," yelled Chua, hoping his bluff would work.

It was his policy never to reveal all he knew. In Chinatown knowledge and information were considered to be of paramount importance. The more one had, the more powerful one was. And he was the most powerful gangster. Through experience he had learned even a little piece of information may one day prove useful.

"Well if that's all you have to say, enjoy your stay," said Philip and rose to leave.

"Okay, wait a minute," relented Chua.

Since he had been unable to fool this man, he was now much more concerned at being away from his business than retaining an insignificant piece of information.

"The man calling himself Shue, had a visitor."

"His name?"

"Tan Chin Chye."

"And what is his specialty?"

"He's the best safe cracker in Chinatown. We call him Light Fingers Chye."

"And what was the job?"

"My sources tell me he didn't agree to do the job himself. He regarded it as being beneath his dignity. He hired some young punk to do it. The young punk had been overheard boasting he was going into partnership with Tan. Stupid idiot. Tan would never be associated with such a third rater. And Tan never engaged in armed robbery but this young kid did."

"And the target?" asked Philip although he believed he already knew the answer.

"The jewelry store that blew up," confirmed Chua. "And before you ask me, I couldn't find out what went wrong. The kid must have used too much dynamite to blow the safe."

"You know that's not true, don't you Chua?"

The hooded eyes of Chua became narrow slits as he yet again upgraded his respect for his questioner. He had never known anyone like him. He seemed to be reading his mind.

'He must have been raised by Chinese to know so much about us,' he thought and shivered a little.

"It's possible both Tan and the punk were set up. It is also possible Tan was killed in the blast."

"That is correct, Chua. It was a diversion to draw the police away from the nuclear bomb. So now you know I wasn't lying to you. The bomb is now disarmed as I told you. Have your men found this man Shue?"

"No. He has vanished like a night shadow when the sun rises. I can only tell you he is not in Chinatown."

"You can go home now, Chua."

He fought against it tenaciously but all his Chinese upbringing and values overcame his willpower. He could not prevent it from happening. The greatly respected and most feared gangster in Chinatown rose to his feet and bowed to Philip.

"Thank you for saving my grandson," he said softly, and stayed bowed until Philip had left the cell.

Once outside the cell an astonished McKay leaned against the wall of the corridor.

"Wow, I've never seen anything like that," he breathed. "I've had many cases in the large Chinatown we have in Vancouver, but I have never seen or even heard of a top boss acting that way. How'd you do it?"

Philip smiled.

"Years of experience at close quarters," he replied. "Firstly, I spent all those years in Vietnam where the Chinese ruled for almost a thousand years; consequently there is a large Chinese population. But much more importantly – my wife is half Chinese."

"Of course – Mei Li. I should have remembered."

They walked back to the meeting room where Douglas was waiting.

"Did you learn anything useful?" he asked hopefully.

"Not really. Only that Red Hand is not in Chinatown. Unfortunately Chua has no idea where he is."

"Do you believe he was telling the truth?"

"I can assure you he was. You should have seen the way Philip handled him. Oh, he was telling the truth all right," averred an admiring McKay.

"In that case I can call off the search teams in Chinatown and transfer them to smaller hostelries in other areas of Manhattan. We have checked the CCTV tapes at all the larger hotels and motels without success. But the smaller places tend to be outside the city. I still don't see how he could have gotten there. Agent Johansson told us he turned onto Lexington. We checked the CCTV tapes at nearby subway stations with no luck. We checked all taxi companies but no one matching Red Hand's description was picked up around that area. He just vanished into thin air. God this is so frustrating, it's driving me crazy."

"Let's agree he didn't vanish. There must be an explanation, but I can't think what it could be," said Philip rubbing his temples.

"You haven't slept for quite some time, Philip. Perhaps you should take a nap for a few hours. I'll wake you if anything crops up," said McKay.

"You're probably right, Hugh. I'm of little use in this condition. And a nap will be infinitely better than sitting here waiting. Watching a clock go oh so slowly around when you have nothing to do is a cruel torment."

Chapter Fifty

A few miles away someone else was watching the clock go round. Paddy had joined Malone and Jackson for a coffee and was impatiently wondering what he would do until three o'clock. He decided he may as well wait in the hospital, so he ordered lunch. Then he forced himself to refocus on the ongoing conversation.

"It was definitely a professional job. The neck had been snapped so cleanly it must have been wrenched by someone well practiced in doing so," said Malone.

"You mean like a professional soldier?" asked Paddy.

"Yeah, exactly."

Malone and Jackson exchanged smiling looks.

"And where were you this morning around three o'clock, Officer O'Neil? With your background you are the perfect suspect," said Jackson with almost, but not quite, a straight face.

Paddy didn't fall for the gag.

"So your hypothesis is a professional killer was roving the fourth floor ward in the middle of the night. That can only mean it was a hit. But who would want to kill a nurse? And why would he do so in a hospital? It would be much easier to do it outside or at her home. It doesn't make sense."

"Hey, take it easy, Paddy. We're supposed to be the detectives," protested Malone.

But the look he gave his partner indicated he had high regard for Paddy's analysis.

"You two realize you have wasted your time interviewing the daytime staff. Don't you? If it was a staff member, which is a distinct possibility, it must have been someone on the nightshift," continued Paddy.

"Thanks, Sherlock. We already came to that conclusion. And before you give us any more of your deductions, we already checked the nightshift register. All women. None of whom has a military background or is known to be a martial arts expert," said Jackson.

Paddy opened his mouth to speak, but Jackson put up his hand to stop him.

"I know, I know, you were going to say there must have been a few male doctors on duty. There were three; however, as is normal, they are on duty for emergencies, and wait in the doctor's lounge on the second floor until called. As far as we know none of them was called to the fourth floor. But we have been instructed to wait until the nightshift shows up to interview everyone. Meantime we have people back at the station running a full background check on the nurse. The initial check turned up nothing unusual. She was a typical young woman living in New York. Making enough money to pay the rent, live within her means, and put a bit away in a small savings account. She had no steady male friend and visited her folks in New Jersey on a Sunday."

Paddy digested this information before asking another question.

"And you're assuming the killing took place on the fourth floor?"

Both detectives looked sharply at him. They had not considered an alternative.

"What do you mean?" demanded Malone.

"It may not be likely, but it is just possible, someone on another floor called the nurse for assistance or something. You told me the body was found in the laundry area. The laundry shoot runs all the way from the top floor to the laundry."

"We'll look into that," said Malone.

"And, no doubt, you'll be interviewing the patients."

"Officer O'Neil, is it your considered opinion a hit man had himself admitted to hospital, waited until the early morning hours, then committed murder?"

"I know it's improbable, but it was only a thought."

"We already interviewed the patients on the nurse's floor. No one seemed to us to be a professional hit man but we sent their info' to headquarters for a more thorough background check. And we confirmed that no fourth floor patient from yesterday has checked out of the hospital today. Before you ask, no, we haven't yet checked the other floors, but we will."

The detectives stood.

"We had better get back to work. Before we go is there anything further you wish us to follow up on, *boss*?" asked Jackson teasingly.

"Sorry fellows, I didn't mean to butt in," said Paddy in embarrassment.

"Forget it Paddy, I'm only yanking your chain," replied Jackson with a grin. "See you around."

"Take care, guys."

Walking to the elevator, the two men looked at one another and chuckled.

"You know, Joe, all kidding aside, Paddy would make a good detective."

"Nah, he's too nice a guy, Charlie. Too often our work finds us in the gutter. And it ain't pretty down there."

"Amen to that."

"Well we better do what the *boss* suggested, and check those other floors," said Malone resignedly.

"I wouldn't be surprised if Paddy came around to see if we were doing exactly that. Let's start one floor on either side of four."

"Maybe I should check in again with the station to see if they've come up with anything yet."

"Good idea, Joe. You do that and I'll get started on floor five."

Little did the detectives know, they had started a rapid train of thought in the mind of a patient on the fourth floor. After being interviewed Ma had returned to his room. He closed the door and put his suitcase on his bed. He checked his weapons and removed the revolver from the bottom of the case. He fitted it with a silencer and laid it handily on top of his other things. He placed a sheathed knife along side it. Then he carefully checked his disguises. He selected the one he had used at the Morristown Airport. He would stride confidently out of the hospital dressed in expensive clothes with a wide brimmed hat pulled over his face. He would use the hospital cane to obscure his limp and affix a false beard to cover his scar. Satisfied he relocked his suitcase and settled back in his bed to think.

While the detectives were interviewing him, they hadn't noticed he was circumspectly studying their eyes. He was confident the eyes showed not the slightest detection of who he may be. However, he believed if they were diligent they would undoubtedly conduct a background check on everyone they interviewed. That was a flashing red light of danger. Such checks would take time. He guessed it would take until the next morning. Therefore as his primary plan he would stick with his original timetable of leaving after midnight. Nevertheless in the off chance the background checks were completed by later today, he would also devise a contingency plan. He closed his eyes in concentration as he went through a series of possibilities. When he opened his eyes he had selected the best option.

First he had decided on the premises upon which his plan would be based.

Item 1: - His long ago carefully planted cover story indicated his name was Wong and he had been born in West Malaysia where a third of the population was Chinese. He had come to Canada as a young man and had taken out Canadian citizenship. He now lived in Toronto. These were sufficient specifics to at least slow down anyone looking for a man born in China and now residing in Vancouver.

Item 2: - Assuming an intelligent investigator still believed Mr. Wong was worthy of further investigation after checking all the names. Such a decision could not be made until later tonight.

Item 3: - The two detectives who had interviewed him would be off duty by that time. Therefore a further check would most likely not be conducted until tomorrow.

That being the case no further planning was necessary. He would go ahead with his primary plan.

Item 4: - Should the police decide the matter could not wait until tomorrow, a different team would be sent tonight. In such a case a brazen plan was essential.

Having established the basic premises he selected the following plan.

Step 1: - If one man was sent he would shoot him and place the body under his covers. Anyone giving the room a cursory check would assume the body was him. Then he would dress in his new disguise, press the do not disturb button and leave the hospital. If two men came he would shoot both and put the second body in the wardrobe.

Step 2: - Hopefully the body or bodies would not be discovered for several hours, by then he would be out of Manhattan.

Step 3: - If an alarm was raised before that time he calculated it would take him ten minutes to execute any investigator, dress in his disguise and exit the hospital. Taxis were readily available. It would take fifteen minutes at most to reach the closest subway station to the parking garage. He would instruct the taxi driver to drop him there.

Step 4: - The police would check taxi companies and find out where he had gone. This would require about fifteen to twenty minutes. They would go to the subway station and check there. That would take another ten minutes. They would also send teams to stations further down the line to stop trains and look for him.

Step 5: - The most likely escape route the police or FBI would consider would be the Lincoln tunnel or the Holland tunnel. Instead he would take a bridge east and drive to the Bronx where he had rented an apartment three months ago. He then had several options. Stay there for whatever time he felt was safe and go south. Or, stay for a while then go back north to Canada where he owned an apartment in Montreal. Or take the Tappan Zee Bridge and go west, before ultimately heading for Mexico.

He didn't have to make a decision at this time. With the benefit of the stolen police radio he could monitor transmissions and make an appropriate choice based on police activity.

Satisfied with his contingencies upon contingencies, he lay back to rest. He felt confident he had thought of every possible eventuality and his escape was assured. He smiled with satisfaction at having outwitted, Phil Hughes, Philip Melville, Hugh McKay, the entire task force and the FBI.

Unfortunately for Ma Guan-lui, the notorious Red Hand, he had not heard of, therefore not taken into account, one other person - Agent Evelyn Pearson.

Chapter Fifty One

At precisely three o'clock, Paddy knocked on Evelyn's door.

"Come in."

Even in his haste to greet her and sit close to her bed, he noticed the difference. She wore a deep pink lipstick, her cheeks were rouged, her eyes appeared more luminous with the careful application of eye shadow and mascara and her hair was beautifully coiffed.

His balloon of delight at her having taken all this preparation for him was burst by her first question.

"Any further developments concerning the murder of the nurse?"

A cloud of disappointment came over Paddy, and somewhat reluctantly he told her all about his conversations with Malone and Jackson. She sat forward, listening intently, and asked several questions. Once the subject appeared to be exhausted, she put her head back on the pillow and thought for a minute.

Abruptly she sat upright.

"Oh, God. I did it again, didn't I?"

Paddy looked puzzled.

"I'm so sorry, Paddy. Here you are giving up your precious day off to visit me; and what so I do? I put on my FBI hat and forget to be sociable. Can you forgive me, Paddy?"

She gave him the coyest of looks. They both burst out laughing.

"But I am so very sorry; and after I spent so much time getting all made up to impress you. You probably didn't even notice."

Another coy look as she fished for a compliment. Paddy's cloud of disappointment was completely dispelled.

"Well I did, and you are beautiful."

Thereafter the conversation was totally uninhibited. They talked for an hour. Then the nurse appeared.

"Time for your afternoon walk, Evelyn. Sorry but you must leave, sir."

"I understand. If I may I'll call you tonight and maybe squeeze in some time to visit you tomorrow."

"Oh, that would be great. Here's the number. It's the nurses' station but they will put you through to me. Can you give me your number?"

Paddy handed her a card.

"The top number is my home phone and the lower one is my police mobile number. Feel free to call me anytime."

"Bye Paddy. And thanks again for the gorgeous flowers."

He waved goodbye and again floated along the corridor on the way out.

At the time Paddy had entered Evelyn's room, Philip was wakening from his nap. He was better rested yet something had tugged at his mind, something he could no longer remember. He had a quick shower and went downstairs to join the others feeling refreshed but frustrated.

"You look better," said Douglas.

"Thanks, sorry for deserting you but I did need that sleep."

"You didn't happen to come up with a solution did you?" asked McKay in a semi-jocular manner.

When Philip's face didn't break into a smile at his comment but rather wore a frown, McKay also turned serious.

"You *did* come up with something."

"When I went to bed something was on my mind. It was a kind of word association. But by then I was so exhausted I must have fallen asleep. Now I can't remember what it was. It was definitely related to one of the last things you said, Larry, just before I went to bed."

"Let's see, what did I say? We checked subway stations – we checked on taxi companies. What else?"

"You said you would transfer men from Chinatown to check other small hotels and boarding houses. You said Red Hand seemed to have vanished into thin air," added McKay.

Philip shook his head at all of those.

"The last thing Larry mentioned is that it was driving him mad. No he didn't say mad, he said crazy."

"Yes that's it! Now I remember. As I undressed I kept asking myself how Ma could have disappeared without being seen. For some reason that word crazy stuck in my mind and I remember a sort of weird word association rattling around in my head before I fell asleep. Crazy led me to mentally deranged and from there to insane. There was something after insane! Think! Philip, think!"

"Well in this city if you were insane you may finish up at Bellevue," said Douglas hoping this would help.

"Of course, of course, well done Larry. That's it!"

Douglas looked bewildered.

"Don't you see? Bellevue is a hospital and the way to a hospital is the same way to disappear off a street. *To be to be picked up by an ambulance*."

Almost before Philip had finished speaking Douglas was on the phone issuing instructions.

Back at Presbyterian Hospital a nurse was giving Evelyn a prim warning.

"You had better put on your dressing gown, there are men walking about the ward."

"Why don't you tell them to bugger off?" responded an upset Evelyn.

Her upset was really caused by her problems using her crutches. She was still not as stable as she wished to be. Her hopes of getting out in the next day or so were rapidly dwindling. This was the true cause of her biting reply.

"I'm sorry. I had no right to take my frustration out on you."

"That's okay, Evelyn. You'll get used to the crutches soon enough."

They were walking along the corridor of the ward as two men came out of a room.

"Excuse me which room number is yours?" asked Charlie Jackson.

"And what business is that of yours?" snapped a still agitated Evelyn.

"This is police business so just answer the question," interjected Malone snapping open his badge wallet.

"Well mine is FBI business. My badge is in my room. Agent Evelyn Pearson is my name. Now what's this all about? Oh, wait a minute, are you the two detectives Paddy told me about? The ones investigating the murder of the nurse?"

"That's right," said Jackson. Are you the one Paddy bought the flowers for?"

"Yes. But why are you here. The murdered woman worked on the fourth floor?"

"This was your friend Paddy's idea. He said the murderer could have come from any floor."

"Smart man, that Officer O'Neil. Have you got a lead yet?"

"Unfortunately, no."

"Nothing at all from the fourth floor?"

"We still have to check out the nightshift staff but nothing from the present staff."

"How about the patients?"

"You and Paddy should get along well together. Questions, questions, questions."

"Sorry, FBI instinct."

Jackson relented.

"Okay, we did check all patients but we didn't spot a hit man amongst them. Most were confined to bed with either serious illnesses or recuperating from surgery. One Asian was doing what you're doing; his walking exercise, going slowly around the ward with the use of a cane. Another two were in the physical therapy roo ---."

"Stop! Stop! Say that again," demanded Evelyn.

The detectives looked at each other in surprise, however Jackson complied.

"Two were in the --."

"No! Not that; before that."

"What? About the guy walking the ward?"

"Yeah. Did he walk with a limp?"

"Possibly. I couldn't tell because as I said he was using a cane."

"Why all the questions? That guy was too skinny to have snapped that nurse's neck," added Malone.

"Think carefully detectives. Is this man about five feet nine, slimly built and does he have a crescent shaped pink scar on his chin?"

"I believe he did have scar, yeah, I'm pretty sure," said Jackson.

Malone nodded his head in agreement.

"Quick let me have your mobile phone. Quickly, quickly," she almost screamed out.

Malone handed her his phone and she rapidly dialed a number.

"This is Agent Pearson. Get me Special Agent Douglas. Top priority!"

"This is Douglas; I can't talk right now I have a major situation, Agent Pearson."

"Listen to me!" This time she did scream. "Our suspect is believed to be on the fourth floor at Presbyterian Hospital Get a team over here immediately."

"Are you certain, Pearson? Have you seen him?"

"No, but I'm on my way to investigate. He was interviewed by two detectives investigating the murder of a nurse on his floor. They gave me the following description. An Asian man, five feet nine, slimly built, with a pink scar on his chin and he was walking with the aid of a cane."

"Good God! Listen carefully, Agent Pearson. Under no circumstances are you to approach this suspect, He is extremely dangerous. We are on our way." He called his control center and barked instructions.

The other two men in the room with Douglas rose out of their chairs in excitement.

"It sounds like it is definitely Red Hand. The description fits him to a tee. Let's go," Douglas almost shouted to Melville and McKay.

He really didn't have to; they were already half way to the door.

Evelyn strode back to her room. Somehow she had miraculously mastered her crutches. Flapping her arms in anxiety her nurse came scurrying along behind her, terrified her patient would fall. The two detectives kept apace, with Malone still holding out his hand to have his phone returned. Once inside her room she grabbed the card Paddy had given her and dialed his mobile number.

"Hello," sang out a still happy Paddy.

"Paddy," she said breathlessly. "The man everyone has been looking for is here in the hospital, masquerading as a patient. He probably killed the nurse. Get back here as quickly as possible. I may need some assistance. I'm heading for the fourth floor."

He didn't have time to reply, she had hung up. Evelyn threw open the door to her wardrobe and pulled out a bag. She withdrew her pistol, checked it, put it in her dressing gown pocket and walked away as quickly as her crutches would allow."

"Where do you think you are going?" demanded Malone. "I could hear your boss tell you to stay away."

"To hell with that. I'm not going to let that bastard get away. I can stand guard until the cavalry arrives. You two can stay here. It could get very dangerous."

That comment insulted the detectives' sense of duty, not to mention their masculinity.

"Why don't you stay here? You wouldn't exactly be inconspicuous on the men's floor. A woman on crutches waving a gun. We'll guard him," growled Jackson.

It was time for Evelyn to compromise.

"Okay I don't want to spook him, but I'm going up to the fourth floor with you. However, I'll stay out of sight and you position yourselves close to his room, but don't go in and don't let him see you."

The intrepid trio set out for the elevator. Two well experienced homicide detectives and a determined FBI agent.

What could go wrong?

Chapter Fifty Two

Almost everything!

As Evelyn was eagerly questioning the detectives on the third floor, they happened to be standing close to the nurses' station. Nurse Evans was goggle eyed at the conversation. Once they left for Evelyn's room, she thought it best to warn her good friend who happened to be on duty on the fourth floor.

"Charlene, get to a safe place. The police are on their way to arrest the Asian man on your floor. He is apparently very dangerous and may have actually killed Lilly. Go quickly."

Charlene was not one to stand by and see her other nurses harmed. She called out over the loudspeaker system.

"All nurses to the station, immediately!"

Ma Guan-lui didn't waste a second. As soon as heard the announcement he immediately began putting on his clothes and false beard. He put his revolver and knife in his overcoat pockets, pulled his hat low over his face and was just leaving his room when he heard an elevator door open. He peeked out of his door and saw the two detectives come out. He quickly stepped back into his room. If he had waited a few seconds longer he would have seen Evelyn being waved out of the elevator.

"Okay, Agent Pearson, it's clear," whispered Jackson.

She hobbled out and managed to quickly enter the nearest room. The surprised occupant stared at her and was about to say something until he saw the gun in her hand.

"Shh, this is a police emergency. Please keep quiet," she urged.

The main nurses' station was opposite the elevator banks. Jackson and Malone crouched down behind a counter with their revolvers drawn. Their eyes were fixed on the room close to the end of the corridor. It was then they noticed four nurses were also taking shelter in an alcove close by. They motioned to the nurses to get flat on the ground.

Nurse Wilson had been settling down a patient who was in distress when she heard Charlene's message. However she waited until her patient was calmer before hurrying to obey. The patient's room was on the opposite wing to the station. As she walked rapidly towards the station she had to pass Ma's room. He was too quick for her and grabbed her as she passed.

With his left arm wrapped around her from behind and his left hand holding a knife at her throat, he marched her out into the corridor. His right hand held his pistol. She was shaking so much he had to hold her upright.

"I know where you are, detectives. Throw out your guns or you will see this nurse's throat slit. And do it now! Malone and Jackson looked at one another, and shrugged in resignation. They knew it could be suicide to do so nevertheless they couldn't stay hidden and watch a nurse being slaughtered: they threw out their revolvers. Each still had a back-up gun strapped to an ankle. They hoped they would have a chance to use them.

"Now stand up and come out into the corridor. Good, now lie face down facing away from me, with your arms stretched out in front of you."

"Damn," muttered Malone realizing this position made it almost impossible to reach his ankle gun.

Once they had complied Ma pushed Nurse Wilson towards the elevators. Keeping an eye on the detectives he pushed the down button.

Agent Pearson had seen all this but had no shot. Nurse Wilson blocked her line of fire. Further complicating things she had to lay down her crutches and was having difficulty holding a shooting stance due to her cast. She tended to wobble. Under these conditions she knew she could not attempt a difficult shot where she had a very limited target to aim at. On the other hand there would be no problem if she had sufficient time for a clear shot. She had to wait for that opportunity.

Impatiently Ma again pressed the button but still nothing happened. He looked at the floor sign above the elevators and saw all three were on the ground level. He realized an emergency procedure had been activated and the elevators were locked on the ground floor. He would have to use the stairs. Ma bent his head close to Wilson and whispered in her ear.

"No matter what happens you will stay in front of me; if you don't you will die. If you wish to live nod your head that you understand."

She did so in a terrified jerky motion.

His first instinct was to kill the detectives but he resisted doing so. His brain told him such a killing would undoubtedly cause the remaining nurses to call down to the ground floor as soon as he headed for the stairs. Having witnessed a cold blooded killing they would assume Nurse Wilson's fate was sealed. Therefore he couldn't bluff them with the threat he would kill the nurse if they raised the alarm. They would believe he would kill Wilson anyway.

He came up with a better plan.

"You nurses in there, come out."

The shaking nurses cowered lower and stayed where they were.

"Maybe this will convince you."

He fired a shot into the wall above them. Plaster cascaded over them and they slowly stood up. Charlene led the way with the others bunched behind her.

"Listen carefully; I will only kill your friend if I have to. Should any of you use the telephone after I've gone, she will die. Do you understand?"

They were too terrified to respond at first. So he screamed at them.

"*Do you understand*?"

They all nodded their heads.

"Good. Anyway you will be busy tending to the wounded detectives."

That confused the nurses, - and the detectives.

He raised his pistol and shot Jackson in the upper thigh. He howled in pain. His cry was mixed with those of the shocked nurses. Nurse Wilson almost collapsed and Ma had to struggle mightily in an attempt to keep her from falling. He still intended to shoot Malone but had to wait until the nurse, who was now around his waist, had been brought erect.

That was the opportunity Pearson had waited for. She hobbled part way out into the corridor and fired. But her cast caused her to lurch to one side and she missed his head. Instead she hit him in the right shoulder. The force of the shot threw him against the wall and the knife dropped from his left hand. Somehow he managed to retain his grip on his gun and on Wilson. Ignoring the pain he raised his right arm and returned fire. Bullets peppered the doorway but his aim was off and Pearson backed safely into the room.

With a super human effort, Ma sidled along the wall towards the stairs still keeping a hold of Wilson. As he moved he left a trail of blood on the wall, and his gun hand hung at his side. Pearson watched helplessly as again Wilson blocked her from taking another shot. Ma was within five yards of the stairway door when it burst open and Paddy O'Neil ran in.

Paddy raised his revolver but couldn't shoot as Ma had swung Wilson around as a shield. He gritted his teeth in pain as he also turned into Wilson to face Paddy. Blood from his shoulder had poured down his arm and was dripping from his hand. Squeezing his soggy hand on the grip of the gun he raised his right arm to shoot. By turning to face Paddy he had exposed part of his back. That's all Agent Evelyn Pearson required.

Three bullets thudded into Ma's back.

Nurse Wilson ran to the other nurses crying hysterically. Paddy edged forward cautiously, his revolver at the ready, his eyes fixed on Ma in case he was not dead. Then his stare was distracted at the sight of Evelyn Pearson staggering forward in an unsteady gait without the use of her crutches. She clutched her revolver steadfastly as she stood over Ma.

With his dying breath, Red Hand stared into her eyes. His own were glazed with shock.

"You're a woman," he breathed in wonder. With his lifelong disdain for women he never could have conceived the ignominy of one ending his life.

His eyes closed and Paddy knelt down to check for a pulse. Feeling none he stood to support the still teetering Evelyn. She threw her arms around his neck and hugged him.

They both took a few seconds to gaze at the body of Ma Guan-Lui, also known as Red Hand. Only later would they learn the full extent of the heinous atrocities he had committed and had planned to perpetrate.

The blazing vengeance which had burned so fiercely inside this terrifying man - Red Hand - had been extinguished by a lady - Agent Evelyn Pearson.

Chapter Fifty Three

Chaos reigned.

Thankfully its reign was short lived.

Patients were peering out of doorways, most of them scared by the sound of gunshots. But human nature can be a fickle and often incomprehensible characteristic. Although most patients were deathly afraid, they had an irresistible urge to see what was going on. The sight of two bodies lying on the floor, bleeding, was at once horrifying and simultaneously intensely interesting. The cascading piercing cries emanating from their mouths were a concoction of horror, fear, and curiosity.

Charlene was the first to take control. She ordered her recently terrified nurses to tend to their patients. Then she immediately called for reinforcements from other floors to assist in quelling the panic.

Joe Malone quickly got up to inspect Charlie Jackson's wound.

"I'll be okay, Joe. Did someone get the bastard?"

"Yeah he's down. I'll check if he's dead, then I'll call it in."

A nurse quickly shooed Malone out of the way and checked Jackson.

"Help me get him into a bed," she instructed.

Once that was accomplished, Malone ran towards Evelyn and Paddy. He paused to confirm Ma was indeed dead.

"Good work, Agent Pearson. I thought we had had it."

"It's Paddy you should thank. If he hadn't arrived in the nick of time I wouldn't have had a shot."

"Yeah, you took a helluva risk standing there unprotected, Paddy. You could have been killed. Why didn't you duck back into the doorway?"

"It all happened so quickly," he replied quietly.

That wasn't the entire truth. Paddy's special forces training had enabled him to take in the entire scene instantly. He noticed Ma's damaged arm and the difficulty he had in holding on to his gun. He saw Evelyn hesitate as she didn't have a clear shot. And as soon as Ma turned to face him he knew the consequences. If he had ducked out of Ma's sight Ma would not have turned. It had been a risk but it had to be taken and Agent Pearson had not missed the opportunity. It had all happened quickly but Paddy was too modest to admit to being willing to sacrifice himself in order to stop Ma.

"How's Charlie?" asked Paddy.

"The nurse immediately applied a tourniquet; I think he'll be fine. I have to call the station then I had better get back to him. Once again congratulations, Agent Pearson."

He thrust out his hand to Paddy who clasped it firmly without letting go of Evelyn with his left arm.

"And thanks to you, Paddy," he said with grateful sincerity, before leaving to make his call.

"Do you want to go back to your room, Evelyn, or stay here until your boss arrives?"

"I have to stay here. If you could help me to a chair at the nurses' station and get my crutches that would be great."

Ten minutes later the reinforced band of nurses had tended to all patients including those who had locked themselves in the bathrooms. Calm and normalcy had been restored. Well – not quite absolute normalcy. There still remained a large pool of blood surrounding much of the body of a slim Chinese man whose eyes stared uncomprehendingly into space. Probably his last thoughts could not grasp why his scrupulous planning had failed, and also, how he could have allowed himself to be bested by a woman.

Some of the nurses had wished to remove the body and clean up the unhygienic blood pool, but the law enforcement officers had unanimously rejected this. Until their superiors had reviewed the scene it must remain undisturbed.

That didn't take much longer. So many people arrived at the same time that Paddy had to once again resort to crowd control. Fortunately the elevators came back on line and he unceremoniously packed most of the crowd into two of them and, over clamorous protests, sent them to the ground floor.

Only McKay, Douglas and Melville were left to survey the scene.

"Where's my cameraman?" demanded Douglas.

"I must have shoved him into an elevator," said Paddy apologetically

"Could you get him back, please?"

"Right away."

"Well that's it. He doesn't look like much does he?" said McKay. "He has a crescent shaped pink scar on his chin but can we be certain it is Ma?"

"Let's look at his foot," said Philip.

As he was removing Ma's shoe and sock he became aware of a rising level of questioning voices. They all looked around and saw what was happening. The reign of chaos had ended, but its throne had been usurped by insatiable curiosity. Patients and nurses were either standing in the doorways of their rooms or actually walking towards the dead body.

"All of you get back inside your rooms – now!" barked McKay.

They scuttled back.

"Who is in charge here?"

"I am," said Charlene.

"Please ensure everyone stays inside."

"Yes sir."

"It's Ma all right. There's his club foot," said Philip.

They looked up suddenly at the sound of approaching footsteps.

"Detective Malone, NYPD," said Joe, as he advanced holding up his badge. "Since I was an eye witness I thought you might like to hear my statement."

"Did you kill him?" asked Douglas.

"No, I did."

They looked around for the source of the voice, but saw no one.

"She's sitting behind the nurses' desk," Joe informed them.

Evelyn managed to stand.

"It's about time you got here, Special Agent Douglas. My leg's really beginning to hurt. Hurry up and take my statement and let me get back to bed."

This wasn't a request she was making of her superior. It was an order.

"Did I not tell you she could be fearsome?" Douglas said to McKay and Melville.

Just then Paddy reappeared with the photographer and a wheelchair.

"Sit here, Evelyn. I'll get you back to your room. These gentlemen can question you there. And you better come along too, Joe. Your statement will be required."

"Thank you, Paddy," she said with a warm smile and laid her hand on his.

Both McKay and Douglas were about to say something at their rank being overlooked. Paddy ignored this and waved them forward.

"Let's go then," he said and marched towards the elevator.

Philip had to smile as he tagged along.

'These Special Forces know how to take command,' he thought.

When all statements had been taken and special thanks given to Evelyn and Paddy, the trio of McKay, Melville and Douglas assembled in the lobby.

"I'll arrange for a plane to take you back to Vancouver, DI McKay. How about you Philip? Do you want to go straight back to Hawaii?"

"If that's not too much trouble. The plane can drop Hugh off first then take me home."

"That's a lot of flying. Don't you want to spend the night in Vancouver?"

"No, I'll go straight home. But first I want to make a couple of telephone calls."

"Me too," added McKay.

"Let's all go back to the safe house. Both of you can make your calls and I can arrange the plane."

Douglas pulled out his phone to alert his people of the situation. Hugh McKay took the opportunity to take Philip by the arm and lead him a few yards away.

"I just wanted to say two things, Philip. First I'll never be able to thank you enough for all you did. I'm sure one of your calls will be to Phil Hughes: will you please also give him my thanks. Tell him I'll call him personally in a day or so. And I rather suspect the leaders of our two great nations will also wish to thank both of you in some way."

"That's not necessary. I'm only glad we managed to get Ma. It's you who should get the praise for leading this mission. You did extremely well, Hugh. What's the second thing you wanted to say?"

"I wanted to congratulate you on your self restraint. When we first saw the body I noticed your hand reach for you revolver. I know how desperately you wanted to put a bullet into him."

"You're very observant Hugh. It was as much for Phil as for me. I promised him I would put a bullet in Ma's head. But I decided a photograph would do."

"I'm confident it will. Phil's a decent, civilized man. The main thing is Ma Guan-lui is dead. The world is rid of perhaps its greatest menace."

"Amen to that, my friend."

Chapter Fifty Four

Philip was eager to get home. Mei Li had told him she was flying back in her uncle's private jet and would be home before he was. As the plane approached the airport in Vancouver the pilot announced he would have to take on more fuel for the onward journey. Philip knew this was inevitable and he could only hope it would be done swiftly.

After deplaning he accompanied Hugh to the airport lounge. There was a surprise awaiting them in the form of Captain Sven Larson. Once he had given congratulations to both men along with long and tightly gripped handshakes he gave them his news.

"The prime minister wanted to see you right away, Hugh. You are to be awarded Canada's highest medal. However I requested a postponement as I have a most urgent matter which requires your personal attention. Once I explained the situation, he readily agreed. I'm afraid you must leave immediately. I asked your wife to pack another suitcase for you. Ah, here it is now."

Hugh McKay's mouth dropped open as Cathy appeared, followed by a man carrying two large suitcases. She ran towards him and hugged him tightly – almost afraid to let him go. Then after a long kiss, she released him to turn to Philip.

"Thank you for looking after Hugh," she said and kissed him on the cheek.

"We looked after each other, Cathy."

"Thanks for coming out, sweetheart. You've probably heard the news that this heartless Swede is immediately sending me out on another bloody case," he said, glaring at his boss, and not trusting himself to say anything further. Berating one's boss in public can be a career ending offense.

"Oh yes I know, and I fully approve," she replied with a sunny smile.

Now Hugh smelled a rat. Something was not right. He looked at his boss for an explanation. So far Larson had done an admirable job of keeping a straight face. He responded to McKay's caustic comment.

"I must inform you, DI McKay, the Vancouver police force would consider it an insult of the highest order not to escort home the man who did most to rid the world of Red Hand. Therefore I am instructing you to do so. You will see Colonel Philip Melville safely home. No, no, I will brook no argument. That is an order."

Now he couldn't contain himself and the officious look on his face gave way to a huge grin. Cathy also found it impossible to keep up the charade. She rushed back into Hugh's arms.

"Phil Hughes called me and said you will be staying with him for ten days. And Captain Larson knows Phil's wife has been in hospital, therefore he is sending me to help look after her. Isn't that fantastic?"

"Is Anne okay?" asked Philip apprehensively.

"Oh yes. She is one hundred percent. This is only the Captain's way of giving both of us a reward. Ten days in Hawaii. I can hardly believe it. You haven't said anything, Hugh!"

McKay was flabbergasted. He didn't know what to say. He stuck out his hand once again to Larson.

"Thanks Sven," he said softly.

Then ever the cop he added, "I'm confident Johnny will handle things until I return."

"I'm certain he will when he returns."

"Returns?"

"Yes, Jeremy Mason left yesterday to accompany the body of Belinda Carson back to her parents for burial. I thought it appropriate we send a representative too and Johnny volunteered."

"That was very good of him. She was a wonderful person."

"God rest her soul," intoned Philip with a bowed head.

"Now let's get your luggage stowed and get you folks on your way," said Larson. "There is one other instruction for you, DI McKay. If you so much as mention the word work during the next ten days, I promise you, you will regret it! And it is only fair to alert you I have a spy who will tell me should you break this rule."

McKay looked over at the happily smiling Cathy who wagged a finger as a warning.

When they arrived in Honolulu, Phil, Anne and Mei Li were waiting for them on the tarmac. A lei was placed around each passenger's neck and after fond greetings they walked to the lounge. There, Phil stood in front of Hugh with one hand behind his back.

"Do you remember a promise I made you last time we flew out here together?"

"A promise? What promise?"

"It related to the complaint you had about out flight."

"I don't recall complaining about anything."

"Yes you did. You complained there were no mai tais on board and I promised I would get you one when we arrived in Hawaii. However we didn't have time. Well I'm a man who keeps his promises."

He produced a large mai tai from behind his back.

"Aloha, Hugh, and thank you for all you did."

"An attendant arrived with a tray of mai tais and handed one to each person."

"A toast to friendship," said Philip.

It was the beginning of the most wonderful vacation Cathy and Hugh ever had.

The time seemed to fly past.

On day eight, they were enjoying a picnic lunch on the beach. As usual the air was filled with laughter. Suddenly it stopped when a gasp escaped the mouth of Mei Li.

"Oh no, not again," she moaned, as she pointed to the road.

She had a sinking feeling in the pit of her stomach, the vehicle she had spotted, belonged to a government agency and, yet again, her husband was being called into action.

They followed her stare and noticed the black SUV with tinted windows, parked at the side of the road, with its engine running. A man got out and waved.

"It's for me, it's George from my office," said Phil and walked quickly towards the SUV.

He briefly listened to George then entered the car. He reappeared a few minutes later and the SUV drove off.

"That was the Director. He had four messages for me. Firstly he wanted to be certain I was taking good care of my guests. I told him they were a pain in the butt so I sent them to a third class hotel."

Everyone laughed and Anne playfully slapped him across the back of his head.

"It's just as well he knows your sense of humor. We have a couple of years until retirement and we need your pension."

Phil's face lost its smile and Anne froze. She knew every move of her husband and waited with baited breath for his next words. Phil noticed this.

"He also told me I had been promoted back to Langley."

They all cried out their congratulations – except Anne, who had no desire to relocate once more.

"However, I thanked him and refused the promotion. He reminded me this was the third time I had refused to go to Langley. He also reminded me that three strikes in baseball had a bad connotation."

Anne's face was showing the strain so he hurried to continue.

"I told him I recognized that, but I still would not go to the Puzzle Palace. Finally he laughed. He said he knew the answer before he offered the job. But it was mine if I wanted it. Then he instructed me to travel Washington to receive the CIA's highest award. With reluctance, he informed me I could stay here, however my grade was increased to the same as that of the position I had refused. Along with that increase would be commensurate salary and pension benefits."

Anne's rush to hug and kiss him sprayed sand on everyone, but no one cared as they also joined in the happy moment.

"As for you, Colonel Melville, you are to accompany me to Washington along with our wives, where you will receive the Medal of Honor from the president. It will be a private ceremony as the entire Red Hand matter is being held as classified."

Once again there were congratulations all round.

"I have kept the best news for last. Hugh, your boss has been promoted to Ottawa and you are to take his place. Johnny will succeed you. And you will be traveling to Ottawa with Cathy to receive your nation's highest honor. There was a message from Sven. He said you would most probably rebel against being taken out of the field; but he truly believes it is the correct move at this time in your career. To ensure your acceptance of this deal, he added you would not want to stand in the way of Johnny's promotion. Would you?"

Tears streamed down the face of Cathy. This was everything she wanted. Her husband would be away from most of the danger and he would spend more time at home with her. However through her tears she stared at Hugh, fearfully awaiting his response.

"It's all right sweetheart, I'll do it."

More sand was spayed as she rushed into his arms.

"This calls for another round of drinks to celebrate. I'll go ask the barman to bring champagne this time," said Philip and strode away.

The two couples were engrossed in happy conversation over Phil's and Hugh's wonderful news. They didn't appear to notice the look on Mei Li's face.

Naturally she was delighted at the recognition being awarded to Philip, but she had the terrible feeling her happiness may be short lived. Twice in the past Philip had come to her rescue. Once in Vietnam and once in Hong Kong. Following each of those times of danger there were times of absolute bliss. She had prayed there would be no further time of danger but Philip had been called on to catch Red Hand. With the success of that mission she was again anticipating the life she always wanted: the peace and safety of being with her wonderful husband. Would it last? She shrugged off such a negative thought as Philip returned with the drinks. Once handed out, Phil Hughes rose.

"I would like to have the honor of proposing this toast," said Phil.

"We are not the only ones to have something to celebrate. There are millions who will never know how much they owe to my friend. Without his enormous talent the world would be a very sad and terrified place. So my toast is to that special man. To Philip Melville."

Philip hung his head in embarrassment. The others cheered loudly and joined in the toast. Mei Li finished her drink then put her arms around Philip's neck and whispered in his ear.

"I am so proud of you my darling and I love you so much."

Philip returned her hug as he held her tightly.

She clung to him – then - like a black panther stealthily pad, pad, padding on his jungle prowl, the bad thought snuck, back into her mind.

"Will this be the last time?"